Penguin Books
The Man from Nowhere

Stanley Ellin was born in New York City in 1916 and graduated from college when he was nineteen, the same year that he was married. In the following years he was a 'pusher' for a newspaper distributor, dairy farmer, teacher, and steelworker, until he joined the U.S. army during the war. After that he began to write; his stories and novels have won many awards, and he himself has won the 'Edgar' Award from the Mystery Writers of America three times. Six of his other novels and some short stories have been published by Penguin: *Dreadful Summit, The Eighth Circle, The Key to Nicholas Street, The Blessington Method, House of Cards* (now filmed), *The Vanishing Estate*, and *The Speciality of the House and other stories*.

Stanley Ellin lives in Brooklyn with his wife and daughter.

Stanley Ellin

The Man from Nowhere

Penguin Books

Penguin Books Ltd, Harmondsworth,
Middlesex, England
Penguin Books Australia Ltd, Ringwood,
Victoria, Australia

First published in U.S.A. 1970
Published in Great Britain
by Jonathan Cape 1970
Published in Penguin Books 1974

Made and printed in Great Britain by
Hunt Barnard Printing Ltd, Aylesbury, Bucks
Set in Intertype Times

to my favourite son-in-law,
George Ellington Brown,
with affection and admiration

1

The car was a grey Jaguar coupé, a low-slung, high-powered brute, its rear seats piled with luggage. When Jake swung it off the causeway in the direction of South Miami Beach the luggage shifted with a squeaking of expensive leather. He reached a hand behind him to shove it back into place.

He glanced at Elinor. 'How long have we been married?' he asked abruptly.

She came out of her daydream with a start and considered the question. 'Six months?'

'Wrong. If we were married on your birthday, which happens to be November tenth, and this is April fifth, it's not even five months yet. How long have we been married?'

'Not even five months yet.'

'Right. And during this five months certain little flaws in your character have naturally come to light.'

'Naturally.'

'Do you know which one bugs me the most?'

'Yes. I talk too much. I'm too confiding. I tell our private business to anybody who comes along.'

'Why?'

'Look,' Elinor said, 'do we really have to go that deep into it?'

'We do.'

'All right then. Maybe it's because of you. I can't get through to you, so I talk my head off to anyone else who'll listen.'

Jake turned down the visor over the windshield against the glare of the setting sun. 'Why can't you get through to me?'

'Because you're a lot more interested in that research and writing you do than me. And there's the age difference. You're thirty-five, I'm twenty-one. You think everything going on in my head is kid's stuff. How does that sound to you?'

'Beautiful,' Jake said. 'Like soap opera in living colour.'

A narrow bridge spanned the twenty yards of Biscayne Bay which separated Daystar Island Number 1 from Miami Beach. A heavy chain across the far end of the bridge barred the way. Jake pulled up before it, and a private guard in dark blue uniform but without jacket strolled up to check his credentials. The man was grey-haired, potbellied, and sour-faced. His shirt was blotched with sweat.

Jake rolled down the window. The humid heat of the outside world was suffocating after the air-conditioned chill inside the car. 'Mr and Mrs Dekker,' he told the guard. 'We've rented a place over on Island Number Two. The de Burgo house. I've got a letter here from Mr McCloy about it.'

The guard read the letter. 'Jacob Dekker?' he said. He came down hard on the Jacob.

'That's right,' Jake said sweetly. 'Any objection?'

'No, sir,' the guard said hastily. 'Just asking.' He pointed. 'That's Seminole Drive. Just stay on it until you hit the bridge to Number Two. Nice to have you with us, Mr Dekker. Mrs Dekker.'

Seminole Drive was as broad as a boulevard and bordered on each side by towering royal palms. The estates along the way were mostly of the hacienda type, but here and there were some places that looked like glass and chromium ranch houses.

'What was all that about?' Elinor asked. 'That Jacob business?'

'He was wondering out loud if I put something over on McCloy. These Daystar Islands are a closed corporation. No Jews. McCloy is president of the works. The chief watchdog.'

'I wonder how they feel about Polacks.'

'Fine, as long as they're married to rich Dutchmen like me.'

There was no one on guard at the next bridgehead, just a small sign announcing that this was Daystar Island Number 2. The road here was Circular Drive, and aside from being bordered by coconut palms instead of royal palms, it could have been Seminole Drive all over again. Jake followed its circle halfway around the island, noting the house numbers painted on rustic boards which were planted at the foot of each lawn.

All the numbers were written out in script: *Twelve – Fourteen – Sixteen*. At *Eighteen,* where the road looped north and he caught a glimpse of Biscayne Bay through the palms, he pulled the car over to the curb and got out. There was no other car on the road, not a soul in sight.

A flagstoned path led over a trim lawn to the portico of number 18. He briskly walked up the path to the house, dodging spray from revolving sprinklers on each side, and rang the doorbell. He waited a few seconds and rang again. While his finger was still on the button the door suddenly opened. A young man stood there, a napkin in his hand, a dark unwelcoming look on his face.

'Yes?' he said.

'My name is Dekker,' Jake said. 'Look, I'm sorry about getting you away from the table like this, but I can't seem to find out where the hell the house is I rented around here. The de Burgo house. It's number seventeen, but so far I haven't seen an odd number anywhere between the bridge and here.'

'Because you drove the wrong way around. Even numbers this side of the island, odd numbers the other side. Anyhow, all you have to do is keep going along the road. Next place is nineteen. Seventeen is right around the bend.'

In the middle of this, the young man's dark expression had suddenly brightened, the hard edge of impatience in his voice had softened. This had nothing to do with him, Jake knew. The young man was watching Elinor come full jiggle down the path toward them.

'Jake!' she wailed. 'My ring!'

'What?'

'My engagement ring. It's gone. And I know where I left it. On the washstand of the ladies' room at the airport. If anybody sees it lying there – !'

'Did you look in your pocketbook?'

Elinor hopelessly held up the open pocketbook. 'I looked. It must be there in the washroom. Jake, if we called up the airport right away – '

'I don't know if the phone's connected at our place yet.' Jake turned to the young man, who had been concentrating hard on Elinor. 'I hate to impose on you, but would it be all right to use your phone?'

'Sure. Come right in. My name's Thoren, by the way. Kermit Thoren.' His hand was against the small of Elinor's back as he ushered them in.

The phone was on a stand in the corner of the dining room. Five people were at the dining table – a grey-haired woman in dark glasses at its head, a middle-aged couple at one side, a youthful pair at the other – whom Kermit introduced with perfunctory waves of the hand as his mother; his uncle and aunt, Senator and Mrs Harlan Sprague; his sister Joanna and Hal Freeman, a friend of the family.

Jake, leafing through the pages of the phone book, observed that Kermit was a fast worker, if not a subtle one. He insisted that the stricken Elinor take his seat at the table, had the Negro houseman bring her a whiskey, and hovered over her consolingly while she emotionally explained to the company what this was all about.

As he dialled the airline's number, Jake saw that everyone's eyes, with one exception, were now fixed sympathetically on Elinor. The exception was young Joanna Thoren. She was covertly watching him as he spoke to the woman at the airline desk in an undertone, describing the ring and asking that someone please check to see if it was still in the ladies' room. He'd wait, he said, until she reported back.

It looked as if Joanna was prepared to wait right along with him. Her head, the hair sheared into a childish-looking tight little cap of curls, was slightly cocked towards Elinor, but her eyes he knew without looking squarely at her, were steadily on him.

Elinor's voice was now a mixture of anguish and resentment. 'And it's not only that the damn ring is worth about five thousand dollars, but it's one of those horrible family heirlooms you have to worry about all the time. My mother-in-law got it from her mother, and the fuss she made about it – !'

She fumbled for her handkerchief and pressed it to her nose, openly weeping. That did it, Jake saw. Joanna's attention was now entirely rivetted on Elinor. Phone to his ear, he instantly turned away from the scene, the tiny transmitter and the sliver of metal which was his tool kit ready in his hand. It was the new universal transmitter, distortion-free and with room-wide range, and he had practiced installing it in his own phone until he had reduced the time needed for the job to the absolute minimum. The practice paid off now.

The job done, he faced the table again. 'Elinor!' he said sharply, and her blubbering diminished to a series of sniffles. 'You know I'm right,' she told him accusingly. 'You know what'll happen when your mother finds out about this.'

'Nothing. And the ring isn't gone for good yet. So will you please, for God's sake, stop carrying on like an infant?'

They left the house ten minutes later – it had taken five minutes for the airline woman to report back that the ring was not in the washroom, then another five minutes was spent in making proper apologies and farewells to the company at the table – and Kermit Thoren accompanied them out to the portico.

He draped an arm around Elinor's shoulders and gave her a commiserating hug. 'Just remember, lady, no ring is worth an ulcer.' Then, arm still over her shoulder, he nodded toward the baggage-laden Jaguar. 'How come the Florida plates?' he said to Jake. 'Have you folks been down here before?'

'No,' Jake said, 'it's a rental.' He bared his teeth in a polite smile. 'But I have a news flash for you. My wife isn't.'

Kermit returned the smile. 'My bad luck,' he said. He casually disengaged his arm from around Elinor. 'Anyhow, welcome to the club, neighbour. This is mostly Caddie and Mercedes country, but I wouldn't drive anything but an XKE like that myself. Come on over when you're in the mood. I'd like to show you some cute adjustments I made on mine.' He disappeared into the house only after they had run the gauntlet of lawn sprinklers and were seated in the car.

'Did you put that gimmick into the telephone?' Elinor asked Jake with concern.

'Yes.'

'When? You couldn't have had enough time to. How did you do it?'

'Like this.' Jake placed a quarter between his forefinger and middle finger and held out the hand towards her, fingers together. The coin slid smoothly in and out between each finger and then back again. He clenched his fist, opened it, and showed her the coin was gone. 'Magic,' he said as he got the car under way.

'It must have been,' Elinor said. 'So then I did all right. I kept the spotlight right where it had to be.'

'You did.'

'I told you on the plane I would. And you weren't really sore about the way I let that horny character play octopus with me? That was just a put-on?'

'That's right. After all, we're supposed to be married. He might wonder about it if I let him feel you up in front of me without showing I didn't like it. Don't ever go by what you hear me say in front of company, Mrs Majeski. I want you to be real good friends with Kermit.'

'It looks like I already am,' Elinor said. 'And it's Miss Majeski.'

'You told me you'd been married.'

'I went back to my maiden name right after the divorce. Now you tell me something. Did you know Kermit drove this same kind of car before we even got down here? Is that why you had that agency deliver this one to the airport all the way from Palm Beach? So you could get to be sort of Jaguar buddies with him?'

'By golly, Miss Majeski,' Jake said, 'you sure do catch on quick.'

2

The streetlights along Circular Drive went on as he pulled the car into the driveway of number 17 and parked before a garage. The lamp-posts were old-fashioned iron stands with translucent globes that produced a soothing golden glow.

He threw open the front door of the house and switched on

the foyer light. He already knew the layout from the plan the agent had supplied. Beyond the foyer a vast living room extended to the French doors of the Florida room facing the bay. Through the French doors, he saw, redly reflected in the last of the sunset, a dining table and chairs, since the Florida room, actually a glassed-in terrace, doubled as dining room. To his right were the pantry and kitchen. To his left was a narrow hallway running the length of the house from front to back. The doors opening off the hallway were, in order, the entrances to a closet, bathroom, bedroom, and study.

The additional telephone under an unlisted number he had instructed the rental agent to have installed was there on the desk in the study. An ultrasonic whistle was warm in his pocket. Now he set the stem of the whistle between his teeth, dialled the Thorens' number, and the instant the last click of the dial sounded he blew a noiseless blast of the whistle into the mouthpiece of the phone.

'– disagree. It's utterly ridiculous, Mother.'

'I said no, Joanna. I meant no.'

The transmission was flawless. From the clarity and volume of the tones, Joanna and her mother could have been speaking directly into the mouthpiece of their phone. Only the almost equal volume of what should have been fainter sounds in the background – the clatter of cutlery on a plate, the squeak and thump of the swinging door between kitchen and dining room – might signal the trained ear that the phone still rested on its stand and that a highly sensitive transmitter was at work in it.

'But Milt and Bobby Webb' – that was Kermit protesting. – 'and the McCloys. Nobody could possibly say we're having an orgy with that collection at the table.'

'What are you doing?' Elinor whispered from the doorway. 'What's that whistle for?'

Jake removed it from his mouth. 'It's sonic. A harmonica bug. You can't hear it, but after you've dialled whatever phone you bugged you blow on it and it activates the bug without ringing the phone. And you don't have to whisper. They can't hear you at the other end.'

He handed her the phone, and she put it to her ear. 'It's

13

Kermit,' she reported with surprise. 'Now it's Mrs Thoren. Hey, look,' she said in alarm and thrust the receiver back into Jake's hand, 'isn't it illegal, listening in like this?'

'Don't let it worry you. Just run out to the car and bring me that pigskin case on the back seat. The top one on the pile.'

'But it is illegal, isn't it?'

Jake said coldly: 'What kind of idiot question is that? Didn't Sherry tell you what this was all about before she handed you the deal? Didn't I tell you on the plane how we'd plant that bug? Why didn't you ask that question then?'

Elinor said stubbornly: 'Because it didn't come through to me the same way. I mean, what it was like, listening in on a bugged phone. And all Sherry told me was that you were an insurance investigator and would pay me three thousand dollars to front as your wife for a month because of a case you're on. But she never – '

'And what she told me,' Jake cut in, 'was that she'd be sending me a girl friend in her place who had plenty of nerve and talent and needed the money in the worst way. You mean she was all wrong about you? Or are you just trying to make me raise the ante, now that you have me in a hole? Now that the Thorens marked you as my wife.'

Elinor looked shocked. 'I never had any such idea.'

'I'm glad to hear it. And get this nailed down tight in that beautiful Polack skull. Bugging a phone to keep someone from swindling an insurance company is only illegal if you're caught at it. And we won't be. Now bring me that bag from the car.'

When she still hesitated he gave her a shove to start her on her way. 'And don't bang it against anything. Handle it like glass.'

The case had the biggest of his tape recorders in it – he had brought along two minis and a Continental attaché case model besides this IBM Executary, the gem of his collection – and before he set up the phone's earpiece against the IBM's induction mike he checked to see if the table talk at the other end of the line was still going on. It was. He started the recorder and left the Thorens to it.

3

'Now what?' said Elinor.

'We bring the rest of the stuff in from the car and set up housekeeping.'

'Well, would you please do me a favour first and tell me what I've gotten myself into? Any play I even had a walk-on in, they at least told me what it was all about before we started rehearsing.'

Jake said: 'For one thing, this is no rehearsal. For another thing, I expected to tell you what's going on as soon as we were settled in here tonight. You couldn't function efficiently if I didn't.'

'Function efficiently,' Elinor said. 'You make me feel like the original mechanical woman. But just for openers, who's trying to swindle the insurance company? Kermit?'

'No,' Jake said. 'His father. Guy named Walter Thoren who got himself killed in an auto crash a month ago.'

'Killed? But if he's dead, what good can you – ?'

'I said I'll tell you later. The whole thing in one piece so it makes sense. Right now, let's get moved in.'

The case with his papers and working equipment he put into the study. The rest of the luggage was lined up on the floor of the bedroom. The bedroom was furnished in colourless good taste and had its own dressing room and bathroom.

Sweating with his exertions, Jake sat down on the edge of the king-sized bed. 'Feels good,' he said. 'Try it.'

Elinor remained standing. 'No, thanks. I'll take your word for it.'

'I see. Miss Majeski, is it your impression that I am now making an unsubtle pass at you?'

'It's been known to happen.'

'Didn't Sherry tell you that when it comes to the hired help my policy is strictly hands off?'

'Yes. Well – ' Warily Elinor seated herself on the bed an

15

arm's-length away from him. 'Look, all this is new to me. You can't blame me for being a little jumpy about it, can you?'

Jake said: 'What's making you jumpy is wondering when I try crawling into bed with you. I won't. That settles it.'

'All right, but how do we arrange things? You move into that next room?'

'After only a few months of marriage to such an adorable sexpot? No, I don't move anywhere. My clothes stay right in here, and none of these doors is ever locked. But I'll sleep on that couch in the study. Just remember there's never to be any bedding showing on it. I'll make it up when I go to sleep.'

Elinor frowned. 'You sound like there's somebody around here who's suspicious of us already.'

'I'll put it this way. The Thorens have reason to be damn suspicious of any stranger who suddenly walks into their lives. We have to get close to that family. We have to move right into it, but quick. If they suspect for one second we're not kosher, we're done for. And you never know when somebody'll drop in to bring a cake and take a good look around.'

Elinor said: 'So wouldn't it have been easier if you didn't have me with you? If you were just sort of a bachelor coming down here to write your book in peace and quiet?'

'No. A healthy thirty-five-year-old bachelor of my type isn't likely to move into a solidly middle-aged, married community like this by choice. The Thorens might have smelled something fishy right off if I walked in there and tried that telephone trick without you along. They're smart enough to have put one investigator out of the game already. My gamble is that they're not so smart that they'll figure his replacement would be a newlywed husband with a cute little wife tagging along.'

'That's us all right,' Elinor said wryly. 'Well, you're in charge. Just tell me which dresser you want, and I'll take it from there.'

After the unpacking she put together a sketchy supper from the basic provisions Jake had instructed the agent to lay in for them. They ate at the kitchen table. When Elinor sat down to it she said: 'Now what about Thoren? How was he trying to swindle your company?'

16

'By committing suicide.'

Elinor's fork, laden with cheese omelette, remained poised in mid-air. 'You're putting me on.'

'Not me, not the Guaranty Life Insurance Company of New York. Last year, February nineteenth, Thoren called on their agent here – that's important to start with: he called on the agent, the agent didn't call on him – and took out a hundred-thousand-dollar life insurance policy with a double indemnity rider attached. You know what that means?'

'Yes. It's double if you're killed in an accident.'

'Right. And Guaranty added its own rider which said the policy didn't go into effect until one year after its issuance. That was February nineteenth of this year. Two weeks after it went into effect, Thoren wound up dead in a car crash.'

Elinor said: 'I get it. If it's suicide the company doesn't have to pay. So it'll try to show this is suicide, no matter what.'

'You're putting it wrong. People who die by violence as soon as their large, double indemnity policies go into effect are, so to speak, suspicious characters right off the bat. And in Thoren's case there was more than the timing of it to bother Guaranty. According to the record, he was driving close to ninety miles an hour on a Saturday midnight when he went off the road and piled into a tree on the MacArthur Causeway here. But according to some people who knew Thoren, he never drove that fast within their recollection and was a hell of a good driver in the bargain.'

'So the company sent you down to see what really happened.'

'Wrong,' Jake said. 'The company doesn't send me anywhere, because I'm not on their payroll or anybody else's. I'm strictly freelance. I invest my own time and money in a case. I get paid off only if I break it.'

Elinor looked startled. 'You mean, all this money you're laying out – my three thousand, the car, renting the house – it's all out of your own pocket?'

'Every cent.'

'But I thought you were on an expense account, like everybody else. This way – well, I guess you know for sure it was suicide, don't you?'

'Knowing it means nothing. Proving it is what pays off. But it was suicide all right. A guy at Guaranty figured that out. Johnny Maniscalco, my contact there. Head of investigations for them, and a very smart operator. Even though the police report said it was an accident, the timing of it and Thoren's driving record put his back up. So he told Guaranty to hold up payment and came down here to look around. One good look, and he knew he was on to something.'

'How?'

'By following up three items in the police report. There were no tyre tracks on the road to show the brakes had been applied, Thoren's body showed no signs of drugs or alcohol at the autopsy, and what was left of the car showed no mechanical failure. To the cops this meant Thoren lost control of the car because he either blacked out or fell asleep at the wheel, which is a logical assumption when you don't have to pay out two hundred thousand dollars for it.

'So first thing, Maniscalco went to Thoren's doctor – a guy named Freeman whose son is that family friend you saw over there – and got his word that Thoren had no record of ever blacking out.'

'But what about falling asleep?' Elinor said. 'How could anyone ever prove he didn't?'

'And that's where Maniscalco really did a job. When he looked over the scene of the crash he noticed that a hundred yards before it, there was a slight curve in the road. Very slight. Maybe five degrees. But when he tested it in his own car he saw he had to manipulate the wheel to keep from going off the road right past that bend. So he knew Thoren was awake one hundred yards before he crashed, which at ninety miles an hour meant two and a half seconds before he crashed. You don't manipulate even five-degree curves when you're asleep at the wheel.

'Since the idea was to get the police to write down suicide in their report, Maniscalco went to them with all this. And after they looked it over, they admitted that yes, there was a small possibility it was suicide. But there was also a big probability it wasn't, and unless he could come up with a convincing answer to the jackpot question he was out of luck.'

'What jackpot question?'

'A reason why Thoren might want to commit suicide. An airtight, credible reason.'

Elinor said: 'But with so much evidence showing, it could be – '

'So much isn't enough. A smart cop is very cagey about labelling an accident suicide without solid proof, especially where a big insurance payoff is involved. Otherwise, sure as hell he'll find himself on the witness stand in court, with the lawyer for the beneficiary slicing him into little pieces. And where the accident involves a healthy, prosperous, well-balanced citizen with powerful political connections, that goes double. Right now, Mrs Thoren's lawyer has everything going for him.'

Elinor said: 'You mean she's suing for payment?'

'She is. And Guaranty has only about a month left to enter a demurrer. And Maniscalco is right in the middle. It was bad enough when he had Guaranty stall on the payment, because that was due as soon as the death certificate and accident report were sent to them. But when the family found out why he was snooping around down here it was even worse, because they blocked him at every turn. Nobody he contacted would say a word to him about Thoren. It was like a hurricane warning had been sent up in south Florida about mentioning the name. You can't blame people for that. Weird as it sounds, even if a man is dead, you can still be charged with slandering him. So with Guaranty blocked off so completely, Maniscalco called me into the case. I'm kind of a panic button for a lot of insurance companies.'

'That's where you lose me,' Elinor said. 'If it means so much to Guaranty, shouldn't they at least pay your expenses? Otherwise, you could just tell them to go jump.'

Jake said: 'I tell them nothing. Matter of fact, they don't even know who I am and don't want to know. That way, whatever I get involved in, their big brass is in the clear. Which is how I like it too.'

'If you come out ahead. But take like this case. How do you know there was even some kind of motive for suicide you could prove?'

'Because I'm convinced Thoren wasn't psychotic. And because I already found out something about him which gives me a lead to a motive.'

Elinor's eyes brightened with interest. 'Woman trouble?'

'Money trouble. Before I told Maniscalco I'd take the case I figured I'd look into the money angle, because there wasn't anything else I could look into from that far away. All he could tell me was that Thoren seemed to have been well-to-do, respectable, happily married, and a good father. A little on the intellectual side, but strong on sailboating, too. And he went in for civic betterment in a big way. Sort of an all-around model citizen, you might say.

'Now, none of this means he couldn't have been living some kind of secret life, but it did mean that if he had any dangerous secrets he knew how to keep them buried. The one thing I could dig up fast without the family knowing was his financial set-up. So I told Maniscalco that if I turned up anything interesting about it I'd take the case. Otherwise, no. And I did.'

'But how, without the family knowing?'

'It wasn't as hard as it sounds. My good luck, Florida doesn't have any regular income tax, only what they call an intangible tax. Once a year you make out an affidavit listing all your holdings and bank accounts and so on, and you pay one tenth of a per-cent tax on the total. So I had a contact in Tallahassee get me copies of Thoren's last few affidavits –'

'Just like that?' Elinor said. 'They're not secret?'

'How secret they are depends on how much you're willing to pay for a look at them. I was told Florida's pretty free and easy in the ethics department, and it turned out I was told right. Anyhow, Thoren's figures showed that up to two years ago he was worth well over three hundred thousand dollars. That January it suddenly went down to two-fifty. This January it was down to one-fifty. Yet he was still getting a fair income from a company he used to own.

'So there was the lead I needed. And between that and the accident stuff Maniscalco dug up, I felt it was a good gamble to take the case. Good gamble meaning you start with a joker in your hand. Now does it all make sense to you?'

'Yes,' Elinor said. 'Except why you call what Thoren had financial troubles. Man, you don't know what financial troubles really are.'

4

After dinner he left her studying the intricacies of the dish-washing machine and went into the study. There was no more conversation from the Thoren dining room coming over the phone, so he replaced it on its stand. He was listening to the tape when Elinor appeared in the doorway.

'Anything interesting?' she said.

'An argument, and we lost. Kermit wanted to throw a little welcoming party for us, and Joanna backed him up, but mama said no.'

'Is that bad? Will it hold you up any?'

'No, I didn't expect that much of a break anyhow. How'd you make out with the dishwasher? Figure out all the buttons?'

'Yes, sure,' Elinor said. 'Only that thing is too much of a project for just two people's dishes. Look, is it all right to make a long-distance call? It's cut-rate time now, and you can take it out of my pay.'

'Long-distance to where?'

'New York,' Elinor said. 'My mother. And my kid. I told him I'd talk to him on the phone tonight.'

Jake had been sitting back comfortably in the big swivel chair behind the desk. Now he slowly came forward in the chair. 'You've got a kid?'

'Yes. Honestly, it won't make any difference in the way I handle the job here. And he's quite a kid. He's – '

'You and the kid live with your mother?'

'Yes.'

'What did you tell her about coming down here?'

'What Sherry told me to. I'm signed up with a theatre group here for a month.'

'All right, stick to that. But don't give your mother this

21

phone number and address. If you want to get in touch with her, do it from our end. You can use the phone in the bedroom. When you're done come back here. I want to show you how to handle all this equipment.'

Elinor still stood there.

'Well?' Jake said.

'Nothing.' Her voice was toneless. 'It won't take long. I'll be right back.'

She was back a few minutes later and listened intently, but with impassive face and cool, remote manner, as Jake explained each piece of equipment in detail. He was gratified to see that she was quick and clever with her hands when asked to demonstrate what she had learned. When he commented on that she shrugged indifferently. 'Can I get some sleep now? It's been a long day.'

He handed her a folder of papers. 'Go through these first. Everything is there that you ought to know about me for conversation purposes. Get it down pat. Otherwise, we could get our wires crossed when we're in company.'

Alone, he went to work on the stage setting. Portable typewriter open on the desk, dictionary and thesaurus next to it, a box of manuscript paper and a dozen sheets of typed manuscript on display around the typewriter. One sheet of typed manuscript he rolled into the typewriter and left as evidence of the author at work.

The stage now set for the duration, the rest of the equipment locked in the closet, he sat down at the desk and dialled Maniscalco's home number in New York. The phone was answered on its first ring.

'Manny?' Jake said.

'Who did you think?' Maniscalco said. 'Did you make contact?'

'Yes.'

'Was the report on Thoren's house accurate?'

'So far.'

Maniscalco said acidly: 'Marvellous. That means they didn't rebuild the house since I put that report together. Was his son there?'

'He was there.'

'You know what I mean,' Maniscalco said. 'Did Sherry hit him right? From what I got about that stud, she's made to order for him.'

'Maybe, but Sherry's not here. She called up just before I left for the airport and told me she was getting married today. She sent a friend to handle this job.'

'Oh, for chrissake!' Maniscalco exploded. 'What the hell got into her? What kind of friend? Some miserable old bagger?'

'No, nobody who ever did this kind of work before. Some kid she worked with in a couple of those off-Broadway shows. A real pin-up, but green. She'll have to learn as she earns. But she'll work out.'

'If she doesn't learn too much,' Maniscalco warned. 'You could always trust Sherry. How much can you trust this one when she finds out what it might be worth to double-cross you?'

Jake laughed. 'You're giving pessimism a bad name, Manny. Anyhow, let me worry about the personnel down here. All I want from you is what you dug up on Thoren's stock transactions. You said you'd have it by today.'

'I've got it. He was selling off chunks of stock about once a month. It started a year and a half ago with sales of around two thousand dollars a month, then after six months it went up to eight thousand a month. Last sale was this January. It was for ten thousand.'

'What about the money? Was it credited to his account or sent to him each time?'

'What you figured. It was sent to him each time. The cheques were cashed for him by the Biscayne National Bank down there. All the same, Jake, that's not proof of blackmail. It could be gambling losses, couldn't it? There's a lot of big-money action around those parts.'

'The percentage says it was blackmail, Manny, so unless you turn up something that says otherwise, that's how I'll play it. If you do turn up anything, don't forget to call me about it.' He gave Maniscalco the number. 'But not too early or often. And no mail at all.'

'I'll leave it to you, Jake. Just remember the bind I'm in,

23

having Guaranty stall on that payment. And it's getting tighter every day. And, Jake, that girl you've got on the job. Once she knows what she can sell to the Thorens – '

'Keep the faith, baby,' Jake said, and replaced the phone on its stand.

He took out a folder from an attaché case. The folder contained a copy of Thoren's insurance policy issued by Guaranty. He opened the policy to its questionnaire and slowly went through the printed questions and Thoren's handwritten answers as he had a dozen times before. Thoren's writing was a minute, tightly disciplined script. It was not, according to the high-priced graphologist Jake had submitted it to, the handwriting of a compulsive gambler, but the graphologist himself, an old pro used by some of the best criminal lawyers in New York, had shrugged away the idea of guaranteeing this. There wasn't enough to go by, there could be concealed factors –

A thought struck Jake. He put the folder down and went into the bedroom. Elinor, decorously clad in pyjamas, was sprawled across the bed, studying the material about him he had given her. She looked up at him.

'I see there's no house rule around here about knocking on doors,' she said coldly.

'None,' Jake said. 'And none about squealing and carrying on like a damn fool if one of us happens to run into the other bare-assed. Now that we've got that settled, I'd like to ask you something about that kid of yours. How old is he?'

'You really want to know?' Elinor said warily.

'Yes.'

She brightened. 'Well, he's only three, but he's one of those kids who – '

'Sure he is. What I want to know is whether having him left any marks on your belly. Any birth striata.'

'Birth striata? What's it your business?'

Jake said: 'Those swimming outfits you took out of your bag were all bikinis. They'll put any marks on your belly right in the spotlight for the Thorens to see. Especially Mrs Thoren, who's likely to know about that kind of thing. So if there are marks, either we'll have to rewrite some of that biography of

24

mine you've got there or switch to one-piece suits. Let's take a look.'

'You don't have to,' Elinor said between her teeth. 'You can take it from me, there are no marks.'

Jake said evenly: 'I take nobody's word for anything in this game, Miss Majeski. Not with what I've got riding on it. Now pull up that jacket.'

Something in his voice made her do it, but furiously, and then, unbidden, she even more furiously tugged down the waistband of the pants so that golden tendrils of pubic hair curled over its elastic. The rounded underbelly showed no marks.

'Well?' she said, and drew her clothing into place.

'All right.' He started to turn away, but when she said, 'Well, I'm glad something is all right,' he turned back again. 'What's that supposed to mean?'

'Nothing.'

'Don't hand me that. The way you said it, it meant something. And you've been putting on a prima donna act for the last hour. What's it all about?'

Elinor said: 'If you have to know, it's about your getting so sore when you found out I had a kid. You wouldn't have given me this job if you knew about the kid before, would you?'

'I didn't have much choice, the way Sherry dumped you on me the last minute. But if I had a choice, no, I wouldn't have given you the job. Kids are a distraction, even fourteen hundred miles away. Sick old mamas in the hospital are a distraction. A husband or boy friend is a distraction if he comes on strong. You can't afford any distractions in this line of work. You have to concentrate on what you're doing every second. One wrong word, one wrong blink of the eye, and I'll be out at least ten thousand in cash without a goddam thing to show for it. If your kid gets a runny nose – '

'Believe me,' Elinor said, 'if he does, you'd be the last one in the world I'd ever tell about it, Mr Dekker.'

5

He woke early and pulled aside the curtain of the study window to look out on the sunlit expanse of Biscayne Bay. The lawn of every house in view ran down to the bay, and at the foot of each lawn was a small dock, most of which had one or two small boats moored to them. On the dock of the house next door, a man on hands and knees was working over what was probably the gear of the sailboat tied up there.

Jake stripped the bedding from the couch and stuffed it into the closet of the study. When he went into the bedroom Elinor was asleep, curled up tightly under the blankets, her head buried under her pillow. She was still asleep when he left the house, dressed in faded chinos, a Hawaiian shirt, and sandals.

A truck with an elevating platform mounted on it was parked beneath one of the palm trees bordering Circular Drive. High up on the platform, a man was hacking away at the foliage with what looked like a machete. 'Heads up,' the man called, and three or four coconuts thudded down into the roadway, followed by lengths of palm frond. One of the coconuts rolled across the road, and Jake went over to pick it up.

He hefted it, and it was like a lead weight in his hand. The driver of the truck, watching this, said: 'It's ready to eat, if you know how to open it. Only trouble is, by the time you get it open you're too tired to eat it.'

Jake walked over to the man. 'That your job? Knocking them down before they come down by themselves on somebody's head?'

'That's the job.'

'Anybody ever get hit with them anyhow?'

'Not that I know of. A car sometimes. You hear about it maybe once a year. Some jerk parks under one of these trees overnight. Next morning he's got a dent in the roof.'

Jake said: 'Still and all, it could be a lot worse if he was driving when it happened. Scare him out of his wits. Might even make him lose control of the car.'

26

The driver shook his head. 'It could, but I never heard of that happening to anybody. Are you the people moved into the de Burgo house?'

'I'm the people,' Jake said.

'Well, you've got four coconut palms of your own in the back there. We'll take care of them during the week.'

'Thanks.'

'No thanks due,' the driver said. 'You're paying the Daystar Association ten bucks a tree for the service. Just don't camp under any of those babies till we're done with them.'

The trees were there to be counted when Jake made his way to the back of the house, along with a solitary royal palm on which a brilliantly coloured woodpecker was hammering away. The lawn underfoot, a coarse, heavy-bladed grass, was flawlessly clipped and still sodden with the night's wetness. Here and there around it were large beds of flowers at least as brilliantly coloured as the woodpecker.

The man tending the gear of the sailboat at the dock next door was now stowing it aboard the boat. He stepped back on the dock as Jake came up. A big man whose features seemed too small for his face, he wore only Bermuda shorts. His hairless, soft-looking body was burned pink by the sun; his nose and lips were smeared with a white ointment.

When Jake introduced himself the man said: 'Yes, I heard you were moving in. My name's Webb. Milt Webb. Say, is it true you're a writer?'

'That's what my publisher tells me.'

'You look more like a pro linebacker to me.' Webb's pursy little mouth twisted in a smile. 'I'll have to admit that's a relief.'

Jake smiled in his turn. 'What did you expect to have show up? Some kind of hippie?'

'You never know nowadays. Not that I was too much worried. McCloy's careful about who he puts up for membership in the Association. It only means trouble all around if somebody who's already moved in gets blackballed and has to pack out again. You're on a lease now, aren't you?'

'Six-month lease, cash in advance,' Jake said. 'Money to be applied to the purchase price.'

'Figure on buying?'

'Yes, now that I've seen the place. This is the first look I had at it. I dealt through an agent.'

'I know. Well, now that we met I can tell you this much. You won't have any trouble when you have to show up before the membership committee.'

'The sooner, the better,' Jake said.

Webb shook his head sombrely. 'It won't be all that soon. The full committee has to be present, and there's supposed to be five on it. There's only four right now. We had a sudden death a little while back. Auto accident.'

'Too bad,' Jake said.

'You can say that again,' Webb assured him solemnly. 'It really was a hell of a thing. One of the finest men you could ever hope to meet, no more than fifty-three, fifty-four, looked as fit as you do, and then – bingo!' He snapped his fingers sharply. 'Walter Thoren. He was a big loss to us.'

'Thoren?' Jake said. 'Oh, Jesus, and we barged in on them – '

'What?'

Jake said: 'Last night. I couldn't locate my place, so I pulled up there to ask about it. My wife and I must have been with them half an hour. They couldn't have been nicer. If I knew about them being in mourning – '

'Oh. Well, they're not in mourning like that any more. It happened a month ago. Not that Charlotte – Mrs Thoren – wouldn't put herself out for you no matter how she felt. A wonderful woman. And he was a wonderful man. One out of a million. What a wallop it was when I heard he was gone.'

'Nice kids, too,' Jake remarked. 'Looked to me like they got a real old-fashioned bringing-up.'

Webb's mouth briefly pouted as if he were trying to drive away a fly that had settled on his upper lip. 'That's what they got all right. But kids today – ' He jerked a thumb at the boat. 'Come on aboard, and I'll set up some drinks. You got any prejudice against starting the day with a vodka and juice?'

'None that I can't be talked out of,' Jake said.

Reclining on the gently heaving deck of the boat, vodka and

grapefruit juice in hand, Webb said: 'Seems like I need a drink any time the subject of today's kids comes up. I had headaches with mine, too. Thank God, they're both married and settled down now. Well, almost settled down.'

'You mean Mrs Thoren can't say that yet.'

'Poor woman. No, she can't. But it was Walter who was really taking the beating. Charlotte's easygoing about things. Walter wasn't. He had very tight standards. Tolerant, yes. But up to a point. You understand what I'm getting at?'

'I'm not so sure I do,' Jake said.

'There's no mystery about it,' Webb said. He made a sweeping gesture in the direction of Miami Beach. 'Jewsville. You know that, don't you? Wall-to-wall Yid. And when one of your own kids waltzes in and announces she's going to marry into them –'

'The son?' Jake said.

'No, the daughter. Joanna.'

'I see. There was a young fellow named Freeman with the family last night. Is he the one?'

Webb said: 'He's the one. Hal Freeman. The complication is that his father's been family doctor for the Thorens and us and lot of others around here for years. Fine doctor, nice, level-headed guy who knows his place, enjoys a good Yid joke as much as anybody else – now how do you tell a man like that his son just isn't wanted around here? Certainly not to be papa to your grandchildren. You can see the fix Walter was in.'

'Tough,' Jake said. 'But how about the Thoren boy setting his sister straight? Kermit. Sometimes a girl will listen to her big brother when she won't listen to anybody else.'

Webb snorted. 'Let me put it to you this way, Jake. You don't mind my calling you Jake, do you?'

'Hell, no, Milt.'

'Well, let me put it to you this way. As far as Kermit is concerned – and I've told it to him right to his face – the only project he seems to be interested in is proving he's champion cocksman of the good old U.S.A. He's worse than useless in a family trouble like this. Matter of fact, he's the one brought young Freeman in the house to start with. They were kids together in school and buddies over in Miami U. and so on. I'll admit this much. In my private opinion, the boy's not too happy about this business himself. But once he knew his father was dead-set against it, why, naturally, he just had to shove it up the old man. He and Walter never did get along.'

'No communication,' Jake said.

'Yeah, that's the word you writers use for it today, isn't it?' Webb finished his drink and helped himself to another, freshening Jake's drink as well. 'Still, it wasn't altogether Kermit's fault. Not by a long shot. If ever a man enjoyed keeping his mouth tight shut, it was Walter. Ask him a question, you'd get an answer. Outside of that, whether it was with his kids or anybody else, he was Silent Joe himself.'

'Not so good,' Jake said.

'Maybe not.' Webb finished half his drink in one long gulp. 'On the other hand, who can tell? When he did have something to say, it meant everybody sure as hell listened. Sort of a natural leader, that man, and without even trying. Ran the Membership Committee here, big wheel on the Civic Planning Association over on the Beach –'

'Planning for what?'

'Oh, to try to keep the whole Beach from being chewed up and swallowed by the real estate interests. The hotel and highrise people. The Association was always trying to block those building code variances you can buy any time you want to stick up an apartment house in somebody's front yard. And trying to keep the hotel owners from ruining the shoreline there any more than they have already. After all, they ruin the Beach, they're knocking down our values right here. But it's an unofficial association. It never carried enough weight to stop the big boys when they wanted to roll.'

Jake said: 'All the same, they couldn't have liked Thoren too much. Someone like that can make himself a real nuisance to the big boys.'

'Yeah, once in a long while maybe. Not that it ever bothered Walter. An absolutely fearless guy. Bert McCloy even talked to me once about what it could mean to have him run as an independent for mayor. But as I told Bert, you have to face the facts. When it comes to running Miami Beach, if you're not one of the Chosen People – you know what I mean?'

'I know what you mean,' Jake said.

6

When he got back to the house Elinor, still in pyjamas, was at the kitchen table with the pages of biographical material spread out before her.

'Eat yet?' Jake said.

'No, I was waiting for you like a good little wife should. I saw you from the back window talking to that man. Who is he?'

'Our next-door neighbour. Guy named Milt Webb. A live one.'

'What's that mean?'

'He's a heavy drinker with a chip on his shoulder. That kind talks a lot. Sometimes they say something worth listening to.'

'Did he?'

'Yes. He's taking it hard because young Joanna Thoren intends to marry that Freeman boy you saw over there with her last night. Freeman's Jewish.'

'Oh. But what makes that his business?'

'Well, aside from his affection for the Thorens, which he talks about too much to make convincing, what finally came through after three large doses of vodka and juice was that Joanna is likely to inherit half the property when her mama dies. Which means her Jewish husband could wind up living right here on Daystar Island Number Two next to the Webbs. And what can you legally do about it?'

'Oh, for chrissake,' Elinor said, 'if that's all people can find to worry about – '

'Not Milt. He's also plenty worried about those Cubans who got away from Castro and landed in Miami across the bay there. He knows for a fact that they're planning to take over Miami just the way the Jews took over Miami Beach. Poor

Milt has a lot of things like that on his mind. No wonder he has to start off the day with a crockful of vodka.'

'He sounds like just another loudmouth lush to me,' Elinor said. 'We're not going to have to be real friendly with him, are we?'

'As friendly as we have to be. Now tell me something. What would you say the odds are on a guy like Walter Thoren committing suicide because his daughter told him she was going to marry a Jew?'

Elinor shrugged. 'How can I even judge? I hardly know anything about him.'

'From what you do know about him.'

'Well, I can't picture anybody committing suicide for that reason. Not unless he was totally kooky to start with. And you told me Thoren wasn't.'

'No, he wasn't. And the statistics on someone killing himself because his child was going to make an interreligious or interracial marriage are zero. Murder for that reason, yes. Suicide, no.'

Elinor said: 'You mean there are even statistics for that?'

'There are statistics for almost everything. And you learn damn quick which ones are important when that's how you pay the rent.' Jake pointed at the papers on the table. 'How are you making out with my life story there? Did you get it down pat?'

'Yes. Want to try me out?'

'Not now. Breakfast first. And make the coffee double strength. The only way to keep Milt talking was to stay with him drink for drink on an empty stomach.'

Elinor went to the refrigerator. 'It won't be much of a breakfast. All we've got is the same as last night. Eggs and cheese.'

'Then make the same thing.'

She did. While she was at it she said: 'First thing I'll have to do this morning is go shopping. Maybe you're hooked on cheese omelette, but I'm not. If you let me have the car – '

'No. You can't use the car because your licence would be a giveaway to your name and address in case of any trouble on the road. That reminds me. You'll have to go through your pocketbook and give me everything that has your name and address on it. I'll put them away for you until we're done here. And we'll go shopping this afternoon. There are more important things to do first.'

'Like what?'

Jake looked at his watch. 'It's almost ten now. At about eleven every morning, when it's nice, the Thorens sit around for a while by their swimming pool. At eleven-thirty you're going to take a walk along the bay and find them there.'

'Suppose I don't? I mean, find them there.'

'It's a percentage play, and the odds say you will. The idea is to get talking with Mrs Thoren. That's where the marketing bit comes in handy. You're new around here, you've come for any advice you can get about where to do your shopping. There's nothing like asking advice from someone to get cozy with her. Then, with that and with the way you've already softened up Kermit, you should be able to wangle a lunch invitation from them. As a matter of fact, you damn well better.'

'Then what?'

Jake said: 'Then it gets a little tricky. You have to let them know you'd love to eat lunch with them, but here I am all by myself sitting over a hot typewriter. Somehow or other, get them to include me in the invitation. Then you phone me, and I'll come right over. Between us both, if we play our cards right, we should be able to get invited to hang around awhile there every day.'

'You really think so? I don't see it. They are hardly what you would call a swinging crowd.'

'I know,' Jake said. 'But they have a swimming pool and we don't. Neither does Milt Webb. If the subject comes up, they don't have to be real swinging to be hospitable about their pool.'

Elinor took her time appraising this, then shook her head in wonderment. 'Talk about computers. Do you have every minute of the whole month figured out like that?'

'It would be nice if I could, wouldn't it?'

3

'No, I think it would be kind of creepy. I don't dig computers very much. Just people.'

'Then you can rest easy, because most of this script has to be made up as we go along. For that matter, we may not even be here a month. I could lick this case or be licked by it any day before then.' Jake saw the alarm in her face as she handed him his plate of omelette. 'Don't let that worry you. You get your money when it's all over, no matter how it comes out.'

She looked relieved. 'Well, all right then. I was already in one show that folded all of a sudden on the road. That was my Christmas present last year, the show folding. Once a year is enough of that for me.'

'No sweat. In this show the producer pays off for the run-of-the-play contract, win or lose. If you deliver.'

'Oh, if it comes to weaseling invitations out of people to go swimming in their pool – '

'There's more to it than that,' Jake said. He dug into his omelette. 'There's a phone in Mrs Thoren's bedroom. When we're over there later on, you have to bug it.'

He saw the fork waver in Elinor's hand. Then she very carefully laid down the fork. Now look, Mr Dekker – '

'Jake.'

'Let's keep it Mr Dekker until we settle this. So you might as well know right now, Mr Dekker, I'm not bugging anybody's phone. Not even if the FBI asked me to do it. And to go sneaking into that woman's bedroom – '

Jake said: 'You're drawing a pretty fine line, aren't you? You'll keep everybody in the room pinned down while I do it, but you won't do it yourself.'

'Well, maybe it is a fine line, but that's how I feel about it. I'd foul the whole thing up anyhow. Why can't you do it?'

'Because,' Jake said, 'it's not likely that a man would bust a brassière strap or tear his stockings and have to go up to madam's bedroom to make repairs.'

'Oh.' Elinor thought it over at length, then said unhappily: 'I'm sorry. I really am. But I can't see it. There must be some other way – '

'That's beside the point, because this is the way I want it done. And it's your job to do it. Let's face the facts, Ellie girl. Three thousand bucks is close to being star money. I'm not paying that for a couple of walk-ons in this production.'

Elinor gave him a strained smile. 'Honest to God, are you really as hard-boiled as you're trying to sound? Knowing how I feel about it – '

'No,' Jake cut in, 'let's not turn this into one of those delightful cocktail-party character-analysis sessions. Just lay it on the line. Do you follow all instructions from now on and stay on the job, or do you say goodbye, Mr Dekker, and take the noon plane back to New York?'

Elinor said cannily: 'And what happens if it's goodbye? The Thorens already think I'm your wife. You can't just pick another wife out of the hat to show them, can you?'

'No, I'll have to handle this solo. It won't be easy, I won't like it, but it can be done.'

'Can it? And how do you explain around here what happened if I go back to New York right after we moved in?'

'Oh, that,' Jake said. 'That's the easy part. After I put you in the cab to the airport, I drop in on Milt Webb and tell him I could use a few more belts of his vodka, because when you looked around this morning you said this wasn't your idea of glamorous Miami Beach, and we had a big fight about it, and you walked out on me. If I know Milt, by tomorrow I'll have everybody on the whole island sympathizing with me.'

'And you would,' Elinor marvelled. 'You really would. Nothing can throw you, can it?'

She abruptly rose from the table and walked out of the kitchen. He waited a few minutes, then went into the bedroom. She was lying across the bed, an arm flung over her eyes.

Jake stood looking down at her. 'I take it you're staying,' he said.

She removed the arm. 'You ought to be glad I have a kid,' she said. 'If it wasn't for him – for what it costs with a kid – but you probably thought about that, too, didn't you? You're so goddam clever about everything.'

'And honest with myself,' Jake said.

'Look who's giving lectures on honesty. In your line of work you can't say a word that isn't a lie.'

Jake told her coldly; 'I said honest with myself. Now try this on for size. Suppose I said all right, you don't have to do anything on this job but a little light housekeeping? Only, since I'm paying three thousand dollars for the housekeeping, I'm entitled to climb into bed with you now and then. No ifs, ands, or buts.' He held up a hand to cut off what she was going to say. 'No, I'm not offering you that deal. I just want you to figure out what you'd do if I did. Be honest with yourself about it, even if it hurts. Then see what you come up with.'

He waited, his eyes fixed on hers, until she turned her head away. Then he said: 'Mrs Thoren's phone is on a separate line, and it's unlisted. When you do the job on it, make sure to get me the number. Now let's go over the floor plan so you know which room is hers.'

7

She called him from the Thoren house at noon with the lunch invitation, and he wasted no time joining the company beside the pool there. Then he watched impassively as Elinor tried to stall off the inevitable. Finally, with condolences paid, with swimming privileges offered and accepted, with the story of the missing ring rehashed, with conversation temporarily dried up, she made her excuses and disappeared into the house. When she came out she gave him the slightest of nods along with a look that wished he were dead. Combined, they indicated that like it or not, she had planted the bug in the phone.

A white-painted cast-iron table stood on the lawn near the pool, a beach umbrella sprouting from the centre of it. Jake had manoeuvered his chair in between Joanna's and her mother's close to the table, with Elinor seated opposite him. Now, after she returned from her mission, she passed by the table and plumped herself down in a lounger a fair distance away. Kermit, who had been in and out of the pool, promptly arranged an umbrella over her and seated himself at her feet. His hand very soon came to rest on her ankle. She let it rest there.

Jake glanced at Charlotte Thoren to see if she was taking notice of this. That pale-lipped, haggard face, shadowed by a broad-brimmed straw hat and masked by oversized sunglasses, was impossible to read. He turned toward Joanna and caught her staring at him.

She reddened and tried to cover her embarrassment with a too-bright voice and manner. 'You don't have very much to say, do you? Are all writers like that? Saving it for their books?'

Jake shrugged. 'If you mean the kind of writers I think you do, you'll have to ask them about it. I'm a ghost-writer. It's a different branch of the business.'

'I know. You write the books, and other people get their names on them. You do the work, they get the credit. That must be awfully infuriating sometimes, isn't it?'

'Yes.'

Joanna waited a moment, then said with mixed irritation and amusement: 'That's all? Just yes?'

'Joanna,' Charlotte Thoren said, 'don't pry. And, Kermit, you will not sit down to lunch in your robe. Not with company at the table. Do get dressed at once.'

'If that's what the company wants,' Kermit said to Elinor, then cheerfully took himself off when she gave him a firm but friendly shove and said, 'Yes, that's what the company wants.'

Joanna said to Jake: 'Do you mind my asking about your writing?'

'No. But I'd rather ask you some questions.' Jake pointed at the feathery line of trees bordering the lawn. 'What are those? Some kind of pine?'

'Not really. They only look like it. They're casuarinas.'

'Easy to tend?'

'I guess so. Why? Thinking of planting some?'

'Could be.' He got up and strolled across the lawn, studying the trees, Joanna close behind him. In the shadow of the gnarled branches, he turned to face her. 'Look, I'm sorry about

37

it, but I got you here on false pretences. It was the only way I could talk to you alone for a minute.'

'Talk about what?'

Jake hesitated. 'I feel like a damn fool saying it, but it's about your brother. The way he's moving in on Ellie. You must have seen it for yourself.'

Joanna looked flustered. 'Well, yes. But Kermit goes around adoring every pretty girl he meets. It doesn't mean anything.'

Jake shook his head. 'Not according to Milt Webb.'

'Oh,' Joanna said. 'Now the enlightenment sets in. You've been getting the word from Mr Webb. Malice, Incorporated.'

Jake said: 'He's malicious, all right. And dirty-minded and bigoted. But watching your brother in action just now, I could tell that Mr Webb sometimes touches on the truth. Not that I'm taking his fine moral tone about Kermit. Hell, I'm the last one who'd have a right to. I went through a time myself – '

'Yes?'

'Funny,' Jake said reflectively. 'It's something about myself I've never even told Ellie. Now here I am ready to spill it to you when we hardly know each other. I guess you can blame yourself for that. How old are you? Nineteen? Twenty?'

'Almost nineteen.'

'Then you're two years younger than Ellie. But somehow you seem older than her. More mature.'

Under her dark tan, Joanna's cheeks reddened again. 'I think Ellie's very sweet.'

'Oh, sure. But like a kid. Like someone who doesn't know how to grow up and become a woman. I wish there were some way you could give her lessons in that.'

Joanna looked grave. 'That's your job, isn't it, Jake? And maybe you ought to start on it by telling her whatever you were just going to tell me.'

'No, I'd rather not. And it concerns Kermit, too. You see, I went through the stud phase myself. A real galloping Casanova for a while, starting when I was only around sixteen. To put it brutally, if it wore skirts it was obviously sent to me by heaven for just one purpose. And the ironic part of it – the part that makes me sick when I think of it now – '

38

'Yes?' Joanna said encouragingly.

'Well, I didn't know it then, but the whole thing was built on hate. It was all a way of putting down my father. I had a picture of him while I was growing up, the noblest Roman of them all, you know what I mean. Then when I was sixteen I found out he was double-crossing my mother with some woman in the neighbourhood. It knocked me right off balance. After that, whenever I scored with a girl it was like landing a punch on the old man's jaw. I had a real hang-up until my analyst straightened me out.'

'You were in analysis?'

'For a couple of years. Until I understood my motivations. And understood I was no unique case. It seems a lot of over-idealistic kids take off in the same direction the day they find out papa isn't a saint. That's why I don't go around passing judgement on people like your brother, the way Milt Webb does.'

'Maybe not,' Joanna said, 'but it certainly seems to me you're passing judgement on my father.' Her small flash of temper instantly melted into warm sympathy. 'Look, I know how natural it is to apply your case to everyone else. But it's wrong to do that, Jake. It's unjust to yourself and them. Believe me, Kermit never had your kind of experience. He couldn't, because my father never gave a damn for any woman except my mother. Honestly, from the way they bored him, I don't think he even liked other women very much. Including some highly attractive ones.'

'Oh, sure,' Jake said bitterly. 'That's what we'd all like to believe about papa, isn't it?'

'Jake, when you sound like that – Look, I've heard friends of his actually kid about it. Old Faithful. And I was right there one night when Nera Ortega – you haven't met her yet, have you?'

'No.'

'Well, when you do you'll see for yourself she's something pretty special. She lives in that place the other side of yours, and her husband's away on business a lot of the time, so she's a little too much on the loose for her own good. Anyhow, when she was over here for dinner one night she got a bit loaded and made a pass at Father. It was nothing, really. Totally harmless. But the way he reacted, Jake, was something to see. I mean, he turned absolutely white with rage. He actually scared her sober. And the very first trouble Kermit got himself into with a woman later on was with her. Do you see what I'm getting at?'

Jake frowned in thought. 'I think I do. You mean Kermit is reacting against your father's morality, not his immorality.'

'I'm almost positive of it. Not that understanding the cause and effect pretties it up any. I'll talk to him about steering clear of Ellie, Jake. That's what you'd like me to do, isn't it?'

Jake said: 'Yes. As if it came from you, not me. It's a lot better than my having it out with him where it could end up with his getting a busted jaw. I have a hunch Kermit's really a very good guy underneath. And he's your brother, Jo. The last thing I'd want to do is get rough with him.'

Joanna measured him with her eyes, then said smilingly: 'I'm glad of that. For Kermit's sake.' Her expression sobered. 'And you're a very good guy, too. But Jake –'

'Go ahead and say it, Jo. After what's been said already, there's no reason why we shouldn't be completely frank with each other.'

'All right, I will say it. Jake, did it ever strike you that you've only exchanged one hang-up for another?'

'I have?'

'Yes. I mean – well, it's your marriage. It's in trouble, isn't it?'

'Is it that obvious?'

'I'm afraid it is. So is the reason for it. How old are you?'

'Oh, thirty-five, my good days. Seventy, my bad ones.'

'You see the way you said that? There it is. That consciousness of age difference is on your mind every time you look at Ellie. That's why you sit there with that hard look on your face, just watching every move she makes, and all pent up inside. It's no good that way. You have to try to relate to her.'

Jake shook his head, 'I do try, Jo, but it's uphill all the way. Believe me, it's not like talking to you. Anyhow, I have that much now. At least, I hope I have. The chance to talk to you when the pressure gets a little too much to take. You won't mind that, will you?'

'No. Of course I won't.'

'Although you won't be around too much longer, I suppose. That boy who was with you here last night – he's the one, isn't he?'

'Last night? Oh, Hal Freeman.' Joanna slowly ran a hand up and down the trunk of the tree they stood under, feeling its texture with her fingertips. 'Well,' she said vaguely, 'we do have sort of an understanding, but who knows? Kid stuff, really. No, I guess I'll be around for quite a while yet.'

Going into the house for lunch, Jake lagged behind with Elinor. 'Did you get that transmitter into the phone?' he asked.

'Yes. And I wish I didn't. I'm scared to even walk in there now.'

'As long as it doesn't show on your face. You're doing fine so far, so don't blow it now. Did Kermit have anything interesting to tell you?'

'What you'd expect. Oh, yes' – Elinor gave him a malicious sidelong glance – 'he said you reminded him a lot of his father. It wasn't a compliment.'

Jake said: 'I'll start worrying when he does compliment me. Did he happen to mention a woman named Nera Ortega?'

'No. You really turned that Joanna on, didn't you? What were you telling her?'

'About her brother's roving hands when he's around you. She said she'd pass the word on to him.'

Elinor said scornfully: 'You think that'll bother him any? Half the fun for anybody like him is knowing he's putting down some stupid husband.'

'I wouldn't be at all surprised,' said Jake.

8

As soon as he could decently get away from the lunch table, he led Elinor home at a quick-step. Back in the study, he immediately activated the transmitter in the Thorens' dining-room phone while she stood watching from the doorway. For her benefit he laid his phone on the desk and planted a monitor next to it. The tired voice which emerged from the monitor was Charlotte Thoren's.

'– *precisely why. And Joanna is right to make an issue of it. It's time you returned to your classes anyhow. You've been away from them long enough.*'

'*Return to them for what?*' Kermit's voice was acid. '*You know graduate school doesn't mean a damn thing to the draft board any more unless you're pre-med.*'

'*Your uncle will attend to the draft board when the time comes.*'

'*Well, I don't know if I want him to. I'm starting to think the army might be a lot easier to take than the kind of nagging I get around here.*'

'*Oh, Kermit*' – that was Joanna, elaborately pitying – '*if you knew how horribly infantile you sounded –*'

'*Infantile?*' Kermit, with outrage. '*What the hell's gotten into you all of a sudden? First you make me out some kind of sex maniac because I –*'

There was dead silence. Jake waited a few seconds, then replaced the phone on its stand.

'What happened?' Elinor said.

'Somebody put in a call to them. It cut off the transmitter. What did you make of that argument?'

Elinor said: 'I guess Joanna must have cut loose about Kermit and me as soon as we were out of there. You don't just sit and watch the pot, do you? You sort of like to stir it up a little, too.'

Jake said: 'I don't have time to sit and watch. And things are shaping up fine for you this way.'

'For me?'

'Yes, because tomorrow we're going over there for a swim, and Joanna's going to be very warm and friendly to you while I get Kermit into the garage to talk Jaguars. She'll want to pump you about me, and you'll play along with that. It's all the opening you'll need to pump her about her father. I want to know especially what he did the day he was killed. How he put in that day.'

Elinor said doubtfully: 'You think I can do that without her catching wise?'

'If you don't work up a sweat about it in advance. Just play it cool, and let me do all the worrying for the team.'

'Oh, sure.'

Jake said: 'Look, I learned something the hard way. The first time Sherry worked with me I told her she'd get fifteen hundred no matter what, and fifteen hundred extra if we broke the case. That was my mistake. She was so hungry for the whole three thousand that she wound herself up in knots and blew everything. That's why it's three thousand now, win or lose. So that you will let me do all the worrying.'

'Including what happens to me if somebody finds out I bugged a phone?'

'Including that. Did you remember to get the number of the phone when you bugged it? I want to make a test run.'

She gave him the number, then said: 'How can you test it now? There's nobody talking in that bedroom, is there? They're all downstairs.'

'You're worrying again,' Jake said. 'Didn't I tell you not to?' He dialled the number and used the sonic whistle. The only response to it from the monitor was a heavy droning sound.

'What's that?' Elinor said. 'Did I foul up something with that gimmick?'

'No, you did a first-class job with it. That noise is what I wanted to hear. It's Mrs Thoren's air conditioner. Most new models are pretty quiet, but I noticed from outside the house there that the ones in those bedroom windows upstairs aren't that new.'

'Noticed it?' Elinor said sardonically. 'Or looked for it?'

'Noticed it. Don't get the wrong idea, Ellie baby. Nobody can think of everything in advance. You'd go out of your skull trying to. The real trick in this game is knowing how to use what turns up along the way.'

'Then I'd sure hate like hell to play poker with you.'

'Too bad, because I was thinking of playing you a few hands for that three thousand you're getting.' Jake looked at his watch. 'So what we'll do instead is go shopping for groceries now. Then around cocktail time we'll see if we can make friends with a lady name of Nera Ortega.'

9

Nera was, as Joanna had put it, something pretty special. A dark-eyed beautiful little blonde with disproportionately hefty breasts and rump, she was possibly thirty at first glance, definitely over forty at second. It was the fine lines on the upper lip and at the corners of the eyes which gave her away. That and the purpled veininess of those otherwise trim legs.

Her husband Fons (*'No, not really,'* he told Elinor, *'but the name Alfonso is a bit overwhelming among friends, don't you think?'*) had been the one to spot them from the window as they strolled the property line between the houses as though survey-ing the premises, and had cordially invited them in for a drink. The house, a Florida variation of hacienda, was almost exag-geratedly Latin-American in its furnishings, right down to the massive pair of bull's horns mounted over the fireplace and the basketlike jai-alai cesta hung on a wall. And the drink turned out to be sangría.

There was also another Daystar Islander on hand, a big, rawboned woman, white-haired and with skin tanned the colour of old leather. Patty Tucker. Mrs Stewart Tucker. Her husband had been Ortega's business partner in South American export and import until his death two years ago.

'Lung cancer, poor lamb,' she said grimly. 'Obviously, I

haven't learned a goddam thing from it, have I?' She chain-smoked ferociously.

Since she was a cheerful and opinionated talker, and since Nera Ortega irritably disagreed with almost every opinion, the conversation moved along briskly. Then Jake mentioned the name Thoren, and it froze solid on the spot. It never completely thawed after that.

The three guests left together. Crossing the lawn to the driveway, where Patty Tucker's bicycle was parked, Jake said apologetically to her: 'I saw you shake your head at me as soon as I opened my mouth about meeting the Thorens, but it was too late. What's it all about between the Ortegas and them? Some kind of feud?'

'That's what it amounts to. Damn shame, too. They were such close friends for years.'

'And one day there was a misunderstanding and it all went bang.' Jake nodded wisely. 'I've seen it happen. Afterward, no one could even say why.'

'Not in this case. No, indeed,' Patty said, 'we all know why. Matter of fact, I was right there when the first shot was fired.'

'Shot?' said Elinor.

'Figuratively speaking, pet.' Patty started to mount the bicycle, then changed her mind about it. She took her time lighting a cigarette. 'What the hell,' she said through the smoke jetting from her nostrils, 'Fons and Nera would kill me for blabbing to you about it, but I'd rather have it me than somebody else with his own fish to fry. The whole thing was ridiculous anyhow. It happened about three years ago. Fons was away on business, and Nera had gone to this dinner party the Thorens gave. Completely informal, family had a few friends, that sort of thing. And a good time being had by all until Nera decided to make a fool of herself, and Walter Thoren blew it up into a total disaster.'

'That's odd,' Jake said. 'Somehow, I had a picture of him as always playing it cool, no matter what. The strong, silent type.'

'Oh, he was all of that. A big, brooding, Scandinavian sort of man. But terribly strait-laced. No boozing it up, no dirty jokes, no fun and games with the girls. And believe me, he had his opportunities. Some of the females in these parts would have been only too willing to help loosen up those repressions.'

'Nera, too?' said Elinor.

'Nera, too. Although for all the good it did her or any of them, they might as well have had a letch for an iceberg. But that night, because she was feeling sorry for herself what with Fons being away so much, and because she was well-liquored when she walked into the house and completely stoned by dessert, she made a weepy, pathetic play for Walter right at the table. And, God rest his Puritan soul, instead of making a joke of it, he told her off the way you'd do a pup that had dirtied your carpet.'

'How awful,' Elinor said. 'I mean, for all of you.'

'It was. But I'll let you in on something, pet. I had the damnedest feeling it was worse for Walter. He looked absolutely sick at having been pawed by Nera even that little bit.'

'And you'd never seen him like that before?' Jake said.

'Well, there'd never been that kind of situation before. Still and all, most of us felt it would blow over in a week or two. We'd get Nera to plead drunkenness, and Walter would go along with it because he liked Fons, and so on. It didn't work out that way. When you were with the Thorens, did you meet the son? Kermit?'

'Yes,' Jake said.

'What did you think of him?'

'Well – ' said Jake.

'Exactly. That boy has been a trial to his family from the day he discovered how dim-witted adolescent girls can be. And, for that matter, some grown-up women who should have known a damn sight better.

'So this young lump of conceit – he couldn't have been more than twenty or twenty-one then – having witnessed that scene at the table, decided Nera was simply demonstrating her need for some male servicing. The very next day he showed up here at the house and went to work peddling his wares. For sheer unmitigated gall – '

Jake said: 'Was she the one who told you about it?'

'She did. She had to, because whenever I dropped in on her, there was Kermit. He hung around day after day like that. She told me that first she thought it was funny. Then it struck her that since his parents, along with the rest of us, certainly knew about it, she could drive them wild by going along with the joke. As far as she was concerned, it was a lovely way of hitting back at Walter. And, of course, she assured me, there was really nothing at all going on between her and Kermit.'

'Was there?' Elinor asked.

Patty made a wry face. 'Well, Fons sure as hell thought so the day he walked in without notice and found them together in a highly compromising position. At least, that's what they used to call it when I was a sweet young thing. Lucky for her, Nera can think fast. She instantly started screeching she had practically been assaulted and never gave up on that story. Even luckier for her, most of the money is hers, so Fons was not that anxious to get a divorce. A little face-saving for him, and Nera was home free. And after the smoke had cleared away, so was Kermit. Walter did all the talking for him, but it was the last time he and Fons ever went near each other.'

Jake said: 'You think he might have paid off Fons?'

'Good heavens, no. Fons would never take that kind of money. Whatever gave you that idea?'

'It was just a thought. When you're the rich father of a stud like Kermit you could be stuck for some heavy cash payments under the table now and then. Hush money they used to call it when I was a sweet young thing.'

Patty laughed. 'Yes, I recognize the good old tabloid style. And trust a writer to think of something like that. It might not be so far-fetched either. It really wouldn't shock me speechless to find out Walter sometimes did pay to keep that boy out of the papers. Anyhow, there it is. Now you know why Fons and Nera took it the way they did when you brought up the Thorens. But don't let it bother you. They're probably sorry already that they weren't more mannerly about it.' She squeezed Elinor's hand hard, and then Jake's. 'You are a pair of darlings, you know. I'm sure they want to be friends with you as much as I do.'

When she had wheeled around the bend of the road and out of sight Elinor said: 'She's nice, isn't she?'

'No. If you're nice you don't go around telling dirty stories about your friends.'

'But you practically wormed it out of her,' Elinor said indignantly. 'And she was only explaining things so our feelings wouldn't be hurt.'

'She was doing it to put down Nera. Their husbands were partners for years. Who do you think her husband had his eyes on any time they were all together? She must have had her bellyful of Nera long ago.'

'Oh, man,' Elinor said. 'You don't trust anyone at all, do you?'

'Not Patty Tucker, for sure. Did you hear her say everyone around here knew what was going on between Nera and Kermit?'

'Yes.'

'Well, the odds are she's the one who let them know about it. And probably tipped off Fons, too, which is why he could catch his wife in the act.'

Elinor said: 'But he did catch her in the act. And I have news for you. If you have the least idea I could ever get to be buddies with Nera –'

'I don't any more. She hated you like poison from the minute we walked in there.'

Elinor looked startled. 'I didn't think you noticed that. Most men wouldn't have.'

'Most men don't have to notice things like that. But I knew right away we'd have to cross her name off your buddy list. No woman like that wants someone like you around. It would be like having a mirror in front of her all the time showing her what she looked like twenty years ago, before the wrinkles set in.'

'Well, I'm just as glad she's off my list,' Elinor said. 'Don't forget it works the other way around, too.'

10

They had an early dinner. When Elinor brought the coffee pot to the table, Jake said: 'You can have your coffee in the study. The Thorens should be sitting down to eat around now. I want you to pipe in on them and get it all down on tape. Remember what I showed you about marking the tape?'

'Yes.'

'Well, anything worth while you hear, mark it right there. That's important. Otherwise, I can be stuck with reading a couple of hours of tape all about the weather.'

'Yes, but how do I know for sure when something is worth while?'

'Use your brain. And if there's any doubt, there's no doubt. Just mark it.'

He remained at the table after she left, his eyes fixed unseeingly on the far wall of the kitchen. When he got around to his coffee he found it cold. He went to the stove, reheated the pot, and had a cup of it, black and bitter, while he stood there. Then he sat down at the table again.

He blinked at the sudden brightness when Elinor walked into the kitchen and switched on the light. She looked at the wall clock. 'It's after nine. Do you mean you've been sitting here like that for two hours?'

Jake said vaguely: 'I suppose so. Did you know Denmark has the second highest suicide rate in the world after Japan?'

'I didn't even know Japan was first. Oh, I get it. I suppose Walter Thoren was Danish.'

'His people were. According to that big obit he got in the paper here, his parents emigrated to Minnesota from Denmark. And that oversized picture on the dining-room wall over there is Red House Square in Copenhagen. It's not that good a picture, you'd hang it up for art's sake.'

Elinor looked sceptical. 'So what? You're not saying people inherit the urge to commit suicide, are you?'

'No, because when Danes and Japanese emigrate, their

49

suicide rate drops down to the local one. But it's interesting that Thoren's mother and father both died the same way he did, in an auto crash. He could have had them in mind when he first started thinking about a way to kill himself that would look like an accident.' Jake got stiffly to his feet. 'How'd you make out with the tape? Hear anything good?'

'That's what I came in to tell you. That Senator Sprague and his wife were there for dinner – her name's Lucille – and most of the talk was just about people in the family and then some politics. But as soon as Joanna and Kermit went away, the senator came down on Mrs Thoren about how she was spending too much money from the estate. He said – '

'No, don't tell me about it,' Jake said. 'Let's hear it.'

From the armchair in the study he watched Elinor reverse the tape. 'I'll start it a little ways back,' she said. 'Then you'll get the whole thing. It's not much altogether.'

' – *send my regards to him, Joanna.*' It was Senator Sprague's professionally mellow tone. '*And remind him to write me when he gets there. Good night, dear. Good night, Kermit. Watch your driving, Kermit.*'

A long silence. A chink of cup against saucer. Then Sprague's voice again, but now barely above ear level. '*Charlotte, there is something you must explain to me. And I don't want you to turn on the frost about this, because I have every right to bring it up. As administrator of the estate – *'

'*Or what's left of it.*' Mrs Sprague, tartly.

'*Never mind that, Lucille. What Walter did with his money is not your affair. Or mine. But this has nothing to do with him. Charlotte, just before Lucille and I left the hotel I got a call from Matthews at the bank. He was very much disturbed. Do you know why?*'

'*He had no right to call.*' Charlotte Thoren's voice was cold with anger.

'*Charlotte, Charlie Matthews has not only been handling your banking for twenty years, he's a friend of the family. When you walked in there this afternoon and calmly drew ten thousand dollars from an account that barely – *'

'*That's enough. I don't want to discuss it.*'

'But ten thousand in cash, Charlotte. In cash, mind you. What conceivable on God's earth –'

'It is my money. I will do with it as I choose.'

'I know it's your money.' Sprague's voice was growing louder. 'Unfortunately, so do a lot of damned snake-oil peddlers who make a speciality of mulcting wealthy widows.'

'Harlan, there are times when you are utterly fatuous –'

The loud squeak of the swinging door between dining room and kitchen. The deferential voice of the houseman. 'I'm sorry, Mrs Thoren. I'll clear away the table later.'

'Now, Raymond, please. We're quite finished.'

'Only with dinner, Charlotte.' Sprague, grimly. 'Not with our little talk.'

His voice faded out of range, was replaced by a thumping of furniture, a clatter of dishes.

Elinor switched off the recorder. 'That's all the talking there was. I tried the bedroom phone afterward, but I only got that air-conditioner noise. They must be settling the argument somewhere else in the house.'

Jake shook his head. 'They're not settling anything. She'll never tell Sprague what she needed that money for. Or anyone else. Not if they string her up by the thumbs and use hot irons on her.'

'How do you know?'

'Because I happen to know what she needed the money for. Thoren was being blackmailed out of every dime he had in the world. In the end, he figured the only solution was to kill himself and make it look like an accident. Then the blackmailer has no more customer, and the money Thoren already paid him comes back to the family by way of the insurance.'

'So?'

'So,' Jake said, 'now it's Mrs Thoren's turn to be blackmailed.'

Elinor sat down hard on the couch. 'Oh, Jesus,' she said.

'I know. It's the one thing Thoren didn't allow for. That whatever dirt he wanted to keep buried was still profitable merchandise as long as he had a wife around who'd want to keep it buried, too, once she was told about it.'

'That poor woman,' Elinor said. 'What she must be going

through right now.' Then she frowned at Jake. 'But look, doesn't that help you? Now you've got someone who really knows Thoren was being blackmailed.'

'I already told you she'll never admit it. She's no fool. She knows damn well that the least hint of it might not only cost her all that insurance money but could bring the dirt right out in the open.'

'It could, too, couldn't it? But dirt about what, I wonder. Him and a woman maybe? Jake, when he put down Nera at that party, maybe he was just covering up for them.'

'No. And I don't want you to start cooking up theories about it, or even thinking about it. It'll make it that much tougher for you to play it cool when you're around Mrs Thoren. Right now, all I want you to do is pipe into her room and stay with it. Use your phone, not this one. Use the monitor, too. Just put it close to the recorder pick-up. That way you won't get your ear stuck to your head.'

Burdened with equipment, she turned to face him from the doorway. 'Jake, please don't get sore about it, but since you do know that poor thing is paying blackmail – '

'Ellie baby, get this straight. If I let on to her I know it, I blow my cover and I'm done for. It would be different if I knew why she was paying the blackmail. Then I could put the thumbscrews on her myself and settle this whole business tomorrow. But I don't. So for the time being, she'll just have to suffer for her husband's sins all by herself. Do you understand?'

'Yes,' Elinor said. 'And I wish I didn't.'

He crossed the room to slam the door shut after her. Then he sat down at the desk with the Xeroxed copy of Thoren's insurance policy before him.

11

The questionnaire of the policy filled two facing pages. He turned to these and flattened them out on the desk. By now his eye automatically slid past any question not worth consideration. All the others, and their accompanying handwritten answers, he went through as intently as if this were the first time he was seeing them.

1. Full name: *Walter Lennart Thoren*
2. Ever changed your name? *No*
3. Residence: *18 N Circular Drive, Daystar Island 2, Miami Beach, Florida*
4. Place of birth: town *St Olivet* state *Minnesota*
5. Date of birth: *October 5, 1915*
6. Marital status: *married*
7. Military service, if any: *U.S. Army from June, 1939 to June, 1942*
8. Occupation: *retired*
12. Former occupation(s) within 10 years: *President, K.O. Sprague Photo-Developing Co. Miami*
13. Amount of insurance desired: *$100,000 at double indemnity*
14. Beneficiary: *Mrs Charlotte Sprague Thoren*
    Relationship: *wife*
    Contingent beneficiary: *son and daughter equally*
25. Ever apply elsewhere for Life, Accident, or Health insurance without receiving it? *no*
26. How many children alive? *two*
    Name, age, and occupation of each:
    Kermit Sprague Thoren, 21, student
    Joanna Lennart Thoren, 18, student

FAMILY RECORD

Father's name: *Frederick Thoren*
   if deceased, age at death: *50*
   cause of death: *automobile accident*
   date and place of death: *2 January 1940, St Olivet, Minnesota*
Mother's maiden name: *Clara Lennart*
   if deceased, age at death: *50*
   cause of death: *same as for father*
   date and place of death: *same as above*
The following Health Record is to be filled out by an accredited examiner only
General state of health: *good*
   use of narcotics: *no*
   use of alcohol to excess: *no*

Any disease of brain or nervous system, heart, lungs, digestive tract, skin, bone, glands, ears, eyes: *no*

History of surgery, if any: *None of consequence. See following re. Identifying Marks*

Identifying marks: *L-shaped scar, 3 inches vertical, 2 inches horizontal, on back, between shoulder blades, from 1st to 5th thoracic vertebrae. Incurred wartime military service*

What clinics, hospitals, physicians, and/or healers has the applicant consulted within the past five years?

    Julius Freeman, M.D.

    Flamingo Drive, Miami Beach, Florida

Medical Examiner's signature: *William McMurtrie, M.D.*

Applicant's signature: *Walter L. Thoren*

Jake turned the page over. On its reverse side was Guaranty's so-far unfulfilled promise to pay the policyholder's beneficiary or contingent beneficiaries $100,000 on surrender of this policy to the insurer along with proof of death, and typed below it was the rider authorizing payment of $200,000 for death by accidental means.

And closing the policy were the two clauses which were, in order, Maniscalco's despair and hope.

A. Incontestability. This policy shall be incontestable after it is in force for a period of one year from the date of its issuance.

B. Limitation of liability. If the insured, within the period of one year from the date of this policy's issue, dies by his own hand, the liability of this company is limited to the value of the paid premium only.

Or as Maniscalco had put it: 'Because of that miserable incontestability clause, we can't even show up in court unless we can prove cold it was suicide. Or even better, get the widow in a back room and show her we have proof of suicide, so she wouldn't dream of going to court.'

In the folder which had contained the policy was also the report from the graphologist who had analyzed Thoren's handwritten answers to the questionnaire. Jake went over the familiar lines of the report with the same close concentration he had given the policy.

Dear Jake,

As I told you over the phone, there are some obstacles to analysis in depth from this kind of material. The machine copy of the policy form, though good, loses the fine shading of the letters. The form itself doesn't allow for true margins. The spaces between lines are too narrow; they would constrain most handwriting. However, allowing for all this, I can still offer the following as statements of fact, and will testify to them in court, if need be. For the usual fee, of course.

What comes clear at the outset is that our subject, Mr T, was intellectually brilliant. I kid you not, Jake, when I estimate that this man must have been up there in the very high IQ class. Narrow as those spaces for answers are on the form, they didn't cramp him at all. And those minute letters are beautifully controlled and legible. A fine scientific mind behind that pen. Putting together various elements of letter formation, I can say that it was a highly inventive mind, attentive to the smallest details, and with a keen power of observation.

Most interesting aside from this is that this was a man with an extremely secretive nature. The neatly looped *a*'s and *o*'s give that away; the knot on every single *a* and *o* has been precisely tied, hard as that was to do within those narrow spaces. This, among other clues, indicates the excessive secretiveness of someone extremely tight-lipped and withdrawn.

What makes this so interesting are the sharp indications in the script that the subject was highly articulate, extremely fluent in expressing himself, might even have had, as the phrase goes, a touch of the poet. This, a contradiction to his penchant for secrecy, suggests to me a man who goes around most of the time wearing a gag he has deliberately stuffed into his own mouth.

Also significant are marked indications of an almost feminine sensitivity along with evidence of a powerful masculine ruthlessness and sense of self-importance. Again an intriguing contradiction.

In answer to the questions in your attached memo, I submit the following:

One. No, there are absolutely no indications of insanity here. And didn't you know the word insanity was out of fashion?

Two. Yes. He may well have held officer's rank in the army. He was – forgive the pun – very high-calibre material.

Three. Obviously, the hypothetical case you set forth in the memo is Mr T's. A man inherits his father-in-law's business, runs it successfully for a while, then suddenly sells out and retires to

Miami Beach squiredom at the comparatively eary age of 49. But how can one gauge from his handwriting whether this is a surprising move or not? He may have detested the business and wanted to escape from it. Then, if he has found suitable hobbies to fill his time after retirement, it would only be surprising if he didn't sell out when he did.

Four. To repeat what I have already loudly assured you over the phone, no, there is not the slightest evidence that he had a gambling streak, by which I suppose you mean that he was a compulsive gambler. At the same time, there's nothing to indicate he didn't take a plunge now and then. After all, you do, and your handwriting, my friend, bears some striking resemblances to Mr T's.

And that does it. Oh yes, when you next meet up with the ravishing Sherry, tell her my offer still stands.

Yours hopefully,

And as a variation on his usual gag where the signature, *Mike Sherman,* would be typewritten, this time Mike had omitted it entirely.

Jake slipped the letter back into the folder, then took a small ruler and well-sharpened red pencil from the desk drawer and bent over the policy form. Very carefully he drew a line under the date of birth provided by Thoren and the date of death he had set down for his father. He also placed neat check marks beside the questions regarding military service and identifying marks.

When he picked up the phone and dialled Maniscalco's home, it was a maid who answered and told him that Mr Maniscalco was out for the evening and no, she didn't know where he could be reached. Could she take a message?

Jake said: 'Yes. And make sure he gets it. Pin it on his pillow if you have to. He's to call Jake whenever he gets home, no matter how late it is.'

At midnight Elinor came in to report that all she had gotten on tape from Mrs Thoren's room was the news broadcast and some of the Johnny Carson show, but the television set had been switched off a few minutes ago. From the sounds coming through, Elinor said hopefully, it seemed likely that Mrs Thoren was preparing to turn in for the night.

Jake said: 'Then you can close up shop, too. But first put that equipment away in the closet.'

'And do the dishes.' Elinor still lingered. 'Jake, I've been thinking about something. I mean, about this blackmail thing.'

'I thought I told you not to.'

'I know, but I couldn't help it. Jake, isn't it dangerous for us if there's a blackmailer around that we're getting mixed up with? Somebody like that could be a real murderous type. If he finds out we're poking into his business –'

'He won't,' Jake said.

'He better not. You might as well know that when it comes to guns and such I'm yellow right down to my toenails. I even hate to be in a play where they have to shoot off blanks.'

'Nobody's going to shoot off anything around here. So forget it.'

'But with that kind of man –'

'Forget it.'

It was two in the morning when Maniscalco finally called. 'What is it, Jake? Something good to report? If it's not, wait'll I sit down and open my tie.'

'Sit down anyhow, Manny, and listen close. I need some help. I need a local boy to work with me who knows this place down here inside and out. Somebody from Miami, but a real pro.'

'A real pro,' Maniscalco said. 'Do you figure to go partners with him, fifty-fifty?'

'No.'

'I thought not. Jake, you know there isn't any pro you can trust in a big deal like this until you split your share with him.'

Jake said: 'I want you to find me one, Manny. If this was up North or on the Coast, I'd know who to sign up in a minute. Down here I might as well be in Hong Kong. All I know is there must be somebody around here who'll play it on the level for a fair day's pay. You've got contacts everywhere. One of them should be able to come up with a name.'

'I don't like it, Jake. I don't even like you having a new girl on that job. How's she working out, anyhow?'

'Good. And you can quit worrying about making any deal behind our backs. She sandbagged herself today.'

'Already? Jake, you are one beautiful son of a bitch. How'd you get her to do it? With a breaking and entering, like Sherry?'

'No, I had her bug a phone. She'll wet her pants if a cop even looks in her direction any time between now and next year. And don't try to duck the issue. I want a first-class man from down here to work with me. You've got the whole day ahead of you to ask around and pick one. When I call tomorrow night you'll tell me who he is and where I can reach him.'

Mama mia, a whole day. All right, I'll see about it. Anything else?'

'Yes. Thoren was in the army from 1939 to 1942, so find out if there's anything shady on his service record or discharge. But quick. And you saw on his questionnaire that his parents were killed together in an auto crash out in the Midwest. I want to know if there was anything peculiar about that crash.'

'What would it mean to us if there was?' Maniscalco said.

'I'm pretty sure now Thoren was being blackmailed. Sometimes a dirty secret goes back a long way into the past.'

'All right, I'll put a man on it right away. But that army record stuff might take too much time. You know what it's like trying to get fast action out of the Pentagon?'

Jake said: 'What I know is that Guaranty has a flock of retired generals on its board of directors. How about telling one of them to go earn his pay for a change?'

'Maybe I will, at that. One way or another I'll get you the stuff in a couple of days. Now level with me, Jake. How does it look to you right this minute? Hopeful?'

'If we don't have hope, baby, life is but an empty shell.'

'For chrissake, Jake, I'm not kidding. How does it look to you?'

'Hopeful.'

Maniscalco let out a long breath. 'Sweetheart,' he said, 'write this down in big letters. If you bail me out of this thing, you not only get win money, but I'm treating you to the best meal in the best Wop restaurant on Mulberry Street any time you name.'

58

'Manny,' Jake said, 'it's your good luck I'm willing to teach you about the finer things in life. So if I pull off this job, you're taking me and my little girl here to The Four Seasons the day we get back to New York.'

12

'Mail?' Elinor said when Jake dropped it on the breakfast table along with a copy of the Miami *Herald*. 'For me?'

'That Sally and Ted postcard from Mexico is for us, the Myra Williams letter from New York is for you. We'll be getting stuff like this every couple of days. It's all fake. You just give your address to this outfit in St Louis, and they take care of the rest.'

Elinor said: 'I'm dazzled. But what's the point of it?'

'To make us look like real folks to any loudmouth postman. And to the help. Tomorrow's our day for the weekly maid and gardener service.'

'Are you sure you want a maid snooping around here? I can easily clean up the place myself.'

'No. I have my own lock on the closet where the equipment and confidential stuff is stashed. The more the maid snoops around the rest of the place, the better. Leave this mail out in the open where she can come across it.'

'And straighten out my dresser drawers too, it sounds like. When do we go swimming at the Thorens'?'

'Eleven sharp. That'll give you plenty of time to work on Joanna while I play kiddie car with her big brother.'

What he got from the two hours spent with Kermit in the Thoren garage taking apart an XKE motor was a large oil stain on his slacks. That Elinor had done better during her session with Joanna was evident from the smug expression she put on as soon as they were out of sight of the Thoren house, on their way home.

'Well?' Jake said.

'Well, it was real wild. I finally got her around to the subject by making up a whole story about how my father died in an accident, too. He is dead, but not from any accident. And how bad I felt, because if I had known what was going to happen I would have been nicer to him. So she – '

'Come on, let's get the show on the road,' Jake said. 'Did she tell you how Thoren spent the day he was killed?'

'That's what I was getting to. It turned out I hit a nerve, because she and her father started off that day with an argument. Or at least he did. He was sitting there at the table with her after breakfast reading his mail, and all of a sudden he cut loose on her about marrying Hal Freeman.'

'Did she tell you it was because Freeman was Jewish?'

'Yes. And she said it probably didn't come as any surprise to me he was, because I must have seen how Jewish he looked. As if that meant anything. I guess it never struck her that so does she.'

'She does?'

'Didn't you notice? Kermit, too. There's that sort of good-looking, brown-eyed, curly-haired type – '

'You know,' Jake said reflectively, 'there's a weird twist I never thought of.'

'What is?'

'Well, suppose Thoren was Jewish? Suppose he decided long ago that going WASP was all he really wanted out of life? He'd be in a sweat if someone threatened to come out with the secret. He'd be wide open for blackmail.'

Elinor said doubtfully: 'Maybe he would be. But to kill himself over it, he'd have to be crazy in the head. You said he wasn't.'

'He wasn't. He was just as sane as everybody else around here. That guard at the bridge worrying about my name being Jake; Milt Webb, the one-man vigilante mob; the Ortegas and Patty Tucker and some of those nasty cracks they pulled about Miami Beach types – '

'I know. They are pretty creepy that way. But so are a lot of people.'

'Including Thoren,' Jake said, 'the one they admired most of all. And for him to be pointed at as a fraud, an outsider, one of the enemy – ? Yes, I think he might kill himself rather than face that.'

'If he was Jewish,' Elinor pointed out. 'And you don't know if he was.'

'No, I don't. And this makes something else I don't want you to worry about. Let's just stick to what he did the day he was killed. Joanna said he was reading his mail after breakfast, all was calm, and then he suddenly landed on her about marrying Freeman. What happened after that?'

'Well, she came back at him as hard as she could. She said the worst part of arguing with him about anything was that he never lost his temper, just stayed ice-cold and used that tone of voice like he was trying to explain something to an idiot. Mostly, she'd cop out after a while by running up to her room, but this time he followed right after her and kept hammering away about how horrible mixed marriages are until she blew up completely and started screaming at him how stupid he was to be prejudiced and what a hypocrite he was, making out he was friends with Hal's father, and a lot of other things she's sorry about now.' Elinor stopped to draw breath. 'He sure was old-fashioned. Back in my neighbourhood, the only thing a mixed marriage means is black and white. And it has to be very black and very white, too. Otherwise, nobody even notices.'

'What neighbourhood does that happen to be?'

'Around Tompkins Square Park. Avenue B near Tenth. It's gone all hippie since they started calling it the East Village, but my mother won't move away. We're still in the same flat she and my father took when they got married. I moved back with her right after the divorce.'

'I figured as much. Did you get the impression there was anything hippie about Joanna and her boy friend?'

'No. Well, she said they smoke pot now and then, but who doesn't? Anyhow, I don't think he rates as much of a boy friend, the way she kept telling me how immature he is. I doubt if she'll ever get around to marrying him. Who she really wants to marry right now is you. She starts to breathe hard whenever your name comes up in the conversation.'

'Because I'm the new Big Daddy image in her life. But what

happened after her argument with Thoren? Did he do anything that seemed out of the ordinary to her during the day?'

'Well, she didn't say it was out of the ordinary, but in the afternoon he went out in his sailboat and didn't come back until almost dark. What makes her sick now is that she was there near the dock when he came in, and when he asked her to help put the cover over the boat, she was still so sore at him that she just turned and walked away without saying a word. And never said a word to him the rest of the evening. Next thing she knew, Kermit was waking her up around three in the morning to tell her he was dead. She told me that she was the only one besides her father to use the sailboat, and now she hates to even go near it. It's been laying there at the dock like that since that day.'

Jake said: 'And she didn't seem to think it was unusual, his going out in the boat alone like that? Or coming in so late?'

'She didn't say anything about it one way or the other. She might have, too, if it was unusual, because she gave me the idea that he was very strong on routine. He had a schedule for everything, and if there was any break in it they all took notice. Like, from the time she was a kid he used to go every Wednesday to a place uptown, Bayside Spa, for a workout and steam bath. She said when he suddenly quit going there it was hard to realize what day of the week it was when Wednesday came around. She wasn't used to seeing him home Wednesdays. Anyhow, you can't set up a schedule for sailboating, can you? Doesn't it depend on the weather?'

'Not altogether. Did she happen to mention when he quit going to that spa for his workouts? How long ago it was?'

Elinor said: 'No. Why? Is that important?'

'It might be. What about that evening, the day he was killed? Did she say anything about what he did that evening?'

'No. And I was afraid to push too hard about it. Dumb as she is, it might have looked kind of obvious by then.'

'What else did she talk about?'

'A lot about you. Some about Hal and Kermit. She warned me about Kermit. Laughing all the while, you know, but not kidding really. That shows you how much brain she has. If I

62

wanted to make a play for somebody's husband, I'd turn my good-looking brother loose on his wife first thing.'

'Women,' Jake said.

In the house, he stretched out on the living-room couch, eyes closed, hands clasped behind his head. Elinor stood looking down at him until he opened his eyes. 'I did all right, didn't I?' she said.

'Fine.'

'I thought so, too. Now tell me why.'

Jake said: 'Because these blackmail suicides run to a pattern. What you got from Joanna tells me Thoren's followed the pattern.'

Elinor looked disappointed. 'Is that all?'

'It's a lot more than you think. It suggests that in that mail Thoren was reading was a message from the blackmailer telling him when and where to make the next drop. A big percentage of suicides resulting from blackmail pressure follow pretty close after that kind of message. They seem to be triggered by them when the victim is near the breaking point. That's why Thoren came down on Joanna so hard about who she married. It was a farewell warning he was trying to give her.'

'But that's just a lot of theory,' Elinor protested. 'It's not the kind of evidence you said you need.'

'The evidence would be the blackmailer's message. Records show that in one case after another, no matter how carefully somebody rigged up his suicide to look like an accident, he wound up leaving a clue to the truth. Possibly in a lot of cases, he didn't even realize he was doing it. It could have been an unconscious act of the ego to show what a sacrifice he made. So after all the trouble he went to, there would be those half-burned or torn-up scraps of message somewhere around. And Thoren had more than his share of ego.'

Elinor said: 'But he died a month ago. Do you really believe you can find any letter like that after a month, torn-up or otherwise?'

'I better believe it,' Jake said.

13

He came right to the point when Maniscalco called. 'Manny, you have somebody looking up that accident where Thoren's parents were killed, haven't you? About any possibility of dirty work there?'

'Uh-huh. I had my boy in Twin Cities drive up to St Olivet first thing this morning. They have a weekly paper, so he'll check through the files around the time of the accident. And it's a small place. He ought to find some old-timers who'll remember the Thorens.'

'Can you get in touch with him tonight?'

'I know what motel he's at. Why?'

'Because there's something else I want him to look up. The religion Thoren and his people were listed under. If it isn't entered on Thoren's birth certificate, he might find an obit or funeral notice about the parents that'll clue us in on it. Can you get him on that right away?'

'Yes, sure. But what have you got in mind?'

Jake explained what he had in mind, and Maniscalco grunted approval. 'No question it's blackmail, Jake. The best part is, if it turns out the poor bastard was paying off because of that religious thing, the family'll think twice before risking exposure in a court case. You know how Guaranty hates to go to court on this kind of non-payment case. No matter how right they are, the publicity always comes out sour.'

Jake said: 'I ought to know it after all the times you've told it to me. Don't you find it touching, Manny, that a great big corporation can be so nervous about some things?'

'My friend, we're all nervous about our image nowadays, especially corporations. And you collect plenty for getting that release from the widow and keeping Guaranty's image nice and shiny.'

'Anything to make you happy, baby.'

'So far I'm not complaining. But all your chips aren't on that one card, are they, Jake? Maybe he was paying blackmail because of the religious thing, maybe not. You have to keep an open mind. It could just as easily have been on account of a woman. Maybe some sharpshooting little hustler he knocked up. Remember that sex is a very strong percentage play in blackmail.'

'I'm taking that into account. Even so, I don't think it would be a female who got the drop on Thoren.'

Maniscalco was silent for a long moment. Then he said: 'I hope I'm hearing right. You think he was a queer?'

'Hell, I don't mean the Fire Island wiggle-ass kind you mean. Not a man like that with a wife and family. But he had some very interesting AC–DC touches. And it doesn't take more than one little impulse in a public toilet to make a disaster. That's why I want to check his service record. For that matter, whatever he said his religion was in 1939 would be entered on it, too. What have you done about getting hold of that record?'

'Plenty. Only they're having trouble locating it. They would, naturally. I'll let you know as soon as they do.'

'Well, tell them to get the lead out,' Jake said. 'And how about the local boy you're supposed to line up for me as a helper? Did you get a tip on somebody good down here?'

'I did. That's what this call was for in the first place. Jake, did you ever hear of a guy named Abe Magnes? Is that name familiar to you?'

'I think so. Didn't he work some headline cases for insurance underwriters a long time ago?'

'That's right. All over the Miami territory. He's the one I lined up.'

Jake said unbelievingly: 'Abe Magnes? But he retired before I even got into this racket. He must be a hundred years old by now. What the hell good is somebody like that to me?'

'Jake, from what my contact told me, Magnes still takes on a job now and then, and he still has more on the ball than most investigators half his age. And he's got a gilt-edged reputation around Miami for being honest. Pay him his price, and he's your man and nobody else's. There's only one hitch. The price. He's good and he knows it.'

'No. I need somebody who can move fast on his feet, not in a wheelchair.'

'Jake, before you give me a hard time about it, at least meet him and see what he's like. I've already had him on the wire, and he said he's willing to talk business with you. And he can offer the one big thing you said you wanted. From what I was told, he knows more about that territory down there than any other living human. And you know that means a lot of time and trouble saved.'

Jake said: 'What I know is that you really let me down on this. All right, considering the choice you're giving me, I have to take a look at him, don't I? Where do I find him?'

'He said it was on the Beach about ten minutes' drive from where you are. The Oceana Hotel. He'll be waiting for you to show up any time tomorrow.'

'If he lives that long,' Jake said.

He went to sleep on the study couch in a bad mood and dreamed accordingly. He was dragged out of a harrowing dream by the sound of his name being called. When he sat up in blackness he saw a thread of light beneath the bedroom door.

He went into the bedroom. Elinor, her discarded blanket and pyjamas on the floor, lay stretched out on her back in the middle of the king-sized bed like a small corpse waiting for embalmment. A sheet was tucked under her crotch and pulled over her to just above the nipples, and every inch of flesh it left exposed glowed fiery red. Her face, a blazing scarlet, was badly swollen. Her eyelids were puffy and half-closed.

Jake took this in with fascination. 'Jesus, what a mess.'

'I know. And there must be something wrong with me besides sunburn, I feel so rotten. Chills and fever and sick to the stomach. I tried to throw up before, but I couldn't.'

'It all comes with the sunburn. Do you mean you were out in that sun with Joanna for the whole two hours without any umbrella over you or any covering at all?'

'Well, she was, so I didn't think about it then.'

'I wish you had, Ellie baby. Tomorrow I wanted you to get her to invite us out in her daddy's sailboat. You have now blown that, but good.'

'Jake, if I feel a little better – '

He shook his head. 'Not a chance. And no use knocking our brains out about it right now. What have you done for that burn?'

'Rubbed that suntan oil with benzocaine on me wherever I could reach. That's why I called you. I hated to wake you up, but I couldn't get any on my back, and it's killing me. And I thought maybe you knew something I could take to stop feeling like this.'

'Sure. The patented Dekker treatment. A couple of sleeping pills to get you over the big jump, and a bottle of ginger ale so you can burp up some of that misery and slow down dehydration. Then we'll finish polishing you up with the oil.'

She downed the pills and drink in meek silence, then yielded limply to him when it came time to pull off the sheet and roll her over on her belly. After he had smeared the oil on her back from shoulders to ankles and replaced the sheet, she sighed gratefully. 'I feel a little better already. You know something, Jake? You're a very nice guy sometimes.'

'Don't mistake competence for a kind heart, baby.'

'Oh, stop being so hard-boiled. It doesn't really scare you to have somebody say you're nice, does it?'

'Yes, if it sounds like it might work up to one of those distractions I warned you about.'

'Distractions,' she muttered. She was lying spread-eagled on her belly, her face deep in the pillow. Suddenly she raised herself on her elbows and looked at him bleary-eyed. 'Look, even if you are a walking computer, there's something I have to tell you. I don't know why. I just feel rotten not telling it to you. So I will.'

'I'm braced.'

'It's about my husband. I never had any. I was never married. There was just this guy from around Tompkins Square who was very big with the guitar and the grass, and when he asked me to move into his pad I did, but when the kid came along he moved out. That's the whole thing.'

'So?'

'So now that I told you about it, I feel better.'

'Good. Have you ever seen the guy again? Does he make like a father at all?'

'No, that's why I moved back with my mother. She said if I didn't have an abortion I could, because she's a real wild Catholic. And it's all right now, because she's crazy about the kid.'

'That's very touching,' Jake said. 'And you'd better stop trying to fight those sleeping pills, because it looks like your head'll fall off.'

She let her drooping head sink into the pillow. 'Miserable computer,' she said thickly.

He waited a minute or two, then turned out the light and went back to the study. He quickly changed from pyjama pants to chinos and left the house through its back door. He glanced at his watch while he stood there in the wet grass giving his eyes time to adjust to the darkness, and the luminous hands of the watch said it was three-thirty.

As soon as he could discern the outlines of the shrubbery, trees, and houses around him, he made his way down the slope of the lawn to where a narrow strip of sand marked the low bulkhead at the water's edge. He followed the sand past Milt Webb's property and to the Thorens' dock. He could barely see the dock but had a clear picture of it in mind: a narrow, unrailed boardwalk which ran out about twenty feet into the bay. Kermit's speedboat was moored along one side of it; Thoren's sailboat, a neat little twelve-footer, lay bow-on to the other side, its stern line tied to a buoy. Its sail had been removed and stored away some place, its cockpit protected by a canvas lashed down over it.

Two boats. But now, surprisingly, there was an addition to the fleet. Alongside the sailboat, stern up against the dock, lay the pale, ghostly length of a big cabin cruiser, all lights extinguished, the soft throbbing of its idling motor barely detectable to the ear. The voices on its afterdeck, sibilant undertones hardly louder than the motor, were impossible to identify.

Jake carefully planted a foot on the dock and tested his weight on it. The board underfoot groaned loudly. He hastily withdrew the foot, moved a few yards away from the dock along the water's edge, and squatted there, eyes fixed on the boat.

He had gotten clear of the dock barely in time. A minute later a figure awkwardly mounted it from the fantail of the boat, picked its way across creaking boards, then quickly started up the lawn toward the house. As it disappeared into the total darkness beyond the pool, the sound of the boat's motor grew louder, rose to a crescendo. Red and green lights flicked on at its bow, a white light at its stern. It started to move away from the dock, and Jake stood up, straining to make out the name on the stern.

'Hey, you!' a voice bellowed. Milt Webb's voice, high-pitched with excitement. 'Don't move. I got you covered. Stay where you are.'

The lights on the boat instantly blinked out, its motor roared deafeningly as Jake whirled toward the sound of the voice. The boom of a gun, the flash from its muzzle, the stinging explosion of sand in his face all seemed to happen together. He sprinted three steps and hit the water of the bay in a long flat dive. When the second barrel was fired he heard the pellets hiss into the water only inches away from him. He went underwater and swam as strongly as he could until his lungs were ready to burst. When he surfaced he was already past Webb's dock. It was an easy swim from there to his own strip of beach in water almost as warm as the sultry night air.

In the house, he flung the chinos into the washing machine, then went into the study and looked up Webb's phone number. When he dialled, the woman who answered sounded in a panic. 'Yes, yes? Who is it?'

'Mrs Webb?'

'That's right. Who is this? What do you want?'

'It's Jake Dekker next door, Mrs Webb. I heard some noise in back of your place a little while ago, and I wondered if anything was wrong. It sounded like Milt calling somebody. If there's anything I can do – '

'Yes, it was terrible. My God, I don't know what the world is coming to. Wait, here's Milton.'

There was the sound of a muffled colloquy. Then Webb came on the phone. 'You heard all the noise, Jake?'

'Yes. I didn't want to say so to Mrs Webb, but it sounded to me like gunshots. What happened? If you want me over there – '

'No, that's nice of you, but you don't have to bother. I took care of it all by myself. So much for those security stiffs around here, when you have to go out in your yard with a gun and protect your own home. Goddam if I don't have something to say to McCloy first thing in the morning about the kind of law and order we're paying for here.'

Jake said: 'Do you mean somebody just tried to break into your place?'

'Not mine, the Thorens'. These goons sneak up in boats sometimes and try a little housebreaking, and so far nobody tagged any of them. I finally did it just now. I scared the boat off, and it left one of them ashore, and I knocked him right into the water with a twelve-gauge.' Webb's voice rose in jubilation. 'In the dark, Jake, and at least seventy, eighty feet away. How's that for shooting?'

'You can't do better than hit what you aim at, Milt. Do the Thorens know about it? Are they up, too?'

'Yes, I was just talking to Kermit and Joanna over there. Soon as I get some clothes on, I'm going back to wait with them for the cops.'

Jake said: 'What about Mrs Thoren? How is she taking it?'

'She didn't come down. It looks like she slept through the whole thing, thank God. Jake?'

'Yes?'

'I've been wondering about something. You told me you did some crime writing, so maybe you know the answer. I mean, about how the cops handle these things. If that body turns up in the bay, do you think they'll let me have any buckshot they dig out of it as kind of a souvenir?'

'It's the least they can do,' Jake said.

14

There was heavy traffic through and around the house in the morning. Miami Beach police and Daystar Islands security men scouting the area, the woman sent by Daystar Service to do housecleaning, a team of gardeners, Milt Webb and his wife, and finally McCloy himself, the ruler of the roost, magnificent in ascot and yachting jacket, come to apologize to these new members of the community for the predawn fuss. And to pettishly make his own investigation of it.

In the privacy of the kitchen, Jake gave him the same account of it he had already given the police – Webb's voice loud in the distance, the sound of shots, the phone call to Webb –

McCloy said challengingly: 'But did you yourself see any boat out there that looked suspicious?'

'You can't see the waterfront from our bedroom here. Even if you could, it was pitch-dark out.'

'Then did you hear any boat coming or going at that time?'

Jake said: 'I have to admit I didn't. What are you getting at? You don't think Webb imagined the whole thing, do you?'

'Well, it's hardly up to me to draw conclusions about that,' McCloy said, but it was clear that he, like the police and security men, already had.

Nothing roused Elinor through all this. When only the maid was left for company in the house, Jake tipped her heavily to attend to Elinor when she did wake, then packed an attaché case and drove across town to the Oceana Hotel.

He found it on the ocean front in the South Beach section of town, a weatherworn, four-storeyed imitation of Mount Vernon, with a high-pillared veranda facing the street. Elderly citizens sat in a row on the veranda, all wearing sunglasses, all bleakly watching the pigeons and seagulls that unsociably mingled in the gutter.

The lobby had an institutional look. At its far end, rows of metal chairs were arranged before a colour television set where contestants with weirdly green and lavender faces were playing a quiz game, but nobody was there to watch the set except the sallow young man lounging behind the registration counter. Without taking his eyes from it, he informed Jake that Mr Magnes was in the penthouse. Take the elevator up to the third, then the stairs up to the roof.

The penthouse turned out to be a tiny one-room kitchenette apartment set like a box in a corner of the roof, and Magnes received his visitor in a pair of drooping bathing trunks and rubber sandals. Small, potbellied, and spindly-legged, with a fringe of white hair around his bald head, a bulbous nose, and small close-set eyes, he looked like an angry duck.

'Some Jake,' he commented. 'You're a Jake like I'm a Shaun O'Reilly. You know, I heard about you even before Maniscalco called me up. From the size reputation you got, I thought you'd be an older man. Did Maniscalco tell you my price?'

'No.'

'I told him to. For one month, give or take a few days, it's ten thousand. In advance.'

'In Monopoly money?' Jake said.

'I like a man with a sense of humour. Ten thousand in advance. I'll put your cheque through my Chicago bank so no smarty bank clerk around Miami can pass the word we're doing business.'

Jake said: 'I've got a better idea. For that kind of money, you can take the case and I'll work for you.'

'Very good,' Magnes remarked to his kitchen sink. 'Not only a sense of humour, but a real expert at making a poor mouth.' He turned his shoe-button eyes on Jake again. 'Sonny, when an Abe Magnes took a case like this, the rule was he split the win money with the insurer right down the middle, and I have a feeling a Jake Dekker don't handle it any different. Which means you stand to make yourself one hundred thousand real American dollars out of this job. Or am I wrong about that?'

Jake said: 'No, only in the way you look at it. Look at it my way. I've already sunk ten thousand into the job. If I don't come up a winner, I'll hurt. If I throw in another ten thousand and don't come up a winner, I'll bleed. I don't like to bleed.'

'Naturally. But I also figure you didn't make your kind of reputation by taking a case you couldn't handle. With help. My kind of help.'

'What kind is that?'

Magnes said: 'For one thing, honest. Do I have to tell somebody like you that in our business selling-out comes easy as breathing? And down here the *momsers* sell you out for bargain rates. I had a stakeout once on a million-dollar phony paralysis case in West Palm Beach. For the three months I was there, I never knew the guy I had on the job with me had tipped them off the second day. And for how much? A lousy hundred dollars. Their sisters they sell to some pimp for fifty.'

Jake shook his head. 'Maniscalco already told me you were strictly on the level. But I need somebody to move around, hunt up contacts, make investigations. And fast. Guaranty wants a release before this thing turns into a court case.'

'My ten thousand covers all that. And where somebody might be needed for legwork or surveillance, I personally arrange for it, so you're completely out of the picture. As for contacts, you tell me who you want to meet, and I'll fix it up. If you want police co-operation – '

'Not on this one. The people I'm working on probably have a pipeline to headquarters.'

'All right, then anybody else. And all this is covered by the same ten thousand. That's the limit you pay me.'

Jake shrugged. 'It's still too much. But I'll take you on an agency basis. By the day, plus expenses.'

'Sonny,' Magnes said with kindly forbearance, 'for one thing, in my fifty years in this business I never worked per diem. I am a talent, not a day labourer. For another thing, that ten thousand rates as a business expense for you. Since you're at least in the fifty per-cent bracket, you save five grand that way on your taxes. And for a final thing, if you walk out without signing me up, you got nobody else to go to. Nobody at all you could trust on a case this big. So tomorrow you'll be back here. And the price will still be the same. So if you consider it from all these angles, we can stop fooling around and get to work.'

Jake considered it carefully from all these angles, then took out his cheque book.

'Good,' said Magnes. 'Now I'll fix us some lunch, and while we're eating you can tell me who's giving Guaranty the finger for a change, and what we can do about it.'

15

The telling, and the playback of the tapes, took up the entire lunchtime and more. Then Jake removed the folders from the attaché case, and side by side at the table, he and Magnes went over each page of their contents.

Magnes closed the folder on the last page. 'So it boils down to three possibilities. The Jewish thing, or he got his hand caught in the wrong fly, or he committed a felony. In my opinion, the first one is very thin.'

'Why?'

'Because it doesn't take the wife into account. If she's paying off now, she knows what he was trying to cover up. For him it would be one thing. But for her it would be something else entirely to cover up at such a terrible cost that she happened to marry a Jew. Still, in this crazy world, who can tell?'

'That's how I'm playing it,' Jake said. 'All I can hope is that those records Maniscalco's digging up will give us a lead there. Meanwhile, I want you to check out some other items.'

'Such as?'

'First, this Charlie Matthews you heard about on the tape. The guy at the Biscayne National Bank. He's a family friend, he knew Thoren's habits, and for two years he was okaying Thoren's cheque for a tremendous cash withdrawal once a month. Now Mrs Thoren cashes a cheque like that for the first time, and suddenly Matthews is all hot and bothered. Find out who and what he is, how he lives, if there was any change in his standard of living recently. Then there's Alfonso Ortega. I want to know just how legitimate he is.'

'Is he a Cuban?' Magnes asked.

'Yes, but he settled down here long before Castro's time. Well-fixed, but the money seems to be mostly his wife's. She rates near the top of my list because of what happened between her and Thoren, but I can take care of her myself.'

'It shouldn't be hard,' Magnes remarked, 'if she's the hot number you said. But you have to watch out. With your kind of setup here, it could be dangerous.'

'Not if Ortega's out of town when I work on her. And he will be. He said something about leaving for Rio this morning.'

Magnes said: 'I don't mean dangerous on account of him. I mean on account of that girlie you got working with you. I'm talking from experience when I say that's always a touchy business. You move into a stakeout with a cute little girlie, you go to bed with her a couple of times, next thing she gets all confused in the head, she begins to think she's your wife. So where she might not even tattle to the opposition for a couple of grand, she'll do it as soon as you come home with lipstick on your collar. Hell has no fury – you know the saying?'

'I know it,' Jake said. 'But you leave her to me and just take care of your end. That's Matthews and Ortega.'

'Any help around the Thoren house with big ears? Or has this high society over on Daystar started to do its own cooking lately?'

'No, there's a husband-and-wife team around the house. Coloured. Been there a long time. He's houseman, she's cook. Raymond and Olivia Beaudry. When Maniscalco was down here he bought some information from Beaudry about the layout of the house and so on, but when it came to family secrets Beaudry clammed right up. Maniscalco went pretty high in his price too, but it was no sale. We'll have to leave it at that for the time being. If you approach Beaudry, and he goes right to the Thorens about it, it'll put them too much on guard. And there are more important things to work on right now. What do you know about Bayside Spa?'

'It's in North Bay Village. A fancy diet-and-health place. You pay sirloin prices, and they give you a spoon of cottage cheese and tell you it's good for your health. Why?'

'Because Thoren used to go there once a week regularly for

a workout, and then he suddenly stopped. I want to know when he stopped. And, if you can dig it up, the reason for it.'

'True,' Magnes said. 'Funny things can happen when the big boys and the little boys get together in a steam room.'

'It's not only that. He started paying blackmail between two and three years ago, which doesn't have to mean he got caught doing something around then. It could have been something that dated from way back, but which nobody thought of cashing in until later. The one sure thing is that the blackmailer made the first contact with Thoren between two and three years ago. And any sharp break in Thoren's routine – like not going to the Spa any more – could tip us off as to just when and how that contact was made.'

'It could be,' Magnes said. He musingly rubbed a hand back and forth over his gleaming scalp. 'It's interesting North Bay Village should come into it. You know anything about the place?'

'No. I don't know much about any place down here. That's what I'm counting on you for.'

'You're counting on the right one. Wait a minute, and I'll show you something.' Magnes removed the dishes from the table to the sink, then unfolded a large street map on the table. He ran a stubby forefinger along a line in the centre of the map. 'Right here in the middle of the bay on the Seventy-ninth Street Causeway, these two islands are North Bay Village. More than any other place in Dade County, this is where the action is. The high-priced action.'

'Operated by the Mob?'

'Plenty of it. Where the causeway runs through it, they call the Strip. There's some independents on the Strip, but in my opinion the best way to get bleeding bowels is to be an independent on the Strip. Anyhow, on the Strip and around it is where you can eat, drink, get a girl, get a boy, get a fix, place a bet, buy a nice new thirty-eight-calibre S and W, and if you're the nervous type, even hire a guy to use it for you. The last couple times I was go-between for the insurer in a big jewel heist, I got treated to dinner on the Strip so I could pick up the stones right there at the table.'

'Is Bayside Spa an independent?' Jake said.

'So they claim. But this Thoren wasn't the only one who went there for workouts. Drop in any time, and you'll see some very fancy hoods doing push-ups. Maybe he did business with them. Then one day they told him either he starts paying off or they spill it all to the papers.'

'Maybe. Do these hoods have any interest in real estate down here? Hotels and high-rises?'

'Hotels,' Magnes said. 'After all, they got to do something with that skim-off money from the gambling out West.'

'Then they'd have reason to come down on Thoren. He was bucking them with that Civic Planning Association of his. He didn't have to be doing business with them. All he had to do was step on their toes and get himself framed.'

Magnes smiled dourly. 'Let me enlighten you about something. This is a tourist town and a retirement town. And the characters who put up the hotels for the tourists here and the high-rises for the retired have it so tight by the nuts that they worry about such do-gooders like an elephant worries about getting screwed by a flea. They own the Beach, they do what they want with it, and if you don't like it, Charlie, go drop dead. Only do it across the bay in Miami, not here, because here we don't have a cemetery. You got my word that the Mob never was turned loose on Thoren because he bothered the big interests here. He couldn't. Not one little bit.'

'If you say so,' Jake said. 'But he was being blackmailed by experts. Big-timers. And where the Mob moves in, they have a vested interest in any kind of operation like that.'

Magnes said: 'This I don't deny. Where you could be wrong is figuring that the blackmailer has to be big-time. A good juicy blackmail setup is something anybody can come across by accident and take advantage of. He can be the little pisher who lives next door and happens to look in your window when the shades are up. If you get stuck on the idea this one has to be a big-time operator only, we could waste a lot of energy walking up the wrong hill.'

'If he could sweat blood out of a guy like Thoren for over two years,' Jake said, 'he was a big-time operator. Thoren had the brains to plan his suicide like a master and the guts to go through with it when the time came. That means that if at any time he had the least chance of killing the blackmailer and getting away with it, he would have killed him. And the fact that he couldn't do it means the blackmailer was right up there in the big leagues. So much so, he's even got Mrs Thoren pinned down now. And no little jerk next door thinks in terms of ten grand a month.'

'On the other hand,' argued Magnes, 'what kind of big-leaguer comes right up to the house in a boat to collect his payoff? If the cops were laying for him, they could have grabbed him right then with the ten grand in his pocket.'

'I didn't say she met him to make a payoff. That was made the day before, right after she drew out the money. What she met him for was because her brother made such a stink about the money being withdrawn. She must have arranged for a meeting with the blackmailer to talk over the problem this brought up. And some other problems. Maybe her husband could hand out that kind of money every month without anybody taking notice, but she sure as hell couldn't. And that insurance money she's been counting on still hasn't been paid to her. My guess is that she either asked the guy to allow extra time before the next payment or to cut the payments down.'

'Well,' Magnes said, 'maybe you're right. But how come you're so sure the payoff was made yesterday? Especially after that boat showed up the way it did.'

Jake said: 'Because that's the pattern. Look it up, and you'll see most of these operations run to form. When payoff day comes, you get your instructions, you put the money together, you drop it when and where you're told, one right after the other. Why the hell would any smart blackmailer want to give you time to think it over, maybe set up a stakeout, maybe have all that dough hijacked while you're carting it around? The game he's playing, he's not calling for any huddles, he wants the ball snapped right away.'

'Sometimes,' Magnes said. 'Not always. Still, in this business, what can you do but play the percentage? So now tell me what's the percentage on finding any blackmail note in that sailboat? In my opinion, he got rid of those notes as soon as he read them.'

'Except the last one,' Jake said. 'The odds are that he had it with him when he was out in the boat all day, thinking things over. Whether he finally destroyed it or not out there remains to be seen. I want to see for myself before I give up on it.'

'Does that mean you'll make another try at the boat tonight?'

'No, I'll hold off a day or two until the excitement around there cools off a little. One last thing. Are there any gay bars running wide-open around here where Thoren might have gotten himself nailed?'

'Right now, no. Right now you need to ask around a little for that kind of action. Two, three years ago, which is what really counts, yes.' Magnes leaned over the map and pointed. 'The two widest open were right here on Alton near Lincoln. You can see for yourself it's a very quick jump between there and the Daystar Islands.'

'What happened to those places? Business troubles or the cops?'

'The cops. Now and then, you understand, we get a terrible rush of morality to the head in Miami Beach. Especially some of those clean-cut-type hotel operators who hate to see customers waste money some place else when they could have an expensive bottle from the bar and a pretty little *fegeleh* sent right up to their room on request.'

'What happened to the guys who ran those two places? Is there any way you can get in touch with them?'

'One, I think, went out to California. The other runs a TV sales and service place somewhere on Washington Avenue. Him, I can look up easy. In his own way, a very nice boy.'

'Nice enough to keep his mouth shut if you ask him to?'

'If I tell him it's because I'm working against the cops, yes.'

'All right,' Jake said, 'sound him out.' He dug into the attaché case and came up with a set of photographs. He handed a couple to Magnes. 'Maniscalco had these made from that old picture they had of Thoren in the paper along with his obit, but it's probably a fair likeness. Show it to the guy and see

79

if he can make any identification. If Thoren dropped into his place now and then, it'll give us something to go on.'

'I'll take care of it along with the rest. I'll phone you as soon as I have anything at all to report.'

'Your calls don't go through the hotel switchboard, do they?'

'Do I look that foolish?' Magnes said. 'I'm on a direct outside line from the day I moved in here thirty years ago. And there wasn't even bugs in those day. Only taps.'

'Do you check the phone for bugs now and then?'

'Every morning, even before I put my teeth in,' Magnes said.

16

Elinor, lobster-red but not quite so swollen of feature, was fetchingly attired in a bedsheet loosely draped around her like a toga. She said: 'What did you tell Milt Webb and his wife about me when they were here this morning? That I was dying of sunstroke or something?'

'No, just the facts,' Jake said. 'Why?'

'Because they must have really laid it on over the grapevine, the way people dropped in after lunch. That poor maid did hardly any cleaning, it was mostly running around and serving them coffee.'

'What people?'

'Oh, first it was the Thorens and that sister-in-law of hers, then Mrs McCloy and some of her friends. And for the big finish, Patty Tucker walked in with Nera while the Thorens were still here.'

'What happened then?'

'Well, Patty took one look around and got Nera out quick. She said something about a lot of shopping to do, so they couldn't stay. But for five seconds it looked like World War Three was getting ready to start right here. I didn't even know Mrs Thoren could look as murderous as she did when she saw Nera.'

'How'd Kermit take it?'

'He looked pretty nasty, too. And that sister-in-law. The only one of them who didn't was Joanna. I think she kind of digs Nera. Nera looked great all right. Especially next to those dried-up females they have around here. Say, where were you while all this was going on?'

'Signing on some extra help. Name's Abe Magnes. An old-time investigator who knows his way around town. Must be way over seventy and comes on like forty. Matter of fact, everybody I saw around that downtown section of the Beach where he lives looks like the Ancient Mariner or his wife. If you're under sixty down there, they call you sonny.'

Elinor said with disappointment: 'You mean that's what Miami Beach is really like? I thought it would be real swinging, like those airline commercials.'

'Well, the further uptown you go, the younger it gets. At least, some places it does. I did some sightseeing as far up as the Seventy-ninth Street Causeway, and it really swings around there. I'll show it to you some day when you can wear more than that sheet.'

'You weren't just sightseeing,' Elinor said. 'Not you. It had something to do with the job, didn't it?'

'Yes. But my end of it, not yours. What did your coffee klatsch talk about? Anything worth filing?'

'Maybe. You know all about the shooting last night, don't you?'

'I do.'

'Well, that was what they talked about mostly. None of them really believe Milt Webb about it. Kermit says he was probably shooting at a sea serpent that came out of a vodka bottle. But I don't know.'

'Don't know what?' Jake said.

'I think a boat did come in at the Thorens' dock last night. Only there wasn't any crook on it, there was a blackmailer looking to collect from Mrs Thoren. And I can tell from that superior little smile on your face that you already thought the same thing as soon as you heard about it.'

Jake said: 'It's not a superior little smile. It's a complimentary little smile because you're a smart girl. How did Mrs

Thoren take it while they were on the subject? Show signs of strain?'

'Total. That's what started me thinking about it, how shook up she looked. Jake, it felt so awful, watching her and knowing what she was going through.'

'Then you're not as smart as I thought. Suppose Thoren had walked into Guaranty's office with a gun and stolen their payroll and stashed it away somewhere? And now Mrs Thoren was trying to get her hands on the loot. Would you feel the same way?'

'It's not the same thing.'

'It's exactly the same thing. Just remember that whenever you feel yourself getting all teary over Mrs Thoren.'

'But you're taking for granted she's deliberately going along with a swindle because she knows he committed suicide. And there isn't anything to prove she does.'

Jake said: 'Except she'd have to be pretty goddam stupid and insensitive not to know what her husband was capable of doing for her sake after being married to him for twenty-five years. You've seen her close up. Do you honestly believe she is that stupid and insensitive?'

It took time for Elinor to come out with it. 'No, I guess not,' she said unhappily.

'All right. Then any time you find your heart bleeding for her, remember she's trying to commit criminal fraud. Maybe that'll ease the pain a little.'

'So what about the fraud we're pulling here?' Elinor said. 'Setting up a phony front, bugging phones, listening in – '

'There's only one answer to that, baby. If Mrs Thoren had been on the level – if she had kissed off that insurance money as soon as she realized she wasn't entitled to it – we wouldn't be here in the first place. Blame it all on her, not me.'

During the evening he drifted in and out of the darkened kitchen, keeping an eye on the Ortega house from its window. Two cars were parked in the driveway there behind the Ortega Cadillac, another was parked at the curb. At eleven he saw that the car at the curb had departed. He waited, and a few minutes later the other two cars pulled out of the driveway and disappeared down Circular Drive.

He went into the bedroom where Elinor was on duty, tuned in to the transmitter she had planted in Charlotte Thoren's bedroom. From the monitor came a voice predicting tomorrow's weather in Dade and Broward counties.

'Get anything from her end besides television?' he asked.

'No. How long should I stay with this?'

'Allow ten minutes after she turns the set off. And don't be surprised later on if that phone in the study wakes you up. Maniscalco's supposed to have some information for me today or tomorrow. If he does call, tell him I'll ring him up first thing in the morning. Leave a note on my desk about it.'

'All right,' Elinor said. 'But where will you be?'

'Out reconnoitring the neighbourhood. I don't know for how long, so don't worry about the time it takes.'

Elinor said: 'With blackmailers coming around here in boats, what's to worry about? Anyhow, before you go would you please do me a favour? Smear that benzocaine glop on my back again? It still feels like I'm being barbecued when I try to lie down.'

She handed him the bottle, and without any display of self-consciousness about her parboiled nakedness, undraped the sheet from around herself and stretched out, face down on the bed. She gasped when he ruthlessly splashed cold oil along her spine and started to rub it in hard. 'Hey, that hurts,' she protested. 'Can't you do it nice and easy like last time?'

'No, nice and easy can get to be too much fun. Let's stick to straight therapy.'

She submitted, groaning, to the therapy. Then with her voice half-muffled by the pillow, she said: 'Jake, when I was talking to the company about you I got to wondering. How much of that résumé stuff you made me memorize is true?'

'As much as can be checked out without too much trouble.'

'You mean you really were a reporter on the *Daily Mirror* back in New York?'

'Until it folded. A whiz kid on the crime beat. And with a by-line sometimes.'

'Then I might have even read news stories you wrote. I used to like the *Mirror* a lot when I was a kid. It had the best jokes of any paper.'

'There are a lot of good jokes in the newspaper business,' Jake said. 'The best one is trying to make a living from it.'

17

Nera Ortega answered her doorbell in glittering hostess pyjamas and one high-heeled slipper. The other slipper she held in her hand. When she saw Jake looking at it she laughed. 'No, it's not a defensive measure. I just sent some company home and you caught me on my way upstairs. There's nothing wrong, is there?'

'Nothing serious. A problem I'd like to talk over with you. May I come in?'

She hesitated. 'I'm afraid it's past visiting hours.' Her speech was flavoured with the faintest Latin accent. 'And Fons isn't home. Or the maid. I'm all alone here right now.'

'I know. I'd just as soon Fons doesn't hear any of this. Or the maid.'

'Oh?' She regarded him quizzically, her lower lip pinched between her teeth. 'And your nice little wife?'

'My nice little wife has been coated with a soothing lotion and stuffed with sleeping pills. She's not in shape to hear much of anything right now. You know, the one bad thing about this Miami climate is that you can't remark how cold it is out and get invited inside on that account.'

Nera looked amused. 'That shows how much you know about the Miami climate. Well, if you can state your problem in twenty-five words or less – '

The huge living room with the bull's horns over the fireplace and the jai-alai cesta on the wall was littered with the residue of a party.

'Sorry about the mess,' Nera said, plainly indifferent to it. She switched on a small table lamp and turned out the bright overhead light. 'If you can't clean it up, hide it. Drink?' She leaned against the portable bar to fit the other slipper on her foot.

'Whatever you're having,' Jake said.

'I've already had my quota for the evening. But it was Scotch and soda. Not too much soda.'

Jake watched her take out the decanter and a glass and place them on top of the bar. 'Sorry,' he said. 'I don't drink alone.'

Nera weighed this briefly, then took out a second glass. She measured off two stiff drinks, added a splash of soda to each, and handed one to Jake. A pair of couches faced each other across the fireplace. He sat down in one; Nera perched on an arm of the other, barely within the circle of light made by the lamp.

Jake raised his glass to her. She mockingly returned the gesture, then downed half her drink in a series of quick gulps like medicine, her face screwed up against the taste of it. With eyes tight shut and mouth wide open, she drew a deep, luxurious breath, savouring its impact. She opened her eyes and fixed them on Jake. 'And your problem?'

'Oh, that. Well, it was how to work things out so that I could wind up here alone with you. And with the lights dimmed and a drink in my hand. Seems to me the problem has now been happily solved.'

'Very funny,' Nera said dryly.

'It wasn't intended to be.'

'In that case,' Nera said, 'please finish your drink and go. I suppose all you writers naturally picture yourselves playing gay caballeros, but this isn't the time or place for any such performance.'

'The best time is always now. The best place is always where you happen to find yourself. Nera, what the hell is your husband thinking about?'

'My husband?'

'Or any husband who'd leave a woman like you alone for weeks at a time while he's off peddling some foolish merchandise. What kind of man is that? If I owned something like you – '

'Oh, this is just too ridiculous.' Nera stood up abruptly and motioned towards the door with her glass. 'Will you kindly get out of here right now? Come back some time when you're not drunk.'

'I'm not the one who's been drinking,' Jake said.

'Then what you're doing – what you're trying to do – is completely inexcusable.'

Jake slid lower on the couch and stretched his legs out comfortably. 'That isn't what you told Kermit Thoren,' he said.

The glass in Nera's hand jerked convulsively. She started to put it down, then changed her mind and drained it with that same quick thirstiness and shuddering distaste before she placed it carefully on the end table beside her. 'So they're still talking about that,' she said.

'They are. Loud and clear.'

'I can imagine. And I suppose it gave you the impression I'd be delighted to jump into bed with the next comer on demand. And you're not one to waste time putting in your application, are you?'

Jake said: 'Don't play games with me. When we got our first look at each other a couple of days ago you knew as well as I did what was going to happen to us sooner or later. And I didn't need stories about you and Kermit to tell me you're more woman than I've come across in a long time. Or to know what to do about it.'

Nera stared at him. Then she dramatically pressed a hand to her breast. 'It's true,' she said. 'From the moment we met I've dreamed only of being in your arms. But now I'm afraid the reality can never live up to that dream. So I think the only thing left to do is call the security man at the gate and have you tossed out of here before I'm terribly disillusioned.'

She walked, a little unsteadily, to the desk across the room and picked up the phone there. She waited, a finger poised over its dial. 'Well?' she said at last.

'Well what?' Jake said placidly. 'Do you think anybody believes Kermit invited himself in here and assaulted you? Or that they'll believe it about me? That includes the security man. What he'll tell you is that if you really don't want to keep getting assaulted every time your husband leaves town, you ought to have the maid sleep in for a change. Or keep a dog on the premises.'

'In three minutes, Mr Dekker, you will find out exactly what he has to tell me.' Her attempt at hauteur was somewhat spoiled by the slight blurriness of the words. 'And, more to the point, what I have to tell him.'

Jake took a long drink. It was not very good Scotch. He said: 'You must be a lousy poker player, beautiful. You should know better than to pull a bluff if there's a fair chance somebody'll call it. It just leaves you standing there with a phone in your hand and egg all over your face.'

Nera made a choked sound. It might have been a strangled cry of outrage, a suppressed sob, or a violent hiccup. Jake put down his drink, crossed the room, and without resistance from her, gently removed the phone from her grasp and placed it on its stand. She did resist, but only momentarily, when he drew her against him. His hand slid over well-rounded buttocks, up under the silk pyjama blouse, and beneath the taut strap of the brassière. She made that choked sound again. 'Please don't,' she said. 'Please go away.'

'You know you don't want me to.'

'I do. You're frightening me.'

'But not very much,' Jake said.

'No, I mean it.'

'Fine. Since I'm forcing you to do this, you don't have a thing to blame yourself for.' Jake unsnapped the brassière, and its strap fell apart. Nera shivered, her breath quickening as he lightly ran his fingertips back and forth over the marks the straps had left. He said: 'You can see you're my helpless victim. Relax and enjoy it.'

'Mother of God,' Nera moaned, her forehead pressed hard against his chest, 'I have a husband.'

'And I'll bet he's a saint on wheels. Right this minute he's probably sitting in that lonely hotel room in Rio reading his Bible.'

'Don't laugh. He's such a good, kind man. And your wife is such a sweet, pretty child.'

'And you are one hell of a beautiful, grown-up woman. Hold up your arms.'

Nera obediently held them up so that he could draw the pyjama blouse over her head. Then with a shrug of the shoulders she released the brassière into his hand. Her swollen slightly pendulous breasts looked enormous in contrast to the girlishly slim waist. Jake cupped a hand around one, and Nera caught hold of his wrist and futilely tried to thrust it aside. 'No,' she said breathlessly. 'Please don't. Not like this.'

'But definitely yes. Like this.'

'I don't mean that.' There was a note of impatience in her voice. 'Let me go upstairs first. I'll call you when I'm ready.'

Whatever went on upstairs gave him more than enough time before her summons to install a transmitter in the phone, open the drawers of the desk with a picklock to find nothing in them worth finding, check the doors of the house to make sure they were tightly secured, and still finish what was left of his corrosive Scotch and soda without haste.

When he entered her room he found its darkness relieved only by the rosy glow of a night light on her dressing table. The bed was a canopied, beruffled four-poster, and Nera, unclothed, had arranged herself on it like a small, blonde Maja Desnuda. 'Turn out the light,' she whispered.

He did, then blindly felt his way across the room in the direction of the four-poster, kicking off his sandals and peeling off his clothes as he went. He found the bed by barking a shin against it.

'Clumsy,' Nera said tenderly. Her hands touched his chest, moved down exploringly. 'Mother of God,' she said with awe. He bent over her, held painfully tight in her grasp, and his nostrils were filled with a scent of flowery perfume, of citron soap, of under-arm deodorant, and, as his lips brushed hers, not of low-quality Scotch, but of a peppermint-flavoured toothpaste or mouthwash. Nera's arms circled his neck and dragged him down full length on her. '*Ay, mi padrillo,*' she moaned, and then engulfed him in peppermint.

Afterward she was in no mood to share either conversation or a cigarette with him despite his prodding, but lay in a stupor of repletion, her hand clutching his. Resignedly, he waited until the increasingly loud, rasping inhalation and bubbling exhalation of her breath signalled she was asleep. Then he detached himself from her and padded out to investigate the upper floor of the house. It had a separate bedroom arrangement; the room adjoining hers was Fons' bedroom. Besides that, there were a couple of guest rooms and a combination library-music room where an extravagant stereo setup occupied most of one wall.

He carefully combed through the closets and drawers of every room without turning up anything of interest. Then in the library-room he found an old-fashioned photograph album, its pages cracked and drying at the edges. Among the pictures in it were a few of the Thoren family, ranging from the time when Kermit and Joanna were toddlers up to their mid-teens, but none included anyone resembling Walter Thoren. Here and there, Charlotte Thoren showed up. Nowhere was there any sign of her husband.

The investigation completed, he went down to the kitchen, made himself coffee and took his time reading the previous day's edition of the Miami Beach *Daily Sun*. When he returned to the bedroom Nera was still sunk in sleep. He stretched out beside her and forced himself to stay awake until, with a gurgle and snort and a restless shifting of position, she gave the first signs of coming out of it. Then he roused her completely in traditional lover's fashion, and she responded instantly and passionately. This time she was ready to share a cigarette and conversation afterwards.

'You're marvellous,' she said with deep contentment. 'Mother of God, what a lovely, dirty mind. I used to wonder what it would be like, doing all those things. I thought people only did them for magazine pictures.'

'You've seen that kind of magazine?'

'Yes, a friend of mine brought me one from Copenhagen. Fons would kill me if he ever got a look at it. Do you want to see it?'

Jake said: 'No, I don't have to. Come to think of it, maybe you should have used it for Kermit's education.'

'Now please let's not get started on that, darling.'

'Does he still come around?'

'He? It makes me sick to even think of him.'

Jake said: 'Poor Kermit. But there must be other men sometimes, aren't there? I don't see how you can keep them away.'

Nera's cigarette glowed brightly for a moment. 'I don't think

I have to tell you I'm a very healthy woman. And half the time I might as well be a very healthy widow.'

Jake said: 'No, you don't have to tell me that. Was Walter Thoren one of the men?'

'Darling, you might get some kind of thrill from pretending I'm the neighbourhood whore, but I don't.'

'Was he?'

'No, he wasn't,' Nera said shortly.

Jake said: 'But you wanted him to be, didn't you? I heard all about that business over there where you made a pass at him right out in the open.'

'Oho, now the light dawns.' Nera caught hold of a handful of his hair and fondly tugged at it. 'You're jealous, you idiot. And of some poor soul who's dead and buried a month.'

'Jealous? Of a man stupid enough to turn you down?'

'Yes, you are. As for his turning me down – well, when I thought about it afterward I was just as glad he did. He was a pretty frightening kind of man, really.'

'Go on. You like to be frightened that way.'

'Only when I know I can control the situation. I don't think it would have been like that with Walter.' Nera raised herself on an elbow and crushed out her cigarette in the ashtray between them. 'I'm beginning to get the feeling it's not like that with you either. I don't mind now, but I'm not so sure about later on. You're just a little bit too much like Walter in some ways.'

'What ways?'

'Attractive enough to make women behave stupidly. Jealous. He was impossible about any outsider having the least influence on Charlotte and the children. Cold and arrogant. Most of all' – Nera was a barely discernible paleness in the black of the room as she straddled him on her knees – 'all head and no heart.' She drew a circle on his chest with her finger. 'Nothing in here. A stainless-steel motor, that's all.'

'Thanks,' Jake said. 'You're a great little ego builder, aren't you?'

'As if your ego needed building. Darling, you are one great big, dangerous, calculating hunk of ego.'

'You don't know me yet. When you do you'll find out what a pussycat I am.'

'Oh, sure. The sabre-toothed-tiger kind. But don't let that upset you. I'd be the last one to deny that you do have your charms.'

'So do you,' Jake said. 'What gets me is why Thoren wasn't hit by them as hard as I was. What did happen when you made that play for him? Granting he had to play it cool in front of everybody, he still could have patted your knee under the table to show he appreciated the compliment. Or knowing you were half-stoned, he could have passed the whole thing off as a joke. But why should he blow up as violently as he did? When a man like that loses control of himself for even a few seconds, there must be some reason for it.'

'I don't know any reason. And I don't see why we have to keep picking at it this way. I'd just as soon stick with the living and let poor Walter rest in peace.'

'Still and all,' Jake said musingly. 'He'd sure make one hell of a character for a story. A natural. Start with that scene at the dinner party, go back and explore the reasons for it – '

'So that's it. I should have known.'

'Well, you can't blame a writer for seeing the story values in a scene like that, can you?'

'I suppose not. But you can't blame me for wanting to be more than story material at a time like this, can you?'

He pulled her down so that she lay sprawled over him, her chin over his shoulder, her cheek against his. 'You know damn well you're a lot more than that.' He slowly ran his hands up and down her flanks and she stirred uneasily. 'Better not start what you can't finish,' she warned.

He clasped his hands over the small of her back. 'What happened? Was it something you did that might have shocked him?'

'Oh, stop dramatizing. What I did was put my arm through his and whisper some nonsense into his ear. And it was hardly a proposition either. It was the most harmless kind of thing.'

'You mean, what you said to him?'

'Yes. I was sitting next to him at the table and hadn't been

91

able to get more than two words out of him all evening. Anyhow, they were all talking about this murder that had happened around here the week before – some millionaire named Farber or Farbstein or something was pulled out of the bay with a bullet in his head, and nobody knew who did it – and I got this Scotch-and-soda impulse to lean over to Walter and say to him: "I know you're the murderer, but if you're nice to me I won't tell anybody." I'll admit it wasn't the brightest remark in the world, but it certainly didn't deserve what he handed me for it. You'd think I stuck a knife into him, the way he reacted.'

Jake said casually: 'And all because of a murder case that didn't mean a thing to any of you. Life's little ironies. I suppose the case was solved right afterward, just to add to the irony.'

'I think it was. No, I'm not sure. Anyhow, what difference did it make one way or the other after the damage was done?' Nera suddenly raised her head and looked around. 'Am I developing night vision, or is it getting light in here? What time is it?'

Jake strained to make out the hands of his watch. 'About twenty to six.'

Nera scrambled off him. 'Time to go. *Ahora. Pronto.* I mean it. Don't settle down and make yourself comfortable there.'

'How about sharing the sunrise first?'

'No.' She hauled him upright. 'Please. You don't know what this place is like.'

'Bright, shiny eyes everywhere?'

'Everywhere. Your wife's big blue ones included.'

He left through the back door. As Nera started to close it behind him he said: 'That word you used – *padrillo*. What's a *padrillo*?'

Nera patted his cheek. 'What you are, thank God,' she said, then quickly pulled the door shut.

18

When he slipped into the house he found Elinor, in robe and slippers, huddled in an armchair in the living room. She looked on the verge of tears as she came out of the chair. 'Oh, Jake, I could kill you. Where were you? What happened to you?'

'You can see nothing happened to me. How long have you been waiting up like this, anyhow?'

'All night, practically. I knew you were somewhere around here because you didn't take the car. And once I started thinking about that and blackmailers and guns, I couldn't sleep.'

'You should have had more sense. Did Maniscalco call?'

'Nobody called. How about some breakfast?' She was already on her way to the kitchen. 'It'll just take a few minutes.'

'Don't bother. I have to make a call, and then all I want to do is catch up on my sleep. You'd better do the same. You look dead on your feet.'

'I am.' She trailed after him into the study and immediately went to work hauling his bedding out of the closet. 'I'll make up the couch for you first.'

He dialled Magnes' number, and while waiting for an answer, got out of his shirt and worked off his sandals against a leg of the desk. Magnes finally answered in sleepy bad humour.

'Yes, I know what time it is,' Jake told him, 'but I just came across something very big. I want you to get on it right away.'

Magnes was instantly wide awake. 'You tried the boat again, after all? You found a letter there?'

'No, it's something else. There was a big murder case down here around two to three years ago. Some wheel named Farber or Farbstein who was hauled out of the bay with a bullet in his head. You know about it, don't you?'

'Farber or Farbstein?' There was a long silence on the phone. 'Offhand, I don't remember such a case. I'll have to look it up.'

'But quick,' Jake said. 'And not only in the newspapers. The police reports, too. And whatever off-the-record stuff you can dig up.'

'Everything. Come over here about noon. I'll have it ready for you.'

Jake said: 'No, I don't want to be seen at your place too often. Pick some tourist place where we can have lunch.'

'Wolfie's,' said Magnes. 'Lincoln and Collins. I'll be at a back table, twelve o'clock sharp.'

Jake put down the phone. He turned and saw Elinor looking at him with an expression that suggested she had just bitten into something strange and wasn't sure how it tasted to her. She said without emotion: 'I don't think it was Joanna you were in bed with. She keeps her fingernails too short to claw up anybody's back that bad. So I guess it was Nera, wasn't it?'

'A very keen deduction,' Jake said.

'A very easy one. It makes it seem kind of funny, too, the way I was sitting here worrying about you all that time. I should have known it was like worrying if Frankenstein's monster carries an umbrella in the rain.'

'Well,' Jake said, 'now you know.'

He went down the hallway to the bathroom, and she followed close on his heels. Shoulders hunched, hands thrust into the pockets of her robe, she watched him plug in the electric razor and go to work with it. Then over the whine of the razor she said: 'Was it Nera who told you Walter Thoren was mixed up in that murder?'

'Not in so many words. It happened to come out while she was talking.'

'I see. And is that how you get women like that to talking so free and easy? By sleeping with them?'

Jake studied his jaw in the mirror, then worked the razor under it. 'What do you mean, women like that?'

Elinor said: 'I mean women her age. Do you have any idea how old she must be? She probably takes those change-of-life pills just to keep going.'

'They must be some pills,' Jake said.

He turned on the water in the glass-enclosed shower, and

steam billowed out into the room. He removed his slacks and underwear shorts and draped them over Elinor's arm. 'One's for the tailor, one's for the laundry bag,' he said, but when he emerged from the shower she was still standing there with the slacks and shorts over her arm. He pointed, and she mechanically handed him a towel.

'Tell me something,' she said abruptly. 'Do you ever do anything just for kicks? I mean, balling, getting drunk, even talking to somebody – do you ever do any of that because you feel like it, not because it would help on a case? You're not always on a job, are you? So what are you like between jobs? You can't be the same as this.'

'Maybe not. But I can't really say what I'm like then.'

Her tone softened. 'Jake, if it's a question of trying to understand yourself – '

'It isn't that. Between jobs, Dr Frankenstein unplugs my electrodes and leans me against the laboratory wall. I'm in sort of a coma then.'

Elinor opened her mouth, then closed it. She gave him a sad, sweet smile. 'I happen to believe every word of that,' she said, and walked out of the bathroom with dignity.

When he got back to the study he found his pants and shorts had been flung on the floor there, and had to step over them to reach the couch.

19

He had trouble rousing himself when the alarm went off at eleven, and even more trouble getting Elinor awake. When she finally managed to raise her head and look at the clock on her night table she said unbelievingly: 'But I've only been asleep four hours. Why do I have to get up now? I can't even think straight.'

'Don't think. Just get dressed. I'm having lunch with Magnes in an hour, and I want you to meet him. If things tighten up later on, you'll have to be my contact with him.'

That opened her eyes wide. 'Tighten up?'

'Relax. All it means is that if some busybody starts taking too much of an interest in my business down here, I can't afford to be seen with Magnes. Then you'll be the one to contact him if its necessary.'

'What good would that do? Everybody thinks I'm your wife. It would be the same as if you met him, wouldn't it?'

'No, because I'm the one they'd keep an eye on, especially if you come on strong as my wife. Now rise and shine.'

Elinor sat up, then collapsed forward like a rag doll, her head almost touching her knees. 'I'll rise,' she said faintly, 'but I sure as hell won't shine.'

He waited until she had dragged herself out of bed before he left her. Ten minutes later a loud wail of despair brought him back into the bedroom. She was sitting at the dressing table, staring at her image in the mirror. 'Jake, look at me. I'm peeling like a leper. It shows right through the make-up. I can't go out looking like this.'

'Look, I'm not arranging for us to meet a movie producer. Just get rid of that make-up and rub a lot of cold cream into your face. When you wipe it away it'll take most of those flakes off.'

She started to protest, then saw his expression in the mirror. She sulkily went to work following instructions. 'You sound like you made this scene before,' she said. 'Are you married, by any chance?'

'I was. Twice.'

'Two lucky girls, no less. What happened with them?'

'Her. It was the same one both times. The first time out, she couldn't stand poverty. The second time, I guess she couldn't stand prosperity. And you can wear that mini you came down here in. That way, nobody'll notice your face.'

Magnes did. Somehow, despite the crowd in the place and the line waiting outside its door, he had managed to obtain for himself a large semicircular booth in the back of the restaurant. He looked Elinor over appraisingly as she seated herself on the banquette between him and Jake. 'A real *tsatskeh*,' he said with approval. 'But that's some burn you caught yourself there, girlie. That wasn't so bright, was it? Look how you're peeling.'

'Well, thanks,' Elinor said coldly.

'And another little thing, girlie. A bagger should not dress so conspicuous that even these old *kvetchers* around here turn and look. In this business, the trick is to make people not look.'

'A beggar?' Elinor said in bewilderment.

Jake said: 'A bagger. A female investigator. What did you get on that Farber or Farbstein killing?' he asked Magnes.

Magnes said: 'The works. It was a killing all right, except the name wasn't Farber or Farbstein. That's what threw me off when you told me about it over the phone. Who gave you those names anyhow?'

'The Ortega woman.'

'Well, she was wrong about it. Did she also tell you Thoren did the killing?'

Jake said: 'She described his reaction when she mentioned it to him. The way he reacted, he must have had something to do with it.'

Magnes shook his head. 'I don't see how. It was an open-and-shut case. The guy's name who got killed was Garfein. Murray Garfein. A nice old guy – a widower – made himself a fortune in cloaks and suits and retired down here to take care of a heart condition. His luck, on his way back from fishing in Key West he picked up a junkie kid hitchhiker, and the kid put a bullet in his head and dumped him in the bay here. They got the kid a week later driving around Jacksonville in Garfein's car and with the gun still on him. They gave him the chair last year. Like I said, open and shut. Could it be the Ortega woman was just talking through her hat?'

'I don't think she was wearing a hat at the time,' Elinor remarked.

Magnes cocked his head inquiringly at Jake. 'The girlie's a comedian?'

'She's a million laughs. Are you sure Garfein was the one Mrs Ortega meant? Remember, that wasn't the name she gave me.'

'You said between two and three years ago. I covered from

last year to almost five years ago, and there was no Farber or Farbstein case. But this Garfein murder matched up every way with what you gave me. It absolutely had to be him.'

The waitress came to take their orders then, and Magnes frowned at Elinor's choice. 'Pancakes for lunch?'

'Will you please stop nagging me?' Elinor said. 'And this happens to be my breakfast.'

'Pancakes are pancakes. With that kind of a shape, you are going to be a fleshy woman later on if you don't watch out.'

'All right,' Elinor said wearily, 'make it a salad.'

Magnes told the waitress to make it a nice whitefish salad and diet soda for the young lady. When she had gone on her way, he said to Jake: 'How did the Ortega woman get that rise out of Thoren exactly? What did she say to him in so many words about Garfein?'

Jake nodded. 'That's what I was thinking about. She said, kidding him, "I know you're the murderer," so I took for granted he blew up because of the suggestion he had killed Garfein. Now I can see it didn't have to mean that. He could have blown up simply because of the suggestion that he was a murderer.'

'And that still convinces you he was?' Magnes said.

'It's even money he was. And the blackmailer not only knew about it, but could prove it in court if he had to.'

'Prove it or not,' Magnes said, 'you still can't afford to give up on the other angles. For all you know, they could be tied in with this one. What I've got on my mind especially is how Thoren's mama and papa got killed in that accident way back when. It wouldn't be the first time a smart young fellow fixed things up to inherit an estate. Did Maniscalco fill you in on that accident yet?'

'Not yet. He should be calling tonight about it. And the service record.'

Elinor said: 'What I'd like to know is why you're both so sure Thoren didn't hire that hitchhiker to kill Garfein. He didn't have to kill Garfein with his own hands to feel like a murderer, did he?'

'Very good,' Magnes said. He tapped his forehead. 'It shows

at least the wheels are turning in there. The only trouble is, girlie, the kind of murder you're talking about is not very practical. You can easy pay off a hitchhiker to kill some driver coming along the road. But how do you make sure the driver will stop and pick up that special hitchhiker?'

Elinor looked at Jake. 'He's right,' he told her. 'What was the date of the Garfein killing?' he asked Magnes.

'February, two years ago.' Magnes pulled a small notebook from his pocket and flipped through its pages. 'February ninth. Which makes it exactly two years and two months ago. They caught up with the kid February sixteenth.'

'All right. And since Nera Ortega said the case was still unsolved when she had her blow-up with Thoren, the blow-up took place that week. And there's a good chance Thoren was hit by the blackmailer for the first time a little before that week. That could have been what had him so on edge when Nera made that crack of hers.'

Magnes said: 'But even cutting it so fine on the dates don't help too much. After all, I just went through the records. You wouldn't live long enough to check out, one by one, every murder and manslaughter and accidental death Thoren might have been involved in before that February ninth.'

Jake said: 'I wasn't thinking of doing it that way. I was thinking of how Thoren suddenly quit going to Bayside Spa. If it turns out he stopped going around there, say, January that year, we'll know we're right on target. It would mean the black-mailer was probably operating out of the spa. That's a big step towards identifying him. I'm taking for granted that if it was someone at the spa who fingered Thoren for blackmail, Thoren would pay up all right, but he sure as hell wouldn't want to go around there and keep the guy company. So he'd give up his workouts there.'

'All right,' Magnes said, 'so suppose the percentage on that pays off, and you do identify the blackmailer. What then?'

'Then the trick is to find out what he had on Thoren. Once I know who he is and the basis for the blackmail, I can break Mrs Thoren down without any trouble.'

'*Shver tzu machen a leben,*' said Magnes. 'Meaning, some

people bought Miami Beach real estate when it was still a jungle here, and some people have to work for a living. As soon as we're done eating I'll go up to the spa and get myself a health treatment. And how about our little girlie here?' He waved a thumb at Elinor. 'You said she was already close to the Thoren family. If she got to talking to that young fellow there about health treatments and the spa, she might turn up something interesting. Or do you think that's too risky?'

Jake said: 'No, she can handle it. I'll drop her off there on the way home. She can thank them for making a sick call as her excuse. Did you get anything on the other stuff I gave you yesterday?'

'So far, not too much. This Charlie Matthews at the Biscayne National Bank is a vice-president there. Very comfortable financially, and with a good reputation. And he's been living in the same place on Brickell Road over in Miami as far back as anybody remembers. Oh yes, I showed that picture of Thoren to the fellow used to run that gay bar over on Alton, and he said he didn't know him. Never saw him around the bar. The other items I was going to start on today, but this Garfein thing held me up.'

'That's my fault,' Jake said. 'Anyhow, you're doing fine so far.'

Magnes said: 'Well, it's not hard when you're doing a job for somebody who knows what he wants. And you happen to be a very lucky young lady,' he told Elinor solemnly. 'Believe me, from the way your boss here operates, I can tell you he is one of the best. What they call around here a real *shtarker*. You listen to him, you do what he says, and you'll be learning the business the right way.'

After lunch, when Elinor had gone off to the ladies' room, he confided to Jake: 'It was a mistake giving you that build-up. I was sorry about it right away. Not that I didn't mean it.'

'Then why be sorry about it?'

'Because she's already got enough of a crush on you. Like I told you yesterday, a jealous woman is a born trouble-maker.'

Jake laughed. 'Magnes, I hate to say it, but when it comes

to spotting girlish crushes, you have to work too much from memory. Better stick to insurance frauds.'

Magnes raised his eyebrows. 'You think so? So why was she sitting close enough to you that if it was any closer she'd be on your lap? And why is it that even when you're only saying it's nice weather she sits and looks at you with the mouth open and stars in the eyes like it was beautiful poetry? Take an old man's advice, sonny, and watch how you handle her. Otherwise, that Mrs Thoren could suddenly drop in on you with a couple of transmitters she found in her phones, and a cop along to explain how it was a felony for you to plant them there. Your little blondie could wreck you in one minute as easy as that. Women. *Meh ken meshugeh veren.*'

'Which means?'

'Which means,' said Magnes, 'that the reason why I'm still so youthful and healthy for all my years is because the women I happened to run across like your blondie would always rather make trouble for some other man.'

20

As Elinor slid out of the car, Jake said: 'Remember the password is Bayside Spa,' and waited until she disappeared through the Thorens' door with a parting wave of the hand at him before he drove off.

Parking the car in his own driveway, he took notice of the sailboat close offshore, with the bare-chested pink bulk of Milt Webb at its tiller. It was moving toward Webb's dock, and when it nosed into the dock Jake was there to tie it up. Webb scrambled to the dock and immediately untied it. Redoing the knot, he said irritably: 'There's a right way and a wrong way. This happens to be the right way.'

'Well, bully for you, admiral,' Jake said. He started to walk away, and when he had gone a few steps Webb said: 'Ah, come on, Jake. You don't have to get sore about it, do you?'

'It looks to me like you're the one who's sore, Milt.'

'Well,' Webb said grudgingly, 'maybe I am pissed off a little at the world in general. Seems like nobody around here believes I really knocked off that crook the other night. Including those Keystone cops over on the Beach. Let me tell you, I've been taking some rough kidding about it.'

'That's a hell of a note.'

'You can say that again. But I'm sorry I took it out on you for no reason. I mean that, Jake.'

'No harm done,' Jake said. 'If I'm going to learn my way around sailboats, I have to start somewhere.'

Webb looked interested. 'Are you serious about that? I mean, about going in for sailing?'

'Sure. But not in anything as big as yours.' Jake pointed at the twelve-footer moored to the Thoren dock. 'I'd say something like that would be about my size right now.'

'The *Carlotta*? She's an Alpha. Dinghy style and damn near unsinkable. Pretty too, ain't she? Walter could really make her do tricks.'

'You think anybody would mind if we went over there and took a close look? Maybe got the cover off so I could see what she was like inside?'

'Mind?' Webb jerked his head over his shoulder to indicate the Thoren house. 'Joanna would go off like a bomb if we tried anything like that. Won't sail her, sell her, or lend her. Happened Walter was out in her right before he got killed that day, and now the girl's made that boat into kind of a memorial to him. That's what I call sick. I guess it goes with her taste for kosher cooking.'

'Peculiar kid all right,' Jake said. 'Anyhow, when you go sailing here, do you just travel up and down the bay or is there any special landing spot you aim at?'

Webb laughed. 'Man, how much of a landlubber can you be? Tell you what. Come on up to the house for a drink, and I'll show you some charts of the waters around here. I've got a pile of catalogues, too, so you can get an idea of what boat prices are like. And you never saw my gun collection, did you?'

Jake managed to get away after only an hour of charts, catalogues, and guns, but when he walked into the house he found Elinor already there. 'That was quick,' he said. 'What happened?'

Elinor shrugged. 'I don't know. I guess I just wasn't wanted around.'

'I take it Kermit wasn't on the scene.'

'Or Joanna. They both went back to college, and she's got a late class today, so he's waiting there to drive her back home. The only ones around were Mrs Thoren and the help. And she wasn't feeling too sociable.'

'Did you get to mention Bayside Spa at all?'

'Yes. I said you used to take workouts in a gym in New York, and that you were wondering if there was any place near here where you could keep doing it. I said we heard Bayside Spa might be a good place, and did she know anything about it.'

'And?'

'And she said, well her husband used to go there at one time, but he quit going when the tone of the place changed. That was it.'

'How did she react when you said Bayside Spa right out loud? Did it seem to hit a nerve?'

Elinor shook her head. 'She couldn't have cared less. Then when she started looking at her watch every two minutes, I figured it was a polite way of telling me to take off, so I did. And you'll notice I didn't step out of line and ask you where you've been all along. You can see I'm a quick learner.'

'From those circles under your eyes, what I can see is you'd better grab a nap now and make up for some of that sleep you lost last night. You've got a lot of listening-in to do after supper.'

'All right.' Elinor turned towards the bedroom, then turned back to face him again. 'I guess I'm not really a quick learner. Where have you been until now?'

'Over at Milt Webb's, looking at blueprints of sailing boats. Surprising how simple they are.'

'So is he from what I've heard,' Elinor said. Her mood was suddenly much brighter. 'Well, if that's your idea of a good time – '

She woke from her nap in time to prepare the usual early dinner, and after dinner, went back to the bedroom to activate the transmitter in the Thorens' downstairs phone. She called Jake into the bedroom a half hour later. When he walked in she immediately put a warning finger to her lips, then pointed at the monitor. The voice coming from it was Charlotte Thoren's.

'– and your father would have agreed. You know he couldn't bear company dropping in without notice. And I wouldn't like the Dekkers even if they had perfect manners. They are not our kind of people.'

'Because they're different and interesting?' It was Joanna, her voice shrill. 'Because they're not like the rest of the walking dead around here?'

'You will mind your tone, Joanna.'

'Anyhow, you're missing the point, Jo.' Kermit, plainly amused. 'Don't you recognize the "not our kind of people" bit? I have a hunch that means they're Nera's kind of people. When she walked in there yesterday and got that friendly hello from Elinor – '

'I don't believe it. That isn't true, is it, Mother? You couldn't be so unfair.'

'Not unless you believe sound judgement can be unfair, Joanna. And I'm not alone in that judgement. Patty Tucker phoned me this afternoon, thoroughly disgusted with her precious friend.'

'It seems to me' – Joanna, coldly – 'that she's thoroughly disgusted with Nera every time she has something to tell you about her. It's positively marvellous how she manages to stay friends with her. Or, for that matter, with us. Come to think of it, how does Patty get away with belonging to both sides when nobody else is allowed to?'

'You know as well as I do, Joanna, that she has no choice about remaining friends with the Ortegas. After all, when Stewart willed her his share of the business he virtually made her their partner. And she wouldn't have to be disgusted with Nera if Nera had the decency to keep her affairs to herself.'

'Now it's coming out.' Kermit, with satisfaction. Then in a

tone of delighted realization: *'Jesus, don't tell me Nera's already hooked Dekker. Not already. But she must have. That's why you're suddenly so soured on him, isn't it? And taking it out on Elinor, too.'*

'I'm telling you no more or less than what I was told. Patty informed me that from Nera's manner and from certain remarks dropped at the lunch table, she knew at once what was going on. When she asked Nera if her new neighbour was involved, Nera was so obviously pleased by the question and so evasive about answering it that she might as well have pointed her finger at the man. That woman actually takes an obscene pleasure in advertising her affairs, and I've had my fill of it up to here. And I can, and will, do something about it.'

'Because Nera told Patty a lot of nonsense?' Joanna, with disbelief. *'And Patty was bitchy enough to repeat it to you? You wouldn't.'*

'And couldn't under any conditions, Mother dear.' Kermit, sardonically. *'Hell, I'd like to see Nera get knocked down and run over as much as you, but you don't have the right to start a purity campaign against her. Anyway, Daystar is hardly the place for purity campaigns. How old do you think Jo and I were when we found out Carol Tobin down the Drive used to run the biggest whorehouse in Miami? Or that Ray Potter was Capone's messenger boy between here and Chicago back in the good old days?'*

'I'm not interested in whatever lurid stores you heard about Miss Tobin or Mr Potter, Kermit. In fact –'

'In fact' – Kermit, sweetly – *'you're just interested in putting down Nera. But you're not taking into account that you can't do that without stirring up a juicy old scandal that also involved me.'*

'Don't be a fool. What I'm saying is that in a few weeks –'

The ringing of the phone in the study suddenly cut through Charlotte Thoren's quietly menacing voice. 'That's Maniscalco,' Jake told Elinor on his way to answer it. 'Just keep getting all this down on tape.'

It was Maniscalco. 'Jake,' he said heavily, 'it's cold and wet up here. And this rotten smog is enough to choke you. How's it down there, you lucky bastard?'

'Full of sunshine so far, Manny, but now it's clouding up fast. What's wrong? Did Thoren turn up clean on every count?'

Maniscalco drew a deep breath and slowly released it into the mouthpiece of his phone. It came across the wire in a mournful, diminishing roar. 'I'll put it like this,' he said. 'Thoren didn't turn up. Period.'

'What's that supposed to mean?'

'My friend, it means that until one happy day in September, 1942, there was no Walter Thoren. That was the day when the Miami *Herald* had a couple of lines about him joining the K.O. Sprague Company down there. Before that, he never even existed. He wasn't born, he didn't go to school, he didn't serve in the army – nothing. Are you beginning to get the idea?'

Jake said: 'I'm not so sure I am. Are you telling me there are absolutely no records on him anywhere? A man like that?'

'Absolutely none.'

'Did they check the other military services besides the army?'

'All of them. They had those computers red-hot working on it. But no dice.'

'Well, what about that guy you sent to St Olivet? Did he go through their birth and death records himself, or did he leave it up to some idiotic clerk?'

'Neither. Because there are no records there dating back before 1940. They had a fire in the town hall that year which destroyed practically all their files. And I know you're going to ask if it was arson, so I can tell you right now it wasn't. It was one of those fluke things set off by lightning, and the building was the kind of dried-out old clapboard that goes up like a matchbox.'

'I see,' Jake said. 'And I suppose when your boy asked around town, nobody there had even heard the name Thoren before.'

'Or the name Lennart, which is what Thoren put down in the policy as his mother's maiden name. You know, Jake, when you think of all the miseries of growing up, it's not bad to start right off in life as a thirty-year-old model citizen. The only thing I'm sorry about is that the guy who figured out a way to do it is in to Guaranty for two hundred grand. And right now, according to four of the most expensive lawyers in this goddam business, it looks like his widow has every chance of collecting it.'

Jake said: 'You mean the incontestability clause holds up even under these conditions? But how can it? I know it bars you from contesting a claim just because a false name was used in the application, but this is a whole false identity.'

'Sure it is, but the only thing we can prove false in court is that statement about army service. And according to those legal geniuses I was locked up with all afternoon, if we wanted to make an issue of that, we had to do it before the incontestability clause became operative seven weeks ago. So what I'd like to know, Jake, is how much this affects the job you're doing down there. I'm not putting it as a challenge. I just want to know how much our chances are hurt because Thoren's a blank before 1942.'

Jake said: 'You're putting it as a challenge. Did those lawyers really shake you up that bad?'

'Not them, Jake. After all, nothing they had to say was that much of a surprise. But a whole team from Claims was there too, shaking their heads at me like I was the one who passed on that goddam policy application in the first place. A bunch of gutless wonders. They won't come right out and tell me to authorize payment, because they smell something fishy here as much as you and I do. What they'd like me to do is give up and authorize payment all on my own. Then they can jump on me for getting them into a useless lawsuit to start with.'

'After thirty years' service? Come on, Manny, you're being paranoid about it.'

'Not me, mister. I hate to tell you how many nice clean-cut college hot shots in Claims would give their right arm for my job, and all of them using that thirty years' service against me. It means I'm too old and pooped-out to handle the job any more. Why not put me out into pasture on half-retirement money right now, before I ruin Guaranty? I'm telling you,

Jake, the pressure at that meeting was enough to make your ears pop. And the one way I can really ream it up these college bastards is to bust this case wide open. So be honest with me. Is there still a chance of busting it open?'

'Hell, there'd better be, considering my investment in it.'

'But could you put enough of the picture together right now, so an outsider could see we had a chance? Claims called another meeting for tomorrow morning with some of the brass sitting in. If I can convince them we have a fighting chance to get a release from the beneficiary before the month is up, at least some of the pressure'll be off until then.'

'All right, I'll do what I can. But I have to go over the policy and all my reports first. It might take a couple of hours.'

Maniscalco said fervently: 'I'll be waiting right here by the phone with the tape recorder all wound up. Listen, Jake, when you look at the date Thoren suddenly turned up out of nowhere – 1942, right in the middle of the war – do you think he might have been a draft dodger on the lam? It makes sense that way, doesn't it?'

'Not enough. For one thing, he wasn't the draft-dodger type. For another thing, he was smart enough to know that being tagged a draft dodger today doesn't mean what it used to. Some of the best people are making it their hobby. It sure as hell wouldn't be worth ten thousand a month to him in blackmail to cover it up, and with suicide for the big finish. Anyhow, don't worry your head about it, Manny. You just light a candle to the saint of insurance investigators, whoever it is, and I'll try to call back before it goes out.'

21

The cardboard folders, Jake observed as he laid them out on the desk, were now beginning to look pretty worn and battered. He arranged them before him, then became aware of the voices from the monitor in the bedroom. He closed his door to cut off the sound, and returned to the folders. He started with an examination of the policy, making notes as he went through the questionnaire.

The door opened, and Elinor stood there. 'Am I bothering you?'

'It depends.'

'Oh. Well, I just wanted to tell you it's all over. I've got the tape marked where you walked out. I can play the rest of it for you whenever you're ready.'

'That won't be for a while. How'd it come out?'

'It'll come out the way Mrs Thoren wants it to. There's some kind of Daystar Island committee meeting next month where they vote on whether you can buy the house or not, and she's lining up votes to make sure you can't. And I want to say you were right about Patty Tucker, and I was wrong. I guess Mrs Thoren's the only one of them who doesn't know what a first-class bitch she is.'

'She knows,' Jake said. 'Well, you don't have to look that depressed about it. It's not your headache.'

Elinor said: 'No, but I kind of liked Mrs Thoren, and right now I can't stand her. How the hell can you ever stand anybody if you're always listening in to what they say in private?' She shook her head as if to clear it of this bleak thought. 'What did Maniscalco have to tell you? Anything interesting?'

'You might call it that,' Jake said. He gave her the gist of Maniscalco's message, and when she looked stunned he said: 'I know. But whatever you're thinking, I already thought. What I have to do now is try and add this whole thing up and give Maniscalco the score. I'll let you know when I'm ready to call him so you can listen in. Meanwhile, phone Magnes and ask him to find out first thing tomorrow if Thoren was a registered voter. Then tune in on Nera Ortega. When I was over there last night I bugged her downstairs line.'

'Well, all right,' Elinor said. 'That, at least, comes as no surprise.'

That was at eight-thirty. It was almost midnight before he stiffly pulled himself out of the swivel chair and went into the bedroom. Elinor, phone receiver and monitor arranged beside her on the bed, was watching Johnny Carson preparing to sell something on the television set drawn up close to her. Jake switched off the set, but the sound of Carson's voice remained loud and clear in the room.

Elinor said: 'That's Mrs Thoren's TV. There was nothing doing at the Ortegas', so I figured you'd want me to stay with Mrs Thoren same as usual.'

'Not watching the set here at the same time,' Jake said. 'That's not how it's done.'

'So now I know. It's just that you can go crazy listening in and not seeing what they're laughing at. And then it wasn't worth seeing after all. Man, that's a square world out there.'

'Well,' Jake said, 'if you want to hear all about a different kind of world, just come inside and listen to what I tell Maniscalco.'

22

He said to Maniscalco: 'Do you have that policy questionnaire handy?'

'Jake, for chrissake, I've been waiting with it in front of me here for the last three hours.'

'Good. Now take a close look at it. First where Thoren put down the date of his birth, and then on the next page where he wrote down the date of his father's death.'

'I'm looking,' Maniscalco said. 'What about them?'

'Look again. I think you'll find the same thing there I did. It's been bothering me every time I went through these papers, but I couldn't figure out why until now. I'll give you one clue. He was emotionally all wound up when he filled those questions in, so he made one little slip which happens to be a very big giveaway.'

Half a minute late Maniscalco said: 'I got it. The first date is written October fifth, 1915; the other one has the day and then the month – second of January, 1940. The European way.'

'Right. And those little hooks on the number ones that make them all look like number sevens is also the European way.'

'What do you know?' Maniscalco said with awe. 'The guy was a foreigner.'

'Well, not strictly a foreigner after living here half his life. But he was a refugee probably. I estimate he landed here from Denmark some time between 1935 and 1940, and those were Hitler years. Refugee time everywhere.'

Maniscalco said: 'It was. And the 1940 I can see. He turned up in Miami in 1942, full-fledged American style, so we allow a couple of years for him to pick up the language. But why the 1935?'

'Because everything on the record indicates he was well-educated. Possibly a university graduate. Which means he was at least twenty when he left Europe. You know, Manny, this was one hell of a man.'

'I'm glad you feel so tender about him, Jake. It's like the whole thing is in the family that way.'

'I wouldn't exactly call it tenderness. But you can't take away from the guy that he created a different person out of himself so perfectly that nobody even dreamed of challenging it. Here's a man who built up an image of himself where he seemed to have a whole social life and be an actively good citizen, while all the time he was really a loner. Look at the way he handled it, Manny. He always kept his mouth tight shut no matter how much he was tempted to talk up sometimes. He locked himself in on Daystar Island here, which is like a high-class isolation ward anyhow. He hand-picked a couple of friends from the people around him and that was all. He made his main activity sailboating, which he could do alone. And he went a long way to keep himself and his family out of the papers. Even that Civic Planning Association he joined to round out the picture of the good citizen must be a stiff. I signed on Abe Magnes and he's checking it out now. I'll bet its membership is that same hand-picked set Thoren was close to on the island.'

'But what's behind the whole cover-up, Jake? Good as your idea looks, you know it makes no sense unless he had some damn good reason for going to all that trouble.'

'He had. Now hold on to your hat, Manny. Thoren came to

111

the States between 1935 and 1940. And somewhere between 1940 and 1942, which is when he showed up in Miami, he committed a murder.'

'A murder? Are you sure? You mean you have evidence of it?'

'If I had evidence of it, I'd be babying Mrs Thoren through a case of hysterics right now so she could sign that release. Just take my word for it. The real Walter Thoren, whoever he was, committed a murder. That's as far as it goes for the time being. What the motive was, or the method, I have no idea.'

Maniscalco said: 'Well, if it comes to that, how about plain, old-fashioned profit for a motive? That ties right in with the sixty thousand bucks he had to pay for his partnership in Sprague's company down there right after he showed up in town.'

Jake said: 'You mean he bought in to that company? For cash?'

'He did. It was in the clipping from the business page of the Miami *Herald* I told you about.'

Jake said softly: 'But you never told me he bought in to the company, you stupid son of a bitch. I've been thinking he made out by marrying the boss's daughter. You should have realized what it could mean if he showed up here with that much money on him, a young guy not even out of his twenties.'

'Jake, be reasonable. It was a small detail as far as I could see, and it happened twenty-six years ago. How the hell was I to know it was even worth thinking about? And it came out now when it mattered, so there's no harm done, is there?'

'No, but there was a lot of time wasted while I was trying to figure out some motive. Any motive. Maybe you are getting too old for that job, Manny.'

'Well, you're not making me feel any younger. What do you say we just stick to the case?'

'I'm the one who's been sticking to it. Anyhow, Thoren committed murder and, as I now learn, wound up with a lot of money. Then he went to work on that new identity. A lot of work, including finding out there was a backwoods place in Minnesota where the town hall had been destroyed by fire

112

along with all the records stored in it. That's how we know the murder was committed after 1940. Because that fire in St Olivet happened in 1940. However he found out about it, he knew that claiming to come from St Olivet took care of most of his background. And he'd want a place in Minnesota because speech patterns in some areas there still have a Scandinavian flavour. So between that and whatever cooked-up identification he needed to prove he was a wounded veteran, he came down to Miami ready to be Walter Thoren, model citizen.

'There's only one hitch to this beautiful setup: someone knew about that murder. And a little over two years ago – I'm calculating it was about January, two years ago – Thoren ran right into that somebody. This we know because of the black-mail. We also know that the blackmailer is now working on Mrs Thoren. Since he'd never be able to do that without telling her the inside story of the real Thoren, it means that right this minute I'm close to two people who know all about Thoren's crime and his true identity. And given a little time, I'll be the third one to have that inside story. I'll hand you the release from Mrs Thoren right after that.'

Maniscalco took his time thinking it over. Then he said: 'You know what I'll do, Jake? Edit this tape a little bit, then run it through for the brass at that meeting tomorrow. I've got a feeling it's the best way to do a selling job on them.'

'A selling job. In other words, Manny, you've got me in a deep hole with the water rising fast. That meeting is to decide whether they give you the go-ahead for another couple of weeks, or whether they send a cheque for two hundred thousand to Mrs Thoren tomorrow afternoon, isn't it?'

'Now, Jake – '

'Save the tears for the brass, Manny. What you can do for me is find out from the Danish authorities whether they have any record of a Walter Thoren emigrating between 1935 and 1940. Also whether any Jewish refugee organization has that name on any list from that period.'

'I'll get to work on it first thing.'

'And on something else, too. Take a look at the question-naire, the second page where the medical examiner put down

8   113

Thoren's identifying marks. Where he described that L-shaped scar on his back. You find it?'

'I found it.'

'Well, since we now know Thoren wasn't wounded in action, there's a chance he was during his commission of the crime. Show the description of the scar to that forensic medicine expert you keep on tap and ask him if he has any idea what kind of weapon might have made it.'

'You can count on me, Jake. Anything else?'

'No. When's that meeting tomorrow?'

'Ten-thirty.'

'Then I'll expect to hear from you by noon. I'd like to know as soon as I can if the water's over my head or not.' Jake planted the phone on its stand and swung around to face Elinor. She was sitting hunched forward on the couch, hands clasped in her lap, looking at him intently. He said: 'You wouldn't mind that too much, would you? Heading back to mama and the kid tomorrow with a cheque for three thousand in your pocket.'

'Well' – she hesitated, the tip of her tongue moving in a small circle around her lips, moistening them – 'I think there's something you ought to know, Jake, because you'll find out anyhow when you get the phone bill. I've been talking to my mother and the kid every night for a few minutes. They're making out fine.'

'I envy them with all my heart.'

'Look, I'm not kidding. It's just that if things are all right at home, I don't mind being down here on the job for the whole time we settled on. It's too early for summer theatre casting anyhow.'

Jake said: 'All we can do is hope Guaranty feels the same way about it. What do you do between stage jobs, such as they are? Modelling?'

'No, I'm not the right size or shape for that. You have to be about six foot tall and weigh ninety pounds. Mostly I'm behind the counter in department stores.'

'Men's departments, I trust? I'm only saying that from the viewpoint of the average male customer. My personal preference happens to be for tall, stately brunettes on the skinny side.'

'That's all right with me. Because mine happens to be for men who cut loose and yell when they get sore at somebody, not start whispering at them like you did with that poor Maniscalco. That's real computer stuff, that terribly self-controlled bit. If you ask me – '

'But I didn't,' said Jake.

Maniscalco called a few minutes before noon the next day. 'You're still in business with me, pal,' he said, all joviality. 'That's the important thing.'

'Fine, now I can stop holding my breath. What's the unimportant thing?'

'That medical expert's report on Thoren's scar. I had a man drop into his office and ask about it first thing this morning. He said odds were it was postoperative. If not, it might have been made by a flanged shovel driven into the back at an angle. Or maybe a bottle, square or rectangular, with the bottom of it knocked off. But he admitted it was all pretty much speculation on his part.'

Jake said: 'And it never entered his speculation that the wound might have been made by a weapon, not an implement? A knife possibly?'

'No, he didn't say anything about that.'

'Did you also ask the Danish authorities and Jewish refugee organizations to look up Thoren?'

'Oh, hell. Jake, I'll get on it right now. Jesus, you should see my desk here. I've got about a dozen active cases piled on it.'

'That's tough. But I'll be very understanding about it, as long as you keep one thing in mind.'

'Yeah?'

'It's this,' Jake said. 'No matter how many cases are piled on your desk, Manny, make sure mine is always the one on top.'

'There, you see,' Elinor pointed out accusingly as he put down the phone. 'You were whispering like that again.'

23

Magnes called late in the afternoon. 'Dekker, we made the breakthrough. The big one. You remember how you figured? If Thoren stopped going to Bayside Spa just before he had that fuss with the Ortega woman, there was a solid chance the blackmailer first bumped into him then and there at the spa?'

'Yes?'

'Well, that run-in with the woman happened around February ninth. And the last time Thoren ever showed up at the spa was two weeks before. January twenty-fifth.'

'Then that was when and where the action started.'

'Wait, there's even more. It also happens that Thoren's pet masseur – the rubber who always worked on him there – went and quit his job the exact same January twenty-fifth. And he had a reputation, this rubber, for being like a mascot to the Mob.' Magnes lowered his voice. 'Look at that. A couple of *yentas* got nothing better to do, they'll take a sunbath right by my window. I think it's better if we get together about this business.'

'Where?'

'Not Wolfie's again, otherwise I'll fill up on coffee and cake between meals. I'll tell you what. Lummus Park is on Ocean Drive where I live. Start walking south along the park from about Tenth Street, and I'll pick you up on the way.'

It was at 8th Street that Jake saw Magnes detach himself from the white-haired and withered audience gathered on the park lawn around an accordionist singing a Yiddish ballad and walk over to a bench facing the sea wall. Jake drifted across the lawn and sat down beside him.

Magnes made a small motion of the head to indicate the gathering on the lawn. 'Don't let that happy music fool you,' he said. 'A bunch of *nudniks,* all of them. Sad people.'

'They don't look it.'

'Then let me enlighten you about it. These are people who

116

when they cash their Social Security cheque at Food Fair they get it all in pennies, so maybe that way they can stretch it until the next cheque. For the rest of their lives, God spare them, every day is panic day. That is not living, sonny. Living is when you can throw away a few dollars at Hialeah, or eat at Joe's Stone Crab, or even take a lady friend to a nice show at the Carillon. If I couldn't do those things when I wanted, you would not be sitting here talking to Abe Magnes. You would be talking to the ghost of Abe Magnes. Like all those ghosts over there waiting for the hearse to come down the street with their name on it.'

'I see. Anyhow, it explains why you hit me up for ten thousand. Especially with the way they've been running at Hialeah this season.'

'That's why,' Magnes said. 'Except that before we're done you'll admit to me you got value for every dollar. Like with this Bayside Spa thing which cost me a steam bath I didn't want and eighty dollars I had to lose in a pinochle game to get in good with the help. But that was top value three ways. We found out about Thoren, we found out about that rubber, and, best of all when it comes to making the next move, we even found out his name is Bert Caldwell and that right now he's holding down a job at the Royal Burgundian.'

'That big yellow and white hotel near the Fontainebleau?'

'The management likes you to say gold and silver. But that's the one.'

'Did you contact this Caldwell yet?'

Magnes shook his head. 'Any contact at the Royal Burgundian is not for me on this job. On some big jewel heists there, I was go-between for the recovery of the stuff, so everybody in Security knows me. This contact you should make yourself. They rent beach loungers by the day there, so tomorrow you take the girlie along with you and make it a nice day around the pool. Then you finish off with a Turkish bath and a rubdown. If you ask for Caldwell, and you let him know you were recommended by some people named Thoren, you should be all set.'

Jake said: 'It makes sense that way. Now let me tell you

117

what Johnny Maniscalco turned up while he was trying to get a line on Thoren's records.'

Magnes took the detailed account of Thoren's life and works with equanimity. 'I'll admit it's not exactly what I expected, but, on the other hand, look what else has been turning up along the way. This Caldwell who was a sweat-bath rubber for the biggest hoods, and Bayside Spa which is not all that kosher, and now the Royal Burgundian which really has a smell to it.'

'Financed by the Mob?' Jake said.

'Sixty percent anyhow. And it's one of those places every big insurance company hates like poison. You know. Where the bellhop spots where the jewellery is kept in the room, then he tells the Brain who lays out how the job should be done, and then he holds the stones until the go-between for the insurance company comes along to settle for so much on the dollar. Teamwork. And the only loser every time is the insurance company.'

Jake said impatiently: 'Maniscalco must have told you how many times I've been his go-between, so you know none of this is news to me. What are you really getting at? That Thoren was tied in with the Mob in this jewel heist racket?'

Magnes said: 'Why not? Isn't it at least possible he was?'

'No. It's like when Maniscalco suggested that maybe he was a draft dodger. Definitely, he wasn't that type. He wasn't this type either.'

'What makes you so sure?' Magnes said. 'Because he was a squarehead, not an Italian or a Jew? If that's what's on your mind, I can tell you right now that with the Mob there is no prejudice except with the coloured. The *shvartzehs* they only let collect the nickels and dimes for the numbers. Everybody else – Jews, Italianers, Irishers, rednecks, even Cubans – they're all free and equal members of the team. Which could have included even a squarehead from Denmark who you yourself say was a killer. True, later on a victim. But first a killer.'

'The killer-and-victim part I'll buy. The rest I'll wait and see about. What about Thoren's being a registered voter?'

'He is. All the way back to 1944. Which, to me, looks like he came down to Miami with the phony papers already in his

118

pocket. It would be too dangerous for him if he had somebody right in his own back yard take care of it.'

'It would. And what about Ortega? And that dead partner of his, Tucker?'

'So far, only that the business is import and export with South America, and it looks legitimate. I have a guy working on it from the inside. In a couple of days he'll give me a report on all the companies they deal with at both ends, the merchandise, the bank balances, and so on. Also, it's true Tucker died from lung cancer a couple of years ago.'

'And that's all for now?' Jake said.

'That's all for now. Tomorrow I want to get what I can on everybody who's in that Civic Planning Association Thoren used as a front. And I suppose you'll be taking the girlie over to the Royal Burgundian and making contact with that Caldwell?'

Jake stood up. 'That's what I'll be doing.'

'Well, be careful she don't get so much sun again.' Magnes said. 'And be careful for yourself, too. Any way you look at it, when you make contact with this guy you are walking into the alligator pool with your shoes off.'

24

What the Royal Burgundian provided them with, besides a pair of lounges and a beach umbrella on its crowded sun deck, was the use of a cabana, a choice of swimming pools, lunch *al fresco*, a steady parade of angular poker-faced models demonstrating the minimum in beachwear, and a tall bronzed beachboy named Eddie.

When Eddie returned from the mission Jake had assigned him and reported: 'Bert's sorry, but he can't book you for a rubdown without a couple of days' notice,' Jake said: 'Try him again, kid. This time tell him he was recommended to me by a Mr Walter Thoren he used to know over at Bayside Spa.'

Watching Eddie go on his way, laying a comb through his

locks as he went, Elinor said: 'Was that a good idea? It'll only make Caldwell suspicious, won't it?'

'Not unless he has something to be suspicious about.'

'If he's the blackmailer, he has plenty to be suspicious about.'

'Except that he's not. He's only the guy who'll finger the blackmailer. And without even knowing it.'

'But, Jake – '

'Not so loud, baby. There are big ears fanned out all around us. Remember, for their benefit you're my cute little wife only wondering when I'm coming through with your next mink.'

Elinor made a noise in her throat. 'The next one. I'll bet I'm the only female around here doesn't have at least two to start with.'

When Eddie reappeared before them a few minutes later, it was to report that everything had been fixed up. 'But Bert says it's got to be right now, Mr Dekker. It's the only way he can fit you in.'

'Right now couldn't be better,' Jake said.

Like everything else about the Royal Burgundian, its sauna was gargantuan in size, lavish in its use of gilded tile and classic statuary. Against this opulence, Bert Caldwell, heavily muscled and with a broad, good-natured face, looked like a farmhand drafted for service in a Byzantine palace.

He said: 'Yes, I knew Mr Thoren for maybe ten, twelve years, and I used to think, well, here's one good for another fifty years, the shape he keeps himself in. Then just like that he's gone. Were you a friend of his?'

Jake said: 'No, my wife and I are friends of the family. We bought a place near theirs, and they've been going out of their way to make us feel at home. When I said something about missing the baths at the N.Y.A.C. they told me to look you up.'

'Yeah. Well, it's nice to be remembered like that. I guess I should have sent them a card when it happened, but you know how it is. Ten, twelve years I knew him. Built something like you, too. He used to have those fatsos around the spa wondering what he was there for, he was in that good condition. Okay, Mr Dekker, you go in the steam room now. I'll be waiting when you come out.'

Jake came out of the steam room pouring sweat, was laid out on a marble slab and scrubbed with a coarse brush and soap, hosed down, and finally led back to the rubbing room with the feeling that every bone in his body had turned liquid.

The rubbing room was long and narrow and blue with cigarette smoke. It contained a dozen tables in a row, most of them occupied. Against the wall at its far end was a larger than life plaster statue of Diana the Huntress on which some-one had planted a straw hat and a pair of sunglasses. Several men garbed in bath towels stood beside the statue brooding over a horse-race sheet.

Caldwell's table was at that end of the room. Jake stretched out on it, and after laving him with oil, Caldwell went to work expertly kneading his shoulder muscles. Jake said: 'You're good at this all right. I can see why Thoren stuck with you all those years.'

Caldwell grunted as he dug in hard. 'Yeah, but it wasn't only the rubdowns. They got those four-wall handball courts over at the spa, and he liked the game I gave him. I could take him maybe three out of five, but it was always close.'

'Was that part of his routine at the spa?'

'Uh-huh. He put in from eleven to four there once a week, and every minute was by the book. You could set your watch by him.'

Jake said: 'Well, he was really sold on you. I suppose you know he never went back there after you quit.'

'No, this is the first I heard of it.' Caldwell dug a thumb into the sole of one foot, then the other. He took each toe in turn and wiggled it as if trying to shake it loose from the foot. 'Now that I think of it,' he said, 'it's not too much of a surprise. When I told them I was quitting there, they paid me extra to hang around that week and like introduce the new rubber to my regulars. But that new guy must have somehow pissed-off Mr Thoren very big.'

'How'd you know that?'

'Because when Mr Thoren walked out that afternoon he was way ahead of schedule, for one thing. For another thing, he looked sore at the whole world, me included. No goodbye tip, no nothing. What the hell, just because the new guy didn't know how to give him a rubdown, he didn't have to take it out on me. I didn't quit the spa to spite him. I was getting a lot more dough to come here.'

'Nobody could blame you for that,' Jake said. 'Did you talk it over with the new rubber afterwards? Ask him what went wrong?'

'Well, I was going to next morning, but he never showed up again. I guess he figured the spa was no place for him if Mr Thoren was the kind of customer he had to handle. Some guys are independent that way.'

Jake said: 'Maybe he was one of those seasonal workers. Up North for the summer, down here for the winter. That kind doesn't worry too much about walking off a job.'

'A snowbird?' Caldwell deftly twisted him over on his back and went to work on his chest and belly. 'Nope, this was one of them nature boys from out of the Everglades. Probably never got further north than the Beach his whole life.'

'Nature boys?'

'Yeah. Swampers from out of the hammocks there. Run swamp boats, do some alligator poaching, but when they're strapped for cash they'll come into the city and take on a job for a while. That's what this one was. A real jug-eared redneck. Only he seemed smarter than most.'

Jake said: 'I guess he's probably back in the swamps now, with no regrets.'

'Most likely. That kind of people, you stick a pair of shoes on them, they get all tensed up. His hard luck to run into Mr Thoren first thing.'

'That's the way it goes,' Jake said.

25

Elinor was not there when he got back to the lounges. She showed up a few minutes later, dripping. 'How'd you make out?' she said.

Jake gave her a warning shake of the head. 'Fine. Where were you?'

'In the ocean. It's kind of seaweedy, but great. There's a million people in the pools and practically nobody at all out there. Come on in with me. We can talk there.'

'In a little while. I want to do some thinking first.'

'Well, if you're not going to do it out loud, I'll go ahead. But don't take too long.'

He did his thinking, then crossed the sun deck to the stairway leading down to the beach. From the head of the stairs he saw that it wasn't much of a beach: a strip of grey sand flecked with patches of drying seaweed. But the surf, despite strands of seaweed floating in it, was an enticing emerald-green, and as far as a hundred feet out where the dun-coloured ridge of a sandbar showed just below the surface, it was shallow enough for the bathers in it to stand at their ease no deeper than their chests. Beyond the sandbar, the water was evidently too deep for standing. A scattered handful of swimmers were out there, bobbing up and down on the waves that crested further inshore.

He finally recognized Elinor as one of the swimmers by her bathing cap, a bright yellow rubber chrysanthemum which looked more ornamental than practical. He went down the staircase and took his time wading out through the tepid water toward the bathing cap. Then suddenly, as if shoved down by an invisible hand, it disappeared below the surface.

It was still not back in sight after the next wave had passed over the sandbar. And the wave following the next.

He plunged through the crest of the last wave and swam as hard as he could in the direction he had last seen the bathing cap. A few strokes beyond the sandbar he caught a glimmer of it below the surface. He took a deep breath and went underwater, to see Elinor and whoever had that unyielding grip on her ankles engaged in a twisting, turning, slow-motion struggle where her body, desperately arching toward the surface, was being borne down away from it to the roiled-up sandy bottom.

The next instant it was all over. The man saw Jake, and

123

despite his immense bulk, torpedoed out of range, then out of sight, with an almost fishlike speed and ability.

Jake pulled Elinor to him and bobbed to the surface with her. She convulsively clasped her arms around his neck, her legs around his waist, straining to draw breath in a series of sobbing, retching gasps. He manoeuvred them towards the sandbar, where he found a foothold barely within his depth. 'Take it easy,' he said. 'You're all right now.'

'Jake, he tried to kill me! If you didn't come along – '

'Sure, sure. But it's a lot more likely he was only trying to scare you. Did you get a look at him?'

'For a second. He's all bald, and he must weigh a ton. Only it's not fat, it's muscle.'

'That's about what I made of him too. Do you think you could spot him, if you saw him again?'

'I don't want to see him again. He's the blackmailer, isn't he?'

Jake said: 'Maybe not the man himself, but he's sure as hell connected with him somehow.'

'Then they know who you are. I told you if you started talking to people about Thoren – '

'Baby, now and then in this game you have to take your chances on a risky move. Otherwise, you just go around in circles.' When Jake tried to detach her arms from around his neck she clung all the more tightly to him. He said: 'All right, tuck yourself into that brassière and let's get going. You can make it to shore now, can't you?'

'As soon as I get my wind. Anyhow, the case is all washed up, isn't it? You said if Mrs Thoren found out who we really were, it would be.'

'No, we've already gone too far for that. We passed the point of no return about three minutes ago. And it wasn't Mrs Thoren who found out who we are.'

'But she will. They'll tell her about it.'

Jake said: 'In that case, why'd they bother to get rough with you? Why didn't they just go and tell her?'

Elinor said pleadingly: 'Even so, it's a bad scene, Jake. Please don't get mad, but I'd just as soon not be with it any more.'

'You mean you'd cut out now when we're really starting to move?'

'I don't like where we're moving. And it'll be a week tomorrow. If you'd settle for a week of the money coming to me – '

'That wasn't the deal.' He held her close with one hand against her back and paddled with the other to keep his footing as they rose and fell together on the gentle swells. Her cheek rested against his, her breathing was becoming steady. 'You know,' he remarked, 'for a girl with such a hard, muscular back, you have an exceptionally soft front.'

'That's a cheap trick, making a pass at me so I'll change my mind.' Her voice was contemptuous, but she remained as she was in the circle of his arm, her cheek against his.

'Oh? Anybody looking at us would say you're the one making the pass.'

'Well, I'm not. It just feels good having you take over after what I've been through.'

'All the same, baby, you fall asleep on me like this, we'll drift right to Havana, non-stop.'

'I'm not falling asleep. I'm just all washed out. Numb.' Eyes closed, she turned her face toward him. Her parted lips lightly brushed his, slowly rubbed back and forth against them with growing warmth. She abruptly pulled her head away. 'No, I won't let you get to me. I wasn't putting you on, Jake. I want to go back to New York.'

Jake said: 'You do that, and you might be followed all the way to your front door by one of these guys. You'll be leading them right to your kid. Then they could really give you fits.'

'I don't believe it. You're only trying to scare me.'

'Baby, didn't you just get shown they're the ones who want to do the scaring? Look, the way I figure it, someone with a hand in this game heard me ask Caldwell all about Thoren and that last day he put in at Bayside Spa. And since that somebody knows Mrs Thoren wouldn't call the police in on this, he doesn't have to be a genius to guess what my angle is. So all he wants to do is neutralize me for a little while. Then Mrs

Thoren collects the insurance money, and he can start bleeding her of it. And it's not like I was a cop. The blackmailers know that once Mrs Thoren collects the money I'm off their necks for good.'

Elinor said: 'I suppose neutralize means scaring you off. But what makes you so sure they'll try that again? Why won't they just shoot you next time?'

'Because they know the insurance company would not only have a good excuse to hold up payment and get a trial postponement, but they'd call the police in on this besides. No, as far as these guys are concerned, the smart tactic is to warn me away. When they see that won't work they might try to buy me off.'

Elinor's eyes searched his face. Could they?'

'What do you think?'

'Oh God, what do I think. If you really want to know, I think you're looking to get me killed. And when I'm laying there dying, you'll prove to me it couldn't happen.'

'That's my girl,' Jake said.

As they came out of the water, Elinor suddenly clutched his arm. 'Jake, that's him. He's the one.'

Jake followed the direction of her finger. Squat and enormously bloated, the man stood in shadow beneath the overhanging stairway to the sun deck, partly concealed by one of the beams supporting the stairway. He moved back a step as Jake turned toward him, and a ray of sunlight coming through the steps momentarily gleamed on his hairless skull.

Jake looked around. The beach itself was empty, the only people in sight the scattered bathers riding the swells beyond the sandbar. He moved toward the man, and Elinor tried to hold him back. 'Jake, I don't want to go near him. Please.'

'Stop that. Do you want him to think he panicked us?'

'He did panic me. Please, Jake – ' But when he pulled free of her grasp she fearfully tagged along a few steps behind him. He walked into the shadow of the stairway and up to the man. It was searingly hot in the sunlight, here it was surprisingly

126

cool. The man stood watching him impassively. He was a head shorter than Jake, and barrel-shaped.

'My name's Dekker,' Jake told him amiably. 'This is my wife.'

Still no expression showed on the round, beefy face or in the pale eyes. 'My name's Holuby. So what?'

'So it seems Mrs Dekker had a bad time of it just now. Almost got herself drowned out there.'

What might have been a glint of humour flickered in the pale eyes. 'Maybe she was in over her head. That's dangerous. People got to be careful about that.'

'And that's a fact,' Jake said smilingly. When he had balled his fist at his side he had left the knuckle of the middle finger protruding beyond the others. He threw the punch short and hard in a straight line, the wedge of the protruding knuckle spiking dead centre into Holuby's massive throat. Holuby grunted. His eyes rolled up so that for an instant only the whites showed. Then he sagged forward and went down on his hands and knees with a thud, his mouth gaping wide, his face purpling, his eyes staring and terrified at his inabiilty to draw breath.

Jake squatted down beside him. He scooped up a handful of sand. 'If I shove this stuff down your throat right now, Holuby, you're finished for good. Just another sad case of drowning. So let's have it. Was it your idea to rough up my wife?'

A string of spittle trailed from Holuby's wide-open mouth. His body heaved, fighting for air. Jake thrust the sand under his nose, and Holuby jerkily turned his head from side to side trying to escape it. 'If it wasn't you,' Jake snarled, 'who was it? Who put you up to it?'

Elinor said: 'Jake, stop it!' She tugged at his shoulder. 'Please, stop it. There's people coming.'

He glanced over his shoulder. Two bathers emerging from the water were veering in his direction. A middle-aged couple, they were looking at the scene under the stairway with frowning concern.

Jake let the sand filter from his hand and stood up. The couple came up beside him and looked down at the figure on its hands and knees gasping like a beached whale. '*Gottenu*,' the woman said. She pressed her hands to her cheeks. 'What happened? What's wrong with him?'

Jake said: 'Nothing serious. He went in over his head and swallowed some water. He'll be all right.'

The man said solemnly: 'Better never to take such chances. Safety first should be the slogan.'

Jake said: 'That's what I just told him.' He pushed Elinor toward the foot of the stairway. 'Let's move, dear. I think we ought to tell one of those pool lifeguards about this.'

She said nothing as she started up the stairs to the sun deck. Halfway up, she suddenly stopped and turned to face him. She said wonderingly: 'You wanted to kill him. You would have killed him if those people weren't there.'

'Like hell I would.'

'He thought so, too. You looked like it. You sounded like it.'

'You ought to know that was an act. Can you think of a better way to make him talk?'

Elinor shook her head. 'It wasn't only that. You were getting even with him for what he did to me, weren't you?'

'That was incidental. Baby, don't ever weigh yourself against anything that's got to do with my job. You're in for a terrible disillusionment if you do.'

'Maybe. Maybe not. Just because you were hung up on a wife who never really –'

'Oh, for chrissake. I'm frying my brains out in this sun, and you stand there handing me lines from old Barbara Stanwyck movies.' He slapped her hard on the rear end. 'Come on, I'll walk you back to the cabana. You can get dressed and wait there while I have another visit with my pal Caldwell.'

He found Caldwell hard at work on a client. 'I want to have a little talk with you, Bert.'

Caldwell continued kneading the body on the table. 'Talk about what, Mr Dekker?'

'Private business. Some place where we can be alone for a few minutes.'

Caldwell gestured at the body. 'Yeah, but right now?'

128

'He'll keep. This is very important private business.'

The sauna's office was lushly carpeted, and was equipped with pastel-coloured office furniture. Around its walls were autographed photos of glamorous clients.

A young man sat behind the smaller of two desks in the room. When Caldwell said to him, 'Just for a couple of minutes, Bubba,' the young man looked Jake over incuriously and strolled out of the room. Caldwell closed the door behind him. 'What's it about, Mr Dekker?'

'It's about whatever happened in that rubbing room after I walked out last time. Somebody there heard us talking about Thoren. As soon as I left, he asked you what you knew about me. Now you tell me who it was.'

'Me? Nobody said a word to me about you, Mr Dekker.'

Jake said patiently: 'There's a gorilla hanging around outside name of Holuby. Squatty guy who might go about three hundred pounds, looks like a pro wrestler. Know anything about him?'

'Sure. 'That's Lou Holuby. He's hotel security for the beach and pool area.'

'They've got funny ideas about security down here,' Jake said. 'This Holuby tried to push me around outside, because somebody in here told him to. And you know who told him to.'

Caldwell heaved a long sigh. 'Look, Mr Dekker – '

Jake smiled. 'When I walked out of here before, I forgot and left my wallet on that table where you keep the oil and stuff. I want that wallet now. I figure five hundred bucks cash and a dozen credit cards is too much of a tip for even a big spender like me.'

'What are you trying to do, Mr Dekker? You know you never left any wallet on that table.'

'That'll be for the cops to decide. And what do you think they'll decide when they look under the mat on your rubbing table and find it there?'

'Find it there?' Caldwell's eyes narrowed. 'You phony bastard, you planted it there yourself just now.' He wheeled toward the door, and Jake said: 'Whether you dig it out of there and hand it to me in front of everybody, or whether the cops dig it out, it comes to the same thing, Bert. I'm a real sorehead. When I'm robbed I make a loud noise about it.'

Caldwell stood with his hand on the doorknob. 'You think that kind of noise would bother me? My record is clean from the day I got down here.' There was no conviction in his voice.

Jake said sympathetically: 'So you were tempted once too often. Tough. But maybe the cops'll be nice about it. Maybe they'll hold off on an arrest and just run you out of town, if that's all right with me. On the other hand – '

Caldwell said: 'All right, it was Frank Milan. He was one of them looking over the scratch sheet right there. He asked if I knew anything about you, and I said no, and that was the whole thing.'

'You're sure?'

'Jesus Christ, Mr Dekker,' Caldwell said desperately, 'if you don't believe me – '

'I believe you. What's this Frank Milan got to do with Holuby?'

'What do you think? Holuby works here, don't he? You mean you don't know Frank Milan owns a big piece of this place?'

'Now I know,' Jake said.

26

At Magnes's suggestion they met for dinner at a Cuban restaurant on Espanola Way, a place which turned out to be a hole-in-the-wall with barely room for its six tables. Most of the conversation at the other tables was in Yiddish-accented Spanish or Spanish-accented Yiddish.

Magnes listened to the recital of the day's events while stuffing himself with chicken stew, black beans, and fried plantains. At its conclusion he said: 'It's no surprise you didn't know about Frank Milan, the way he ducks publicity. He came down here with Owney Madden and Frank Erickson when they put up Tropical Park racetrack maybe forty years ago. He was muscle for them. Now he's on top of the Mob. Also a very good friend with Meyer Lansky. It shows you how nice people get along with each other down here.'

Jake said: 'So he's on top of the Mob. But what about him running some blackmail as a personal sideline?'

Magnes belched delicately and patted his lips with a paper napkin. He shook his head. 'Frankly, I don't see it. He's one of those hoodlums, y'understand, who in his old age likes to put on a very high-class front. Golf, the grandchildren in college, the works. For him to get mixed up personally in blackmail makes no sense. With what he's got in the bank, he needs that kind of trouble like a *loch in kop*. A hole in the head.'

Jake said: 'He's the one who sicked Holuby on me. That means he knows about Thoren and the blackmail setup.'

'That much I grant you. Also that you were right when you figured some pro is handling the blackmail. The way I see it, that hick from the Everglades – that sweatbath rubber – was the one who spotted who Thoren really was. But a character like that could never handle it so good, no matter how much larceny he got in him. So what did he do? He cut in some guy from the Mob who could help him make a big-money thing out of it.'

'And that somebody cut in Milan.'

'I still say Milan wouldn't want any part of it personally. But you have to understand nobody in the Mob could run such a fat concession unless Milan okayed it. That's why Milan had to know about it. Then you come along and talk about Thoren, so Milan figures to protect the guy running the concession by giving you a dig. If you're harmless, so ducking the girlie is a practical joke. If you're not, it's a warning. And after what you did to Holuby, they know for sure you're not harmless.'

Jake said: 'How far do you think Milan would go to protect his man?'

'Not too far. Killing is out, because then the heat comes on and the publicity. A beating, an auto accident, what happened to the girlie in the water – you could figure on stuff like that. Your hard luck he owns a piece of the Royal Burgundian and hangs around so much with those big ears.'

'Your hard luck too,' Jake observed, 'if he thinks it's worth having me tailed.'

'I know. What's on your mind, sonny? That because it's a *groisser shisser* like Frank Milan, I'll lose my nerve? I'll maybe let you down?'

'The thought might have crossed my mind,' Jake said.

Magnes made a gesture of dismissal. 'So now you can stop worrying about it. If people like Milan bothered me, I'd have been out of this line of work while I still had all my teeth.'

Jake said: 'That's good to know. It means the only thing left to worry about now is how we locate some guy who worked for one day as a rubber at Bayside Spa over two years ago and then took off. He might not even be listed on any of their old employment records.'

'For that matter,' Magnes said, 'he could be in Rio right now, with such a nice, regular income from blackmail.'

'I don't think so. From what Caldwell told me, he was a genuine yokel. Not the kind to roam too far from home. But that won't mean anything unless you can get into those employment records at the spa and dig up who he is. You know the exact date he put in his one day there – January twenty-fifth – so all you have to do is look up that day. You can get to those records, can't you?'

'I'll get to them,' Magnes said. 'But what's the chances of this yokel telling you all about Thoren while his mobster partner is holding a gun to his head?'

'Better than even, if I can get enough on him. If I can really get evidence that he's a blackmailer, I can probably make a deal with him. Either he tells me the whole thing, or I tell the cops what I know.'

Magnes pursed his lips. 'That's some tightrope you'll be walking. Do I have to give you a little reminder, you won't only be putting the squeeze on him but also on that mobster partner of his?'

'You don't. Right now all you have to do is find out who the yokel is and where he is. Anyhow, from the way Caldwell made so much of this guy being a swamp rat who'd stick close to the Everglades, it looks like whatever crime Thoren committed must have been committed around there. It narrows it down that much at least.'

'You think so? The Everglades covers a terrible lot of territory, sonny.'

'Not for people to live in, from what I've heard. Can you dig up a contact who knows his way around it?'

'Naturally. But first I got to find out who that rubber was, so at least we'll know who we're looking for that likes to live with alligators in the front yard. I'll see if I can get into those employment records at Bayside first thing tomorrow.'

Jake said: 'And what about that Civic Planning Association Thoren was tied in with? Did you get any more on that? And Ortega's business?'

'Some. Ortega's business, at least from the books, looks legitimate. Export–import, but mostly export. That Association is legitimate around the edges.'

'A front for something?'

'Well, it's supposed to be for making Miami Beach beautiful, but it's strictly for making Daystar Island people happy. It's like a private little club, with McCloy and some others from Daystar Number One and Number Two running it. So if there's bother about more taxes for the Islands or open housing or anything like that, they put the pressure on. They get some big politician to make a speech at their meeting and hand him a couple of grand for it which is really a payoff. One thing they don't like is outsiders should mix in their business.'

'They sound like Thoren,' Jake said.

27

Elinor opened the door to let him in, then slipped its chain back into place. She looked angry and a little dishevelled. She said: 'That Kermit must be psychic or something about his timing. You just missed him. He's all I needed after that Holuby monster.'

'Did he give you a bad time?'

'Medium bad. Trouble was I wasn't sure how you wanted me to handle him. I mean, mostly I can handle somebody like that, but I didn't know how much you'd want me to put him down.'

'Not so much that he'd steer clear of us afterward.' Jake looked at his watch. It showed a quarter past nine. 'How long was he here?'

'About an hour. He said he came over to ask us to supper there tomorrow. When he found out you weren't in he made himself right at home.'

'That's interesting,' Jake said. 'The supper part. Now why would his mama hate us so much one day and then okay an invitation like that the next day?'

'Maybe because the blackmailers told her who you really were, and she wants to get together with you about it.'

'At a dinner party?'

Elinor said: 'Then I don't know why. And don't think it was easy keeping it straight in my mind that I wasn't supposed to know she was sore at us. I almost said something to Kermit about it before I remembered. And that damn monitor was still tuned in on their phone when he walked in here. I thought it was you, so I answered the doorbell without turning it off. If anybody started talking over in the Thorens' dining room, Kermit would have heard it on the monitor for sure. Man, I was real shook up until I could get inside and cut it off. And he must have thought from the way I was shook up that it was because of him and his curly hair. After that, there was no holding him.'

Jake said: 'You mean the recorder's been dead for the last hour? We don't have anything on tape from Mrs Thoren's room for that whole time?'

'Look, I just explained to you –'

'Sure you did. Now just get hooked in on Mrs Thoren's phone quick. Did they say anything at dinner worth hearing?'

'No. What did Magnes have to tell you about that Frank Milan?'

'About what I expected. He's a big shot in the Mob. Now get on that transmitter.'

He watched her activate the transmitter to Charlotte Thoren's phone, then went into the study and sat down behind the desk without turning on the light. He leaned back in the big swivel chair until it was tilted at its most acute angle and put his feet up on the desk. After a long while he heard the squeak of the bedroom door and saw Elinor silhouetted against the light from the bedroom. 'Jake?' she whispered.

'I'm not asleep. You can turn on the light.'

She switched on the desk lamp. 'It's almost half past eleven. Can I cut out on Mrs Thoren now?'

'Not yet. Did you get anything from her end so far?'

'Nothing worth marking on the tape. Around ten o'clock the cook was up there, and Mrs Thoren gave her a lot of instructions about what to buy at the market and such. Then she watched TV for a couple of minutes, then turned it off. It's been pretty quiet since. Just some moving around.'

'No late news? No Johnny Carson show?'

'No. Maybe she thought this was a good night to catch up on her reading.'

Jake said: 'If she did, it'll be the first time since we've been listening in. That's a break in the pattern all right.'

'Except it's not much of a pattern, is it? I've only been listening in on her a few days.'

'It's still a pattern.' Jake swung his feet to the floor with a thud and let the chair tilt him upright. 'Jesus, what is it with you and Magnes? Anything I say, you two seem to think is some kind of challenge to a debate.'

Elinor said indignantly: 'Jake, that's not so.' Then she looked at him with narrow-eyed speculation. 'And that's not what you're really bugged about right now, is it? It's something else.'

'I suppose it is. It's what that miserable Caldwell told me today. He really scrambled the picture.'

'How?'

'He said in effect that Thoren was identified by the kind of swamp character who always sticks close to home. Some alligator-wrestler from the boondocks who could just about make it from there to Miami and back. In that case, if that

135

guy witnessed whatever Thoren did thirty years ago that was worth blackmailing him for, it was done somewhere around this area.'

'So what?'

'So it knocks the hell out of the theory I've been going on. From what I put together, I assumed Thoren was a refugee or immigrant who landed in the States between 1935 and 1940 and settled down in the Midwest. The Midwest, because he showed such familiarity with it in that cooked-up background of his. Then he committed a crime there, made a big haul – at least the sixty thousand dollars he paid for his partnership in the Sprague Company – and ran down here to hide out permanently under a new identity. That way it makes sense. This way it doesn't. Let's say he committed the crime in this area. Then why stay around here afterward?'

Elinor considered this. 'You still think he was a foreigner?'

'What he wrote in his policy application and how he wrote it says he was. And nothing has turned up to prove otherwise.'

'Well then, maybe this is the only part of the country he knew. Maybe he was afraid to go some place else where he wouldn't know his way around.'

Jake said impatiently: 'For a man with that amount of brain power – ' He stopped short and looked at Elinor blankly. 'Brain power. A highly educated Dane who could have spoken fluent English even before he landed here. He didn't need a couple of years to master it so he could pass as an American. All he needed was enough time – a month or so – to rig up that phony identity. He bought into Sprague's company in September, 1942. Put everything together, and he could have hit town here around that summer, right in the middle of the war.'

'Could have,' Elinor said doubtfully.

'I know, but it's a probability that explains why nobody around here knew him in his real identity. Another good probability is that he wasn't a refugee at all, where he'd be under the supervision of some organization. He came here for his own good reasons.'

'What reasons?'

Jake said: 'Your guess is as good as mine, baby.' He picked

up a pencil and scratched the nape of his neck with its eraser. 'Wartime. A man with a real good scientific and mechanical head on him. Somebody sent here on military research? Hell, no, he'd be under even tighter supervision that way. Leadership qualities. A natural leader. A military instructor? Still the same thing.' He aimed the pencil at Elinor. 'What else can you think about him that might fill the bill?'

She gnawed her lip as she considered this. 'Well, he had to be great on detail, didn't he? I mean, the way he planned every little thing when it came to changing his identity and all.'

'I know. That's what made me think of the military mind at work. From the first time I went through his dossier, I had a picture of him somehow being the real colonel-of-the-regiment type. But a combat man. Maybe Air Force.'

'But you just said he couldn't have been in the service.'

'I still say it. But he sure as hell should have been, from the picture I have of him. Take the way he was about boats. A natural-born naval officer. Big man on a –'

Elinor waited for him to finish that. At last she said: 'What is it, Jake? You think he was a navy officer?'

'I can't help thinking it, it's so damn perfect. But the same thing still holds true. If he was in the service, he would never have hung around here after changing identities. Any branch of the service is too tight to allow for that. You'd always be bumping into people who knew you if you stayed around. And down here was very big with the military during that war.'

Elinor said: 'But why did it have to be the navy? There's all kinds of boats, aren't there?'

Jake stared at her. 'All kinds of boats.'

Elinor said defensively: 'Yes. I mean, well, like freighters. And he liked sailing more than anything. It was his bag.'

'It was, wasn't it?'

'So if it makes sense, why sit and look at me like I'm some kind of kook?'

'Baby, that's not how I'm looking at you. I'm looking at you with awe because it makes so much sense. I'm thinking you just zeroed in on the biggest and best probability of all. An officer on a freighter. Maybe captain of one. Why not?'

'And then he happened to get mixed up in something, and afterward – '

'No,' Jake said, 'I don't think it happened to him. I think he made it happen. He was the kind of man who'd have everything worked out long in advance. Like that phony identity, for instance. He could have landed here from abroad with forged credentials ready in his pocket. With a good idea of what this town was like. Of how to get the money, and what to do about it afterward.'

'More probabilities?' Elinor said.

'And subject to change without notice. But that's how I make my living, baby, betting on probabilities. Only this one you'll be checking out.'

'Me? Jake, if you think I'm any Sherlock Holmes because I came up with one good idea, you are really ringing the wrong number. And I'm scared stiff of characters like Holuby and Frank Milan. I'd be watching for them over my shoulder all the time.'

'You don't have to, because I'm the one they're concentrating on. And you don't have to be Sherlock Holmes to go through old newspaper files. That's the whole job. Tomorrow morning we drive over to some big department store in Miami. From there, you head for the main library in town and work through the *Herald* files backward from September, 1942, to say, May of that year. You'll be looking for a news story – it might only be a few lines in the middle of the paper – about a ship's officer disappearing from a boat docked here, and you'll do it page by page, not skipping anything. Slow and steady, that's how it's done.'

Elinor said: 'It sounds like a barrel of laughs. All the same, wouldn't the police have records about it? Or maybe Magnes could do it? I don't like to be any place all day without you. Maybe they're concentrating on you, but I'm the one Holuby tried to drown.'

'He'd have a hard time doing it in the library. And I can't go to the police for this kind of information, because Milan probably has contacts on the force, and I wouldn't know who to trust there.' Jake stood up and peeled off his shirt. 'Now bring that monitor and recorder back in here and lock them up in the closet.'

'I thought you wanted me to listen in some more.'

'I do.'

'Just with the phone stuck to my ear?'

'Right. Just like you were making a call home to mama.'

'Ah, Jake, if you're bugged because I call home every night – '

'No, I'm not. I think it's very touching you're such a devoted daughter and mother. But I'm going out now, and if anybody happens to drop in here a little later – like security men or cops – I don't want that equipment in sight.'

Elinor said with alarm: 'Why should cops come here? What are you talking about?'

'Now don't start making a thing out of it. I want to look over Thoren's sailboat. I still feel he might have left that last note from the blackmailer there. The records show that happens sometimes in suicide cases like this, and I can't afford to pass up even an odds-against bet right now.'

'But security men and cops?'

'Hell, if you're freaking out just because I try to exercise a little foresight – '

'I'm not freaking out. I'm only scared something'll happen to you. And if you're getting me ready to have the cops walk in and tell me they shot you – don't.'

'I don't have to. What might happen is that they'll bring me in with them and ask you to identify me. And maybe ask you if I'm in the habit of taking moonlight dips in the bay. And you'll say yes, I am. And that's the worst that can happen.'

'Are you sure about it?'

'I'm sure. I wouldn't even have to take that much into account if it wasn't for that stupid Webb next door blasting off with his gun the other night and stirring up everything around here. They might have tightened security in this section because of it.'

'I see,' Elinor said. 'So all I have to do is sit there with that phone stuck to my ear and wonder how much they tightened security.'

139

'That's all.' He got out of his clothes, and with Elinor trailing after him, went into the bedroom and put on a pair of bathing trunks. She followed him back to the study, where he rolled a pocketknife and miniature flashlight into a plastic pouch and thrust it into the belt of his trunks. Finally she said: 'Did you know that bay is all polluted? You can get all kinds of things swimming in it. Joanna told me so.'

'Considering the people I'm dealing with,' Jake said, 'I'm probably immune by now.'

28

He left the house through the back door, locked the door, and planted the key on top of its frame. Standing there, he saw that Milt Webb had lately taken his own precautions against possible invaders. A drop light had been run from Webb's house to a nail driven high up into a palm tree in the middle of his lawn, and the unshaded bulb cast a light which extended in a wide radius to the waterfront. Jake stepped off the bulkhead into the water, and using a sidestroke which allowed him to keep his eyes fixed on the boundaries of the lighted zone, tried to stay clear of it as he covered the distance to Thoren's sailboat.

The boat turned out to be as buoyant as a cork. When he grasped the rail near the stern and pulled himself up, the rail dipped under water. Then the boat rolled back the other way, going stern down and bow up. The dock creaked loudly as the bow line jerked at it; there was a sudden splashing of wavelets against the bulkhead.

Jake froze there until the sounds had faded away, then hauled himself on to the narrow deck beside the cockpit. Flat on his belly, he took out the flashlight, cupped a hand over it to shield the beam, and examined the line tying one corner of the protective canvas cover to the handrail. The knot was a sea-manlike job. He undid it, then slipped into the cockpit beneath the canvas and pulled the canvas back into position over him.

There was a couple of inches of warm, slimy water in the

cockpit. As he stretched out in it on his back, something gently nudged the sole of his foot. He shudderingly pulled the foot back, then turned the flashlight beam in its direction. It lighted up a plastic container there, shifting back and forth as the boat rolled. He jackknifed himself around to get at it and pulled open its cover. Empty. Running the flashlight beam under the overhang of the deck, he saw a smaller container dangling from a cup hook screwed beneath the stern decking. He lifted it off the hook and aimed the light into it. It was about the size of a one-pound can and half full of scraps of paper, cardboard, cellophane wrappers, and paper matchbook covers.

He probed the stuff with his finger. Damp, but not sodden. He carefully picked out a scrap of paper and others adhered to it. Holding the light close to them, he saw that the lettering on them was a little blurred, but legible.

He got the watertight pouch from his belt, and holding it between his teeth by its flap, he worked the contents of the container into it. There was a sudden, deafening explosion of sound in his ears. He almost dropped the container, managed to grab it in time, but some shreds of paper spilled from it into the water he lay in. The noise quickly receded in the distance. A big jet flying low in or out of Miami International airport. He emptied the last of the container's contents into the pouch, then propped himself on an elbow and patiently went to work salvaging, piece by piece, the bits of paper in the water. With the pouch back under his belt he crawled from under the canvas, tied it down again, and noiselessly slipped into the bay.

Back in the house, he went into the kitchen and emptied the pouch into a large skillet. He carried the skillet into the study, set it on the desk, and turned on the desk lamp. 'Jake?' Elinor called.

'In here.'

'Are you all right?' She came pattering barefoot into the study, clad in pyjamas and with her hands held out before her like a sleepwalker. 'You are all right, aren't you?'

'Couldn't be better.' He looked at her outstretched hands. 'What happened to you?'

'Nothing. I was all wound up, listening in on that phone and

141

thinking about you getting shot, so I tried to do my nails. I couldn't even finish them, I was so shaky.' She watched him stir apart the damp pile of paper on the skillet, spreading the pieces evenly. He lowered the lamp so that the heat of the bulb was diffused over the skillet. Elinor said: 'Is that stuff from the boat?'

'It is. Lucky he was one of those compulsively neat characters, not the kind to go heaving litter overboard. But that figured.'

'You really think the note from the blackmailer is there?'

'It could be. When it's all dry we'll fit it together and find out. One good sign is the way he tore up these pieces so small. You don't usually take that kind of trouble with a grocery list.'

Elinor said: 'I hope not. The kind of job it'll be putting it together, I'd hate it to come out a grocery list.' She suddenly waved a hand back and forth before him. 'I almost forgot. The phone.'

'You mean the transmitter was cut off? Somebody called her?'

'No, even more than that. Kermit came into her room, and she had a talk with him. Jake, she's taking off some place, and only Kermit and Joanna are supposed to know where. Somebody did tell her who we are, I'll bet on it. Now she probably thinks the best thing to do – '

'Slow down, baby. There's no sense blowing a gasket about it. Did she say where she was going?'

'No.'

'Not a word about it?'

'Not while I was listening in. All she said was that when the cheque for the insurance money came he was to forward it to her immediately. Then he started walking out, and she called him back and said to remember he and Joanna weren't to tell anyone at all where she'd be. She came down on that very hard. And he said wasn't she overdoing it a little, and she said Dr Freeman told her absolute peace and quiet was vital for her right now, and this was the only way to get it. Jake, you don't think the doctor really told her to go away, do you? It was somebody from Frank Milan, wasn't it?'

142

Jake said: 'Most likely. But she probably got the doctor to say a trip would do her good. Then she'd be covered if anybody checked with him about it. Did she say when she'd be leaving?'

Elinor shook her head. 'No, but earlier in the evening she gave the cook all those instructions about going shopping tomorrow morning. That could mean she wouldn't be here herself.'

'It could,' Jake said. 'Which is why Kermit came across with that dinner invitation. He knew she'd be gone by then, so it was safe to have us over.' He looked at his watch. 'Twelve-thirty. However she's travelling, she's not likely to leave before five or six in the morning at the earliest. Otherwise – ' He picked up the phone and dialled Charlotte Thoren's number. As soon as he heard her say in a tense whisper, 'Hello. Hello. Who is it?' he hung up. 'We're that much ahead of her anyhow,' he told Elinor. 'She's still here.'

Elinor said: 'But you can't keep her here. So what happens if she's not around when you want her to sign that release?'

'No sweat, baby. I just look her up wherever she is.' He picked up the phone again and called Magnes. While he waited for an answer he prodded apart drying scraps of paper on the skillet with his finger. 'Yeah?' Magnes said sleepily.

Jake said: 'Trouble. Mrs Thoren's getting ready to take off, maybe first thing in the morning. I want a man on her who knows how to handle surveillance work. A pro. Can you get me somebody right away?'

'In an hour. A very good boy. He even got a passport on him covers any place you don't need a visa. Taking off, hah? You know what that means?'

'I know what it means. But it probably won't be a passport job because the blackmailers won't want her that far away from them. Furthest away might be some place like the Bahamas. Does Milan's mob have any setup there?'

'Some say yes, some say no, because maybe that new *shvartzeh* government there put too much heat on them. Anyhow, best thing for my boy is to wait in his car near that bridge from Daystar Number One to the Beach. He'll pick her up when she hits the Beach. You know her licence number?'

'There's two numbers,' Jake said. He flipped open his notebook and read the numbers to Magnes. 'He shouldn't have any trouble spotting the car. Either a cream-coloured Jag sports model or a black Mercedes coupé. It'll pretty sure be the Mercedes, with her son or that houseman driving. She's a grey-haired woman, very thin and washed-out looking, wears oversized sunglasses even in the house.'

'There's other ways off that island,' Magnes pointed out. 'Cab, hired limousine, even a boat. They got something at that dock besides the sailboat?'

'Yes.' Jake thought it over. 'You know what I drive, don't you?'

'I saw it.'

'Then describe it to your man, and if he sees anything likely coming across the bridge with me close on its tail, that'll be Mrs Thoren. Whichever way she heads when she gets over on the Beach, I'll cut in the opposite direction, and he can pick her up right where I leave off. It might even convince her nobody is following her.'

'And if it's by boat?'

Jake said: 'You'll have to have somebody cover that, too.'

'But not in an hour. The one I can get has his boat in a marina down on Fourth Street. For him to go down there and bring the boat back to Daystar would take at least a couple of hours.'

'Just tell him to make it as quick as he can. He won't have any trouble finding the place here. The guy next door has a big light burning in his back yard, and it's the next house north of that. But tell your man to lay far enough offshore not to get spotted. This guy Webb who put up the light is gun-happy.'

'I'll tell him. This is some *tummel*, all right. She knows all about you, you know all about her, and both of you got to go around with a straight face like you don't know anything. That is some smart pro working on her, sonny, to fix things up like that. You know what? With such a head on him I wouldn't be surprised if he made a deal with her. She hands over all the insurance money to him when she gets it, and in return he'll

144

lay off her for good afterward. Nobody even has to account for that money, because there's no taxes on it.'

'I already thought of that,' Jake said. 'So make sure your boys know what they're doing every minute.'

29

He planted the phone back on its stand and said to Elinor: 'Get the picture?'

'Yes. What'll you do? Watch out of the window for her to come by?'

'No, I'll wait outside in the car.' He yawned widely, his eyes watering. 'I don't think she'll make any move until morning, but when she does I have to be right in back of her.'

'But that means sitting there at least five or six hours. The way you look, you'll never be able to stay awake that long.'

'It's the way I feel, too. But there's not that much of a rush. I'll catch some sleep now, and you wake me up at three. Then it'll be your turn.'

'I don't feel sleepy,' Elinor protested. 'I'd rather wait in the car with you.'

'You'll do what I tell you to. And you'll start by hooking the phone into the monitor and bringing it up full volume. That'll amplify any sound in her room so you'll be able to hear a hair-pin drop on the carpet. Then if you hear anything that sounds like she's up and doing, wake me quick. If not, wake me at three. I guarantee you'll be sleepy by then.'

He showered, scrubbing himself hard to cleanse off any residue of bay water. When he went into the bedroom Elinor was sitting cross-legged on the bed, the phone locked into the monitor on the night table beside her, a magazine propped against the monitor. She was peeling an orange, and the room was full of its sharp scent. 'Want some?'

'No. All quiet with Mrs Thoren?'

'All quiet.' She stuffed a segment of orange into her mouth and just managed to get it down as Jake started toward the study. 'Jake, that's foolish. I mean, you can't even turn around on that couch. There's enough room in this thing so you can be comfortable for once.'

He didn't dispute the point. He fell into bed beside her, giving himself up to sleep as soon as his head touched the pillow. The next thing he knew, she was softly rubbing her fingertips back and forth over his forehead. 'Hey, it's three o'clock.'

He sat up and shook his head to clear it. 'Still all quiet at the other end?'

'Still. Want something to eat before you go out?'

'No, hungry is better if you have to stay awake. Now get some sleep yourself.'

The windows of the car were fogged opaque by night dampness. He went over them with a rag, then got behind the wheel. By backing down the driveway a few yards, he found he had a view of the Thoren house front from where he was.

He slid down in the seat, eyes fixed on the house. With the passing of time, moisture again formed on windshield. Pale golden light from the street lamp coming through the rear window reflected droplets of water trickling down it. After a while he got out of the car and used the rag on the glass again. He had just gotten back behind the wheel when he saw Elinor running across the lawn toward the car. She had changed from pyjamas to dress but was barefoot. She slipped into the seat beside him and said breathlessly: 'There's nothing wrong, Jake. I just couldn't stand being alone in there.'

'Nerves?'

'Yes. I tried to go to sleep, but as soon as I turned the light out – '

'Keep your voice down, baby. Otherwise you'll have Milt Webb scouting around here with a machine gun.'

Elinor said in a whisper: 'I'm sorry. Anyhow, as soon as I turned the lights out, all I could think about was Holuby grabbing me and pulling me under. And when I tried to think about something else, it kept coming up all blackmailers and gangsters. That was even worse. I mean blackmailers and gangsters are only supposed to be like in the movies, but these are for real.

146

They make such a big thing out of smoking pot, but how about them?'

'The logic is on your side. And now that you got it off your chest, how about getting back into the house?'

Elinor thrust her arm through his. 'I'll feel better staying here. Right up close to all that muscle.'

'I won't.'

'Yes you will.' She leaned against him, his imprisoned arm pressing against her breast. 'Look, I know all about what happened when we came here last week. I made like Doris Day, so you made like a computer. But you don't have to any more, Jake. You turn me on, I turn you on, so it doesn't make sense that way.'

'Baby, not even Elizabeth Barrett Browning could have put it into more beautiful language. But get this into your head. What turns me on is Mrs Thoren. Especially Mrs Thoren sitting there with a ballpoint in her hand, waiting for me to show her where to sign a release form.'

'All right, so go be a computer about her. Not about me. I wouldn't believe it anyhow, after what happened yesterday. I mean, the way you landed all over Holuby because of what he did to me. So you're just as human as anybody else, aren't you?'

'At least.'

'Then why don't you stop trying not to be?'

Jake said: 'For one thing, if I got too human with you right now, Mrs Thoren could come rolling by and I'd never know it.'

'I didn't say right now. And suppose you didn't know where she was going? If you wind up with all the information you need to make her sign that release, you can just give it to those lawyers at Guaranty. Then they could win the case in court with it.'

Jake said: 'Except there's not a chance of my giving it to them. The merchandise I'm selling is a release, not information.'

'Oh,' Elinor said, disconcerted, and when Jake said, 'That's the word for it, all right,' she said defiantly, 'Well, that still doesn't change anything between us, as far as I can see.'

When she started to fall asleep in a series of nervous twitches, her weight slowly bearing more and more on him, her head sagging over to rest on his shoulder, he put an arm around her shoulders and kept it there until the car windows misted up again and he had to get out to clean them. It took some trouble to get her propped into the far end of the seat then – she was completely out and as limp as if she were boneless – and he left her that way when he got back into the car.

The grey of dawn lightened the sky a little after five-thirty. A few minutes later a shaft of sunlight struck the glazed, earth-coloured tiles on the roof of the Thoren house. The sunlight might have been the signal for departure, the way the black Mercedes suddenly appeared in the driveway of the house. From what Jake could make out at that distance, Charlotte Thoren was behind the wheel, and there was no one else in the car.

He already had the Jag's motor turning over when the Mercedes, moving fast, flashed past him, squealing as it rounded the bend of Circular Road. Trying to time his own departure to the split second, he had forgotten Elinor completely. As he shot the car down the driveway in reverse, she was flung forward, her head banging hard against the dashboard. The Jag leaped forward with a snarl like something jet-propelled, careened around the turn past the Ortega house, and headed into the straightaway leading to the bridge to Daystar Number One, but the Mercedes was already out of sight.

Elinor had so far not made a sound. Jake glanced at her. She was clutching her forehead with both hands, her face screwed up with pain.

'Are you all right?' he asked.

'I don't know. I guess so.' Still clutching her head, she peered dazedly through the windshield. 'What happened? Did you see them go by all of a sudden?'

'Not them. Her, all alone.'

'But where is she?'

'Over on Island Number One by now. We have to close up on her before she gets clear of it, or she can go right past that guy Magnes has waiting. She is one hell of a driver.'

The Mercedes didn't come into sight again until Jake made

148

the last turn of the road circling Daystar Number 1. Then he saw it approaching the bridge over to the Beach, slowing down to take the hump of the bridge smoothly. He moved up on it fast, yelled: 'Watch it!' to Elinor as he took the bridge in a leap and a bounce, caught a glimpse of the guard's open-mouthed, astonished face as he went by, and was only half a block behind the Mercedes as it headed down the street to the intersection of North Bay Road. At the corner of the inter-section, aimed in the same direction as the Mercedes, he saw a car double-parked, poised and waiting. An unobtrusive blue Buick, a few years old, it's driver's elbow – all that could be seen of him – resting on the window sill.

'Magnes' boy,' Jake said. He slowed down a little and touched the horn. The Buick instantly went into motion and took up the pursuit of the Mercedes with a surprising burst of speed. 'There's more motor in that baby than it came out of the factory with.'

By the time the Mercedes made the northward turn into Alton Road, it was already a full block ahead of him, the Buick midway between them. Jake swung southward into Alton, drove a couple of blocks along it, then pulled up to the curb. Across the street were the greens and sand traps of a golf course. It was only a little after dawn, but a pair of golfers were already trudging across the green, dragging golf carts behind them.

Elinor said: 'Won't she catch on pretty soon about the other car following her?'

'She might. It won't make any difference. She's known since yesterday that we're on to her.'

Elinor shook her head somberly. 'It must feel awful being followed around like that.'

'It does. It's not bad for breaking down somebody's nerve after a while. Let's see your head.'

She leaned toward him and lifted her face for inspection. At the hairline was a swollen, reddening bruise. She winced when Jake ran a thumb over it. He said: 'You'll live. It'll be black and blue there, that's all.'

'Thanks for the consolation.' She gave him a look of triumph.

'You know, that's the first time I ever saw you scared about anything.'

'Well, what the hell. Magnes's guy was expecting me to show up right behind her. If I didn't – '

'I don't mean that,' Elinor said. 'I mean the way you looked at me when I banged my head. I saw it. You were in a real panic because you thought I was hurt bad.'

'I panic easy,' Jake said.

30

Between gaping yawns at the breakfast table Elinor said: 'When will you know where she went?'

'As soon as that guy can get to a phone without losing her and call Magnes. It might be ten minutes from now. It might be ten hours.'

'But he can't keep watching her all the time, can he? Twenty-four hours a day?'

Jake said: 'No, but if he has to he'll get somebody from a local agency to double up with him. There's no place in the world where you can't get local talent to back you up on a surveillance job.'

While Elinor slept he went to work, bleary-eyed, sorting out the now dry scraps of paper gleaned from Thoren's boat. He wound up separating it into four sections: wads of cellophane, bits of cardboard, writing paper, and what had to be the remnants of a stamped envelope.

That done, he started piecing together the fragments of envelope, working outward from the stamp and cancellation mark. Before it was completely reassembled he could make out that it had been addressed in large, ineptly formed block letters to *Mr Walter Thoren, 18 S. Circular Drive, Daystar 2, M.B., Fla.* It bore no return address.

Jake ran strips of transparent tape across it to bind it together, then bent the desk lamp low over it and studied the blurred postmark. Finally, with the aid of a reading glass, he

150

deciphered it. *Miami Beach, March 6th*. March sixth was one day before Walter Thoren's death.

'You pretty little thing,' Jake said to the envelope.

He went into the kitchen, washed down an amphetamine with a glass of orange juice, and brought another tablet and glass of juice into the bedroom. Elinor was under the blanket, knees drawn up to her belly, head, as usual, under the pillow. 'The human lungfish,' Jake said. 'Come on, start surfacing. It's after nine.'

When he removed the pillow she feebly clutched at it. 'Ah, Jake, I can't wake up. It's no use. I just can't.'

He tossed the pillow aside. 'Then get this pill down. It ought to carry you as far as the bathroom anyhow.'

Elinor managed to prop herself on one elbow. She looked at the pill through barely open eyes. The bruise on her forehead, Jake saw, was now completely black and blue. 'What is it?' she asked suspiciously.

'A benny. Bottled insomnia. Open your mouth.'

She did, and he popped the pill into it. She took a long swallow of juice. 'You're sure in a good mood,' she said. 'What happened? Did Magnes call up about where Mrs Thoren is?'

'No, I just worked out a jigsaw puzzle with Thoren's waste-paper. I think I have the envelope the last blackmail note was mailed in. And don't settle back to sleep again. You have to get to town and work on those newspaper files.'

When he pulled off the blanket he saw she had given up altogether on nightclothes. The narrow areas that had been covered by the bikini were strikingly pale against the rest of her. She dragged herself across the room and leaned over the dressing table to peer into its mirror. She gingerly touched a finger to the bruise. 'Look at that. First sunburned so it almost killed me. Then drowned. Now this. I'll never make it back to New York.'

'You'll make it back. But I have to admit you are more accident prone than most, baby.'

'Me?' Elinor said with outrage. 'You call Holuby an accident? And the way you drive?' The phone in the study rang,

151

and she instantly forgot her outrage. 'I'll bet it's Magnes,' she said eagerly.

'Or Maniscalco,' Jake said. 'Looking for me to build up his confidence again.'

It was Magnes. 'Dekker, for a man my age to get one heartburn after another is absolutely no good. Take my word for it, the whole next week every mouthful of food I swallow will turn to acid in me.'

'Your guy lost her,' Jake said. 'Only three hours, and the stupid bastard lost her already.'

'He didn't lose her.'

'Then what are you moaning about?'

'He never had her. From the beginning, he didn't have her.'

Jake said: 'What kind of car does he drive?'

'A Buick. A blue hardtop.'

'Then he had her from the beginning, Magnes. I was right there in back of her, and I gave him the horn, and I saw him take off after her. What are you up to? Am I supposed to pay you bonus money now to find out where she's holed up?'

Magnes said coldly: 'Sonny, before you go around calling people a sellout artist, you want to listen to everything they got to say. So listen. I am calling you from Mount Sinai Hospital where my boy is laying with stitches all over his head and maybe a fracture. And with a nice little wife sitting here like it's *ek velt*. Like it's the end of the world for her. Because the one you saw driving that Buick was not my boy. My boy was on the floor in back of the car out cold and with his head split open. That's how some meter maid found him when she looked in the car where it was parked uptown.'

'For chrissake, how did he get himself into a spot like that.'

'How? Because around five a.m. a car pulls up where he was waiting for the Thoren woman to show, and a couple plain ordinary guys get out and flash him a police badge. They tell him he was reported by somebody lives on the block as a suspicious person and what's he up to? He shows them his credentials, he tells them he got a job tailing somebody coming off Daystar, and they tell him to get out so they can frisk him. All friendly, y'understand, even some joking. And while one

152

of them is frisking him, the other one knocks him over the head. That's all he knows. Next thing he's in Mount Sinai with his wife sitting there and crying her eyes out. She's marked down as next of kin on his I.D., so they went and got her to the hospital right away. So she called me up, and here I am.'

Jake said: 'A police badge? The real thing?'

'That's what he told me, and this boy is no *shmendrik*, Dekker. Believe me, he knows from the real thing. What wasn't real maybe was the guy with the badge. It could have been some hood got hold of it, one way another.'

Jake said: 'Does your man know Holuby? Maybe one of those guys was Holuby.'

'No, because that was what I asked him first thing. He don't know Holuby, but he says it wasn't any wrestler built like a tank. He says both of them looked like plain ordinary people.'

'That's a helpful description. Where the hell did this genius learn his business? From a correspondence school?'

'Now listen to me, sonny – '

'Don't bother to cook up excuses for him, Magnes. All you have to do is clean up the mess he made. Meaning, find that woman for me quick. The last I saw of her she was all alone in the Mercedes, driving north on Alton at six a.m. Now you take it from there.'

'Take it where? You want me to check the airlines and railroad? A waste of time. If she was alone in the car, odds are she wasn't taking any plane or train, she was probably heading somewhere upstate. Or she's already there by now.'

Jake said: 'All right, you've got the car's licence number, and you told me you've got contacts all over the state. Now how about peeling off some of that ten grand I paid you and turning them loose on this?'

'Dekker, be reasonable. There are anyhow a million motels and hotels along the way, even figuring only as far as Palm Beach. To check them, I would need the whole FBI put together. The smart thing is to concentrate on this end. Somebody here has to know where she went. Like those kids of hers. That's who to work on.'

'Which makes it my job, doesn't it?' Jake thought it over.

153

Then he said sourly: 'Nice how it works out. Your boy drops the dish, and I sweep it up. All right, I'll do what I can. Meanwhile, you go over to Bayside Spa and find out who that rubber is and where we might locate him. That way, I'll be getting at least a dime's worth out of my ten grand.'

'I'll drive over there as soon as I make arrangements with the doctors here about my boy. As for that ten grand, sonny, you already got plenty of value from it and you'll get plenty more yet. Rest assured.'

Jake said: 'We'll see. One thing, Magnes. If you happen to meet up with Frank Milan, and he tells you he's on the police force, don't believe him. Not even if he shows you a badge.'

He slammed down the phone before Magnes could answer that. When he turned he saw Elinor standing in the doorway, her face clouded with concern. 'What the hell are you supposed to be posing for?' he demanded. 'Living statues? You should have been dressed by now.'

'Jake, that's not fair. It's not my fault if somebody else fouls up, is it?'

'And will you can the chatter for once and just do as you're told?' He moved toward the doorway, and Elinor hastily backed away from it, hand outstretched to fend him off. He stopped in his tracks and stared at her unbelievingly. 'You must be kidding,' he said at last. 'Do you really think I meant to belt you?'

'I don't know. You don't see how you look right now. You scare me when you look like that.'

'Then unscare yourself. All I want to do is get into the bathroom and shave. And you're out of character anyhow. From what I heard, Polack women liked to get belted now and then.'

'Well, they don't. Not the ones I know. Just try being nice to them. You'll do a lot better.'

'I see,' Jake said. This time she stood her ground warily as he approached her. When he cupped a hand under each plump breast and hefted it as if calculating its weight, she remained rigidly unmoving, her arms at her sides. 'You mean like this?' he said.

154

'No.' She angrily struck his hands away. 'I don't mean like a doctor. Or a butcher. I mean like people. I guess that leaves you out, doesn't it?'

'Does it? When Kermit invited us to supper tonight, what did you tell him?'

She looked bewildered at this abrupt change of subject. 'Kermit? I said it was up to you. Do you want to go over there tonight?'

'You heard what I told Magnes about loosening up Kermit and Joanna about where their mama is. The sooner we get to work on it, the better.'

Elinor's face darkened again. 'And what does that mean? Look, if you think I'm crawling into bed with Kermit so he'll start telling secrets –'

'Baby, you've got a lot to learn. It's the ladies who dig the pillow talk afterwards. It makes them feel they haven't been used, they've been sharing something beautiful. With the gentlemen, the warm-up time is when they talk too much. They can be real gabby while they're figuring their chances of getting your zipper down. Afterwards, they'd just as soon watch the Late Late Show on TV.'

Elinor's lip curled. 'So the only reason I don't have to go to bed with Kermit is because he might not be in a talky mood afterwards. Thanks a lot.'

'Save your thanks. You know goddam well I'd never try to shove you into bed with Kermit or anybody else for any reason.'

'You're all heart, Mr Dekker,' Elinor said.

31

During the drive to the Miami causeway she maintained a stony silence. Then, as it seemed to dawn on her that he was driving with an eye always on the rear-view mirror, she suddenly said: 'What do you keep looking in the mirror for? You think somebody is following us?'

'That Chevy with the six-foot aerial, a couple of cars back. He picked us up as soon as we got off Daystar.'

She turned to look through the rear window, and Jake said sharply: 'Stop that. Get around here and keep your eyes front. I'm the one they're worried about. You show you know what's going on, and they'll start worrying about you, too.'

'What do you mean, start worrying? It was me Holuby tried to drown, wasn't it? Look, do you have to leave me alone all day when they're after us like that?'

'There's only one guy in that car. I leave it to you which of us he's after. And when I drop you off at a store to do some shopping, that'll settle all questions in his mind about it.'

Elinor said: 'But what about you? After what you did to Holuby – '

'Nothing'll happen to me. And if it does, there's an account book along with the rest of my stuff in that closet back in the house. There's an entry in it about the three thousand dollars coming to you for professional services. That'll hold up as good as contract when my estate is settled.'

Elinor said angrily: 'That's very funny, but you know I wasn't thinking about the money.' She narrowed her eyes. 'And if you're so sure nothing'll happen to you, why'd you mark it down before you even paid me?'

'Because income-tax time is coming. When my accountant figures up my estimate for the year, he likes to know all my business expenses. That's the way he is. A walking computer, just like me.'

Whatever she had in mind to say to that she sullenly kept to herself.

Jake pulled the car up to the curb near Burdine's department store on Flagler Street. The Chevy with the tall aerial, he observed, passed him by, but then double-parked half a block ahead of him. Its driver remained behind the wheel.

Jake pointed past it. 'See that white building down there, right on the bay front?'

Elinor, her eyes on the Chevy, said: 'I guess so.'

'Don't guess. And quit worrying about that guy. When I

take off he'll follow me. I'm trying to show you where the library is. That white building.'

'I see it.'

'Good. And what's your job there?'

Elinor closed her eyes. She made a slow circling motion with her forefinger as if zeroing in on the answer. 'Going through the 1942 newspapers. Start in September and go backward to May. Anything about a ship captain who disappeared off his boat down here.'

'A ship's officer. It doesn't have to be a captain. If you find anything that fits, phone me right away. If not, I'll pick you up here at six.'

'That's a long time, Jake.'

'You're not getting paid by the hour.' He took her hand, pressed an amphetamine tablet into its palm, and closed her fingers around it. 'Comes lunchtime, have something at a counter around there and then take this. It'll keep you going in high gear.'

'I'm already in high gear from the last one.'

'When it wears off you'll slow down to a crawl. Take this one before that happens.' He counted off twenty dollars from his money clip. 'This is shopping money. Kill half an hour in the store here. Buy something while you're doing it.'

'Twenty dollars' worth?'

'As long as it's something you can carry with you. Don't arrange for anything to be delivered. I don't want somebody ringing the doorbell and claiming to be a delivery man even if he is. Got it straight? And for chrissake, don't look down the block at that car. Just walk right into the store.'

He waited until she was lost in the throng entering the store, then drove home. The reflection of the Chevy was in his rearview mirror all the way. It disappeared only when he had crossed the bridge to Daystar Island Number 1.

32

He had stored Thoren's envelope and scrap paper in glassine packets and locked them in the closet of the study. As soon as he was in the house he took them out and went to work on them again. The packet of cellophane wads was easily disposed of. The wads, when opened and flattened out, turned out to be a collection of cigar wrappers. He held each one up to the light and went over it with the reading glass, but the only thing imprinted on them was the manufacturer's name.

He was about to empty the packet of notepaper scraps on the desk when he heard a knocking at the back door of the house. He swept the packets into a drawer of the desk and went to the door. The outline of the figure showing through the glass curtains was flagrantly female. Nera Ortega.

He opened the door. 'Howdy, neighbour,' he said, but remained in the doorway, blocking it.

Nera gave him a quick, artificial smile, the ripe lips turning up at the corners for an instant and immediately turning down again. 'My turn to ask for an invitation to visit?'

'You picked a bad time, ma'am. I'm working now.'

'Writing a book?'

'At least trying to.'

Nera said: 'You know, it's marvellous how convincing you make that sound. Only you may as well get used to the idea that none of it convinces me. Not one little bit. I catch on slow, Mr Dekker, but sooner or later I do catch on.'

'What?' Jake said blankly. 'What's this about?'

'You. And what's going on behind that honest face. But I'd rather talk about it inside. You owe me a drink anyhow.'

Jake glanced over his shoulder. 'If my wife –'

Nera flashed him that brief, tooth-baring smile again. 'Your wife was with you when you drove away about an hour ago. She wasn't with you when you came back. So she isn't here to worry about it one way or the other.'

'That your hobby? Peeking from behind the window curtains?'

'Sometimes,' Nera said. 'Well?'

He shrugged in resignation and led the way into the living room. When he took out the bottle of Scotch from the bar cabinet Nera said: 'No, not this early in the day. For high noon, a martini. I'll bet you mix a great martini.'

'Sorry, but martinis are a slow, sociable drink. You can see I'm not in a slow, sociable mood right now. Whether you believe it or not, lady, I've still got a day's work ahead of me.'

'Ah, but what kind of work?'

Jake looked at her quizzically. 'You seem to have your own ideas about that. Suppose you let me in on them.'

'*Corta eso,* tiger. I'm your friend. There's no need to play games with me.' She took her Scotch and water and settled back on the couch. She emptied half the glass without drawing breath, then waved it slowly from side to side at him like a metronome. 'Walter Thoren had a big insurance policy. About half a million dollars, from what I heard. Now Charlotte is having a lot of trouble trying to collect from the insurance company. They even sent down a man a few weeks ago – some fat little Italian snoop from New York – to prove it wasn't an accident at all. When he went away Fons said to me: "Don't worry, they're not giving up that easy if they really think there's something queer about Walter's death and they can save themselves half a million dollars by proving it." What do you think of that, tiger?'

Jake said. 'What am I supposed to think of it?' He frowned at her. 'Wait a second.' His voice was unbelieving. 'Is it your bright idea I'm some kind of mystery man sent here to replace your fat little Italian snoop?'

'My very bright idea.' Nera closed one eye tight and aimed a beautifully manicured forefinger at him. 'You might as well know right now, sweetheart, that I have police blood in me. Papa didn't make his million the easy way, from sugar plantations back in Cuba. He was a cop. Started from the bottom and worked his way up until he was Machado's biggest and best cop. And in case you don't know it, next to Machado, Batista

159

was nothing. And I am Papa's girl. I have a head for these things.'

'And a beautiful one. But mixed up. Too much Walter Thoren on the brain, I'm afraid.'

'Sure. Because you put him there. The first time you and your wife came over to the house, who was it started asking me questions about Walter? And the other night in bed of all places, who was it asking me about him again? I never talk about him to anybody – especially about what happened between us – and suddenly there I am, telling you all about it.' Nera slapped her forehead with the heel of her hand. '*Ya eso es más de la cuenta*. That's when I should have started wondering what you were up to. But it wasn't until last night that I did.'

'Last night?'

'A swimming party in the bay all alone, hey? In that filthy water which could poison you?' Her eyes widened with mock apprehension. Her voice fell to a whisper. 'First we sneak out of the house and look all around to make sure no one is watching. Then a nice swim in the dark all the way to the Thorens' for some quiet snooping. Only it's not completely dark since that idiot Webb lit it up. Where I sit by my pool it is, but not where you swim in the bay. And it wasn't the first time you were on that kind of swimming party. Another time was when Milt scared somebody away by shooting at him. He thought it was a robber, but I could tell him different now, couldn't I? When I was looking out of the window because of the shooting I saw you sneak back into your house, not go out of it.'

'Through binoculars?' Jake said.

'No. But I do use a pair sometimes for bird-watching. Especially for watching chicken hawks done up in pigeon feathers.' Her face became mournful. She dramatically pressed her hand to her breast. 'Forgive me, *chino*. But can you blame me for wanting to watch your every move, knowing how passionate you are about me?'

'So that's it?' Jake nodded wisely. 'That's what's behind all this nonsense. You're sore because I haven't kept in touch with you. You've been steaming about it until there's blisters showing.'

160

'Look, mister – '

'Oh yes, you have. You've been wondering what happened between us that night to cool me off so fast. Had it been that much of a letdown for me? No, it couldn't have been. So now you come up with some crazy reason for it which at least soothes your pride. I'm a secret agent, God help me. All I wanted from you was information about Walter Thoren, not an affair. So I couldn't have cooled off on you, because I was never heated up in the first place.' Jake planted his hand on his chest, mimicking her gesture. 'Of course,' he said with broad sarcasm, 'the fact that I have a full-time writing job to work at and a full-time wife keeping an eye on me wouldn't have anything to do with it, would it?'

Nera sat staring at him in awe. 'My God, listen to him,' she said. Then she gulped down the remainder of her drink and thrust the empty glass at him. 'You'd better fix me another one of these, pal. *Paluchero*. After that song and dance, I really need it.'

'Why? Because it'll be easier to stay sore at me if you get stoned?' But he refilled the glass and handed it to her. 'Let's face the facts, beautiful. I'm not your problem. You are.'

'Sure I am.'

'Yes, you are. It's a problem all right when a woman like you can underrate herself the way you're doing. When she can't appreciate the impact she has on a man. It can lead her to cook up some pretty wild theories about why he doesn't send flowers every day, instead of letting her be logical about it.'

'Uh-huh. But I don't underrate you, tiger. Not for a minute. And I don't think Charlotte Thoren does either.'

'Charlotte Thoren. I can see this gets better as it goes along I suppose she was up there at your window taking turns with those binoculars.'

Nera said venomously: 'I wouldn't let that smug, self-righteous bitch put a foot in my house, and you know it. But it so happens Patty Tucker was over a little while ago, and she was full of Charlotte's latest.'

'And now it's Patty Tucker too? Jesus, this is beginning to

sound like one of those mass delusions they had in the Middle Ages.'

Nera said tiredly: 'Oh, why don't you quit playing dumb? It's starting to bore me. And why aren't you drinking? I'm being sociable about this. You might as well be sociable about it to.'

'I am not drinking, dear, because I'm on little pink pills which I took to keep awake so I could finish a writing job I contracted to do. And if I sound dumb about your delusions maybe it's because I don't know what the hell you're talking about.'

'Don't you? Well, I'm talking about some interesting things Patty had to tell me this morning. One was that when she stopped off at the Thorens' on the way over, she found out Charlotte just went off on a trip by herself and doesn't want anybody to know where.'

'Including Kermit and Joanna?'

'They were leaving for school, so Patty didn't have time to pin them down. The only thing she got from them was that it was doctor's orders. But when she called Dr Freeman from my place, he said Charlotte was fine last time he saw her a week ago, and it was her own idea to go away like that. Nerves, she said. All he did was tell her to go ahead if she felt it would do her good.'

Jake said with amusement: 'So you and good old Patty put your heads together and decided Mrs Thoren must have discovered I was on her trail and therefore took it on the lam.'

Nera said sweetly: 'No, Mr Dekker, I did the deciding. All by myself. In private. And that wasn't until after Patty also told me that a couple of days ago Charlotte went to the Daystar membership committee and ordered them to get you off the island pronto. And when they said they couldn't take any kind of legal action until someone was elected to fill Walter's seat on the committee, she said they could appoint her to it then and there. Which, as it turned out, they couldn't. Now you tell me why she was so wild to get rid of you, and then, when she couldn't, she suddenly goes away herself. Especially when she's having trouble collecting the insurance on Walter and must know just as well as Fons that there's an investigator on the job around here.'

'Oh, no,' Jake said. 'And to think I'm the one writing the books.'

'Uh-huh,' Nera said. 'Writing books. That'll be the day.'

He crooked a finger at her. 'Come on. I want to show you something.'

'I've already seen what you have to show me, remember? And I don't play matinées.' Her face was very pale now, her nostrils flaring. 'You really are a contemptible son of a bitch, aren't you? Climbing in bed with a woman to get information from her. Or is that your way of paying for the information?'

'That does it.' He took the glass from her hand and put it on the table. Then he caught hold of her wrist and brutally hauled her to her feet. 'Fun is fun, but only up to a point. Now we're going to set the record straight.'

'By twisting my arm off?'

'By showing you something I didn't intend to show anybody for a long time to come. But if that's the way it has to be – ' When he pulled her down the hallway to the study she tried to hold back, then followed on skittering little steps. In the study he gestured at the display on the desk. The typewriter with the incomplete pages of manuscript in it, the open box with the other pages of manuscript, the stack of typing paper. 'What do you think that is?'

'I don't care what it is. And let me go. You're hurting me.'

He thrust her up against the desk. 'Go on, read it,' he said in a hard voice.

She did, near-sightedly leaning over the typewriter. Jake pulled other sheets of manuscript from the box and spread them out on the desk. 'Take a look at these too.'

She glanced over them. 'I suppose it's some kind of book,' she said sullenly.

He opened a desk drawer and pulled out a cardboard folder. He turned back its cover and held it out toward her. 'And what does this little document look like?'

Her eyes went over it. 'It says it's a contract for a book.'

'From whom?'

'All right, it's from the Donaldson and Friar Company. Publishers. In New York. Does that make you happy?'

'Not completely,' Jake said. 'When was it made out?'

'Last year. And it's for five thousand dollars. And you're writing a book.' Her tone was now one of baffled apology. 'Jake, will you please stop carrying on like this? Look, I don't know what got into me. Or maybe I do. I have been thinking you made a fool of me, and I started off the day with a couple of drinks – '

'Another member of Milt Webb's breakfast-out-of-the-bottle club?'

'You don't have to be so stuffy about it. When you live my kind of life, maybe you're entitled to join the club.'

'Not if it means turning paranoic every time you raise your elbow.' Jake released her wrist, and she stood rubbing it, watching him grimly stack pages of manuscript together again. She finally said: 'Please stop behaving like this. Please.'

'Why? The other night I thought you and I were on to something special. Something very good. But if it's going to be one emotional fit after another over any lousy coincidence that comes along, who needs it?'

'Maybe I do.' Nera moved up close to him and placed her hand against his cheek. 'And there won't be any more fits.'

'Lady, with your hot Latin blood and your kind of imagination – '

'Listen to me, darling. I swear there won't. Is that better?'

Her hand still rested against his cheek. Jake drew her other hand over his shoulder so that they stood body to body. She was a foot shorter than he was. The elaborate spun-gold coiffure tickling his nose was brittle with hair spray and gave off a faintly acrid smell.

He said: 'I'll settle for it. But that imagination will have to be toned down, beautiful. Insurance investigators. Walter Thoren a suicide. Hell, if there was any chance of that – '

'I didn't say he was a suicide.'

'That's the impression you gave. And if he wasn't, why should there be trouble about the insurance?'

'Because,' said Nera, 'he might have been murdered.'

'Thoren? I thought he died in a car crash.'

'He did. But it wouldn't have been very hard for someone to make the car crash, would it? Monkey around with the brakes or something like that?'

Jake laughed. 'Of course. If you say so, dear.'

Nera pulled away from him, but not forcefully enough to make him release her. She said annoyedly: 'Will you kindly not sound so condescending about it? I'm serious. It could have happened that way.'

'Meaning Charlotte Thoren arranged it so she could collect her husband's insurance?'

'No. Somebody else did. And not for the insurance.'

Jake said dryly: 'I see. A homicidal practical joker. Like I'm a secret agent.'

'I told you I was sorry about that, didn't I? Anyhow, if you saw it from my point of view, you'd know it wasn't such a wild idea really. Not with Charlotte trying so hard to get rid of you.' Nera knit her brow over this. 'Why, Jake? What does she have against you?'

'Not me. Elinor.'

'Oh?'

'And ah. She was watching her son react to Elinor. And Elinor react back. Happily.'

'Knowing Kermit, I should have thought of that,' Nera admitted.

'Except it's so much more fun dreaming up murderers and spies.' Jake patted her back. 'But we're all over that phase now, aren't we? From now on, no more make-believe. Only the facts, ma'am. How about it?'

'How about it.' Nera repeated scathingly. 'Do you have any idea how infuriating you are when you take that tone?'

'Better to infuriate you than have you sounding off like some kind of psycho. Not that you don't make an exceptionally lovely psycho.'

This time she did push herself free of him. 'What are you doing tonight?' she demanded. 'Taking another of those midnight swims in the bay?'

'I might.'

'Well, don't. That water really is polluted enough to give you some kind of horrible skin thing. My pool isn't.'

Jake looked doubtful. 'You mean we get all nice and cosy together in the moonlight so you can chew my ear off about why you think Walter Thoren was murdered?'

'You can humour me that much, *chino*. I just want you to tell me how psycho I am after you hear something very intriguing about Walter.'

'Some programme. It sounds like a ball.'

'Oh, it can be,' Nera assured him, 'once we get this business of Walter settled.'

'I'll be there,' Jake said.

33

As soon as he closed the door behind her he went back to the study and activated the transmitter in her livingroom phone. A couple of minutes later he heard the quick sharp click of heels on tile, and then Nera's voice. *'Maria? Where the hell are you? Maria!'*

'Señora?'

A machine-gun volley of Spanish followed, and Jake, after uncomprehendingly taking it in for a moment, cut off the connection and dialled the Thoren house. The deep, warm voice that answered was redolent of life on the old plantation. 'The Thoren residence. Raymond speaking.'

'This is Mr Dekker, Raymond. Is Mr Thoren there?'

'No, Mr Dekker, he's out. But he said you might call. Can I take the message?'

'You can. Tell him thanks for the dinner invitation, and we'll be there. What time should we make it?'

'By seven, Mr Dekker.' The voice was considerably cooler now. 'Is that all?'

'That is all,' Jake said.

He emptied the packet of Thoren's notepaper scraps on the desk and went to work on them. It was slow going at the start, and it took over an hour to discover he was not trying to assemble a single large sheet of paper but three smaller ones. He went into the bedroom, pulled out the cardboard stiffeners from three shirts, and then tediously assembled and taped down the borders of pages, one to a cardboard. It took another hour just to finish this job, the amphetamine working both for and against him. It gave him a sense of sharp perception, and at the same time, had his nerves increasingly on edge. He was debating whether to risk a stiff drink on top of the pill when the phone at his elbow rang. He picked it up, and Magnes said instantly: 'Don't talk. First check for a bug, then call me back. It'll probably be a QCD-two-way if it's there, not a harmonica.'

Jake disassembled the phone, reassembled it, and dialled Magnes's number. 'Nothing there. What'd you do, turn one up at your end?'

'A souvenir from some phony TV repairman. My luck, when I came in, a *yenta* on the top floor here told me she saw a stranger walking downstairs from the roof, so I checked right away. A beautiful job. Even the phone cord was twisted the way I left it.' Magnes sounded as if he warmly approved this kind of expertise. 'Believe me, sonny, the trouble they're taking, they are playing for that whole two-hundred-grand insurance in one lump. They ain't looking for any handouts from it once a month.'

'And you still think it isn't Frank Milan's operation?'

'Positive. All right, let's say ninety percent positive. His people, his facilities, yes. But not him personally. Meanwhile, we're not doing so bad ourselves. I can now tell you definitely that that rubber at Bayside Spa – that one-day replacement there – was the guy who put the finger on Thoren and started the whole blackmail thing going.'

'You mean you got his name from their employment records?'

'No, but what does it show if the daily payroll record for that one day is all of a sudden missing? If it's not with the rest of those records?'

Jake said impatiently: 'Somebody in on the deal lifted it. But what's the good of knowing – '

'Sha. Sha. There's a copy of it with the accountant. He keeps copies of all Bayside's stuff in his own office until the tax people give him the okay. I already made a cash deal with him for it. He'll have it for me by tomorrow. How are you making out locating the woman?'

Jake said: 'I'm taking my girl there for dinner tonight. If she handles it right, she might get sonny boy to unload where his mama is. How about you? Did the cops get around to questioning your boy in the hospital yet?'

'Naturally.'

'Did he mention Mrs Thoren or the kind of car he was supposed to be tailing?'

'He didn't mention her, and he told them he was supposed to be tailing a white Continental. So if somebody on Daystar drives a white Continental, I wish them luck when the cops drop in to ask them about it. They also put some pressure on me, but not too much. With me – as long as it ain't a murder or a big heist – they don't come down too hard. They know I got a bad heart condition, so if I get too much upset I could, God forbid, drop dead in front of them.'

'Nice of them,' Jake said. 'All right, keep in touch with me. And keep checking for bugs.'

He was about to put down the phone when Magnes said: 'Wait a second.' Then, after a silence which lasted considerably more than a second, he said abruptly: 'About that girlie, Dekker. Tell me it's none of my business, but this happens to be a very sweet kid.'

Jake said: 'A living doll. What's on your mind, marriage or adoption?'

'Very funny,' Magnes said mirthlessly. 'So if you want to know what's on my mind, I'll tell you. If it was my daughter, she wouldn't be here with you on any job like this.'

'She sure as hell wouldn't,' Jake said. 'After all, Magnes, if she was your daughter, she'd be at least fifty years old.'

34

All three messages pieced together from the shreds of notepaper turned out to be in Thoren's minute, meticulously formed hand-writing. Jake took his time comparing each with the envelope addressed to *Mr Walter Thoren, 18 S. Circular Drive* . . . As far as he could make out, there was no resemblance at all between the script used in the messages and the clumsy block lettering on the envelope.

Of the three messages, one was largely comprehensible. A list with each item followed by a lightly pencilled check mark.

> *thermos*
> *cigars*
> *rations*
> *chart and rev.*
> *trans.*
> *pen*
> *twls*

The other two were totally incomprehensible.

One read:

> *m ltd w b 2*
> *m mc ltd b 3*
> *ltd bl b 4 to*
> *ev 6.0*
> *1.0 2nd fl*

The other:

> *f c dayb 15*
> *225 y 007 deg*
> *fr bb r 1*
> *f lt 7 ft*
> *Meloy cb Meloy cb 5*
> *disc*

Jake laid the cardboards to which they were taped side by side and compared them closely. The number 7, he saw, did not have the Continental stroke through it here as it had in

Thoren's insurance application, but the number 1, in each case here, had that small serif, that tiny fishhook at its head, that it had in the application.

He slipped a piece of paper into the typewriter and copied the three messages. Then he took out the Greater Miami phone directory. There were a couple of Meloys listed, both at addresses across the bay in Miami.

He dialled Magnes. 'Does the name Meloy mean anything to you?' he said without preliminary. 'Meloy with an *e*.' He spelled it out.

Magnes gave the question some thought. 'Nothing,' he said at last. 'What's it about?'

'It meant something to Thoren. I put together that torn-up paper I found on his boat and the name's down there.'

Magnes said incredulously: 'You mean the blackmailer signed his name to a payoff note?'

'Come on, Magnes, would he be that thick? There are three notes here, and none of them was written by the blackmailer. Thoren wrote all of them himself. But there's an envelope too, and from the look of it I'm pretty sure it was from the blackmailer.'

'So now you know. The paper with instructions where to make the drop, Thoren got rid of for good. Naturally. I told you that's how it would be.'

'Maybe. But two of these notes might be his copies of the instructions. They're in some kind of code, and the only thing loud and clear on them is that name Meloy. It's also in the phone book. Twice. Check out those names for me fast. If they don't pay off, ask around and see if anyone by that name has some connection with the Mob.'

'I don't think so,' Magnes said. 'It's not a name I ever heard anywhere. But I'll find out.'

35

Swinging the Jaguar into North Bay Road towards the causeway at Fifth Street, Jake saw the familiar Chevy with the
elongated aerial move away from the curb and fall into place
a few car-lengths behind him. Despite the heavy Miami-bound
traffic, it expertly held to this position across the causeway as
far as Watson Park Island, where the sunset was blindingly
reflected from the silver skin of the sightseeing blimp moored
there.

Now it started to move up on him. Whether he turned north
or south when he hit Biscayne Boulevard on the Miami shoreline, the Chevy's driver was ready to turn with him.

They crossed Watson Park and headed over the last stretch
of water to the mainland. Jake bided his time, an eye on a
station waggon moving up in the next lane. Then, as the station
waggon came parallel with the Chevy on his tail, he suddenly
pulled across in front of it, bringing it to a screeching, horn-
honking stop. The Chevy's driver realized what was happening
a moment too late. The next instant he was past the Jaguar,
and Jake came down hard on the gas and swung back across
to his original lane, now directly behind the Chevy.

They were in the bottleneck entrance to Biscayne Boulevard,
where the Chevy's driver had no room to reverse their positions.
At the green light on the boulevard he slowed briefly as if in
a last desperate hope of luring the Jag after him, then made
the logical decision to turn south toward Flagler Street and
the shopping section. Jake promptly turned north. He cruised
along the boulevard for a few blocks, then left it and worked
his way in a southward arc to the library through a district of
shabby wooden and stucco buildings that looked as if they had
been weathering there unpainted since the year Miami was
founded. A solidly Cuban section. A large sign in one store
window along the way announced *English Spoken Here*.

The library stood in the middle of the bay-front park, and
Elinor was waiting outside it. She covered the distance to the

car in a panicky sprint, her knee occasionally banging the large package she was carrying. She scrambled in beside Jake headlong, heedless of the view she offered passers-by on the sidewalk. 'Man, don't ever do that to me again.'

Jake got the car moving. 'Do what?'

'You said you'd pick me up at six. It's quarter after now. Do you know all the wild things you can think of happened to somebody in fifteen minutes? I even called up the house a couple of minutes ago. I was all ready to hear some cop tell me they found you laying dead there.'

'Obviously they didn't. How'd you make out with the newspaper files? How far back did you go?'

'About three months. September and August and most of July. That was some war they were running in 1942, wasn't it?' Her voice was shrill and strained. 'Did you know the Germans and Japs were winning practically everything then? There were even German submarines right up and down Florida. And Jap planes getting ready to bomb California. I never heard of any of that stuff in school.'

Jake glanced at her. 'What's wrong with you?'

'Me? Nothing. What makes you think there is?'

'You sound funny.'

'Well, I don't feel funny,' Elinor said explosively. She started to cry. 'I was so goddam scared something happened to you,' she blubbered. She pulled a handkerchief from her pocketbook and worked it around her eyes and nose. 'Who needs it?' she demanded fiercely. 'A girl has to be out of her mind to get turned on by you. I mean, Andy's father at least had some feelings.'

'Andy's father? Who's Andy?'

Elinor said with elaborate patience: 'Andy happens to be my kid, and I've been living with you a week, and you don't even know his name yet. So that shows you, doesn't it? And maybe his father's bag was just guitar and pot and hanging around, but he did have feelings. Real feelings. And you don't. I thought you did, but after the way you were to me this morning I know a lot better. Because you don't.'

'Baby, I estimate there are anyhow five or six people across

172

that bay who are doing all they can to cut me out of a hundred thousand dollars coming to me. You'd be surprised how deeply I feel about them.'

'About the money. Because you are absolutely, totally money-oriented. Isn't that the truth?'

Jake whistled softly. 'That is some fancy language. Where'd you pick it up? From Andy's father before he walked out on you and his kid?'

'Never mind him. Isn't it the truth?'

'Well, to put it in the words of the great Joe E. Lewis, I have been rich and I have been poor, and believe me, rich is better.'

'Sure it is. But it would be even better for you if you just once got turned on by people, not money.'

'That's a very profound thought,' Jake said. He motioned at the package in her lap. 'What turned you on in the store?'

'Shoes. They were on special, so I got three pairs. I was only going to get one and give you the rest of the money back, but it was such a bargain I spent the whole twenty. Now I'm glad I did.'

'So am I. It'll give you a choice of what to wear for dinner tonight.'

'At the Thorens', I suppose?'

'At the Thorens'. And remember to be properly surprised that mama isn't there when we walk in. If we tie some conversation on to that, they might let slip where she is.'

'And if they don't?'

'I'll try to break us up into twosomes for some private chatter later on. But be careful how you work around to the subject of mama's hideout. If Kermit gets the least bit suspicious, that door closes for good.'

Elinor said: 'How about you and Joanna? She knows where her mother is too, doesn't she? Or do you just go walk with her in the moonlight so she can tell you in private how wonderful you are?'

'I always bet win and place, baby. But the fact that I'll be trying to wheedle family secrets out of Joanna doesn't let you off the hook. Kermit's your target. You concentrate on him.'

'That'll be a lot of fun,' Elinor said with distaste.

She caught sight of the lipstick-stained, half-empty glass of Scotch and water on her way through the living room. She picked it up and examined the stain. 'Nera Ortega, I bet.'

'You bet right.'

'And what could she have been doing here, as if I didn't know?'

Jake said impatiently: 'You don't know. Now go on and make yourself beautiful. You've got about fifteen minutes for it. And if someone asks about that bruise on your forehead, tell them the truth. I came down on the brake too fast.'

She let it go at that. But seated before the dressing-table mirror doing her face as he got into a fresh shirt, she suddenly said: 'What don't I know? She just came around to make a pass at you, didn't she?'

'No, she didn't. She is a very shrewd cookie about some things, our señora. She already suspected there was something fishy about Thoren's death, and she took it from there and figured out why I was really down here. I had a sweet job talking her out of it.'

Elinor stopped working on her face. 'How?'

'A friend of mine in New York runs a small publishing house. He keeps me fixed up with a phony book contract just for emergencies like this. It worked before. It worked this time.'

'And that's all it took? A phony contract and some talking? She sure must have been anxious to believe you.'

'Baby, I don't like the nagging-wife bit. It brings back some highly unpleasant memories. So knock it off. Permanently.'

'Well, you can't blame me for – '

'Did you hear me?' Jake said with slow, hard emphasis. 'Either knock it off for good, or get the hell back to New York right now.'

Elinor turned to look at him, and what she saw in his face seemed to shock her. 'You don't mean that. Not really. Yesterday when I wanted to go back home you told me it could be dangerous for me and the kid. We'd be kind of hostages for you. Things didn't change all that much in one day, did they?'

'No, they didn't. But I've had it up to here with your hang-ups. Because what they're leading up to is that you will be the little lady in charge of my methods and morals, and I will be the goon who has to keep apologizing for them. That kind of comedy I can do without. So either change your attitude or pack in and take your chances on what happens to you and the kid in New York. You can count on me for the plane ticket and cab fare to the airport.'

'You mean,' Elinor said, 'it wouldn't bother you if something did happen to me or the kid?'

Jake shrugged. 'You're the one who just explained I had no feelings. How could it bother me?'

Her shoulders sagged with relief. 'So that's it. That's what's bugging you. Jake, you know I only said it because I was so mad at what happened between us this morning. It's been eating into me all day. But don't you think I can –'

He held up a hand. 'Now don't start swinging all the way in the other direction. I didn't say you were wrong about me, did I?'

She gave him a pale smile. 'All right, rub it in.'

'Baby, you are delusion-prone. I am not rubbing anything in. I am trying to tell you in plain language that while I'd hate anything to happen to you or your kid because of this Thoren deal, I'd hate just as much paying you three thousand dollars to reform my character. Matter of fact, I'd feel the same way if it came free. You want to make it with me for kicks, okay. You want to show me how the love of a good woman ennobles a man, start packing. It's as simple as that.'

Elinor's face was scarlet. 'And I suppose you think I'm kind of simple, too. I suppose you expect me to say how sorry I am for the way I feel about you. Felt about you. All I have to do now for my three thousand dollars is just be Mata Hari when you tell me to and one of your harem when you're in the mood. And keep on doing the cooking and housework in between, not that you even notice all the trouble I take with them.'

'Jesus Christ,' Jake said helplessly, 'there you go again.'

'That's right.' Her voice was so choked with rage that she almost croaked the words. She swallowed hard, then took a long, slow breath to get control of herself. 'Because that's what

I'm doing. I've had it. I'm going.' She compressed her lips and narrowed her eyes at him, then discovered that one false eyelash, only partly attached, was dangling in her line of vision. She ruthlessly plucked it away. 'But suppose – just suppose – I don't go straight back to New York? Suppose I stop off at the Thorens' first and tell Kermit all about you? Especially about bugging those phones. Would you still be all that hard-boiled if the cops came around to ask you about it? Do you think you could put them down as easy as you put me down?'

'It seems to me,' Jake said, 'that you'd have some questions to answer yourself about bugging phones.'

'I only did it because you made me. And if I tell them about it, they'll let me off. It would be worth it to them. Don't you worry about that.'

'Maybe,' Jake said mildly, 'maybe not.' He stood there frowning at her, and she stared back at him defiantly. Finally he said reflectively: 'Funny thing. Magnes told me this could happen, but I told him no, it couldn't. Not with you. There was too much woman there, I told him. She knows we're doing a dirty job and might have to get our hands dirty, and she knows the problem her being around poses for me, but she'll play it cool. She'll show understanding.' He shook his head ruefully. 'I still don't see how I could misjudge anybody that badly. Or maybe I just don't want to believe I could.'

'Oh, no,' Elinor said between her teeth. 'You mean, first you're rotten about everything, and then you somehow lay it on me?' She suddenly shifted from outrage to suspicion. 'And what problem do I pose just being around? What's that supposed to mean?'

'Not a thing. Forget it. And you don't have to stop at the Thorens' to turn me in to Kermit. You can do it right over the phone here.' He moved toward the hallway, head down, shoulders slumping wearily. 'I'll be inside.'

'Wait a second. Don't you go dropping heavy hints and then tell me to forget it.'

Jake faced her from the doorway with a woeful, crooked little smile. 'Baby, look at yourself in that mirror. When something like that walks into a man's life he could be made out of stainless steel, and it would still get to him. And no matter what you think, I'm not really made out of stainless steel.'

'Are you trying to tell me – '

'I'm not trying to tell you anything. What's there to tell? That I was wrong in not letting you know about this from the start? That because of our setup I thought it would be taking advantage of you to get an affair going; it would be dirty pool? Hell, anybody goes against nature like that deserves what he gets.'

Elinor pressed her hands to her cheeks. 'This is crazy. This is absolutely crazy. Only two minutes ago – '

'I know what happened two minutes ago. You stepped all over my pride, and I hit back. That, I am not sorry about.'

'Telling me to get the hell out? Telling me it didn't matter what happened to me or my kid?'

'I was ten miles deep in love with my wife. She put me down once too often, and that was the end of it for us. She got the kid, too, and I loved him as much as you do yours. But with a man, pride has to come first. He isn't much of a man without it.'

Elinor looked dazed. 'You've got a kid?'

'A great kid. Nine now. Almost ten. What's so surprising about it?'

'I don't know. I mean, I guess I just didn't think of you that way. You see him, don't you? You're with him sometimes. A kid needs that.'

'I know. And I do what I can about it. But when she re-married she picked a guy with a million dollars and a jealous streak. It's no accident that a lot of my visitation days are made miserable for the kid before I get there and after I go. They're both doing their best to turn him against me.'

'But that's awful, I'd never do that with Andy.'

Jake gave her a look of tender appreciation. 'No, you wouldn't. That's the way you are. No mean streak at all. Maybe that's what kept me from crawling into bed with you first chance I got. I'm not much used to your kind of woman.'

'Oh, Jake, you make such a thing out of that, but you knew

about my kid. And you knew how I felt about you. That sure didn't put me up there with the Virgin Mary.'

He shrugged ruefully. 'So I blew it.'

'But it was my fault, too. Because I did put you down. I was just jealous, that's all. I still am. I can't stand the way you are with other women. It kills me.'

'Baby, Nera Ortega is only one other woman. And you know my half of the relationship is strictly business.'

'Maybe the reason for it is strictly business. Not the rest of it.' Elinor made a helpless gesture. 'Now I'm nagging you again. I can hear myself doing it, and I can't stop. You've got me so balled up I don't know what I'm doing.'

'Well, how do you think I feel? The last thing in the world I wanted was for us to get emotionally involved before this job was finished off. Maybe I'll have to take a walk in the moonlight with Joanna. For sure I have a date with Nera later tonight to get some information out of her. She said something about Thoren's having been murdered, and I can't let it go at that. How easy do you think it'll be for me to put on an act for her or Joanna, the way things shape up between you and me right now?'

Elinor sniffed. 'You like putting on that kind of act. Any man would.'

He walked across the room, cupped her face between his hands and raised it so that her eyes had to meet his. 'Sweetheart, with you around, a man sure doesn't kill time with the little girls and the old ladies out of choice. Or like to watch you come on strong for someone like Kermit Thoren from across the room. But that's the way it is.' He pressed his lips to hers, and she gave an involuntary start and shiver. When she began to respond more warmly he pulled away. 'We'll have to watch that quick acceleration while we're on the job. Now stick back that other eyelash and get yourself set for action. We're ten minutes late already.'

She unwillingly turned back to the mirror. She forced herself to smile at his reflection in it. 'It's not the acceleration,' she said. 'It's the way you can come down so quick on those brakes that worries me.'

36

But there was no action at the Thorens'. No information forth-coming about the dowager's whereabouts. Instead of a cosy, readily interchangeable foursome at the table, there were six. The added starters were Hal Freeman, Joanna's boy friend, and a big, handsome, redheaded girl, an old flame of Kermit, who attached herself as tightly to him as Hal did to the glower-ing Joanna. Evidently uninvited, to judge from Joanna's reac-tion, they took over the evening as if determined to put these newcomers in their place.

When, a little before eleven, Jake caught the first whiff of a cigarette Kermit and the redhead were now sharing, he gave Elinor the high sign and they took their departure.

Outside the house, she said: 'That was pot. Did you smell it too?'

'Yes.'

'Is that why you wanted to get away so fast?'

'That's why.'

'Well, I think it was a mistake. They might get high enough to talk about anything you want. Even about where Mrs Thoren is.'

'I doubt it. Anyhow, next thing I'd be invited to share a joint with them, and I can't afford to play games like that on the job. And if I turned down the offer, I'd really be showing my generation gap.'

Stepping from the lawn to the hard surface of the road, Elinor caught hold of his hand to steady herself. She did not release it as they started down the road. She said: 'I think you're wrong. I don't mean about them testing your genera-tion gap, I mean about the way it would come out. What-ever you did, you'd come out fine, and Kermit and Hal would look like kids. That's how it was going all night there. I liked it.'

'They are kids. And while we're on the subject of juvenile vice, my knowing little East Villager, you might answer a question for me. By any chance, do you have some stuff stashed away around our place?'

Elinor hesitated. 'Some. I'll dump it down the toilet first thing, Jake. Unless – '

'No unless,' Jake said.

Back in the house, he watched her empty the packet of marijuana and Zigzag papers into the bowl and flush them away. He said: 'Now, for being so co-operative, you can go to bed and catch up on your sleep. Just dig in and enjoy it. Tomorrow it's back to the library and finish up on those newspaper files.'

'What about you? The way you look, you're as beat as I am.'

'I am. But I already told you I have to have a talk with Nera tonight.'

Elinor said sulkily: 'I know. About Thoren getting murdered. You don't really believe that, do you?'

'No. But she does, and I have to find out why.'

Elinor sat down on the edge of the bed and watched in silence as he got into swimming trunks. 'When'll you be back?' she said at last.

He shook his head in disappointment. 'I thought we were done with that kind of question.'

'I'm only asking. What's wrong with just asking? I'm not trying to make anything out of it. All I want to know is when I should start worrying.'

'Never,' Jake said. 'Let Mrs Thoren do all the worrying for us Daystar folks.'

37

The Ortegas' swimming pool and terrace were surrounded by a high, tightly meshed hedge of casuarina. The only light on the terrace came from the lemon-coloured glow of a mosquito-repellent lamp. Two lounges had been arranged side by side some distance from the lamp, and Nera reclined on one. She

180

was entirely in shadow. Only the glimmer of lamplight in her eyes showed that she was awake and watchful.

She said in greeting: 'I wondered if you'd be here,' and when Jake said, 'That's what I was wondering about you,' she asked with amusement, 'What would you have done if I hadn't been?'

'Taken a swim in the pool and gone home. I'd figure you had a good reason to play it safe right now.'

'Not that I changed my mind about us?'

'Not for a second,' Jake said, and she laughed softly.

'Go have your swim anyhow,' she said, and plucked at the waistband of his trunks. 'And you don't have to be so formal with me. You can take that off.'

'How about you?'

'I'm already as informal as I can get.' His eyes were becoming accustomed to the shadows, and when she drew apart her robe in demonstration he could see she was wearing nothing under it. 'But I never go in before the summer. I don't enjoy cold water.'

The pool, when he pulled off the trunks and slipped into it, turned out to be as warm as the bay. He lazily swam its scant length back and forth a few times, then hauled himself out. Nera was waiting there for him with a terry-cloth bath sheet. He wrapped himself in it and stood peering through the darkness in the direction of his own back yard.

'What is it?' Nera said. 'Expecting company?'

'No, just wondering how you kept track of me through those hedges. You said you were watching from beside the pool here, but it's like trying to see through a brick wall.'

'Not if you're over by that opening where the drain pump is.' She nudged his knee with hers. 'You think I was lying about it? Come see for yourself.'

He did, and saw that the narrow opening in the hedge allowed a fine view along the bayside by the bulb suspended over Milt Webb's lawn. But its light did not quite extend as far as the Thorens' dock. It was impossible to make out the outline of the sailboat moored there.

'You see?' Nera said. 'I like you very much, *chino*. I don't lie to people I like very much.' She led him back to the lounges.

181

'That towel must be soaked by now. You'll be better off without it.'

He tossed the damp towel aside and stretched out on a lounge hands clasped behind his head, eyes closed. Nera sat down beside him. 'You going to sleep, mister?'

'It depends. If you're warming up to that wild story about Walter Thoren's death you threatened to tell me, I might.' He patted the adjoining lounge. 'How about moving over here? Save Walter for your analyst. I've got better things in mind for us.'

'After I tell you about Walter. Look, I am not psycho on the subject, darling, and I will not have you going around thinking I am and being terribly kind to me about it. Now open your eyes.'

'I listen with my ears.'

'Then make sure you're listening. Jake, I'm serious. This thing about Walter is not funny. It's frightening.'

He opened his eyes. 'Why?'

'Because it's very likely Walter's car was deliberately fixed so it would crash. Next week – tomorrow – it could be Fons. It could be any one of a dozen people close to Fons.'

'Including you?'

'Including me.'

'So you must have told the police all about it. And since they know – '

'They don't know. We didn't go to them. It would be very awkward if we did. They'd find out who certain people are and what they're doing, and it's not altogether legal. It has to do with Fidel. With the movement against him here.'

'Castro?'

'Naturally Castro,' Nera said impatiently. 'How many Fidels do you know?'

Jake pushed himself up into a sitting position. 'Let me get this straight. You mean Thoren was somehow tied in with the anti-Castro movement? That he was working for the CIA or something?'

'Not the CIA. *Avispa*. And he wasn't working for it. He just helped it as an adviser.'

182

'*Avispa?* What the hell is *Avispa?*'

'An organization of Cuban freedom fighters. The most vital one really. Not like those others that go around collecting money and using it just to make a big noise here in Miami. It's front line. It does all kinds of sabotage in Cuba. Sugar refineries, oil plants, factories, anything. It wasn't too effective at the start, but after Fons got Walter involved in it, it really made Fidel sweat. Between the army experience Walter had at that kind of thing and the sort of brain power he had anyhow, he was brilliant at it.'

Jake said dryly: 'I see. So brilliant that some of Castro's boys decided he had to go.'

'Yes, whether you believe it or not. Oh, you make me furious. And you're a writer, too. But if something out of the ordinary – '

'Hold it, beautiful. I'm not saying things out of the ordinary can't happen. I'm just saying this thing couldn't. There's way too much stacked against it.'

'Such as?'

'Such as we both know Fons and Thoren hadn't had anything to do with each other the last few years. So if Fons was his contact with it, Thoren didn't have anything to do with this *Avispa* outfit for the last few years. Why would Castro's boys take the risk of killing him now when he hasn't been doing any damage to them all this time?'

'Because he was doing damage to them all this time. Do you think he'd put aside his idealism just because he had a quarrel with Fons? Last year alone, he met with leaders of *Avispa* at least three or four times to go over their plans. And Fons never had anything to do with that part of it. His job is only to help raise money and buy materials. He has no head at all for stuff like machinery and explosives. But Walter knew everything about them. What explosives to use, where to plant them, everything.'

'But he wasn't involved in the actual operations, was he? All he did was the planning.'

'All he did.' Nera's voice was scornful. 'You make it sound like nothing. But if you had any idea how much his plans cost Fidel – '

183

'Hell, I'm not trying to take any credit away from Thoren. But you just said he was outside the organization and only had contact with its leaders. So who sold him out to the Reds? One of those leaders?'

Nera said despairingly: 'I don't know. All I know is it's been ruinous for us since Walter died. Everyone in the leadership is afraid to meet with the others now. They all wonder if one of them isn't a Communist agent. Or it could be someone Walter knew outside of *Avispa*. Some Judas he should never have taken into his confidence.'

'From what I've heard about him, he was not a man to take anyone into his confidence about anything.'

'That's true in a way. But he might have made one little slip, and that's all that's needed. Look at me right this minute. Look at the way I'm telling you all this. Do I really know you well enough for that?'

Jake said solemnly: 'No. All you know about me is that I'm a spy sent by some insurance company to investigate Walter Thoren's death.'

Nera put a warm, lotion-scented hand over his mouth. 'Don't make fun of me. I told you I was sorry about that, didn't I? But now I think you can see how I got such ideas in my head. Blame them on what happened to Walter.'

He pushed the hand aside. 'Sweetheart, I still say your theory about him is all wet. And the only one I blame for anything is Fons. Where did he come off letting you in on this *Avispa* thing anyhow? If he had kept it to himself – '

'Fons? Let me in on it?' Nera snorted. 'Angel, I happen to be the one who involved Fons in it. I am the one whose property in Havana and Cienfuegos and Camaguey was stolen by the Reds. Half of everything I owned in the world, not even counting the rents they brought in. Fons has no blood in him. He's a gentleman. An aristocrat. That's why Papa bought him for me. So he could have aristocratic little grandchildren who would be invited to join the most exclusive clubs in Havana. After all, what more could a big, tough cop from out of the provinces want than aristocratic little grandchildren? Except that my husband was never man enough to make them. Involve me in *Avispa?* That *fuñio?* When Fidel showed what a thief and murderer he really was, all my precious husband wanted to do was sit and look sad.'

'But not you.'

'No, not me? Why? Do you dislike me for having some guts?'

'What do you think?'

Nera's hand moved over his shoulder to the nape of his neck, gripped it painfully hard for a moment, and then released it. 'If you must know, I think it's damn lucky you and I married the people we did. We're too much alike, *chino*. If we'd ever married each other, there would have been a couple of heavenly days to start with, and all the rest would have been hell on earth.'

'I'm not so sure. And I'm still not so sure you have the right slant on Thoren's death.'

'Now you're just being stubborn.'

'Because there's still too much about it I don't understand. Like, how come Thoren let himself get involved in *Avispa* at all? Did he have investments in Cuba too?'

'Mother of God, does it always have to be money? The only money that came into it was what he gave Fons for *Avispa* when it was started. He always gave generously to the movement. Then one time he asked exactly what *Avispa* was doing, what its function was – at that time it was sending small planes over the cane fields to destroy the crops – and when he found out what the operation was he was very much affected. You know what a cold man he was, but Fons told me you could see him light up with interest. He told Fons in strictest confidence that he himself had been a demolitions expert in the army during the war in Europe and believed his experience might be valuable to the movement. So at a party here one night, Fons took the chance and introduced him to some of the *Avispa* leadership. It worked out fantastically well. They'd get him the plans of whatever refineries and plants were to be destroyed, and the instructions he gave them paid off again and again. Now, how much do you think it would be worth to Fidel to get rid of someone like that?'

'Plenty,' Jake admitted. He rubbed his jaw reflectively. 'But an army man? Are you sure? Somehow, I had the impression he had served in the navy. The way he was about boats and sailing, he was a natural for sea duty.'

'Well, he said it was the army. But that hardly – '

'And he saw combat in Europe?'

'He said he did. But what difference does any of that make? Can't you keep your mind on the important thing? He was a danger to the Reds and they killed him. That's the important thing.'

Jake said: 'How about what's-his-name, your late partner, Patty Tucker's husband? Was he involved with the movement too?'

'Stewart? No. He contributed sympathy, that's all. He was very tight with his money.'

'And Patty?'

'The same. And if you're wondering if one of them betrayed Walter, I can tell you neither had the least idea he was working with *Avispa*.'

'All right then, how about Mrs Thoren? Did she know what her husband was up to?'

'Charlotte? Well, she never gave any signs of it, but she probably did. Walter had complete faith in her.'

'So there is a chance that without realizing it she was the one who – '

'Without realizing it?' Nera's voice was rich with meaning. 'That would be stupidity. Whatever else that woman is, darling, she is not stupid.'

'Hell, are you trying to tell me she deliberately connived at her husband's death?'

'No, I am not. I am only saying Charlotte is not stupid. Far from it. She is exceptionally clever and calculating.'

'And rich, too, when she collects the insurance. How much did you say it amounted to?'

'Half a million. At least, that's what Patty thinks. But Charlotte is hardly what you'd call a pauper now, even without the insurance.'

Jake said: 'All the same, if she soured on her husband for

186

some reason, she had nothing to lose and a lot to gain by turning him into Castro's hatchetmen. And according to your friend Patty, she has been acting pretty strangely nowadays. How about that business of suddenly taking off and disappearing this morning? When someone's played Judas – '

'Darling, please. Don't even talk about it.'

Jake said sympathetically: 'I know. But face the facts, Nera. The woman's running away and hiding is a bad sign. And it shows her up as a lot less rational than you'd like to believe, suddenly picking some place at random to hole up in. Clever and calculating people don't behave like that.'

'And neither did Charlotte. Take my word for it.'

'You mean she'd head straight from some special destination? She knew where she was going before she started?'

'Yes. Don't forget, darling, Fons and I were close to her and Walter for a long time. I can read her like a book. As soon as I heard about it, I could guess where she went. What's even more interesting is that it's a place Walter detested. I was there for a week with her – oh – ten or twelve years ago.'

'Some hotel?'

'No, a little house her father left her outside Belle Glade. A vacation cabin on the lake there and disgustingly primitive. The Spragues came from around there originally, and Charlotte had terribly sentimental memories of it. Walter was furious at her going there with me that week. He hated the Everglades.'

'Hated it? That's putting it pretty strong, isn't it?'

'If you'd known Walter, you wouldn't think so. He wouldn't even drive through it on the Trail to the west coast. Whenever we went holidaying to Naples or Tampa with him and Charlotte we'd have to take one of those little planes that are always cracking up in the swamps. I guess he felt about the Everglades the way I feel about snakes. He never went to the cabin that I know of.'

'But she did, now and then?'

'Once with me, two or three times by herself. She told me it was like a refuge to her, but I suppose it was hardly worth a scene with Walter. So whatever she has on her mind, she's probably there right now.'

'Sounds logical, the way you put it.'

'And what about the rest?' Nera said. 'About what happened to Walter? Doesn't that also sound logical now?'

'I guess it does.'

Nera leaned toward him. 'And I'm not psycho about it, *chino?* I was not making up wild stories?'

'No, you aren't. And weren't. But you have put me on the spot, lady. Now that I know all this, what am I supposed to do about it?'

'Nothing, for God's sake. Just keep it to yourself. But I am alone a lot, and if I need help for any reason, it's good to know you're right next door and I can call on you for it. It's very comforting to have a big brute like you next door.' She patted his belly. 'Very.'

'In that case – ' Jake said, and put an arm around her waist.

'Wait,' Nera said. She got up, walked around to the other lounge, and lay down on it on her back, robe thrown open. 'Now,' she said firmly, 'make love to me the way you did the other night. Slowly. Then I'll do it to you. There's no need to hurry, is there, darling?'

'None at all,' said Jake.

38

It was after four when he made his way back to the house. The desk lamp in the study was lit, and on the desk was a note that said *J. Maniscalco called. Very woried.* He shredded the note into small pieces and dropped the pieces into the wastepaper can. Then he sat down at the dask and dialled Magnes's number.

Magnes answered the phone in a hoarse whisper. 'Don't tell me who it is, sonny, because I already guessed. You know you're killing me with your kind of hours?'

'Well, hang on a little while longer, grandpa, because I have a lead on Mrs Thoren. I want a couple of men put on it right now. And I mean as soon as I hang up.'

'Take it easy, it'll be right now. Where's the place?'

'A cabin on the lake at Belle Glade. What lake is that? Where's Belle Glade anyhow?'

'Upstate, maybe seventy, eighty miles. Lake Okeechobee. A big one. Like an ocean.'

'All right, just get it straight that this time I want two men on the job. They'll start back to back at the lakefront close to town and move out along the lake in opposite directions. And remember to give them the licence number of that Mercedes. If and when they spot the woman, I want them to stay there out of sight and keep an eye on her.'

'Both of them?'

'Both of them,' Jake said ominously.

Magnes sighed. 'Ten thousand dollars, but the way manpower costs today, I'll be owing money before this *tzimmis* is over and done with. All right, they'll be up there before it's light. Oh yeah, and you can forget about those Meloy people you wanted me to look up. They're clean. Very respectable citizens. They couldn't be who Thoren meant in those notes.'

'Then keep looking,' Jake said. 'And I want to see you tomorrow about those notes. Two o'clock at Wolfie's.'

He went into the bedroom and switched on the lamp on the night table. Elinor was sleeping sprawled on her back, her arms flung wide, the blanket tucked under her chin and exposing her feet. She was snoring softly. With each exhalation a strand of hair which had fallen over her open mouth stirred and fluttered.

He patted the sole of her foot until the snoring broke off with a gurgle and gasp and her eyes opened.

'What did Maniscalco call about?' he asked, and Elinor said faintly, 'Nothing from Denmark about Thoren.' She cleared her throat. 'They checked all the records they could. Nothing.'

'Is that what Maniscalco is worried about?'

'Not just that. He said to tell you he was very worried about the whole situation. He sounded like it.'

'Hell, he always does.' Jake got out of the swimming trunks and into pyjama pants. 'He'd sound like that if he won the Irish Sweepstakes. And there are two *r*'s in worried.'

'I thought it looked kind of funny,' Elinor said. She pushed herself upright with one hand. With the other, she held the blanket modestly clutched to her chest. 'How did you make out with Nera? I mean, what did she have to say?'

'Plenty. I'll tell you about it tomorrow.'

'After you got me all awake like this? You might as well tell it to me now.'

He seated himself on the foot of the bed and told it to her.

Elinor said sceptically: 'She sounds like somebody on a bad trip. You believe any of that stuff?'

'Some. We know from the papers that outfits like this *Avispa* have been hitting Cuba where it hurts, so there's no reason to doubt that much of what she said. Or about Thoren having been a demolitions expert and giving them advice. But I also know for a fact that Thoren committed suicide, and it didn't have anything to do with helping burn down some sugar refineries in Cuba.'

'Jake, if you think the rest of it is true, maybe that's what the blackmailer had on him.'

'Baby, what the blackmailer had on him happened about thirty years ago, before there was any Castro. And even if I'm all wrong about it, and Thoren was threatened with exposure as a guy who helped plan sabotage in Cuba, it wouldn't have bothered him nohow. He'd figure to be voted a medal for it by Congress, not indicted.'

Elinor considered this, then nodded solemnly. 'I guess that's so. Because nobody here has any idea of all the good things Castro is doing in Cuba. All you get is lies about him.'

Jake gave her a long, contemplative look. 'Now my day is complete. I take it Fidel is one of your heroes?'

'Some. Mostly, I dig Che.'

'That figures. And I'll bet Andy's father wrote some pretty keen songs about Che to sing around the East Village.'

'Well, he didn't, but what if he did? It so happens he made the scene all over Cuba and South America. Anybody who makes the scene there digs Che.'

'Anybody? It seems to me there's a couple of hundred thousand Cuban refugees in these parts who might not.'

Elinor said heatedly: 'Because they don't know any better, that's why. And with somebody like Nera, it's because she's just sick. She is decadent. And you know why she told you all this hokey stuff? Because she's hot for you. Because she is just itching to have you think she's a poor, frightened little thing with the big, bad Commies after her.'

'Now that is a fact,' Jake said.

Elinor looked at him blankly. 'You knew about it?'

'Baby, it would be hard not to, the way she comes on so strong. If I don't show up there again pretty soon, I wouldn't be surprised to get a late night call from her, asking me to report there and protect her from some mystery man she saw near the house with a bomb in his hand. She's so damn devious and heavy-handed, all mixed together, that it's funny. At the same time, she's got a real poisonous streak in her. Like trying to score against Mrs Thoren by implying she connived at her husband's death. You can't get much more poisonous than that.'

'You can't? Well, she thinks we're married. How about getting you out of bed with your wife so you'll get in bed with her? That's not just talking poisonous.'

Jake craned his neck to see the clock on the night table. He said brightly: 'My, my, almost four-thirty. Sleepy time, and here I am, getting you all wide awake and fired up. And you have a date to do research early in the morning, too.'

'Don't be cute. If you want me to shut up, just say so.'

'Then I'm saying so.' He wearily stood up. 'Now how about moving over and giving me some room? I won't crowd you. There's enough room on this thing for four.'

'You can have it all. I'll go finish my sleepy time on the couch inside.'

Jake said flatly: 'Well, I sure as hell won't. No more waking up with a broken back for me. And I thought we came to an understanding. I wish you'd settle it in your mind, one way or the other.'

She seemed to wilt under his hard-eyed appraisal. 'I know.' Her voice was suddenly anguished. 'Jake, listen. After you went next door I was laying here and thinking about it – I mean, about where you were and what was going on there – and I kept getting sicker and sicker in the stomach and finally I had

191

to run to the bathroom and throw up. I couldn't stop. My throat is still all sore. How can I go along with any understanding that makes me throw up? It just doesn't make sense.'

'Well, what does make sense to you? Having Andy without benefit of clergy? Getting high on pot? Giving three cheers for Che? You're willing to buy that kind of stuff, but when it's me and my job you come on like some goddam stupid little Polack convent novice. That's what doesn't make sense.'

'Yes it does, the way I feel about you.'

Jake clapped a hand to his forehead. 'Now I get it. It's a plot. Sherry secretly hated me, so she sent you here in her place for revenge. If she only –'

'That's right. Stand there stinking from that fifty-dollar-a-bottle perfume and be funny about it.' Elinor awkwardly got to her knees on the bed, still clutching the blanket to her. She pointed at him. 'And you know what made me even sicker? Talking to that Maniscalco. Because what you were doing with Nera was just doing a job for him. You know what that makes him?'

'And me,' Jake said. He patted her cheek before she could draw it away. 'And you, Sister Sanctimonious. And everybody in the whole world except noble characters like Andy's father and Che. It's all right. I'll take the couch. Gladly.'

He went into the study, pulled the bedding from the closet shelf and flung it on the couch. He was tucking the sheet into place when Elinor came to the doorway, swathed in the blanket.

'Jake?' she whispered, and when he didn't answer, she said pleadingly: 'Jake, I'm sorry.'

'I'll credit it to your account. Now beat it.'

'Please, Jake, don't be like that. I have to tell you something.'

He switched out the light and stretched out on the couch, face deep in the pillow. Elinor felt her way across the darkened room until she was standing over him. 'It's something I never told any man before in my whole life, not even Andy's father. I mean, you just don't tell it to anybody who comes along. It's got to be somebody who really makes you blow your mind. So now I'm telling it to you.' She drew a long breath. 'I love you. I wish I didn't, but that's how it is. And that's what the trouble

192

is. When I even think about you I'm in a bad way. When I'm around you it's that much worse. So I open my big mouth and shove my foot into it. Half the time I want to kill you, the other half I want to climb into bed with you, and either way I keep saying something wrong. That's not my fault. Honest to God, I don't see how people ever say anything right to somebody they love. How do they?'

Jake rolled over on his back with an effort. He looked up at her through one barely open eye. 'Most people don't have your problem. They go on a romantic jag when they're kids, and then they grow up. And growing up means seeing things as they are, taking them as they come. Those who don't can make a stiff pain of themselves.'

'I know,' Elinor said mournfully. 'I guess you're still mad at me, aren't you?'

'I'm not sure. I am so dead tired right now, baby, that I can't get my feelings sorted out. But tomorrow –'

She patiently waited a long time for him to finish that before she realized he was sound asleep.

39

In the morning he delivered her to the Jordan Marsh store near the Miami exit of the causeway, gave her another twenty dollars' spending money, and added to it cab fare for the trip to the library and back to the house when she was finished with the newspaper files.

During breakfast and the drive to Miami she had managed a strained cheeriness, evidently in response to his own casual dismissal of last night's passage between them. Now she looked dismayed. 'You mean you won't pick me up? I'm supposed to go back home alone?'

'Yes. What's left of the library job won't take you all day, and I might not be home if you phone me to pick you up. Don't let it worry you. Matter of fact, you'll probably be better off that way.'

'Why will I? Jake, you're not going out looking for trouble, are you?'

'Who has to look for it? Now go on, be a good little wife. Buy some more shoes and then get on the job.' He reached across her to push open the car door, but instead of climbing out directly she turned her face up to him with a sort of hopeful expectancy, and he gave her a lingering, unhusbandly kiss. Then he drove home to catch up on the rest of his sleep. The green Chevy with the conspicuous aerial, he observed, was as close behind him on the way back as it had been on the way out.

He got to Wolfie's at two and nursed a glass of ice water at the usual back table until Magnes arrived fifteen minutes later, badly winded. Magnes was coatless, and the chest and back of his shirt showed broad patches of sweat. He wearily slid into the banquette seat beside Jake and mopped his face with a sodden handkerchief.

'Some business to be in for a heart case,' he said. 'First I got tied up settling things with this accountant from Bayside Spa. The one who has the old payroll sheet with that sweatbath rubber's name on it. It cost an arm and a leg, but now we know the rubber's name was Earl Dobbs and the home address for him on the sheet was Ocean Drive near Biscayne Street right here on the Beach. So even if the address was from three years back, I drove down there to see if maybe he was still around or if somebody remembered him. It's a boarding house from the Year One. A miserable dump. Not so many customers, but plenty of palmettoes.'

'Palmettoes?'

'Those king-sized cockroaches we got around here. The Chamber of Commerce thinks if you call them palmettoes, it don't sound so disgusting to the tourists. Anyhow, this weasel that owns the place remembered all about Dobbs. Not only that, he thinks he spotted him a few weeks ago right there in a bar on the corner. Only when he went over to say hello, the guy took one look at him and headed out of the door. So in my opinion, this was positively Dobbs, and he positively did not want to be spotted by somebody that knew him.'

'Then why does he stay around that neighbourhood?'

'He most likely don't. The weasel says he came to put in a night at the dog track, which happens to be right across the street there. He says this Dobbs was a real nut about the dog races.'

Jake said: 'What would make him doubt at all it was Dobbs?'

'Something which also fits in with our angle. Dobbs three years back, he says, was a real *dorfying*. A peasant such as you wouldn't believe. But in the bar it was no more peasant. The same *dorfying* face, but very expensive clothes. And when he ran outside he got behind the wheel of a very expensive car. So it looks like this is one sweatbath rubber who somehow came into money inside the last three years. And do I have to tell you whose money?'

Jake shook his head. 'It would be a hell of a coincidence if he wasn't our man. What else did you pick up about him?'

'He's about forty-five, fifty years old. A six-footer, but skinny like a pool cue. Big pointy nose and not much chin. Mortimer Snerd in the flesh. But to me' – Magnes abstractedly started to polish the tines of his fork with a paper napkin – 'I don't know. To me, what sticks in the mind is the dog-track betting. It gave me kind of an idea. Maybe *meshugeh*, maybe not, I happen to think not.'

'An idea about what?'

'About who Dobbs' partner could be. The big-timer who figured how to make a beautiful ten-grand-a-month blackmail out of what was maybe a two-bit shakedown. The way I see it, this could be a hood, name of Gela. An enforcer for the Mob. Not only is this real old-fashioned muscle who would break your back for laughs, he is also Frank Milan's nephew. It so happens Milan's real name is Gela.'

Jake said: 'So far, so good. How'd Dobbs' being a dog-track nut lead you to think of Gela?'

'Call it an inspiration. In the Mob, Gela's nickname is Pooch. Pooch Gela. And a pooch means a dog. So while the weasel is telling me about Dobbs and the betting, it suddenly came to me maybe Gela got such a name because he's a dog nut too. I

195

called up a contact right there from the boarding house, and he told me yes, Gela's a very big man for the dogs, that's how he got the name. So to me, at least, it ties him in with Dobbs. What do you think?'

Jake said without enthusiasm: 'I don't know. It's like putting money on a horse because of the way it's name sounds.'

'So what about Gela being Milan's nephew?'

'That's something, not a lot. If Milan's not running the black-mail, just lending a hand to someone who is, it doesn't have to be a relative. It could be anybody close to him. And Gela sounds like just another strong-arm guy. This kind of elaborate black-mail deal is way out of that class.'

Magnes put down the fork and irritably went to work on a spoon. 'What's to say a strong-arm guy can't have a little ambition, too? And maybe a little brains to go with it?'

The waitress came up. She said good-humouredly to Magnes: 'Ready to order now, Mr M., or do I wait until the end of the *shmoos?*' and left with their orders.

Magnes nodded after her. 'A lovely woman with four lovely kids, and her husband walked out on her. I located him for her, so now at least he's paying support for the kids.'

'That's very touching,' Jake said. 'Anyhow, I don't think Gela's much of a lead. It's up to you, if you want to put a man on him.'

'You mean pay for the man out of my end?'

'Why not? You said my ten grand covered all expenses.'

'I thought that was coming. Look, sonny, from this job I am already paying hospital expenses for one guy, and I got two more living it up in Belle Glade, and now I probably got to have somebody help me hunt up this *verkockteh* Earl Dobbs. When I told you all expenses I did not mean you should fix me up with a payroll like General Motors.'

Jake said with malice: 'The more you invest, the more you speed up the job, so the more you'll have left out of that ten thousand. But if you don't think a bet on Gela is worth backing – '

'All right, let's forget it.' Magnes made a sweeping gesture of dismissal. 'You think I'm making a wild guess about something, I won't argue. Now what about those notes from Thoren? Is there something I'm supposed to do about them?'

'First look them over and see if they make any sense to you.' Jake laid the copies of Thoren's three notes on the table, and Magnes, silently mouthing their syllables, studied them in turn. Then he said: 'This one makes some sense. Thermos, rations, cigars, charts – it's like a list of what to take on the boat when he went sailing that day. These other two definitely look like code. You want my opinion, you'll give them to a code man to work on.'

Jake said: 'That happens to be my opinion, too. But can you get me a first-class man around here? And not somebody on the cops.'

'Sure.' Magnes folded the notes and held them poised. 'Out of your end.'

'Out of my end,' Jake said.

Magnes tucked the notes into his shirt pocket. 'Code,' he said sourly. 'That's all we need to stall the works real good. And we don't even know how much we're on the right track so far with anything.'

Jake said: 'Take it easy. Last night I had another little talk with the señora next door and heard enough to know we're on the right track.' He recounted the significant parts of the talk, and concluded: 'So a lot of maybes are sure things now. Like Thoren committing the crime in the Everglades thirty years ago, and Dobbs witnessing it. That's why Thoren wouldn't even drive through the Everglades. Because it was the scene of the crime, and he might run into Dobbs there. Another thing is that he lied when he told Ortega he had been an army demolitions expert who saw action in Europe. Mrs Ortega shook me up with that at first, and then I realized Thoren must have been lying. He never saw action in Europe.'

'Because they can't turn up a service record for him? Maybe it was under a different name.'

'Under any name. He was here in Miami by the middle of 1942. We didn't get an army into Europe until long after that.'

Magnes said: 'Suppose it wasn't our army? Suppose it was maybe the Danish army?'

197

'If it was, he wouldn't have seen action either. In case you don't remember it, the Nazis walked in and took over Denmark without a fight.'

'I can see you're a regular history book, *tokkeh*. So what does it all mean in a practical way?'

'It means for sure Thoren lied in the insurance application about that big L-shaped scar on his back being a war wound. I'll swear to it now he got that wound back in the Everglades about thirty years ago – twenty-seven or -eight years ago, to be more exact – and Earl Dobbs was there to see him get it. One thing that's been bothering me all along was how somebody who hadn't seen Thoren since 1942 could recognize him so easily. But when Thoren laid down on that rubbing table, and Dobbs got a close look at the scar, he must have had the past come right up and hit him in the face.'

Magnes nodded thoughtfully. 'It adds up. It adds up.'

'It does. But I have to know who Thoren really was and exactly what crime he committed. That's what'll give me clout in making Dobbs co-operate when the time comes. Once he believes I have the goods on him and will turn him in for blackmail unless he backs me up in getting Mrs Thoren to sign a release, he'll co-operate.'

Magnes raised his eyebrows in inquiry. 'And the silent partner? The big-timer who Frank Milan is doing favours for? Even if it turns out he ain't a natural-born murderer like Pooch Gela, how glad will he be to get dished out of two hundred grand?'

'I know. So the trick is to hold both him and Milan to a stand-off until the release is signed. After that I won't be sticking around to hear their complaints. If you're smart, you'll clear out of town for a while, too, after it's all over.'

The waitress placed their sandwiches before them, and Magnes regarded his without appetite. He remarked: 'I went once to this Serpentarium place down around Homestead. That's where this guy grabs these cobras and rattlesnakes and holds them down by the neck, and this good-looking girlie – all the girlies there are very good-looking, only with a scientific head on them – she puts a jar by the snake's mouth so the guy

198

can make it squirt poison into it. All of a sudden I got this feeling I'm right down there on the snake farm again, only now I'm the one holding the snake by the neck.'

'You knew what you were getting into from the beginning,' Jake pointed out.

'Which shows I'm not as smart as I look. You got somebody tailing you all the time?'

'Sure. Guy in a green Chevy.'

'Mine is a green Olds. You think maybe green is like school colours for Frank Milan?'

Jake said: 'It's the colour of money, so why not? Did the guy in the Olds follow you down to Dobbs' old boarding house?'

'He followed me there and back here, and right now he's probably playing two-handed pinochle with your guy. This is Miami Beach, sonny, not Miami. A small town with water all around it. If somebody wants to tail you and don't care if you know it, he can do it like watching a baby in a crib.' Magnes pressed his denture tighter into his upper jaw with a thumb and took a bite of sandwich. 'So now I'll ask you something. How about our girlie?'

'Our girlie?'

'Your girlie, my girlie, when you blew your cover to Mrs Thoren she's no more use here. So how about paying her off and shipping her back to New York? Around here, she is only a sitting duck.'

'I'll think about it.'

'What you'll be thinking about, sonny, is how nice it is to have a beautiful *zoftik* little blondie doll climbing all over you like a puppy dog whenever you snap your fingers. I don't even blame you. *Ahlevai*, I should only be young again. But in this town if you want to get laid, any fellow looks like you and with folding money in his pocket can take his pick. Amateurs or professionals. He don't have to go depend on some dopey, big-eyed kid who, the way things shape up, would be better off back in New York from the start.'

'Now you sound just like Mrs Ortega,' Jake said.

40

He made sure the green Chevy was following when he pulled away from the restaurant and headed uptown along Collins. At 21st Street, he parked in the lot across from the Miami Beach library, a small, handsomely designed cultural oasis surrounded by gaudy restaurants and shabby strip-tease joints. Small as it was, its stacks turned up a fat volume on cryptography, and he spent an hour trying to match the curious system used in Thoren's notes against likely samples in the text before he gave up the job as hopeless.

Then, the green Chevy always in his rear-view mirror, he once more headed uptown on Collins, this time on a test run which carried him to Haulover Cut, the northernmost limit of the island, and back again. Going and coming, he tried every trick in the book to cut loose from his shadow, but without any luck.

He got home close to dinnertime and found Elinor already there, hard at work in the kitchen, her transistor on the table blasting away deafeningly. He switched it off. 'I could hear this thing from the driveway. With all that noise going on, baby, you could have the cavalry gallop through the door and never know it.'

Elinor said apologetically: 'I didn't think of it that way. I left it on loud so as people would know somebody's here, and they wouldn't come sneaking in. And you'll have to wait a little for supper. I didn't heat it up yet, because I didn't know when you'd be back.' She heaved her shoulders almost up to her ears and let them slump again. 'If you'd be back.'

'I'll always be back. Did you find anything at all in those newspapers about a ship's officer disappearing off a boat here?'

'Nothing. Jake, I was wondering about that ship's officer bit. If Nera said he was an army man –'

'He wasn't.'

'Oh. Well, anyhow I went all the way back to the beginning of May, 1942, and there was nothing there. Where were you today? Did they find Mrs Thoren yet?'

'I was with Magnes. No, they didn't find Mrs Thoren yet, but Magnes found out who the guy was first started blackmailing Thoren. Redneck by the name of Earl Dobbs.'

'Well, all right,' Elinor said.

'Except for one little thing. Magnes is being tailed full-time by one of Frank Milan's boys, and still he headed straight for the boarding house Dobbs used to stay at. So now they know we've worked our way right up to Dobbs. They'll probably try to hide him out the same as they did Mrs Thoren. Not that I blame Magnes too much for it. It's tough to shake off anyone tailing you around this town unless you cross over to the Miami side. I tried it just now, so I know.'

'You mean somebody's tailing you full-time too?'

'It's nothing to turn green about, baby. The opposition wants to keep in touch with developments, that's all. They know the case is set for trial in a couple of weeks and Guaranty would rather pay up than stand trial, so they just want to make sure there are no surprises coming up to spoil the party.'

Elinor put her hands on her hips. She said menacingly: 'But there are surprises coming up for them, aren't there? You might as well know, Dekker, anything happens to you I won't just turn green. I am going to have real loud Polack hysterics.'

Jake laughed. He sat down on a kitchen chair and motioned to her. 'Come on over here.'

She gave him a speculative look, then walked over to him. He pulled her down on his knee and put an arm around her. She sat there stiffly for a moment, then relaxed against him. 'You like me today, don't you?' she said.

'Why not? You're a likeable kind of girl today.'

Elinor said placidly: 'I'm a sellout, that's what I am. A real fink. Because you know what you are? You're Establishment. I always had a feeling some day somebody would come along – maybe like John Lennon or Paul Newman – who'd make me completely blow my mind. I mean, totally atomize me. I never thought it would be somebody Establishment.'

'They're not Establishment?'

'No. Because it's not if you get way up there that counts. It's how you relate to the world.'

'I see,' Jake said. 'And I relate to it all wrong.'

'Yes. But as long as you relate to me all right, I don't mind. That's why I'm a fink. You know what I bought with that money you gave me this morning?'

'A hair shirt?'

Elinor giggled. 'No, but you're close. Come take a look.'

She led him to the bedroom and pointed at the box on her dresser done up in Jordan Marsh wrapping. 'Now what do you think it is?'

'A black lace nightgown?'

'This time you're not even close. It's for you. It's a present.'

It was a handsome Pucci sports shirt. 'This is one hell of a present,' Jake said. 'Baby, don't you know it's dangerous giving members of the Establishment presents like this in a bedroom?'

He was on the bed mouth-to-mouth with her, his hand moving slowly up her thigh under her skirt, when the phone in the study rang, and Elinor said: 'Aw, that's not even funny.'

The caller was Magnes, his voice a hoarse whisper. 'Dekker, I'm down here in Coral Gables. In a drugstore. I just got done with that code man I told you about. You want me to read you what's in those notes?'

'You mean he doped them out already?'

'While I stood there. The only thing slowed him up a little was he started laughing so hard.'

'Laughing?' Jake said. 'What the hell are you getting at, Magnes? What's in those notes?'

'What I'm getting at, sonny, is when I told you Thoren never left anything in writing about being blackmailed, I was right. Your luck this code man not only handled such jobs for the FBI for ten years and he's a big criminology professor down here at the university, he also sails a boat all the time around here. And he says these two notes are Coast Guard chart corrections, line for line. They give them out so you shouldn't crack up your boat. Like take this first line, *m ltd w b 2* and so on. From what he wrote down here, it means Miami lighted whistle buoy number two and Miami main channel buoy number three and lighted bell buoy number four were changed to flash every six seconds with a one-second flash after. And Meloy ain't anybody you can call on the phone, it's the name of a channel you go sailing on. It's all like that. Chart corrections, only Thoren copied them down in abbreviations. You hear, *shtarker?* Because for all my chasing around with them and making myself look like a fool, these notes got nothing to do with blackmail. But Mr Earl Dobbs got plenty to do with it, so now I'll go find him for you.'

With that, he hung up.

41

'What's wrong?' Elinor said.

'Nothing.' Jake stood looking at her abstractedly. 'Except that your skirt's all twisted around.'

She twisted it back into place. 'Sometimes you don't have as much of a poker face as you think. What did he tell you about those notes?'

Jake said: 'Seems that they don't have anything to do with Thoren's making a blackmail payment the day he was killed.' He dug his fingers through his hair. 'I don't get it. The envelope I found along with them is dated March sixth. It was delivered to him on the seventh, the day he died. It must have had something in it.'

He abruptly sat down at the desk and flung open the drawer which contained the packet of cardboard scraps from Thoren's wastepaper can. He spilled the scraps on the desk. Minute bits of slick-surfaced grey cardboard, with a black imprint showing on them here and there.

Elinor said: 'You going to work to that stuff now? What about supper?' She hastily added. 'Not that it matters.'

'No, it doesn't. I'll tell you when I'm ready.'

The job took him longer at the outset than it should have, because, confusingly, some of the lettering as it emerged seemed to be printed sideways. Once that became a clue instead of a complication, things went faster. In the end, what he had lying before him, neatly taped together, was a fifty-cent ticket issued by the Miami Beach Kennel Club for one admission to a grandstand reserved seat. That sideways printing at each end of the ticket indicated that the seat was Number 9 in Row P, Section D. There was also the notice that the ticket was good only on that date for which it was issued, but there was no date given. However, there was the information that this was *Day of Racing 55*.

Jake dialled the track's ticket office. It took the woman at the other end of the line time to understand that he wasn't applying for a refund on a ticket. 'I'm sorry, sir, it's only good for the racing date shown on it. We can't make refunds or exchanges for it after that date.'

'I know that. All I'm trying to find out is what the calendar date was for your fifty-fifth racing day.'

'Oh, the calendar date.' There was a long silence. 'It was March seventh. Is that all?'

'It's enough,' Jake said. 'March seventh. Thank you, lady. And may the Lord continue to shed his bounties on you.'

In the darkness of the living room he found Elinor on the couch, legs curled under her, watching a drama being played out soundlessly on the big television set. He said: 'Set busted?'

'No.' The light from the screen gave her eyes a catlike luminescence when she raised her head to look at him. 'I was worried the noise would bother you. Anyhow, I was only watching to see if any friends of mine showed up in the commercials. I wish I could get some commericals to do. Those residuals are great. How'd you make out with your picture puzzle?'

'All right.' He sat down beside her, and she immediately pushed up tight against him and drew his arm around her waist. She said: 'I know you. When you say all right like that, it means a lot better than all right.'

'Maybe it does this time. There was a ticket to the dog track mailed to Thoren in that envelope. I have an idea that told him when and where to make the blackmail payoff. Probably those payments were always made at whatever dog track was operating at the time. There's three or four around here split up the season among them.'

Elinor said doubtfully: 'A payoff in a place like that? I mean, with so many people around?'

'I know, but that crowd might have been Dobbs' best protection. I'm positive Thoren would have killed him if he could have caught him alone somewhere.'

'I guess he would. Not bad, finding all that out from one little ticket.'

'And more. Magnes told me today who he thought Dobbs' partner was. That one little ticket says he might have been right.'

'Who did he say? I'll bet that big slob Holuby.'

'No, a dog-racing fan by the name of Pooch Gela. Very close to Frank Milan. And a professional gunman. That ticket of Thoren's puts him right into the middle of the picture.'

Elinor gently rubbed the crown of her head back and forth against his jaw. 'Even so, better somebody like that than a monster like Holuby.'

'You're going by appearances, which could be a mistake. Holuby's not as tough as he looks. It's probably the opposite with this guy Gela.'

'Holuby is so as tough as he looks. Only you're even tougher, so how would you know. Do you still like me?'

Jake tightened his arm around her. 'I still like you.'

'I turn you on, don't I?'

'You turn me on.'

'I'm glad. Jake, you remember where we left off when Magnes called up?'

'I don't have to, because I'd just as soon start all over again from the beginning. But not now. First I want that supper you owe me, and then I'd like to get to the dog track before the last race and look it over.'

'Yes, sir. I can go along, can't I?'

'No, sweetheart, what you can do is stay here in case Magnes calls. It won't take me long.' He thrust his arm out into the pallid light from the television tube and studied his wristwatch. 'It's not nine yet. I'll be back in plenty of time for the eleven o'clock news.'

Elinor said reproachfully: 'That's not what I want you to have on your mind at eleven o'clock. All right, come on in the kitchen and talk to me while I get things ready.'

She stood up and hauled him to his feet. After she had switched on the room light he went over to the television set and turned it off. It was as if his finger on that button triggered a chain reaction. He was facing the French doors that were wide open to the Florida room beyond. The windows of the Florida room offering a view of the bay were not solid panes of glass, but horizontal strips of it, each slightly overlapping the next. In lightning succession, he saw a strip of glass disintegrate, glittering splinters of it flying inward, heard the high-pitched whine of an angry hornet fill the room for an instant, and, superimposed on that sound, the distinct crack of a rifle.

'Get down!' he yelled, and when Elinor still stood there in frozen bewilderment he hit her with a flying block, shoulder into belly. She went down under him with a gasp, her face agonized. He rolled clear of her, and before she could make any move, threw an arm across her to hold her down. Straining to catch her breath, flat on her back, she was in a perfect position to see the next bullet slam through the top of the framed Van Gogh print on the far wall. Shards of glass spilled from the frame, the picture swung wildly back and forth on its wire and then followed the glass fragments to the floor with a crash. The hole in the wall behind it now showed clearly. It was a large shapeless hole with a thread of plaster sifting from it like a fine talcum powder.

Elinor stared at it. 'They're shooting at us,' she said as if trying hard to comprehend this. Her voice rose. 'They're really shooting at us!' With a sudden convulsive strength she pulled free of his restraining arm and lurched to her feet. 'Bathroom,' she said between her clenched teeth, and headed for it before he could grab her.

He swore, and crouching low, got to the wall switch and flicked off the room light. Then, still in a crouch and holding as close to the wall as the furniture permitted, he made his way to the Florida room. There was no other shot. There was what might have been the drone of a high-powered boat moving out of range on the bay.

He opened the door to the back yard an inch, lay down on the floor, and from that position, reached out and pulled the door wide open. By the light Milt Webb had strung up he had a shadowy view of the yard. Nothing menacing showed there. He stood up and cautiously went outside. Saturday-night company was being entertained at both the Webb house and the Ortegas'. Bright lights showed in the windows of both houses, and the company, soundless as the picture Elinor had been watching on television, could be seen having a time of it.

He went back into the house, closed and locked the door, and drew the drapes over the windows. In the living room, he closed the French doors and threw their finger bolt. When he turned on the light again he saw for the first time that the door frame itself was made of metal. Centred in it overhead was a raw gouge, a gleaming metallic channel. The first bullet had hit there and then ricocheted. He searched around the floor until he found it. It looked to be a .30–30 and still had most of its shape. Climbing on a chair, he gouged the other out of the wall with his pocket knife. This one was almost shapeless.

Standing there, he became aware of the sounds from the bathroom. When he opened its door he saw Elinor kneeling prayerfully before the toilet bowl. He squatted beside her, his hand clamped tight against her sweat-soaked forehead as she went into another spasm of retching. As soon as the spasm had passed she pushed the hand aside. 'Go away. Please. I don't want you here now.'

'Don't be silly,' Jake said.

It was another bad ten minutes before she got the spasms under control. She emerged from them with her face red and swollen, eyes puffy, hair lank with sweat. He sat her down on the toilet lid and did what he could to make facial repairs with a damp washcloth. 'Better now?' he asked.

'I think so,' she said weakly. She gingerly prodded her lower ribs. 'It hurts here, but that's where you banged into me.'

'If you'd hit the floor when I yelled, I wouldn't have had to. When you hear a gun go off like that, baby, remember the best place to be is flat on the floor. And if you want to heave up, do it right there on the carpet.'

'I didn't want to. I couldn't help it.' Her eyes opened very wide, the lids fluttering. 'Jake, they were really shooting at us. They were trying to kill us.'

'Not if you go by the angle those bullets took. They were deliberately aimed high. Didn't I tell you the last thing they want is to knock me off so Guaranty would have something to take to the cops? And have a beautiful excuse for stalling on the payment to Mrs Thoren?'

'That's what you want me to believe. Maybe you even believe it yourself. But I don't. If you're staying on this job, I want you to call the cops in. You have to. Honest to God, Jake, what's wrong with doing it when things get this hairy?'

'You shock me, sweetheart. A member of Che's fan club talking about the fuzz so tenderly?'

'I don't care. I don't want you dead, that's all. Do you know what I thought when I saw that picture come down off the wall? It was wild. All I could think was it might have been you with a hole through you laying there dead, and we never even made it with each other!'

'Always to wonder, never to know.'

'All right, if you want to be funny about it, I'll call the cops myself.' She stood up unsteadily and made her way into the bedroom.

Jake followed, and when she sat down on the edge of the bed and picked up the phone on the night table, he shook his head at her. 'Don't do it, baby. Now or any time. Don't even let the thought enter your mind.'

'But why?' she demanded fiercely. 'Mrs Thoren knows who you are now, so what difference does it make if they know?'

'Put that phone down.'

She hesitated, then unwillingly obeyed. Jake sat down beside her and clasped her hand in his, fingers interlaced. He said: 'Listen to me. I get my cut of that insurance money when I personally turn over to Maniscalco a release signed by Mrs Thoren. That's my contract with him. I don't get a dime if the police move in on this and dig up enough so that they change the official report on Thoren's death from accident to suicide, because then Maniscalco won't need a release any more. It's as simple as that.'

208

'No, it isn't. Because if you've done all the work – '

'Maniscalco's not paying me for my work, he's paying me for that release. And nothing would make him happier than to see this thing settled by the police, with me left out in the cold. Hell, he's a company hero if I pull it off for a fifty per-cent cut and save Guaranty a hundred thousand. Picture the kind of hero he'd be if he could save them the whole two hundred thousand.'

Elinor said slowly and emphatically: 'I don't care about him. I just don't want anything to happen to you.' She dug her nails into his palm. 'Look at me. The last time I threw up I was about ten years old, and I ate too much junk in the movies. Now I'm like doing it all the time on account of you. On account of your crazy job saving money for a rotten insurance company. I always thought when somebody fell bang in love the trip was all guitars and rosebuds. So just look at me.'

'I'm looking,' Jake said, 'Well, what do you want to do about it? Do you want to go back to New York right now?'

Her hand suddenly went limp in his. 'Didn't you tell me that could be dangerous for my kid?'

'I have a summer place out on Long Island. I think it could be handled so you and your mother and the kid move in there without anybody knowing about it until this is all over. And with the whole three thousand that's coming to you.'

'Is that where you'll go after you're done here?' Elinor said. She was watching his face closely. 'I mean, if I'm staying out there, should I kind of expect you to show up after a while?'

'To keep the three of you company? I'm afraid not.'

'Suppose they went back to the city, and it was me alone?'

'Hell, that's a long way off, sweetheart. We've got plenty of time to hash it out.'

'Jake, it's not a long way off. Maybe I shouldn't even tell you this, but what scared me almost as much as all that shooting was the way you walked in on me before, so happy about figuring out what that dog-track ticket meant. About the way the job was getting done. All of a sudden I could see the curtain start to come down, and for the big finish we're saying goodbye to each other at Kennedy. But it shouldn't be that way. Not for us. And all I'm asking you to do is say so.'

'Baby, sometimes you are too simple to believe. Don't you know how easy it would be for me to look you straight in the eye and say it and not mean a word of it.'

'I don't care. Say it anyhow.'

He stood up. 'What I'll say anyhow is that there's no racing here Sundays. If I don't get over to that track damn soon, I'll have to wait till Monday to take a look at it.'

Elinor said stubbornly: 'Then at least tell me one thing. Would you feel sorry if I did go back to New York right now? Honest to God sorry?'

'Oh, for chrissake, you're still being simple about it.'

'Jake, please answer yes or no.' With her eyes glistening too brightly, she looked ready to burst into tears. 'Wouldn't you feel rotten if I went away? Don't you want me to be here with you?'

He stood there gnawing his lip in indecision. 'Yes,' he said at last.

She sniffled a few times, a sort of hiccupping sniffle, then wiped her nose with the back of her hand. 'So all I have to do,' she said, 'is just learn to keep my stomach under control.'

42

They bolted a stand-up supper of cold leftovers and beer, and even with her mouth full she managed to make it clear that there had to be one small change of plan. Daytime was different, but hell or high water she was not going to sit alone at night waiting for him in any house full of fresh bullet holes. If Magnes called and didn't get an answer, he'd just keep calling until he did. So what difference could it make if she went along to the track too?

In the end, she was with Jake when he went out to the car and discovered that both its front tyres had gone flat. And each

210

tyre, he saw on close investigation with a flashlight, bore the mark of the blade that had been driven into its whitewall.

He stood up and dusted his knees. 'Looks like somebody keeps trying to tell us something, doesn't it?'

'That's how it looks,' Elinor said in a strained voice, then quickly assured him: 'It's all right. You can see I'm not letting it get to me.'

'That's my girl.' Jake prodded a deflated tyre with his toe. I'm one spare short, but there's no use calling the garage now, if I want to get to the track before it shuts up. We'll take a cab.'

He phoned for one, giving the dispatcher Milt Webb's name and address, then waiting with Elinor on the curb at the foot of Webb's driveway. In the cab, he had her sit low when they crossed the bridge to the Beach and tried to keep his own head out of sight. He got a glimpse of the green Chevy parked near the corner of North Bay Road. As far as he could make out when he risked looking back through the rear window a few blocks later, it was not following the cab.

The Miami Beach dog track was located at the very foot of the island, bordering the ocean. It looked from the outside as coldly utilitarian and downright ugly as an old-fashioned factory, and its enclosed stand, cheerless as a public garage, littered with torn-up betting tickets, crumpled newspapers, and refuse from the refreshment counters, wasn't much better.

A mixed crowd filled it. Elderly whites, the kind of seedy, worn-out people who made up much of the South Beach neighbourhood around here, a sizable number of Negroes, more than Jake had seen gathered together any place since landing at Miami International, and a sprinkling of Latins, most of them youthful. The prevailing mood, by and large, seemed to be glum.

One whole side of the grandstand was sections of seats with a view of the track through ceiling-high windows. Jake drifted in that direction, and Elinor, thrusting her arm through his, said: 'Man, this is like a funeral. You mean these people are supposed to be having fun?'

'Well, everyone to his own misery, but I'll have to admit it's a lot grimmer than the horse tracks I've been supporting.

Maybe it's got something to do with dogs looking so sad to start with. And this sure as hell feels like poor people's country.'

'What are we supposed to be looking for in it?'

'Section D, Row P, seat nine. But not so anybody would know we're looking for it.'

He found Section D at the head of the stretch near the entrance to the building where they had come in. Row P was its topmost row, separated from the floor of the stands by a waist-high iron railing behind it, and seat 9 was in the middle of it. That seat and the one next to it were the only empties in the row.

Jake positioned himself at the railing not far from them, ostensibly studying through the window the tote boards on the track's infield. One board listed the odds on every possible quiniella combination. The other, which listed mutual odds, also had a timer on it which indicated that five minutes remained before the eleventh race. On the track, handlers in white yachting caps and green shirts were parading muzzled greyhounds in double file to some syrupy tune coming over the public address system.

Elinor leaned close to him and said in an undertone: 'You think Dobbs and Gela are using those seats? That they're around here somewhere?'

'Dobbs might be. Not Gela. He'd never keep company with Dobbs in public.'

'So what'll you do? Just wait?'

'I'll wait. And meanwhile try to work out an interesting problem you brought up.'

'Me?' said Elinor. She sounded rather pleased with the idea.

'You. Remember you asked why they'd use a public place like this to pick up the money?'

'Uh-huh. And you told me Thoren would have killed Dobbs if he could, so the safest thing was to pick up the money right in the middle of a crowd.'

'And I still say it. I'm sure Dobbs was stuck with all the dirty work, like mailing the tickets and picking up the money, while Gela was the silent partner. But look at the way this place is lit up everywhere like Broadway at show time. And Dobbs is supposed to be a standout physically. Very tall and skinny. After he took the money and walked away, it would be a cinch to follow him and knock him off sooner or later.'

'And not get caught?' Elinor said.

'And not get caught. If I was in Thoren's shoes, I could have done it a dozen times over in all those years he was being bled. Right outside on the street where there's not much light or in the parking lot across the way where it's really dark. Or tailed him around town until I got him alone somewhere. Do you mean to tell me that in all those years Thoren never once found the chance to do that? Suicide was his only out?'

'Well, I suppose when he had the chance he didn't have the nerve to go through with it.'

'Which is what I've been thinking,' Jake said. 'The only trouble being that it doesn't sound like Walter Thoren.'

Elinor said tartly: 'So now you – ' Suddenly she turned on a rapturous, wholly inane smile, and said through it: 'Jake, don't look around. That man over there in back of you is the one works for the Thorens.'

'Raymond? Did he see us?'

'He must have. He's talking to somebody, but he's staring right this way.'

'The one he's talking to. Is it a tall, skinny white man?'

'Just the opposite. Black and beautiful. And she is not a man, that's for sure. Jake, do you think he's mixed up in this?'

Jake put his arm around her waist and turned her in the direction of the track. He pointed at the tote boards. 'Maybe. Maybe not. Either way, what you do now is look at those boards out there and pick something to bet on. The sellers' windows are across the floor. I'll wait here for you while you buy the ticket.'

'But what ticket? I don't even know what it means on that board. That quiniella-odds bit. And right now I'd just as soon not – '

Jake cut in sharply: 'Will you stop being so goddam thick-headed? You're supposed to be an actress, aren't you? Well, start acting. And a quiniella's when you try to pick the first two dogs across the line. There's eight dogs running, so go over to one of those windows and give the man any pair of different numbers from one to eight. And this money.'

He was handing her the two dollars when the deep, almost theatrical baritone behind him said: 'Evening, Mr Dekker. Mrs Dekker. Didn't know you went in for the dogs.'

Jake turned. In contrast to the largely dour, casually clad throng around them, Raymond was impeccably clad in jacket and tie and wore the expression of someone well content with the way things have been going for him. Jake said: 'Why, hello, Raymond. No, this is our first time. Mrs Dekker thought she'd like to try her luck,' and Elinor instantly followed by making a long face and saying dolefully, 'Only I'm not having any, Mr Beaudry. I hope you're doing better than I am.'

'I can't complain, Mrs Dekker. You betting quiniellas or mutuals?'

'Quiniellas.'

Raymond said with fatherly kindness: 'Well, now, I put my money only on the nose, regular style. You try it my way and see what happens.'

Jake prodded Elinor hard in the spine with his thumb. 'And you'd better get your next bet down now, dear. That clock says the windows close in a couple of minutes.'

He watched her move off across the floor. Others watched too, some lowering their programmes to focus on her as she passed, and Raymond said disdainfully: 'No manners at all. See a nice young lady go by and look at her popeyed that way.' He cocked his head at Jake. 'You don't mind my saying it, Mr Dekker, the clubhouse section is where you ought to take Mrs Dekker. The Terrace Lounge.' The voice was warmly solicitous. 'You try it next time. Good food and drinks while you watch the action. And the right kind of people.'

Jake said: 'Now, that's what I call a strong recommendation. Or could it be more than a recommendation?'

Raymond looked politely inquiring. 'Beg pardon?'

'I was asking whether you were advising me to use the clubhouse after this, or strongly advising me not to use the grandstand. Like the difference between the positive approach and the negative, if you know what I mean.'

Raymond knit his brow. 'I'm afraid not, Mr Dekker. Seems to me like six of one, half a dozen of the other.'

Jake looked him over, then amiably said: 'I guess it is at that. And judging from the dinner last night, you know your food and drink. I'm only sorry Mrs Thoren wasn't able to enjoy it with us. By the way, did she get in touch with the family today? Let them hear how she's feeling? Mrs Dekker and I have been a little worried about her.'

Raymond's face went completely expressionless. 'That's nice of you, Mr Dekker. No, she didn't call. If she does, I'll tell her you asked about her.'

'I'll be glad to tell her myself. Mrs Dekker's been thinking she'd like to send a card or a little gift, but we don't have the address. If you knew it offhand – '

'Sorry, but I don't, Mr Dekker.' There was no note of regret in the voice. There was a veiled contempt in it.

Jake took out his billfold. With deliberation he partly extracted a ten-dollar bill from it, then replaced the ten and drew out a twenty. He folded the bill in half lengthways and slipped it between his fingers in conspicuous view. 'It's too late to put anything down on this race,' he said, 'but it would be worth something to get a good tip on the next. Or on any kind of winner you can think of, dogs or otherwise.'

The veiled eyes briefly took in the offering. Then Raymond dug into his hip pocket and brought out an immense roll of bills. He opened it, and with the same deliberation Jake had exercised, he peeled two twenties from it. He held them out. 'Now that is a coincidence, Mr Dekker. Enough to make you wonder. Here I was, just getting ready to ask you the same thing.'

A bell rang, and the stand was suddenly plunged into darkness, although the track itself remained brilliantly lit by floodlights. Handlers ran from the starting boxes into which they had just placed the dogs and scattered to posts along the inside rail. Raymond said softly in Jake's ear: 'You bet on the rabbit, Mr Dekker. You never lose that way,' and Jake was aware that he was gone.

'There goes Rusty!' bellowed a voice over the loudspeakers,

215

the toy rabbit on its rod skittered past the boxes, and the dogs hurled themselves after it in a maniac burst of speed. Jake leaned over the railing and looked along Row P. Outlined against the glare of floodlights were two forms occupying the hitherto empty seats, and one of them looked to be tall and skinny. There was a rising sound of urgent, pleading voices around him, an explosive yell, and the lights went on again inside the stand. The couple occupying those seats were women. Housewife types. The tall, skinny one wore curlers in her greying hair.

Jake turned, trying to catch sight of Elinor in the crowd. Then he saw her pushing her way toward him. Finally in the clear, she came up to him in a rush. 'Jake, are you all right?'

'Sure.' He pointed at the betting ticket clutched in her hand. 'A winner?'

'No. Where's Raymond?'

'He took off when the lights went out. What did you think when they went out? Did you catch on?'

'I caught on to a couple of things.' Her tone was resentful. 'Like, you wanted me to go make a bet so I wouldn't be around you in case anything hairy got going. Isn't that so?'

'Maybe it is, but I'm talking about those lights.'

'I know. I thought of it right away when they went out. I even thought how it must have been fixed for Thoren to sit in the last row. Soon as it went dark, Dobbs just leaned over that railing and took the money. Then he had time to go get lost before the lights went on again.'

'Especially,' Jake pointed out, 'if Thoren's planted in the middle of the row where he can't get out easily himself. And Dobbs most likely passed the money to Gela right there and got his cut later on. I'm taking for granted Gela had brains enough to always stay in the background. I doubt Thoren even knew Dobbs had any partner.'

Elinor said: 'So it was just the two of them. For sure, Raymond didn't have anything to do with it, did he?'

'Not for that sure. He is a much smarter cat than he'd like The Man to believe. And he's carting around a roll of bills that would sink him if he fell into deep water.'

216

'So what?' Elinor said defensively. 'Other people carry a lot of money on them too, don't they?'

'Other people?'

'You know what I mean. White people. I bet you wouldn't be so suspicious of them just because they had a lot of money in their pocket.'

'Sweetheart, if you're accusing me of judging Raymond too harshly because he's coloured, forget it. He could be king of the honkies, and I'd still wonder why he came over for a friendly chat when I know damn well he's not that fond of me. Besides, you're the one who made a big thing of mistrusting him when you saw him looking our way. Now, all of a sudden – '

'Because I had an insight. As soon as you started talking to him, I knew I was wrong to make a big thing of it. I was like demonstrating very deep-rooted prejudice. Only I didn't realize it until I heard how you sounded.'

Jake said: 'Now I am like confused. How did I sound? Like George Wallace?'

'You called him Raymond. His name happens to be Mr Beaudry.'

Jake said: 'I stand corrected. In return, you ought to quit thinking a man might not have brains and nerve enough to be part of a highly successful blackmail ring because he happens to be coloured. That's what I call very deep-rooted prejudice.'

Elinor looked blank. Then she said uncertainly: 'No, it isn't. I mean, you're just turning it upside down.'

'Right side up.' He removed the ticket from her hand and tossed it away. 'No use taking a losing ticket home. Now let's get going.'

'It was only half losing.' Elinor pointed at the odds boards on the track. 'I picked number three and number five on account of your age, and the five won. Only the three came in way back, and they don't pay for half right, do they?'

'Not on quiniellas.' He took her arm, but she held back.

'Jake, it says only six minutes till the next race. Can't we stay for it? I think three and five'll be lucky this time. I'd like to put one more bet on it.'

'Not with my money, sweetheart. I don't have the courage of your convictions.'

'All right, then I'll buy my own ticket. Anyhow, that way I keep it all if I win.'

They went outside after she bought the ticket, and watched the race from the rail near the finish line. A fine dirt raised by the pack sprayed the railbirds as the greyhounds went under the wire, number five in the lead, number three lagging far in the rear, and as Elinor brushed the dirt from her shoulders she said bitterly: 'No-good, rotten dogs.'

'Now you sound like an expert,' Jake said.

43

He woke to the sound of a torrential rain beating against the bedroom windows, looked at his wristwatch and saw it was twelve noon. Then he became aware that Elinor in her sleep had not only gathered his entire share of the blanket around her, but had, by some legerdemain, managed to extract his pillow from beneath his head and plant it over her own. She was sleeping like that now, head sandwiched between both pillows.

He got into pyjama pants and slippers, went into the study and dialled Magnes's number. No answer. He had better luck with a garage, after trying several, and arranged for replacements for the Jag's front tyres. The arrangements settled, he phoned Magnes again. Still no answer.

In the Florida room, he found the curtain against the broken window sodden, the floor beneath it a spreading pool of water. He taped a bath sheet over the window, mopped up the pool, and swept up the fragments of glass. The bullet hole in the living-room wall he covered with a large, ornately framed Boucher print from the bedroom, and finished off his house-keeping by cleaning up the glass and plaster on the floor. The torn and shattered remains of the Van Gogh he disposed of in the waste bin.

One o'clock. He made another futile try at getting Magnes on the phone, then showered and shaved and went back to bed, where Elinor was still asleep with her head in the pillow sandwich. When he reclaimed his pillow and planted it under his head, she stirred a little. Then she said, barely exhaling the words: 'What time?'

'Almost seven.'

'Is not. Went to bathroom eight o'clock.'

'If you want to be argumentative about it,' Jake said, 'it's after one. Time to get up and make breakfast. I'm starved.'

She peered at him through one half-open eye, then smiled broadly. 'Mmm,' she said.

'My sentiments, too. But I can't live on love, so you'd better start renewing my strength quick. Skip the eggs or pancakes. Make it a steak and trimmings.'

'Mmm,' she said again. 'Steak's not defrosted.' She opened both eyes wide. 'Is that rain?'

'Total.'

'Do you have to go out in it?'

'Not until I can get in touch with Magnes. So far, no luck.'

Elinor said contentedly: 'Rainy Sunday in bed.' She rid herself of the encumbering blanket and, naked, wormed her way up against him. 'Maybe you can't get in touch with him for a couple of days. We could have a bed-in and protest something.'

'And what would a sellout like you have to protest? Hell, you've been completely corrupted by the Establishment. You even bet on dog races.'

Elinor raised herself on an elbow and propped her chin in her hand. She said seriously: 'You know, I was thinking about that. If they keep records, and you find out from them what two numbers win most of the time – '

'Oh my God,' Jake said.

'Well, wouldn't you win most of the time, too, if you kept betting on those numbers?'

'Of course. I'll tell you what. Instead of letting you put the track out of business, I'll book your bets for you myself. Just give me the numbers you want and the two dollars, and we'll see how you make out in the papers next day.'

He kept his face impassive while she studied it suspiciously. Then she shook her head. 'If you want to do it that way, there must be a catch to it. You'd probably wind up with all my money, wouldn't you?'

'Better me than the track. Always keep it in the family, I say.'

She laid her head on his chest and draped an arm and a leg over him. 'That sounds nice. Family. Do you like the way I look first thing in the morning? That's supposed to be the real test.'

'All I ever see of you first thing is a pillow. I'm surprised you haven't suffocated to death long ago.'

'No, because there's a place to breathe in between them. I've been doing it since I was a little kid. I slept on a couch in the front room, and my father and his friends used to play cards all night with that big light burning. But do you like what you see first thing when you can see me?'

'I like it.'

'I like the way you look, too. All over. I love it. I am in love, love, love. And I'm not gentle in my mind about it either. It's like all strobe lights going around in it.'

'Breakfast,' Jake said.

'In a little while.' She slowly rubbed her leg back and forth over him. 'Doesn't that get you excited? Sure it does. I can tell it does. See? You don't need any steak at all.'

44

Half an hour later, wearing nothing more than a hair ribbon, she went in to make breakfast while he tried another call to Magnes. When he sat down to the table, Elinor said: 'Was he in?'

'No. And you ought to put something on. You are sure as hell going to burn one of your vital assets bending over the stove in that condition.'

She looked down at herself. 'The only thing's likely to happen to me is getting black and blue marks from you.' There was a garish bruise on her lower ribs in addition to the now fading one on her forehead. 'Anyhow, I'm only going around like this to hold your interest.'

'Well, you're holding it. I get a thrill every time you lean over that frying pan. Did you ever play in one of those skin shows? The new, new, new theatre bit?'

She shook her head. 'I answered some calls for them, but I never made it. Those calls were a real bad scene. I mean, the creepiest kind of people telling you to get undressed right there in the office, and you had to do it. And they'd have their creepy friends sitting around just to look at you for kicks. And I don't think any of them had enough money to back a kiddie show for the PTA.'

'Show biz,' said Jake.

'I know. But it's better now because some people in Equity got sore and made them stop. I mean, they can't make you get undressed right in the office any more, and it's different if you do it on stage. You don't mind that.' She put his plate of bacon, eggs, and French fries before him. 'How does that look?'

'Almost as appetizing as you.'

She served herself and sat down at the table. 'Well, you deserve it. I mean, not only to build up your strength again, but because I was expecting the house to be a mess from last night, and you cleaned it all up. Only where's the Sunday paper? Didn't they bring it today?'

'I suppose so, but I didn't bother to go out and get it. If it's been lying out on the doorstep since six this morning, it'll just be pulp by now.'

But later, when he was in the study taping a detailed recitation of the case to date, she came in triumphantly with the bulky Sunday edition of the Miami *Herald*.

'Dry?' Jake said.

'They had it in a big plastic bag all tied up tight. I guess they deliver that way any time it rains. You want to look at it now?'

'No, you can have it. I'd like to finish this first.'

He finished the tape, played it back, and went into the living room, where Elinor was stretched out on the floor, sections of the paper scattered around her. She said: 'Jake, what was the name of that organization Thoren was helping out? The one Nera told you about. Wasn't it *Avispa?*'

'It was.'

She rattled a section of the paper at him. 'So listen to this. The guy who used to be head of it died yesterday. Emilio Figueroa. And a few years back, the government almost put him in jail for buying one of those little baby submarines like the Japanese used in World War Two and fixing it up to fight Cuba, only they dropped the charges.'

'Let's see that,' Jake said.

He read the brief news story and then the half-column given Figueroa on the obituary page. Emilio Figueroa, long-time associate of deposed Fulgencio Batista, combatant at the Bay of Pigs, founder of *Avispa*, a leading organization of Freedom Fighters against the Castro terror, dead of a heart attack at sixty. Five years ago, raised funds for the purchase and reconstruction of a wartime Japanese two-man submarine for the smuggling of saboteurs and their equipment into Red Cuba. Was indicted for illegally arming the boat, but the indictment was later dropped on a technicality. Counsel for Figueroa had been the office of State Senator Harlan Sprague.

'Sprague,' Jake said. 'Thoren's brother-in-law,' and Elinor said mournfully, 'I had to go bring in the paper. Now I probably spoiled the whole rest of the day for us.'

'Spoiled nothing. This happens to be a stakeout, not Honeymoon Haven.'

'Well, all right. You don't have to sound that hairy about it.'

'Forget how I sound. There's something you told me about those old newspaper files you researched that ties in with this news story. Now what the hell was it?'

Elinor shrugged. 'Only that there wasn't anything in them about a ship's captain disappearing here. A ship's officer.'

'No.' He sat down on the couch and leaned forward towards her. 'Now listen. Don't say a word, just listen carefully. I picked you up at the library, and you got into the car all wound up because I was late, and you started talking off the top of your head. Just chatter. First it was about my being late, then something about the war. World War Two. But what was it you said?'

'Well – ' She arranged herself into an approximation of the lotus position and broodingly scratched an elbow. 'Well, didn't you ask how many of the newspapers I went through, and I told you?'

'You told me more than that. Something about the war. The fighting. Come on, concentrate.'

She tried, but quickly gave up on it. 'It's no use, Jake. I can't think when you sit and look at me that way. Anyhow, what could be so important about what I said? It didn't have anything to do with Thoren, did it?'

'Yes. I have this feeling you somehow tied him in with the news story about Figueroa.'

'Oh, a hunch.'

Jake said: 'Sweetheart, a good solid hunch simply means you've fitted some pieces of a puzzle together in your mind quicker than you can think. Somehow, what you said that time fitted together Thoren and Figueroa for me, as far back as World War Two. Now do you see why it's important?'

'I suppose so,' Elinor said doubtfully. Then she suddenly lit up with excitement. 'Wait a second. Submarines. That's what I told you about. There was a big fuss because some papers here gave out that German submarines were coming right up to Florida, and the government said it was supposed to be a secret. Jake – ' She reached out and rocked his knee back and forth. 'Hey, are you listening? What are you looking so glassy-eyed for?'

'Submarines,' Jake said wonderingly. 'Son of a bitch. A submarine.'

'Not just one. A lot. That's what surprised me, because I kind of thought the war was all in Europe and Japan, but here they were, right around Florida. And in California they were worried about Japanese planes bombing them. I told you that too, didn't I?'

'Yes. But it's the submarine part that counts. Don't you see? If Thoren was the big idea man for *Avispa*, he could be the one

223

who came up with the plan for smuggling saboteurs into Cuba by submarine. And he was too damn intelligent and practical to just pull any such idea out of his hat. He could have had experience in that line. And that ties in with my feeling that before he showed up here in Miami, he had something to do with ships.'

'Submarines?'

'Submarines are ships. And during the war saboteurs were being landed from them all around the world. Remember, according to Nera he was a demolitions expert.'

Elinor said: 'According to Nera he was an army man too. What's somebody like that doing in a submarine?'

'Getting transported to where his mission was. There's no contradiction in it. Matter of fact, it clears up what I thought were contradictions in what Nera told me. It proves she really was levelling with me.'

'Oh sure, you can always count on Mrs Ortega in the clutch.'

'And you. If it wasn't for you, sweetheart, I might have passed right by that Figueroa story.'

Elinor said too sweetly: 'It's so kind of you to mention it.' The sweetness became unmistakably acid. 'But I wouldn't be that sure about Nera levelling with anybody. Like that army man bit. Thoren would be kind of a hero in the army, going out on those missions, wouldn't he?'

'Probably,' Jake said. 'If he pulled them off.'

'So what's a hero doing, walking away from the action and going into business right in the middle of the war?'

'Some heroes were carried away from the action. That scar on his back – '

Elinor cut in sharply: 'You've been saying all along that scar on his back wasn't any war wound. And that if he had been in the service, he would never have settled down here after he pulled off a murder or something, because Miami was all full of the military during the war. So it looks to me like you put together a good solid theory about this case, and then Nera comes along and kicks it all apart with one cute little foot. I mean, all that stuff she handed you about Thoren and the army and sabotage and *Avispa*. Man, if you buy that package, you are buying a whole load of contradictions. You know that, don't you?'

'What I know, sweetheart, is that there's a strong smell of personal bias in your analysis.'

'So? That still doesn't change anything, does it? If you go along with what she says, you're still stuck with all those questions and no answers.'

Jake said coolly: 'That's my worry. I told you from the start, it's none of your concern whether I break this case or not. And considering this isn't show business, you might as well put some clothes on.'

'I knew it,' Elinor said to his departing back. 'I knew as soon as I opened my big mouth about Figueroa, the whole rest of the day would be spoiled.'

It was an accurate prediction in more ways than one, Jake found. The garage man showed up and not only brutally over-charged for the two new tyres, but was much too curious about what had happened to the damaged ones. When Elinor called McCloy about the broken window, he made it icily clear that he was not the Daystar janitor, and that the Service Department was the one to call on for repairs. And when the service man arrived to grudgingly replace the broken glass, he took notice as well of the gouge overhead in the doorway between the Florida room and the living room and remarked pointedly that old Mr and Mrs de Burgo had lived in this same house for twenty-two years and never left an inch of damage to show for it. That cost him the fat tip Jake had ready in his hand, and when he went out he slammed the front door hard enough to loosen its hinges.

Meanwhile, there was no response to the phone calls to Magnes made every half hour.

At Midnight Jake made the last call and went to bed, Elinor, in pyjamas, giving him an excess of space for himself. He lay there sleepless, his eyes fixed unseeingly on the glowing hands of the clock on his night table. Occasionally, as if to demon-strate that she was also wide awake and actively rejecting him, there was a sharp little flurry on Elinor's side of the bed. A

15   225

shifting of position, punching of the pillow into shape, kicking of the blanket straight.

At two o'clock he slipped out of bed, went into the study, and softly closed the door behind him. He took out Thoren's dossier and read it through carefully line by line, making notations on a pad as he read. Finished, he went into the living room, poured himself a large belt of Chivas Regal, and brought it back to the study. Luxuriously stretched out in the swivel chair, feet on the desk, glass of Scotch in hand, he went through the list of notations, giving each item long and hard thought. Then he dropped the pad into the folder along with the rest of the dossier, locked it away, and went into the bedroom.

He stood at the foot of the bed for a minute, but there was no sound of deep, regular breathing from it, only an intense silence. 'Are you awake?' he whispered, and Elinor said in a flat voice, 'No.'

'Too bad, because I've got some news.' He felt his way along the bed and turned on her lamp. She immediately flung herself away from him, face buried in the pillow. He sat down beside her and pulled her around to face him. Her eyes glimmered wetly, her nose was pink, there were the marks of tear stains on her cheeks. 'Crying,' Jake said. 'A big girl like you.'

'You mean a dumb Polack like me, don't you?'

'No. Let's say a highly emotional Polack.'

Elinor struggled to a half-sitting position. 'That's just beautiful coming from a manic-depressive like you. You think you're not because you always play it so cool?'

'Was I really that rough on you?'

'No, you were nice and smooth, like an ice cube. All you did was stop talking to me or even looking at me, but since I obviously don't have any feelings, what's wrong with that? I just have to remember that when everything's so warm and cosy one minute, it could be the deep freeze the rest of the day. And if somebody gets in bed with me and doesn't even know I'm there, well, that's the way it is for the hired help when the boss has business on the mind.'

'Sweetheart, there are times in a man's life when sex – '

'I'm not talking about sex. I'm talking about just lying there nice and quiet and holding people. Even just saying something to them.' She slid flat again and closed her eyes. 'What's the use? You don't even know what I'm talking about. It's not your fault. Men like you don't know how women feel about things, that's all.'

'They're emotional,' Jake said. 'The way I felt when I hit the answer to all those annoying questions you raised about Thoren. That's what I came in to tell you about, but if you're not in the mood – '

Elinor opened her eyes. 'You hit the answer?'

Jake took her hand. She made the smallest motion to pull it away, then let it rest limply in his grip. He said: 'An army officer, a trained saboteur, travelling in a submarine to an important mission. A combat man who suddenly shows up in Miami with a lot of money and goes into business here right in the middle of the war. The most upright and uptight citizen of Daystar Island Number Two, but when you check him out, there isn't one record of his existence before 1942. And none of it fitted together until I just happened to ask myself what the hell direction that submarine was travelling in on its way to that mission.'

'Direction?' Elinor said. 'What's that got to do with it?'

'Everything, sweetheart. That was a German submarine, and Walter Thoren was a German saboteur who never got home again.'

45

Elinor said warily: 'Are you putting me on?'

'No.'

'Jake, it sounds crazy.'

'Until you try it on for size.'

She moved over to make room for him. 'All right, tell me about it.'

'After you fix me up some sandwiches and beer.'

She squinted at the clock. 'At four o'clock in the morning?'

'Manic-depressives are always hungry in the manic phase. I talk better when I'm not hungry.'

'You think you're not a real case?' She got out of bed and drooped against him, her arms over his shoulders, her forehead against his chest. 'Dr Jekyll and Mr Hyde. Some day I'll kill both of you.'

At the kitchen table, watching her transport supplies from the refrigerator, Jake said: 'You get a feeling sometimes – it was the feeling I got when you were telling me about Figueroa and came out with the word submarine – that a light's been turned on, but it's in the next room and the door to it is shut. And I couldn't get it open because too many things in the case did look like contradictions. Then all of a sudden I had a brainstorm. I remembered something from way back that could be the answer to the whole mess. It wiped out every contradiction on the spot.'

'Was that when you jumped out of bed and went inside?'

'That's when.' Jake looked at her quizzically. 'You certainly take a highly personal view of this, don't you?'

'Well, I thought you couldn't stand being in bed with me. I mean, because I couldn't fall asleep and I was keeping you awake or something.'

'Hell, no. I went in to look over everything I had on Thoren. The idea of his being a German agent during the war solved the whole mystery about his background, but it looked just too damn wild. But everything I had on him fitted in with that idea. Every single item. Anyhow, what I remembered that put me on the right track was an anniversary article about World War Two the *Mirror* printed a little while before it folded. A twentieth-anniversary piece about the Germans landing saboteurs on Long Island during the war. It's funny how the mind works. When you mentioned the word submarine it put me right back at my desk on the *Mirror* one night, looking over a paper fresh from the press and trying not to get the ink on my fingers while I was reading a story in it. Only I couldn't understand why I should have that kind of weird recollection right then. I was going crazy all day trying to see why.'

'I know,' Elinor said dryly. 'I was there.'

'Well, you were a martyr to a good cause, because all of a sudden it came to me, and that opened the door wide. Operation Pretorius or Praetorius it was called. And I knew it was in early 1942, because it had to be twenty years before the paper folded, which was 1962.'

Elinor held a bottle of beer poised over his glass. 'You mean they had some fighting right there on Long Island in the war?'

'No, the whole thing was a foul-up from start to finish. One of the Germans in it who came from America originally tipped off the FBI as soon as they landed, and they were all grabbed right away. They were all executed, too, except that one. He got a jail term.'

'I don't understand. If all of them were caught, where does that leave Thoren?'

Jake took her wrist and tipped the bottle of beer into his glass. 'That's a good question. For sure, he wasn't with the Long Island bunch, so he had to be with another unit that landed somewhere else. I know if I was running German Intelligence, I'd never put all my eggs in one basket, especially with an operation like this. I'd figure to co-ordinate at least two or three landings in case one was knocked out of action. Thoren had to be in one that hit the coast right around here.'

Elinor looked pained. 'But now you're just guessing. I thought you had everything all settled for sure.'

'Almost. You'll be the one that settles it for sure. This morning you're going back to the library – '

'Again? They're already tired of me there.'

'Too bad, because they'll have to bear with you one more time. But this time you won't go hunting through all those files. You'll just look up Operation Pretorius or Praetorius in the index and take it from there. What I want most of all is confirmation there were other landings. Especially one in south Florida. After that, whatever information there is on it.'

'Uh-huh,' Elinor said. She sat down across the table, planted her elbows on it and cupped her chin in her hands. 'Well, goodbye.'

'Goodbye?'

'I'm thinking what happens if it turns out there was no landing in south Florida. I mean, when you go around hating me for it. It makes it easier to say goodbye now before you get back in the deep freeze.'

'Don't worry. There was a landing.'

'Thanks. I was hoping you'd say there wouldn't be any deep freeze.'

'And either Thoren voluntarily walked out on the operation and took cover as a good American citizen, or we pinned him down so tight he had to do it, which was more likely the case.'

'We?'

'The FBI, Army Intelligence, whoever. The way I see Thoren, he wasn't the man to quit on a mission without good reason. He must have been jammed into a corner where he had no choice about it. That's where Earl Dobbs enters the picture. He was there when Thoren tried to break out of his corner and killed somebody at it. A perfect witness against Thoren for the rest of his life.'

Elinor dropped her hands to the table. 'Wait a second. You've been saying all along Thoren killed somebody to get all that money he showed up with.'

'I know. That was one of the things that kept misleading me. Now I'm sure he didn't have to kill anybody for money. The top man of the squad who landed on Long Island not only had a complete set of false documents to cover his background, he also had a fortune of American money on him. Thoren probably rated top man of his unit. He'd have had a bagful of cash on him in that case.'

Elinor said: 'So if he didn't kill anybody for money, maybe there wasn't any killing at all. He could just have been black-mailed for coming here as a German agent.'

'I doubt it. Not with the kind of blackmail he was paying. And with the way he ended up killing himself. Fact is, if it came out twenty-five years after the war he had landed here as an enemy agent, he was in good shape to ride it out publicly. If he hadn't done any damage before he gave up on his mission, he'd be as likely as not to get an amnesty. Remember, he turned into a high-class citizen, his brother-in-law is a big politician, he'd have a lot of sentiment on his side to let bygones be bygones.

230

All he'd have to do is say how much he hated Hitler in the bad old days. Match that against giving away every penny you have as blackmail and finishing off with suicide, and I think Thoren would have gambled on riding it out. But there's no statute of limitations on murder. And if you kill somebody when you're out of uniform on a sabotage or spy job, you're guilty of murder. No sentiment about it, no letting bygones be bygones. Just a life sentence in jail. And some big trial lawyers cleaning you out of whatever money the blackmailers didn't already get.'

Elinor picked up a soggy roll, squeezed it, and put it down with an expression of distaste. She said: 'Well, I think it's kind of sad about him, but not much. Mrs Thoren's the one I feel sorry for. She doesn't have to worry about jail or anything, and she still has to pay blackmail to keep it out of the papers.'

'And to collect her insurance,' Jake pointed out.

'I didn't think of that. So what do you do now? Tell her all this? Break her down and make her sign the release that way?'

'I've been wondering about it. It might be worth the try, if I could pull a strong enough bluff about having real evidence to back me up. It might be the last straw for her, the extra pressure that would break her down. It would be a lot better if I could break down Dobbs first, then use him as leverage against her. The only trouble either way is that I don't know where the hell she is right now. I can't cash in on any of this if I can't sit her down in a chair and stick a pen in her hand.'

'Well, Magnes has those two men – '

'And where is he right now, for that matter? He's my contact with them. How do I know how they're making out, if I can't get in touch with him?'

'Jake, you think maybe something happened to him?'

'No.'

'How can you be so sure? I mean, an old man like that, and with a heart condition. And all that running around he's doing.'

'He's getting paid plenty for running around. And he'll still outlive us all.'

He held out his empty glass, and Elinor took another bottle of beer from the refrigerator. She drew his foot out from under the table with hers, then sat herself down on his knee and poured each of them a glass of beer. She drank off the top of hers and emerged wearing a moustache of foam. 'I like that,' she said with a small nod of her head.

'Beer?' Jake wiped away the moustache with his thumb, and she gave him a quick, sharp nip of the teeth *en passant*. 'Or my thumb?'

'No, the way you're always so sure of everything. It's kind of like having emotional muscles to go along with these others. But you make mistakes too, so you're not really a machine. I like that extra.'

'Satisfied all around,' Jake said.

'Uh-huh. And sleepy.'

In bed, she backed up against him and drew his arm around her waist. 'But just holding,' she warned. 'I'm too tired for anything more exciting right now.'

'To tell the truth,' Jake said, 'I'm glad you are.'

46

When they pulled up before Jordan Marsh's, Jake said: 'You know the routine, don't you?'

'Yes.' Elinor ticked it off on her fingers. 'Hang around in the store awhile and buy something. Take a taxi to the library. Look up Operation Pretorius or Praetorius. Call you at the house when I'm ready.'

'Good. But there's one change. If you don't get me on the phone, keep calling every now and then. But don't go home by yourself. Don't even walk outside the library. Take a book into the reading room and sit there until I show up.'

She smiled at him crookedly. 'They weren't just trying to scare us the other night, were they, darling? They were just aiming bad.'

'No, those were strictly scare tactics. But there's no reason you have to be scared like that again. You wait there until I show up, no matter how long it takes.'

'If it takes too long, I'll be dead from hunger anyhow.'

'Not a chance. While you're in the store buy a box of candy or something to hold you over. I'll make it up to you tonight. We'll go celebrate in some classy restaurant.'

'You're that sure we'll have something to celebrate?' Elinor said.

'If not, I'll take you out just to show you off.' He put his arm around her, and when she raised her face to his, he said: 'And husbands and wives don't kiss goodbye with their mouths open.'

'Only because the husbands are chicken,' Elinor said. She kissed him with abandonment, then said: 'Is that the car that's following us back there? That green one?'

'That's the one. Persistent but harmless.'

'And all dirty.' She opened the door, slid out, and put her head to the window. Her smile was a little too bright. 'You'd think anybody tailing a Jag like this would at least polish up his car.'

Back in the house, he tried Magnes's number, drew a blank, and went to work adding to yesterday's tape his analysis of Walter Thoren's identity. Then he ran off a duplicate of the completed tape, which he carefully wrapped and sealed and addressed to his own apartment in Manhattan.

A little before noon the phone rang. Nera Ortega, muttering something unintelligible.

'What?' Jake said.

She raised her voice to a loud whisper. 'Idiot, you don't have to yell. I am telling you Fons is suddenly home. A dear friend of ours just died, and Fons came back here for the services. There'll be no more swimming parties for a while. Understand?'

'Yes.'

She lowered her voice again, so that he had to strain to make out the words. 'But in a week – ten days at most – it'll be all right again. Still interested in swimming?'

'Yes.'

'I'm glad to hear it.' Nera laughed under her breath. 'You really are a remarkable swimmer,' and hung up.

Five minutes later when the phone rang again Jake moved

233

towards it without alacrity, then realized it was the unlisted phone in the study that was ringing. He almost knocked it off the desk, grabbing for it. Magnes.

'Jesus Christ,' Jake said explosively, and Magnes cut in: 'Listen, Dekker. Saturday night for your sake I had to put away so much booze I almost drowned in it. Last night I slept out in the boondocks in a house which, you'll excuse the expression, you wouldn't keep in the back yard for a crapper. So don't say anything now we'll both be sorry for. Just be grateful I found Mr Earl Dobbs for you. You want to hear all about it?'

'I have to get something to the post office right away. I'll go over to your place right from there.'

47

On his way across town to Ocean Drive, Jake pulled up to the post office on Washington Avenue and watched the green Chevy double-park further down the block. Then, holding the package of tapes in conspicuous view, he sauntered into the post office and saw to its mailing. He walked out of the post office no less conspicuously empty-handed.

Magnes, in bathing trunks and straw hat, was taking his ease in a beach chair outside his rooftop hutch, dripping sweat. He looked sunken-eyed and haggard. 'Did you eat lunch?' he said in greeting.

'Forget lunch,' Jake said. 'What about Dobbs?'

'I told you I found him, didn't I? He's holed up where we can get to him any time.'

'And Mrs Thoren. Did your boy scouts turn her up yet?'

'Sooner or later. Belle Glade is a big town, sonny.'

'Is it?' Jake said pleasantly. 'You wouldn't by any chance be holding out on me about Mrs Thoren, would you? Working some interesting little angle of your own?'

Magnes said without rancour: 'From anybody else that would be an insult. From you, somehow it comes natural.' He pushed himself out of the chair. 'Come on inside. Maybe you can skip lunch, but I can't. Especially after what I went through the last couple days.'

Inside, he busied himself putting up canned soup and a pot of coffee and setting the table for two. 'Saturday night,' he said, 'after I phoned you, I went to that crummy bar Dobbs liked near the dog track and settled down there. Thank God, around three, four in the morning, the bartender points me out a guy who used to hang around there with Dobbs. So I made friends with the guy. Turned out he once ran a gas delivery truck that stopped at a town, Crosscut, out in the swamps, which is where Dobbs lives. He even went hunting with him a couple of times, because Dobbs got himself a little shack on a hammock near Crosscut which is a good place for hunting. I'm dying for sleep already, but the guy tells me if I'll stop by his house in my car so he can pick up a couple of rifles, he'll show me in Crosscut where Dobbs lives, maybe I can meet him right away. I had let on to him I was in real estate and I heard Dobbs had some nice cheap property for sale out in the boondocks, so his idea was he could help me close a deal for it and get a few bucks for himself for being middle man.'

'Did you meet Dobbs?' Jake said.

'No, the old geezer in the house next to his – house, shmouse, you wouldn't keep pigs in it – said Dobbs was out in the swamps, he was staying at his shack there. You got to drive a swamp buggy out to it, and he didn't know the way. Anyhow, he said he didn't.'

Jake said: 'Just as well. The man tailing you might have been told to do something about it if you ever got together with Dobbs. He followed you out to Crosscut, didn't he?'

'I wouldn't swear to it.' Magnes placed two bowls of soup on the table and sat down to his. He tore a piece of black bread in half and buttered it thickly. 'Thank God, my doctor don't believe in cholesterol. You even been out on the Tamiami Trail?'

'No.'

'Well, it's like driving in a tunnel, you know what I mean. Straight across to the Gulf, the canal on one side, the swamps on the other. You want to tail somebody on it, you could stay a mile back of him and still not have a worry. The one place to watch out for is where Route 94 cuts off south from the Trail about forty miles out of Miami. Crosscut is a few miles down 94. And I didn't see anybody back of me on it.'

Jake said: 'It would be a break if you did shake him off. But that was yesterday morning. Where the hell have you been since then?'

Magnes took a large bite of his bread? 'Where? Believe it or not, I was hunting in the swamps with my *shikker* friend from the bar and that old ragbag from next door to Dobbs. My rummy is up to his eyeballs in booze when we walk out of the bar, and he's got a bottle along with him in the bargain. By the time we get to Crosscut he's like my brother. He's falling all over me with love. So he puts my car keys in his pocket, I'll have to stay and hunt with him and the old man. Tell him no, he aims his gun right at me, because I don't love him the way he loves me. So I went hunting all day for deers and half the night for alligators, and I slept at the old man's place on a mattress, it stunk so much from piss I had to hold my nose to fall asleep. When we got back here this morning I dumped my *shikker* off at Flagler Street, and I went to see what the government people have about that hammock where Dobbs's shanty is. The old man had told me it's just called Dobbs Hammock, and it turned out there's no such place on the government maps. The government man said maybe one of those Monroe County game wardens could find it in a swamp buggy. Anyhow, Dobbs still got to come back to Crosscut regular for supplies, so that don't matter.' Magnes waggled his spoon at Jake. 'And you don't have to sit with such a look on your face, wise guy. You think it's a joke an old man with a bad heart goes through such a *mishegas*?'

'Me?' Jake said innocently. 'You're reading me wrong, Magnes. What I'm thinking is that some people have all the luck.'

'Oh sure. That kind of luck I gladly wish on Nasser.'

'All the same, there are people who go shooting and people who get shot at. Who would you say are the lucky ones?'

'Shot at?' Magnes said. 'You?'

236

'They put two slugs through the back window of the house Saturday night. And sliced up a couple of tyres on the Jag.'

Magnes pursed his lips in a silent whistle. 'So the party is getting rough. Were they shooting for keeps?'

'Probably not.'

'The girlie all right?'

'Fine.'

Magnes said accusingly: 'But at a time like this to leave her alone somewhere, Dekker? When they're starting to move in on you?'

'I told you she was fine. She's at the library over in Miami checking out the latest on Thoren, and nobody'll bother her there. Now do you want to hear the latest, or do you want to go hold her hand?'

'I'm listening. And if you don't like cold soup, you can eat and tell me at the same time.'

Jake told it in detail, starting with the discovery of the ticket to the dog track and winding up with his analysis of Thoren's past. When he had told it all, Magnes sat in morose silence for a long while. Then he said softly: 'A dirty, rotten Nazi. A butcher. A soap maker. You know what? So help me God, I'm sorry he's dead. A hundred times better if he was alive, with those hoodlums squeezing a little blood out of him every day of his life.'

'You don't seem very much surprised about him,' Jake remarked.

'Why should I be? If it turned out he was a Jew living some-how on Daystar Number Two, I would be surprised. But that a Nazi shouldn't be right at home there?' Magnes shoved his plate away. 'I got no appetite any more.' He pointed a bony forefinger at Jake. 'And his wife knows what he was, Dekker. My one satisfaction now will be seeing she don't collect a penny of that insurance. And his kids don't see a penny of it. So far, this has been a job of work for me. From here on, I give you my word, it'll be a positive pleasure.'

Jake said: 'That's my good luck. And what about Raymond Beaudry? You think there's any chance at all he's tied in with Gela and Dobbs?'

'No.'

'He's in a good position to be their tip-off man, right there in the middle of the family. And meeting him at the dog track like that – '

'I still say no. Remember, this *shvartzeh* has been with the family for years, but the blackmail didn't commence until Thoren ran into Dobbs. Dobbs is the one to nail down. And fast. I'll contact a game warden about taking us out to this hideout of his, and I'll send another man up to Belle Glade to help locate the woman. I'll have it set up tomorrow both ways.'

Jake said: 'What you'll do is cool off and play it my way. I still have to find out exactly what Dobbs had on Thoren before I put the squeeze on him.'

'The Nazi business. Illegal entry. Why should it have to be more than that? Because you made up your mind Thoren was involved in a murder? You futz around with that angle, Dekker, you're only wasting time.'

'Magnes, I know Thoren by now damn near as well as he knew himself. If he was faced with anything but a sure long-time jail sentence, he would have battled it out. This is a guy who had no nerves. He was hard as nails. So ten-thousand-a-month blackmail and then suicide for the wind-up says he must have pulled something that would get him that sentence.'

Magnes lowered his chin to his chest and peered at Jake from under his eyebrows. 'You mean it's like two of a kind? No nerves, hard as nails – you figure you know what he would do, because you know what you would do?'

'What I figure is not to show my hand to Dobbs until I fill it. When I tell him to come along with me and have Mrs Thoren sign that release or else I turn him over to the cops, he has to know I'm not bluffing.'

'And what about the lady?'

'She's got no choice at all. Either she signs away that money to keep the story hushed up, or she doesn't sign and loses out on the money anyhow when Thoren's death is declared a suicide. And gets the story into the papers in the bargain.'

Magnes narrowed his eyes. 'That's very fancy chess playing, Dekker. But why? You want to give this woman a break, keep-

238

ing it out of the papers? Or is Maniscalco the kind would cut you out of your payoff if you don't personally hand him her release?'

Jake said: 'He claims I have to hand him a release because it's the only way he can get Guaranty to authorize payment to me. I claim he'd cut me out of a five-dollar payoff if he could.'

Magnes nodded wisely. 'I thought that was it. What it comes down to is you're selling him that release. So all right, but I don't want to be stuck with whatever you promise the woman. The way I want it, you get the release and take the plane back to New York, and then I go to the newspapers with the whole story. Daystar Number Two don't like publicity except when they run a fancy party for charity? *Chob dir in bod.* They'll get publicity from this until it comes out of their ears.'

'It's up to you,' Jake said. 'Once I'm gone, you can do what you want about it.'

'I will. But there's still one other thing on my mind. Pooch Gela. Who do you think shot up your place? Who lost the Thoren woman for me because he put my boy in the hospital? You show your hand to Dobbs, and first thing he runs right to Gela.'

'If I'm stupid enough to let him. For that matter, Gela's in a bind, too. He must know that if he knocks me off, Guaranty will really tie up that money tight. And work right along with the cops down here.'

'He must know,' Magnes said heavily. 'Also he must know to spell cat c,a,t, but I wouldn't bet very much on it. Still, this is your lookout. But what about the girlie?'

'What about her?'

'You told me you'd think about sending her back to New York. I notice she's still around.'

Jake shrugged. 'That was her choice.'

'Her choice. Did you tell her the heat was on? Did you tell her it could get even hotter before this job is cleaned up?'

Jake said: 'I didn't have to. She knows everything there is to know about the job. And she was right there when those slugs came through the window.'

'Naturally. Where you are, she wants to be. This is a baby,

Dekker. An infant. She don't know anything except she's crazy about you. But if, God forbid, one of those bullets went through her head, it wouldn't bother you? You'd take such a risk just to get a little piece now and then? Because don't tell me it's more than that.'

'I don't have to tell you anything, Magnes, except that for someone who hates to waste time, you're wasting a lot of it. How about getting back to business?'

'Is that your answer? The girlie stays, no matter what?'

'Yes,' Jake said. 'As long as she wants to.'

Magnes looked at him curiously. 'The way you say it – Tell me the truth, Dekker. Am I wrong about it? That kid means more to you than I figured?'

'If there's a wedding, Magnes, consider yourself invited. But don't stand and wait too long for it to happen.'

'A wedding.' Magnes bobbed his head admiringly. 'Very slick, the way you duck a question. Because I happen to know such things don't matter *bubkis* nowadays, even with a nice girl from a respectable family. She picks out her man, she buys a bottle of pills, and she'll skip the wedding part. But why duck the question? You think it's a disgrace to have some real feelings for a woman?'

'That was quick,' Jake said. 'A minute ago she was an infant.'

'True. Because if she chases after you like somebody in a fan club, she's an infant. But if she really means something to you, she's a woman. Either way, Dekker, a professional killer got that house on Daystar marked. You want to keep the girl around, at least get her away from there. I can fix it up so she'll stay in a nice hotel without a soul knowing. Better that than to leave her alone in your place any more.'

'I'll think about it,' Jake said, and when Magnes threw up his hands and said, 'Ahh, go talk to a wall,' Jake said, 'That's what I seem to be doing right now, isn't it?'

'All right, big man, so we'll talk business. What business?'

'I want you to arrange a meeting for me with Frank Milan.'

'Some joke,' Magnes said.

'And soon. By tonight, if you can.'

'By tonight. And tomorrow morning I'll fix it so you can eat breakfast with the Pope.'

Jake said: 'One reason I signed you on was because you guaranteed you could contact anybody down here for me. With no exceptions. And Milan's not hiding out. He was right there next to me in that sauna at the Royal Burgundian.'

'Sure. And if you said hello to him there, he might even say it back. But if you said two words more, you'd be hustled away from him so fast you wouldn't know how it happened.'

Jake said coldly: 'You're not so bad at ducking questions yourself. Now let's have it. When's the soonest I can get together with Milan?'

'When he's done having you checked out. And believe me, if he's even interested in having you checked out considering what he already knows, it would take at least a few weeks.'

'You know that's not soon enough,' Jake said.

'You're the one in a rush. For him it's soon enough.'

Jake thought it over, then abruptly pushed back his chair and stood up. 'Where's the phone? Not the hotel phone, your private line. I want to call Maniscalco. You can charge it to me.'

'Him? You think he could do any better than me when it comes to making contacts down here?'

'No, but there's somebody else here who can get me together with Milan. Only Maniscalco has to back up my play.'

Magnes cocked his head inquiringly. 'Somebody else? Who else?' He pointed at the bedside table. 'On the bottom shelf there. You just lift the cloth. You mean you're working with somebody else down here I don't even know about?'

'No, it's just kind of a buddy of mine. A guy who takes a lot of interest in me.' Jake dialled the number, told Maniscalco's girl Friday who it was, and was handed over to him without delay. 'That you, Jake?' Maniscalco went into a spasm of coughing and said through it: 'Lousy cold. You're lucky to be down there out of this cruddy weather. What's the word?'

'The word is somebody might check me out with you today, Manny. Will you be in the office the rest of the afternoon?'

'And half of the night. But what –'

'No, just listen. Whoever it is, you'll have to tell him I'm on Guaranty's payroll as an investigator and I collect bonus money besides. Ten per cent. And if he asks if I'm married, tell him I am. You got that?'

There was an ominous silence. Then Maniscalco said: 'I got it and I don't like it. You know our agreement. We never use your name, you never use our name. That still goes.'

'Manny, for once in your life don't be such a goddam company man. This is important. It has to be done.'

'Nothing has to be done that winds up with Guaranty backing up any free-lancer. You want them to do that for you, sign on with them. You start working here any day you name. You want to play it solo, don't ask them to bail you out. That's the name of the game, Jake. You can't have it both ways.'

Jake said softly: 'You chicken bastard, if you don't go along with me on this, you'll blow the whole case. And I'm just about ready to wrap it up.'

'Wrap it up?' Maniscalco went into another fit of coughing and finally brought it under control. 'You mean you've got the goods on Thoren? He was really being hit for enough blackmail to make him suicide? What's the story?'

'That I'll tell you after I hand you the release.'

'Oh? You're that far along with it, you're already playing cagey? That sounds like happy news, my friend.'

'So far it is. If you want it to stay happy, cover for me when you get that call, Manny. Don't think about it until you lose all your nerve. Just do it.'

Jake banged down the phone, and Magnes said irritably: 'So tell me. Who's this old buddy can get to Frank Milan in no time at all? Do I know his name at least?'

'I don't even know it myself,' Jake said.

48

From the vantage point of the hotel's porch, the ancients seated on it beadily watching every move he made, he looked up and down Ocean Drive for the green Chevy with the elongated aerial. Then he saw it. South of the hotel a big building was under construction, a luxury condominium according to the sign posted before it. Its skeleton extended from Ocean Drive almost to the tide line, chewing up a large hunk of open beach. A truck parked in front of it was unloading steel pipe, and the aerial of the Chevy showed behind the truck.

Jake walked down the block to it. The car's closed windows and the heat ripple from its exhaust indicated that its driver had the motor turning over and was sealed inside in air-conditioned comfort. He was young, in his mid-twenties at most, and had a long-nosed, narrow face, the eyes too close together, the hairline moustache doing nothing to beautify it. He seemed overdressed for his job in a plaid sports jacket and broad, vividly coloured tie.

If he was disconcerted at the way Jake was studying him through the window, he didn't show it. Face blank, head back against the headrest, hands limply draped over the steering wheel, he sat there and let himself be studied. But when Jake pulled open the door and leaned inside, he moved fast enough. The sudden hard pressure drilling into his chest, Jake saw, was the muzzle of an automatic. The hand gripping it was noticeably white at the knuckles. 'What the hell you think you're doing?' the driver snarled.

Jake remained as he was, half in, half out of the car. He said amiably: 'Looking for a few words with you. Better in here than out in that sun. You can fry your skull bald in that sun.'

The driver's face screwed up in disbelief. 'Wha'?' It sounded like the drawn-out, ascending blat of a muted saxophone.

Jake said: 'Ah, come on. You know me, I know you, what do we have to play games for? And I don't pack a gun, and I'm not trying to make any deal with you where you double-cross Frank Milan, so relax. Put that thing away and let's talk.'

'Mister, you want to know something? You're bugs.'

'Not enough to be worried about an automatic dug an inch deep into me. Where'd you learn about guns anyhow? You ought to know you can't fire an automatic jammed this hard against anything. A revolver, yes. Not this thing.'

The man flashed a quick look down at the gun in his hand. When he looked up his expression suggested that he was both shaken by this information and suspicious of it. 'You crazy bastard,' he said in alarm as Jake relentlessly forced himself into the seat against the thrust of the gun, 'You're just askin' for it. Get outa here.'

Jake said: 'So you really didn't know it.' He clamped the man's wrist in an iron grip to keep the gun jammed into himself. Then he carefully reached back with his other hand, found the door handle and swung the door shut behind him. 'Of course, if you could get a little room for this thing, you could put a hole right through me. Then Frank would hand you your head on a plate. The orders were just to tail me, not nail me, weren't they?'

The man desperately tried to pull back on the gun. All he succeeded in doing was wedge himself deeper into the tight corner between the steering wheel and the seat, his back against the door there, Jake crowding him almost body to body. 'You crazy bastard, leggo, you hear?' There was panic in his voice now. The car was cold with the air conditioner working full blast, but a heavy sweat suddenly showed on his face.

Suddenly he jabbed bony fingers at Jake's eyes. Jake blocked the hand in mid-air and slowly, steadily turned it back against the wrist until the man yelped with the pain of it.

Jake maintained the steady pressure, at the same time making sure the gun stayed wedged tight into his ribs. He said: 'A little more of this, and you wind up with a broken wrist. Is that what you're trying for?'

'No, no, for chrissake. Just leggo, that's all.'

'First you let go of the gun.'

244

It fell to the seat between them. Jake released the man, gave him a stunning backhanded slap across the face that banged his head against the window, and moved clear of him. He picked up the gun. It was a 9-mm. Luger, but from the imprint on the blue steel barrel, a Smith and Wesson. It was fully loaded.

The man watched this dazedly. He was breathing hard, and a trickle of blood oozed from one nostril. He sat in numb acquiescence as Jake pulled a wallet from the inside breast pocket of the sports jacket and flipped through it. 'So you're Anthony Aiello,' he said. 'Tenderfoot enforcer.'

Aiello said with repressed fury: 'You're a cop, ain't ya? The son of a bitch that stuck me on this job never told me you – '

'No, I'm not a cop.' Jake tossed the wallet into the glove compartment. 'What son of a bitch stuck you on this job? Frank Milan?'

The fury instantly evaporated. In its place was an intense wariness. 'Me? What would I have to do with Frank Milan?'

'That's true. It would be somebody under him. But it's all the same to me, Anthony. Whoever it is, you're going to get me together with Frank Milan right away. See that phone booth down the block? We're going over there, and I'll give you all the change you need, and before you get out of that booth I'll have a date set up with Mr Milan some time today.'

'Oh sure.' Not even Magnes could have said it with more scorn. 'That's me. Frank Milan's private secretary.'

'That's what you were just promoted to. Now pull this heap around to that booth. Shoe leather costs a lot nowadays. We'll save what we can of it.'

'You pull it around to that booth, mister. Because what I think – '

'I don't want you to think, Anthony. I don't want you to strain a muscle in your head. All you do is what you're told. Meaning, somebody up there can get me together with Frank Milan right away. And you're going to convince him he has to do it.'

'Suppose I can't?'

'You'll laugh when I tell you. We drive down that side street where nobody'll see the action, and I cold-cock you with this gun butt, and take all your clothes off right down to the last stitch. Then I walk back to this phone booth with them and your car keys and call the cops and tell them there's a pervert exposing himself in his car, and where to find you. If you want to tell them how it happened when they come rolling up, go right ahead. If you don't the possibilities are even funnier. Especially when it gets back to the Mob what happened when the guy you were tailing got tired of it.' Aiello was leaning back against the door, fumbling for its handle, and Jake took him by the necktie and yanked him away from it. 'Don't do that, Anthony. You should know better than that by now.'

Aiello snuffled, trying to staunch the trickle of blood from his nose. 'What I know is if you're not a cop, you crazy bastard, you should be.'

Jake backhanded him again. 'I have a name, Anthony. What is it?'

'Dekker, for chrissake. Dekker.'

'That's right. And I'm an investigator with Guaranty Life Insurance in New York, and my boss is a guy named John Maniscalco. And I want to meet with Frank Milan right away. Got all that?'

'Yeah, I got it.'

'Good. Now do we make a phone call, or do we play it for laughs?'

It took Aiello a long and apparently harried time to complete the call, with Jake standing half wedged into the booth with him as overseer. A withered little crone leaned on a cane behind Jake for a while, waiting her turn at the phone, then snapped, *'Vehr geharget, grobbers!'* whacked the booth with her cane, and wrathfully hobbled away.

Aiello finally hung up the phone. 'They said make it four o'clock over in Nappy's Lounge. On the Strip. Maybe he'll be there.'

'Four o'clock?' Jake said. 'That's almost two hours.'

'Ah, man, you heard me talkin' my head off, didn't you? What more do you want?'

246

Jake said soothingly: 'That's the truth, Anthony. It shows the kind of ingratitude you meet up with sometimes. Now I'll borrow your car, so I can drive up the street there to where mine is parked. You can pick it up there. The gun I'll keep.'

'Yeah? You walk in on Frank Milan with that on you –'

'Me?' Jake said. 'I told you I never carry firearms, Anthony. I just collect them.'

49

He restlessly marked time in the house until three-thirty, then phoned Maniscalco. 'Did anyone check me out, Manny?'

'About twenty minutes ago. Guy from Southeast Credit Bureau. In person.'

'Did you back me up?'

'I backed you up, God help me. I told him you're with Guaranty for fifteen thousand a year plus ten percent of any claims you prove fraudulent. Jake, for chrissake, Southeast is one of the biggest credit-rating outfits in the country. A week from now every IBM card around with your name on it will have Guaranty coded on to it too. Hold on a second.' Maniscalco's voice suddenly went diminuendo. 'Honey, forget those forms. Just go outside in the hall, close the door after you, and wait there. That's right. Until I call you.' The voice picked up volume again. 'Jake?'

'Yeah?'

'Now if you get caught pulling something raw, Guaranty is dragged right into it. You know what happens to me then?'

'If I pull something raw. And get caught at it.'

Maniscalco snarled: 'Ah, who do you think you're talking to. You probably got bugs in every phone around Miami by now, and taps to go along with them. You told me yourself you had your girl bug the Thorens' phone. Suppose she gets in a mood to hold you up for it? I can just see the brass on the top floor here when the law walks in on them.'

'No sweat, Manny. This is a special kind of girl. And as soon as the job is done, you can tell Southeast I resigned from your lousy company. That'll straighten out those IBM cards.'

Maniscalco tried to talk through a coughing fit, finally surrendered to it, and came out of it wheezing. 'You said a week, maybe less than a week. Does that still go?'

'Yes. Did Southeast ask if I was married?'

'No, but I threw it in for free. Less than a week, huh? Let's hear about it. I've got some time on my hands right now.'

Jake laughed. 'That's not even a good try, Manny.'

He put down the phone and stood considering Anthony Aiello's gun which lay on the desk before him. After due reflection, he removed its clip, wrapped it in a handkerchief, and locked both clip and gun in the closet.

Then he put on the Pucci shirt Elinor had provided and his best jacket, and headed uptown in the car to 79th Street.

50

Nappy's Lounge was keyhole-shaped. A long, narrow room, bar on one side, cocktail tables ranged along the other, led to a spacious circular dining room. The dining room seemed to be completely empty, but the bar was doing a good business. Most of the stools at it were occupied, and the occupants gave the impression of being uniformly middle-aged, well-fixed, and low-voiced. There were no women at the bar, but a pair of exotic-looking brunettes sat at one of the cocktail tables sleepily nursing tall drinks. One of them, caught in the middle of a huge yawn when Jake turned her way, snapped her jaws shut and gave him a professional smile. When he showed no response she luxuriously went ahead with the yawn.

The man seated on the stool nearest the entrance must have been keeping tabs on the place by way of the mirror behind the bar. He swung around on the stool and walked over to Jake. Despite the dim lighting of the room, he wore dark glasses. 'Yes, sir,' he said. 'Anything I can do for you?'

Jake said: 'I don't know. I'm supposed to meet someone named Frank Milan here. Is he around?'

'You Mr Dekker?' the man said, and when Jake said he was, the man said: 'Then he's around.'

He led the way to the dining room. At its entrance, a maître d'hôtel in dinner jacket, looking as sleepy as the two girls at the cocktail table, was standing before a lectern, checking through the reservations book on it like a conductor going through a score before a concert. 'Dekker,' the man said to him, and the maître d'hôtel signalled into the dining room. A couple of thirty-year-old all-American types, almost too clean-cut, emerged from it, and one of them said apologetically to Jake: 'Hope you don't mind, Mr Dekker, but we have to make sure you're clean. No weapons, no taps, no tapes. Just a formality, of course. In the manager's office, please.'

It was a formality executed with painstaking care. In the manager's office they had him strip down to his shorts. Then they went through his clothing and everything in its pockets, not missing an item. He observed that they paid special attention to his watch, ballpoint, key holder, and belt buckle. When he was again fully clothed he was led into the dining room.

The two men sat on a banquette at one side of it, out of view of the bar area. One was small and slight, well-tanned, silvery-haired, and sad-faced. The other was large and grossly fat, pale, bald, and even more sad-faced. There was no one else in the room.

The large, pale man gestured at Jake's escorts, and they moved away and sat down at a table near the entrance. No one suggested that Jake sit down. The man said curtly: 'I'm Aaron Katzman. This is Mr Milan. I am his legal representative, also his personal representative, so whatever you have to say, please say it to me. Also, please say it fast.'

Jake took his time pulling out a chair and seating himself directly opposite Milan. He said: 'I expected to have a private talk with you, Milan.'

Milan looked like a lizard basking in the sunlight. He gave the impression of being either deaf or totally uninterested.

Katzman said: 'Some of those people out in the bar are waiting for important appointments with Mr Milan. If you do not want to do things the way he prefers, please grant those people the courtesy of not delaying their appointments further.'

'That's quite a mouthful,' Jake said. 'Do I gather from it that this is Mr Milan's office and that he doesn't go in for privacy? That might seriously inhibit me.'

Katzman said: 'Anything discussed here will be kept absolutely confidential. And I trust Mr Milan does not need some kind of fancy-shmancy office to impress you. Now will you kindly speak your piece?'

Jake kept his eyes on Milan. 'My piece is that Mr Milan is at least partly responsible for having my wife almost drowned, in having shots fired into my home, and in having me tailed twenty-four hours a day by would-be tough guys who carry large guns. Confidentially, I don't find any of it very funny. Especially where it involves my wife.'

Milan studied his fingernails with mild interest. Katzman looked as stern as his blubbery face permitted. 'Dekker, I must warn you – '

'Counsellor, I am here on a mission of peace. By the time you get done meddling in it, there will be only desolation and sorrow. Now keep your mouth shut for a minute and listen. I was sent to these parts by Guaranty Life Insurance of New York to investigate a fraudulent claim entered against them by the widow of someone named Walter Thoren. I am sure none of this comes as a surprise to either of you. Or that a relative of Mr Milan called Pooch Gela – '

'Who?' Milan's voice was a deep, rasping growl. 'Who'd he say?' and Katzman said, 'Angelo. He means Angelo.'

'Oh, Angelo.' Milan nodded. He smiled a faraway smile, the old uncle smiling at the escapades of a harum-scarum nephew.

Jake said to him: 'Let's quit playing games, Milan. This morning I sent a complete report on the case so far to my boss at Guaranty, John Maniscalco. It tells everything there is to tell about Angelo's involvement with Thoren. So if anything unpleasant happens to me now, my company will turn that information over to the authorities here and demand a full investigation of how and why. They will really kick over Angelo's can of worms. And you're down on the record too, as more or less covering for him.'

The faraway smile remained fixed on Milan's lips. Katzman showed open horror. 'Dekker, these statements are not only insulting, they are absolutely slanderous.' He slapped a hand on the table. 'Absolutely. I don't understand Mr Milan's forbearance at this moment. A respected member of the community to patiently sit and let himself be slandered so vilely?' The orotund voice became almost tender. 'This man cannot be made of flesh and blood to take it the way he does. He must be made of iron.'

Jake said to Milan: 'For chrissake, how can you stand having this clown around?' and Milan said slyly: 'What's the matter? You think you're smarter than he is?'

'I'll let you decide that. Listen to me, Milan. Get it straight that I'm not trying to threaten you, because I know damn well you're too big for that. And I'm also willing to believe you're too big to be personally cutting in on Angelo's blackmail racket. So you're not my concern. He is. When I get a release from Thoren's widow my company hands me a ten per cent bonus for it. I want that money quick, and Angelo is holding up the works.'

'Threats are threats,' Katzman cut in ominously, 'no matter who they're directed against.'

Jake disregarded this. He said to Milan: 'I'll lay it on the line for you. You know as well as I do that Thoren's insurance was for two hundred grand, so my ten per cent comes to twenty grand. If you advise Angelo to take a vacation trip far away for the rest of this month, I'm willing to hand you a healthy slice of my percentage. Five thousand dollars cash. Five thousand just for being Angelo's friendly family adviser. How does that sound?'

He waited. Milan sat smiling at him, then inclined his head toward Katzman, who, miraculously, no longer showed any signs of temperament. Katzman planted his elbows on the table, knitted his fingers together, and regarded Jake over them. 'Five thousand dollars to give advice to a nephew is too

251

much. A dollar would be too much. Family advice should come free. I don't know about your family, but in Mr Milan's family, good will prevails. Blood is thicker than water.'

Jake said gravely: 'Then maybe Mr Milan has some worthwhile enterprise I could invest in. Like a fresh-air fund for delinquent nephews.'

'Mr Milan is connected with many enterprises. But as an investment in any one of them, five thousand dollars would be too little. A drop in the bucket. The very smallest investment, the very least that would be worth his consideration' – Katzman pursed his lips and looked up at the ceiling as if the answer might be written there – 'would be, let us say, exactly nineteen thousand eight hundred dollars.'

'Practically my whole bonus? You have to be kidding.'

'Dekker, you are the one who offered a deal. If you want to withdraw the offer for the time being, goodbye and good luck. After all, tomorrow is another day.'

'Not so quick, Katzman. Call it curiosity, but I'd like to know how you hit on that particular figure. Why nineteen eight and not the whole twenty? Out of charity?'

'Out of necessity. Hand a man a nice piece of cash nowadays, and too many people worry about it. Especially income-tax people. So as not to worry them, you will sign a demand note which states that Mr Milan has loaned you eighteen thousand dollars at ten percent. Then, when you give the money to him, it goes on the books as the repayment of a loan. Do a little arithmetic in your head, and you will see that the principal and interest of this loan add up to nineteen eight. Not twenty. Certainly not the five you offered.'

Jake worked his hand back and forth over his mouth. He saw Katzman glance at his watch. He said: 'Ten thousand is my limit. And no phony demand notes.'

'The price is nineteen eight, Dekker. And if you're ready to meet it, I happen to have the note all made out and ready to be signed.' Katzman drew a folded sheet of paper from his pocket and tossed it on the table. 'Go ahead and read it. Nineteen eight, payable on demand. Never sign anything without reading it.'

252

'All I'm buying, Katzman, is goodwill, and without any guarantee it can even be delivered. If Angelo doesn't want to listen to uncle, uncle is still holding my note for almost twenty thousand dollars. I'd have to be out of my mind to go for that kind of deal.' Jake turned to Milan. 'Ten thousand, the day I lock up the case. It's as simple as that.'

Milan, still faintly smiling, looked at Katzman. Katzman's shake of the head set his series of chins wobbling. He said flatly: 'Nineteen eight. And a note to make the cheese binding. But why does it have to come out of your pocket? Put it to your company. They should be glad to settle a two-hundred-grand case so cheap.'

Jake said: 'Can I also put to them that I saw Angelo board a plane for a vacation in Palermo, starting tomorrow morning?'

Katzman's mouth drew down. 'As you said, you are buying goodwill. What form it takes is up to Mr Milan.'

'Then it's no deal, Katzman.'

Katzman said blandly: 'That's how you feel right now. Tomorrow or the day after, who knows? Sometimes things happen that can make a man change his mind overnight.'

Jake stood up. He braced his fists on the table and leaned forward toward Katzman. 'What's that supposed to mean, Counsellor?'

'It means that if you change your mind, don't stand on ceremony. Just knock on the door. Mr Milan is always interested in a sound proposition.'

Jake said: 'For your sake, you fat bastard, let's hope that's all it means.' He turned to go, but Milan said, 'Hey, you,' and he turned back again. Milan's smile was now broad enough to reveal the uneven edges of yellowed teeth. He jerked his head in Katzman's direction.

'You still think you're smarter than him?' he asked.

51

Adjoining Nappy's Lounge was a big seafood place. Jake phoned Magnes from there. 'How quick can you fix me up with a room for the girl?'

'Before you can wink an eye. Fifteen, twenty minutes. It's about time you got around to it, Dekker. What name do I book her under?'

'Use hers. Make it a suite for Mr and Mrs Jacob Majeski.' Jake spelled it out. 'But the place has to be over on the Miami side, and on the bay so I can get to it by boat. Another thing. I know it's short notice, but I want you to find me a girl who'll take a plane to New York late tonight and stay over there a few days. Someone who looks like my girl.'

'For a quick switch?'

'Yes. So she doesn't have to be her twin. Just small, blonde, and well-stacked.'

Magnes said: 'Is it all right if it's a professional from an agency I know?'

'If it has to be. Get on it now. I'm up on the Seventy-ninth Street Causeway. I'll stop by at your place in about twenty minutes to work out the details.'

Caught in the five o'clock traffic where it looked as if every car on the Beach was stacked bumper to bumper in front of him, he needed forty minutes to make the trip. Magnes took one look at him when he opened the door and promptly said: 'Cool off. Everything is all fixed up.'

'What are the arrangements?'

'Expensive. The place is the Argyle East on the bay over in South Miami. Bedroom, sitting room, and private terrace for ninety bucks a day. Everything de luxe. She can check in whenever she's ready.'

'How about protection?'

'Best thing about the place is it don't cater to the hoods, which is why I picked it. But I'll still talk to Security there about keeping an eye on her. And I already lined up a girlie for that trip to New York. You didn't say what flight, so I picked the Northeast ten p.m. If you want, I can change it.'

Jake said: 'No, it'll do fine. Tell your bagger to be in the ladies' room nearest to the Northeast counter at quarter of ten and carrying a pair of sunglasses in her hand for identification. And to take only a flight bag along. She'll be given her ticket and money there, and I'll throw in enough extra so that she can outfit herself in New York.'

'I figured something like that. I told her fifty a day, all expenses included, so you'll know what to give her. Now let's hear what happened to shake you up like this. My guess is somehow or other you got to Frank Milan, and he shoved his thumb right in your eye.'

Jake said: 'That was one eye. The thumb in the other was from a shyster named Aaron Katzman. Milan's fat mouthpiece. Do you know anything about him?'

'Dekker, everybody in Dade County knows about him except maybe the tourists. This is the guy figured how to make the hoods who moved in here respectable with their skim-off money from Vegas and the Bahamas, and, once upon a time, Havana. He's in with some of the hotel people and builders and union bosses, and he ties the hoods up with them so nobody can even figure who's got a piece of what action any more. A real barracuda. And close to the biggest politicians in Miami and here on the Beach. Anyhow big enough so he was under indictment three times already, and he walked out laughing every time.'

Jake said: 'I should have known. I've met a lot of lawyers and most of them creeps, but I never met one before who practically admitted complicity in a blackmail ring, tried to extort money from me, and then threatened me with violence if I didn't pay up.'

'Threatened you?' Magnes said. 'Or your girlie?'

'Same difference. The point is that this guy knows the inside story about Thoren as well as Milan does, and neither of them could be happier about it. You people run quite a town here, don't you? This place could give Tijuana lessons.'

Magnes shrugged. 'Who's arguing? A complete hundred

per cent rotten it's not, but I'll have to admit it's about as rotten as it can get. On the other hand, you can't beat the climate.'

'Except during hurricane season. Last point on the agenda. That guy you know with the speedboat. Would he be available for a job tonight?'

'Him or somebody else like him. Don't worry about it. Give me a couple hours, and I'll fix you up with a fast boat and a deaf and dumb driver any time. When do you want him?'

'Midnight at my place,' Jake said. 'Twelve sharp. It's the first house north of the one with the big light in the back yard. And tell him to ease up on the horsepower and keep his spotlight off when he pulls in. My neighbours are jumpy to start with. I don't want him to panic them.' He pushed open the door. 'What's a good eating place near that library in Miami? Something with a little glamour.'

Magnes considered this. 'You could do a lot worse than the Columbus roof. On the boulevard about Northeast First Street. Good eating, and you get a very nice view of the Beach from there.' He added, deadpan: 'You only see the buildings, not the people.'

Anthony Aiello must have parked his green Chevrolet well out of range this time. Jake was halfway home before he caught sight of it in the mirror. He made sure it was with him until it pulled up at its usual station near the bridge to Daystar Number One.

In the house, he stuffed five hundred dollars into an envelope and thrust it into his pocket. Then he hauled out two of his biggest suitcases and quickly packed them with everything Elinor had brought with her, a raincoat and head scarf going in last. These suitcases and her flight bag he planted on the rear seat of the Jaguar. He went back to the house, pulled out Elinor's own two empty valises and loaded them into the trunk of the car.

Passing the green Chevy when he recrossed the bridge to the Beach, he observed that the driver was not Aiello now, but a moon-faced, unmoustached blond, so apparently the night shift had taken over. He led the Chevy across the cause-

256

way and down Biscayne Boulevard to the Columbus Hotel at First Street, where he turned the Jaguar over to a parking attendant. Then he walked to the library across the boulevard slowly enough for the moon-faced blond to mark his destination without trouble.

Elinor was at a table in the reading room, a clutter of books and magazines before her. A tall, skinny boy with an unkempt mop of hair and a scraggly beard had managed to work his chair so close to hers that they sat almost head to head. He was talking to her in an undertone, one hand gesticulating passionately as he talked. She was focusing on an open magazine as she listened. The expression on her face was one of mixed irritation and amusement.

She caught sight of Jake, and her face lighted up. He walked over to the table, and she said, 'Hello, darling,' with the aplomb of a long-wed housewife greeting her mate on his return home from the office. Her companion looked at Jake. 'Well, maybe they do,' he said to Elinor, and made his way off without waiting for an introduction.

Jake sat down in the freshly vacated chair. 'Who was he? What was that all about?'

Elinor said: 'Well, I've been telling him to quit hanging around, because my husband would be here soon and he's very jealous, and he said they don't make jealous husbands any more. I guess he changed his mind about that fast when he got a look at you. Poor kid.' She moved close to Jake, her thigh warm against his. 'You don't know how you look when you're feeling hairy. It's like a thunderstorm building up.'

'Did he ask what you were doing here?'

'He isn't one of the bad guys, if that's what you're worried about. He's just a kid, goes to Miami University. Anyhow' – someone behind them made a shushing sound, and Elinor lowered her voice – 'anyhow, the big thing is you were right about Thoren. Every which way. I mean, the submarine operation and everything else.'

'I was? But I told you to call me in that case. Why didn't you call?'

'I did call. I've been calling every hour since three o'clock.

And it's half past seven now, so I would have called in another half hour again. I didn't think you were home all day.'

'I just came from there. You must have missed me, coming and going. Then it's definite about Thoren? But he didn't go under that name then, did he? He couldn't have.'

'He didn't.' She gestured at the collection of literature before her. 'It's all here. The only thing you were wrong about was the name of the operation. It wasn't Operation Pretorius, it was Pastorius. One submarine landed at Long Island and two down here.'

'Did you take notes on it?'

Elinor patted her pocketbook. 'It's all here too. And all about who Thoren was and what he was doing here and how he met up with Earl Dobbs. The whole thing. Do you want to hear about it right now?'

'No, while we eat. Remember that victory celebration I promised you? We'll have it now.'

'Now? Without going home to change?' Elinor looked down at herself in dismay. 'I don't think I'm dressed for high living this way.'

'You'd be dressed for it in a flannel bathrobe and with your hair in curlers,' Jake said, and she enthusiastically bumped his shoulder with hers and said, 'You convinced me. Let's start celebrating in a nice restaurant and then go home to bed and finish celebrating there. Jake, it still works. When I saw you walk in just now I took right off. I mean, right into orbit. It's wild, man.'

They were outside the library doors when she suddenly clutched his arm. 'My package,' she said. 'I almost forgot,' and ran inside again to retrieve the Jordan Marsh box from the checkroom. Crossing the park to Biscayne Boulevard, she waved it at him. 'Guess what it is.'

'Not another present for me, I hope. It's your turn.'

'Hey, that's right. You're wearing my shirt, and I didn't even notice. It looks great on you. But this package isn't for you. It's for both of us. Go on and guess.'

Jake saw the moon-faced blond man standing on the sidewalk at the foot of the path. As they approached him, the man slowly sauntered away. 'Go on and guess,' Elinor said. 'Take a chance.'

'A black lace nightgown?'

'Well, if you keep guessing the same thing all the time, you have to be right sooner or later.' She squeezed his hand. 'But wait'll you see it. Naked is nothing compared to it.'

52

The twilight view of Miami Beach from the Columbus roof was all Magnes had said it would be. As lights went on along the causeways and then in distant hotels and highrises across the bay, Elinor said: 'Now that's what I call timing. How far away is it?'

'I don't know. At a guess, about five miles. What'll you have to drink?'

'Beer, if you don't think it's kind of crude for a celebration. And some rolls or something right away. I'm starved.'

When the waiter had gone off with their order she pulled a collection of crumpled notepapers from her pocketbook and arranged them before her. By the time she had them organized to her satisfaction, the waiter was back again. She said to Jake with her mouth full: 'How do you want it? Just the parts about Thoren and Dobbs, or Operation Pastorius from the beginning?'

'Both. But boiled down to the essentials.'

'Mmm.' She studied the notes. 'Well, in 1942 this officer in something called Nazi Party Intelligence, Overseas Organization, gave a plan for sabotage to the German High Command. And they gave it to Admiral Canaris of High Command Intelligence. The idea was there would be three submarines sent to the United States, and each one would have four sabotage experts on it. The first' – she peered closely at the slip of paper in her hand – 'oh, the first objectives for the men landing on Long Island were to destroy railroad communications into New York City and to blow up the Niagara Falls power plant. Then men landing in north Florida were to destroy railroad communications around Jacksonville, and the ones landing in south Florida were supposed to sabotage the submarine base in Key West. Then all of them would meet in the Tennessee Valley and sabotage the Alcoa plants there. That was the main objective, because that was our biggest aluminium works, and we needed aluminium for airplanes. Only nothing worked out right.'

'Which was what I remembered of it,' Jake said. 'One of the men in the Long Island party turned them all in to the FBI as soon as they landed. Right?'

'Right. That was George John Dasch. He was head of the Long Island bunch, but he knew all the plans for everybody. So everybody was captured right away except one man from the south Florida bunch. And everybody captured, except Dasch and a guy named Burger who proved he had been forced to go on the mission, were electrocuted by the American army in August, 1942. Those two went to jail.'

Jake said: 'And the one who escaped was our pal Thoren. But under his real name, it must have been. What was it?'

'Walther Stresemann. I mean, it had to be because Walther Stresemann was the one who got away. He was in charge of the south Florida bunch, too, and that makes it sure. The north Florida submarine landed at Ponte Vedra Beach near Jacksonville on June seventeenth. The south Florida one with Stresemann on it was the last to come here. That was June twenty-first. They put Stresemann and the three men with him ashore at Juno Beach near Palm Beach, and next day those three were caught, but he got away. Now comes the best part, because it's all about him.' Elinor planted her elbow on the table and propped her chin in her hand. She stared long and hard at Jake. 'You know you're a genius?' she said solemnly.

'Yes.'

'Well, I can see that's something we'll argue about.' Abstractedly, she stuffed a piece of roll into her mouth. 'I mean, like you really are. When Sherry told me about you she said you were smart, but it takes more than just smart to figure things out the way you did. Almost everything you finally

260

figured out about Thoren was right. And you hardly had anything to go on.'

Jake said: 'I had more than it looked. And some luck. And you to come up with a couple of inspirations.'

'You mean that? I really did help?'

'You did. Now what about Thoren?'

Elinor returned to her notes. 'Where was I? Oh, he got away But they had the roads blocked to the north, so he headed south. What made it hard for them was that he had a valise with eighty thousand dollars in it which was supposed to cover expenses for his unit, so he had enough to keep buying beat-up old cars for cash and throw the FBI off the trail that way. Between Palm Beach and Miami, he bought three different cars. He had been fixed up with a driver's licence and army discharge papers and whatever else he needed to pass himself off as an American, but from what I make of it he didn't have to use any of that stuff while he was on the run. That's why there was no record anywhere of the name Thoren, which was the one on his papers.'

'What about the language problem?'

'There wasn't any. He got out of college in Germany in 1935 able to speak good English, and then he went to the Univeristy of Minnesota here for a year and for another year to MIT before he went back to Germany. No language problem at all.

'Anyhow, the FBI and army people after him thought they finally had him bottled up in Miami, but he got away and headed for the west coast of Florida on the Tamiami Trail But when you're on the Tamiami Trail –'

'I know,' Jake said. 'Once you're on it, there's only one way off before you hit the coast. Route 94. When he realized they were on to him again and had blocked the way to the coast, he took 94 into the town of Crosscut.'

Elinor said: 'You see? You're making like a genius again. But that's what happened. And that's where Earl Dobbs comes into it. And his Uncle Jesse. Stresemann put a gun on them and made them hide him out. So they did. Like on a little island right in the middle of the swamp there.'

'Dobbs Hammock.'

'Dobbs Hammock. But that night the uncle tried to kill Stresemann and get away. He hurt him bad with a broken bottle, but didn't kill him, and in the end the uncle got shot to death and Earl Dobbs – he was only a kid then, fifteen years old – got a bullet in him that made it look like he was dead too. He almost was by the time the FBI found out about this island and how to get to it. And by that time Stresemann was gone for good. Just took the Dobbses' boat and disappeared. They hunted all around the swamps for him, but they never found any sign of him or the boat, so they wrote him off as dead. I mean, what with being wounded so bad, and the alligators and snakes and all, it made sense that way. But of course he wasn't dead. Somehow he made it back to Miami and became Walter Thoren for good.'

Jake said: 'You have to admit he was something of a genius himself, wasn't he?'

Elinor shook her head. 'Maybe. But I don't dig geniuses that go around shooting old men and kids.'

'You don't think Fidel and Che ever did anything nasty like that?'

'No. They wouldn't.'

'Remember,' Jake said, 'you don't have to pull the trigger yourself to be the killer.'

Elinor knit her brow over this. Then she said unhappily: 'I don't know. I mean, if they did anything like that, it's because they were leading a people's struggle, weren't they?'

'Sweetheart, that's very pretty, but Thoren could offer even a better excuse. He was trying to stay alive, which happens to be the name of the game. And he won the game with all the odds against him. Give him credit for that at least. This guy had brains enough and guts enough and cool enough for ten people. His hard luck he didn't finish off Earl Dobbs then and there.'

'Ah, Jake – '

'No, I'm not crying over what happened to Thoren. I'm just sorry that when he was finally brought down it had to be by a couple of hyenas like Dobbs and Gela. He probably thought the same thing when he saw he was at the end of the line.'

Elinor said: 'And Mrs Thoren is probably thinking it now, wherever she is. Magnes didn't find her yet, did he?'

'Not yet.' Jake pointed at the notes. 'Is that the whole story?'

'Uh-huh. Unless you want all the details about everything. Like this Admiral Canaris they brought the scheme to at the start said it was flaky, but nobody listened to him. They said go ahead anyhow. Stuff like that.'

'No, we can skip the details.'

'Yes, sir. Then that's the whole story. Any questions?'

Jake thought it over. 'Two questions. First, what did German Intelligence have in mind for these guys if they pulled off their mission? Were they supposed to be picked up by submarines at some later date? Brought back to Germany?'

'No. They were supposed to settle down separately here and make out however they could. This Operation Pastorius was their whole thing for the war.'

'I thought so. I have a feeling that if they were ordered to report back to headquarters, Thoren would somehow have done it, even if he had to build his own submarine.' Jake pointed at the notes. 'Mind if I have them for the files?'

Elinor handed them to him. 'As long as you don't mark them for spelling. I'm a terrible speller. Even when I copy words, I spell them wrong. What's the second question?'

Jake leaned back in his chair to give the waiter room to serve them. He watched Elinor daintily harpoon a large shrimp, slosh it around in sauce, and engulf it.

He said: 'I like a girl who doesn't pick at her food. You've got cocktail sauce on your chin.'

She dabbed at it with her napkin. 'What's the second question?' she said around the shrimp.

'How would you like to be a kept woman?'

She smiled at him. 'I am a kept woman. I like it.'

'I mean kept in style. A suite in a luxury hotel, a charge account at the shops downstairs, call room service for champagne and caviar, total decadence. I'm serious about it.'

She looked at him searchingly. 'You don't sound like it, but I guess you are. Why, Jake? You think they'll try shooting up the house again?'

'I'm not sure what they'll try. But Gela knows I'm almost ready to put the whole case together, and he's not going to take it like a little gentleman. I'd feel better if you were out of range, no matter what he tries. You've finished your part of the job, so now you're only an innocent bystander, and there's no reason for the innocent bystander to take any chances getting hurt. You can see I'm being completely honest about it.'

'No, you're not. You're only talking about me, but you'll be right in the middle of everything. Jake – '

'Take it easy, sweetheart. I've told you more than once Gela won't do anything that Guaranty can jump on as an excuse to block payment. He has to depend on intimidation, not a power play. And you happen to be someone he can use to put leverage on me. If you're off the scene, no leverage.'

'Off the scene?' Elinor said. 'I thought you were talking about a hotel right around here.'

'I am. The Argyle East on the bay a little further downtown. The trick is to get you in there without anybody knowing about it. We can do it right after dinner.'

Elinor said: 'But what about you? It sounds like I'm supposed to stay there alone. I don't want that. I want you to be with me.'

'Some of the time I will be.' He rested his hand on hers. 'You don't think I'm keeping you around just for show, do you?'

'I hope not. But you said somebody's always following you. So he'll follow you to the hotel and know where I am. I might as well stay with you.'

Jake said: 'Right now, the best thing that can happen is for someone to follow me. The way it works, I take you to the airport, pick up a ticket in your name for a flight to New York – Mrs Dekker being your name – and check your luggage through. Then you go into the ladies' room. Magnes has arranged for an agency girl to be waiting there. She'll look something like you – at least from a distance – and she'll be carrying a pair of sunglasses in her hand so you can spot her. She becomes Mrs Dekker and goes right out to catch the plane. You wait awhile, then take a cab to the Argyle East and check in as Mrs Elinor Majeski. That's the whole deal.'

'But where will you be? When will I see you?'

'After I leave you I'll drive back to Daystar along with the guy tailing me. Argyle East is on the water. I've booked a boat to take me there at twelve o'clock. I don't know how fast you can travel on the water here at night, but I should be at the hotel somewhere between twelve-thirty and one. I'll have the boat wait for me. Five a.m. I go back to Daystar.'

Elinor made a sound that was half-laugh, half-tearful sniffle. 'You sound like some kind of crazy commuter.'

'Not for long. Once we turn up Mrs Thoren, we'll nail down the case quick. The way things are, the only other choice would be for you to go back to New York, with some muscle-bound agency man to pick you up at Kennedy and then hang around the house as watchdog until I'm done here. And I'm not offering you that choice. I want you here.'

Elinor gave him that searching look again. 'You really do, don't you?'

'Sweetheart, the amount of trouble and money this setup takes – '

'I know. I sort of twined myself into your heartstrings after all, didn't I?'

'Only since you've been properly corrupted. All I aimed to do all along was save a soul for the Establishment.'

'Oh, sure.' She sat smiling at him. Then slowly the smile faded. 'Jake, tell me something. What happens after the job is done? I mean, to us? I know we've been through this already, but things are different now aren't they?'

'Seems like they are.'

'But I've still got a kid. And he needs me. I need him too, for that matter. Do you see what I mean? It's like this package comes two to a set.'

'Why should it have to, sweetheart? The kid has a grandma to take care of him. There are nursery schools. And you'll have plenty of time to drop in on him and give him a dose of TLC. Every day, if you feel like it.'

'Feel like it? Darling, this is my kid. You don't just drop in on your kid when you feel like it. That would be a bad scene. You know it would be. You've got a kid of your own you're hardly ever with. How do you think he feels about it?'

There were some crumbs scattered on the table between them. Jake picked them up one by one and arranged them in a straight line. While he carefully checked the line with his knife blade, he said: 'For the sake of accuracy, there's something you might as well know right now. I don't have any kid.'

Elinor said blankly: 'But you told me –'

'That's right. But do you remember when I told it to you? How you were carrying on about walking out on me and turning me in to Kermit Thoren and the cops about bugging phones? As far as you were concerned right then, I was Frankenstein's monster on the loose. I had to think of something to say that would at least make me look halfway human to you, and that was it. About having a kid. About not being allowed to see him.'

'Jake, you shouldn't have. You didn't have to. I never would have walked out on you.'

'That's easy to say now. You forget what you were like only a little while ago. For all her brave talk they didn't come any more uptight than my girlie. Even Magnes knew that after only one look at you.'

'I don't care what he knew. I just want you to know I never would have done anything to hurt you. I never will.' She compressed her lips and nodded once, very firmly. 'But I'm glad you told me the truth about it now. I mean about not having a kid. That's really a meaningful relationship, when we tell each other the truth about everything, isn't it?'

'Heavens to Betsy, yes.'

'It's nothing to joke about,' Elinor said reproachfully. 'Especially when I'm wondering about some of the other things you told me. Like being married twice to the same woman and getting divorced both times. Was that the truth?'

'It was. I seemed to have a compulsion to keep marrying that woman. It's all gone now.'

'Because of me?'

'Well, you've offered some sound therapy, Doc.'

'That's what I thought,' Elinor said. Then she said wistfully: 'But it doesn't change the one big thing, Jake. This package still comes two to a set.'

'A mother's heart,' Jake said. He checked the line of crumbs with his knife blade again, then swept them up on the blade and dropped them into his plate. 'What the hell, I've got a great big brownstone in Manhattan all to myself. You can keep the kid chained in the cellar. It's a little damp, but he'll get used to it.'

'Oh, Jake – '

'I know. It is a beautiful gesture, isn't it? I'm already wondering how I got conned into it.'

'You are not.'

'Oh yes, I am. And how's your mama going to take the arrangement, considering she's already watched you share a happily unwed relationship that didn't wind up very happily?'

'She'll take it the same as the other time. She'll yell at me and call me names, and then after a while she'll be dying to see the kid, so she'll ask us over and cook us a big Polish supper. That's how she is.'

'Jesus, what a package. Now there's three in the set. And heartburn.'

'Mama's a great cook, so there won't be any heartburn. Jake, when I'm at the hotel would it be all right to call up home every day, same as at Daystar?'

'Sweetheart, you can call home every hour, if that's what you want. I told you that at Argyle East, the world is yours. But it won't be all roses, because the one thing you can't do is go out of your room. Is that clear? The chain stays on the door, you stay in the room, and only licensed help is allowed in. Two rooms and terrace, that is. Even if you feel you're going stir-crazy, that's how it has to be.'

'*Che sera sera,*' Elinor said airily. She held up her glass of beer. 'Here's to finally catching up on my reading. Anyhow, if you ever saw the way I can sleep when no one sets the clock, you'd know I'll make out just fine.'

53

Jake pulled the Jaguar away from the Columbus and parked beside a hydrant down the block. He said to Elinor: 'Now we're going to do everything by the numbers. You know what that means?'

'Yes, sir.'

'Good. There are two bags in back with all your things in them. Open them up.'

She kneeled on the seat and leaned over to do it, her rear end high in the air. When Jake braced his arm across it to hold her steady, she said, 'Hey, wow.'

'Keep your mind on business. I'll be bringing this stuff along with me when I go to the hotel later on. Meanwhile, put whatever you really need of it in your flight bag. It's on the floor there. Your raincoat and a head scarf are packed on top of one of those suitcases. When you're done loading the flight bag, put them on.'

Wearing the raincoat and scarf, she finally settled back in her seat, the flight bag on her lap. As he got the car moving she opened the Jordan Marsh box and stuffed the nightgown into the flight bag. She said: 'It wouldn't be any good if you brought it along with you, because I want to look real decadent when you show up. What's the next numbers?'

'I'll tell you when we get to the airport.' He turned north toward the 36th Street Expressway to the airport and saw the green Chevy swing around the corner after him. 'Nothing to worry about. Everything is lovely.'

'If there's nothing to worry about, why do I keep feeling I have to pee all the time, but I really don't? And I keep getting cold shivers. But everything is lovely.' She moved against him and slid her arm through his. 'I've never been happier in my whole life. Scared stiff and never happier. What an adorable, crazy, mixed-up kid I am. Don't you think I am, Jake? Where's the brownstone you own?'

'Uptown on the East Side. Sixtieth and Lexington. And if I had known how two bottles of beer would hit you –'

'It's not the beer. It's you and the brownstone.'

'And the kid chained in the cellar.'

Elinor put her head on his shoulder. 'He'll get used to it,' she said contentedly.

Coming up the ramp to the Northeast departures platform, Jake said: 'We're back to the numbers, soldier. Are you tuned in?'

She released his arm and sat up straight. 'I guess so. Jake, suppose that girl from the agency isn't here?'

'I'll stand by when you go into the ladies' room. If she's not there, come right out, and I'll call Magnes about it. But she'll be there. This kind of assignment is too sweet for her to blow.' He handed Elinor the envelope with the five hundred dollars in it. 'This is the sweetener. You give her this and your ticket. You switch coats with her and give her that scarf to wear on her head. You trade around the stuff in your flight bag, so she can carry yours. And your pocketbooks go into the flight bags. Actually, you won't have to concentrate on every detail, because she'll know what to do. If you think costume changes in a show are something, wait'll you see a professional make this kind of change in nothing flat.'

'But she still can't look that much like me. So when she walks out –'

'She'll walk out fast, with shades on, carrying your bag, wearing your coat and head scarf, and with a handkerchief to her nose like someone who just caught the cold of the year. Which is why you'll put on your shades now. And while you're at the ticket counter you'll keep your handkerchief working. Hell, sweetheart, don't you have any confidence in me?'

'You know I do.' She put on her sunglasses and looked at him mournfully over them. 'I just don't have any in me.'

He stopped the car at the entrance to the terminal. 'There's still time to do it the other way,' he said. 'You'll have a ticket to New York in your hand and plenty of money in that envelope. All you'd have to do is walk into the plane.'

'But you don't want me to, do you?'

'No.'

'And I wouldn't, even if you did want me to. So why are we wasting time?'

She worked the handkerchief hard while the ticket was being made out and her two empty valises being checked through. The final touch came after Jake saw to her seat reservation and then led her aside for a farewell kiss. She waved him off. 'No,' she said in a muffled voice through the handkerchief, 'I don't want you to catch my cold.'

Jake said: 'Watch the overacting, dear. Anyhow, whatever you've got, I've already caught it,' and kissed her at length. Then he said into her ear: 'Remember to wait about fifteen minutes in there after you make the switch, then get right into a cab. And when you sign in at the hotel your name is Mrs Majeski. And you don't step out of your room, no matter what. Anything you want, you order from downstairs by phone. That's all the numbers there are.'

'And you'll be at the hotel by one o'clock?'

'I'll be there.' He gave her a broad wink. 'Now that my wife is going out of town, I can really swing.'

'Men are such beasts,' Elinor said.

He watched her disappear into the ladies' room, clocked off two minutes on his watch, and left the terminal. Driving down the ramp to the expressway entrance, he searched for the image of the green Chevy in his rear-view mirror, but didn't see any. He slowed down, and a battered Rambler tailgating the Jaguar almost went into it. Its driver thrust his head out of the window. 'Damn fool!' he bellowed. 'More money than brains!'

Jake put his own head out of the window to answer, but then, a few cars behind the Rambler, he caught sight of the green Chevy. He pulled his head back in and drove to the Beach at a moderate clip, whistling tunelessly to himself all the way.

54

Back on Daystar, he recounted the story of Operation Pastorius over the phone to Magnes, made out a cheque to Elinor for three thousand dollars, straightened whatever in the oppressively empty house needed straightening, and packed his flight bag with some necessaries of his own for overnight use. Shortly before twelve he carried the two suitcases loaded with Elinor's things from the car to the head of the dock, along with the flight bag. A few minutes later he heard the snarling crescendo of a high-powered motor out in the bay and was blinded for an instant by the glare of a searchlight swinging in his direction. The light flicked off, the sound of the motor faded. Then a sleek inboard appeared out of the darkness, running without lights, the sound of the motor now no more than a muted purring. It came around in a wide turn and drew up broadside against the dock with a feather touch. 'You the passenger?' said the shadowy figure behind the wheel, and Jake said: 'That's me.'

He set the luggage in the stern, jumped aboard as the boat drifted clear of the dock, and felt his way into the bucket seat beside the skipper. Under reduced throttle, the boat quietly moved south toward the arches of the Venetian Causeway. A few minutes of this, and the searchlight suddenly went on, its beam cutting a brilliant white track through the darkness ahead. The motor roared wide open, and quick acceleration pressed Jake's shoulders back against the seat. They went under the causeway full flight, water hissing beneath the hull and never slackened speed until they were approaching the Rickenbacker Causeway far down the bay. Here the boat swung toward the Miami shore and a line of high-rises made visible by their lighted windows.

The skipper pointed. 'That there's Argyle East on the bay. Argyle West's beyond it over on Brickell Avenue. Same dock though. You want me to stand by at it?'

Jake said: 'I want to be picked up about five a.m. You can do whatever you like as long as you're here then.'

'I'll be here.' Under the dock lights, Jake got his first good look at the man. His close-cropped hair was white. His face was distorted, its skin badly seamed and with a curious shine as if freshly lacquered. The man took notice of Jake's scrutiny and ran his fingers down a gleaming cheek. 'Burnt,' he said laconically. 'All skin grafts.'

'You used to race boats?'

'Nah, used to run hooch in from Bimini, Prohibition time, until some hijackers caught up with me and done this. Tied me up in my boat and set it on fire. New York fellers. They always played extra dirty.'

'So I've heard,' Jake said.

The dock area was deserted, the lobby of the hotel almost so. He signed in as Jacob Majeski on a card Elinor had already signed, and refused the offer of a bellhop to carry the bags. The suite was 15C on the fifteenth floor.

He knocked on the door of 15C, and almost at once it was pulled open against its chain and Elinor's eye squinted at him through the opening. The room behind her was in darkness. 'Wait a second,' she said breathlessly. 'Don't make a move until I tell you to.' She closed the door, he heard the chain released, and waited. Then she called: 'All right, you can come in.'

He pushed open the door. Lights were on now, and Elinor stood posed in the centre of the room directly under the glitter of an ornate chandelier. She was wearing a floor-length black chiffon nightgown designed in the Empire mode, the waistline high and tight under her breasts. It was just this side of being completely transparent.

Jake said: 'Well, like hey wow.'

'Isn't it?' Elinor said delightedly. She pirouetted, the skirt spiralling around her legs, then leaped at him and threw her arms around his neck. 'Jake, I missed you. Did you miss me? Tell me the truth.'

'Considering it's been all of three hours, I managed to bear up pretty well.'

'No, you didn't. You couldn't wait until you saw me again.'

272

She allowed him to detach himself and bring in the luggage from the hall. Then she said resentfully: 'But that woman Magnes hired didn't look anything like me. She's at least as old as Sherry – '

'Almost thirty? What did she do? Show up in a wheelchair?'

'No, but you know how Sherry looks, and this one didn't. She looked like a lady wrestler. A real bull dyke. Nobody'll think she's me.'

'Yes, they will.' Jake carried the two valises into the bedroom, and Elinor followed with the flight bag. 'She didn''t make a pass at you, did she?'

'Well, there wasn't time for a real pass, but when we were changing around coats and scarves, there seemed to be an awful lot of extra hands all over me.'

Jake peeled off his jacket and shirt. The front of the shirt was damp from spray. He said: 'Ever experiment along those lines?'

'No, I don't dig Lesbies. Besides, I was saving myself for you.'

'From all the way back?'

'From as far back as I can remember. I always knew you'd come along. Did you know I'd come along?'

'Yep.'

'You did?'

'I did. Sometimes at the end of a bad day I'd say to myself: Dekker, your life is unbelievably complicated. What could possibly make it more complicated? Obviously, I was waiting for you to come along.'

'Ahh, you're a rat.' She watched him get out of the rest of his clothes. 'But built. And that white part around you makes it look like you're all lit up there. That reminds me. You know the terrace outside? Well, it's all closed in except the front, so nobody can see you there. Now I can finally get tan all over. I always wanted to get tan all over.'

'Watch it, sister. I've seen what happens when you get too much sun. This time you could fry some very important parts.'

'I'll be careful. But this whole place is wild. There's a little refrigerator under the TV, and a whole stereo in the wall, and the shower stall has about forty nozzles in it, and look at this.' She stepped up on the big double bed. 'I mean, this mattress. It feels hard as a rock, but watch what happens.' She hauled the nightgown up to her knees and did a series of high bounces. 'It's like a trampoline. It's a trip all in itself.'

'Talk about miscalculation,' Jake remarked. 'I thought life at the Argyle East would have a maturing effect on the girl. Kind of polish her up. And what happens? She goes right back to the kiddie playground stage. She'll never shape up.'

Elinor stopped bouncing. 'You sound like my grade adviser used to in high school. Jake, you know what tomorrow is? It's Tuesday. I mean today. It's already Tuesday.'

'What about it?'

'Don't you remember? Tuesday is when we get those cleaners and gardeners and exterminators at the house. And if you didn't mind, I could go – '

'No, you couldn't. They'll all do fine without any supervision. You'll stay right here and suntan your fanny. You're finished with Daystar Island Number Two. That's where the job is, and you're done with the job.' He fished the three-thousand-dollar cheque from his wallet and handed it to her. 'That's it. Paid in full.'

She looked at the cheque, then, with concern, at him. 'You still want me to have this? Even with the way things are with us now?'

'That was the deal, wasn't it?'

'I know, but, well, it's like a paycheque. And I'm not hired help any more. I thought you just wouldn't bother about it.'

'Oh, in that case,' Jake said and reached for it, but she held it up away from him. She said: 'Not that I won't keep it. I need some for Mama, and there's clothes and stuff for the kid, and most of it'll be put away for his school later on. I'd just as soon take it out of this and not ask you for money.'

'And when this is all gone?'

'Then I'll ask for more, and you'll be glad to give it to me because all you're interested in is my happiness, aren't you?'

'No.'

'Yes, you are.'

'Yes, I am. You know, it certainly saves a lot of trouble, the way you handle both ends of our conversation. Now come down off there like a nice big girl, put that cheque away, and get the hotel operator on the phone. Put in a call for me at quarter of five.'

'Oh, Jake. So early?'

'Darling, I am the one who'll be getting up and getting out. If I know you, you'll be sound asleep with your head under the pillow when the phone rings.'

'But you'll wake me up if I am, won't you?'

'It depends on how energetic I feel. You are not an easy waker.'

Elinor stepped off the bed. 'I will be this time. I know what. I'll take the side with the phone. Then I'll have to be the one who answers when it rings.'

So, when the call came, he had to reach across her to get to the phone. He left her still sleeping while he gathered his clothes together and went into the bathroom to dress there. She came in as he was towelling himself after a hasty wash. She stood swaying, head down, chin on her chest, hair fallen forward over her eyes like a sheepdog's. 'Did the phone ring?' she said in a blurred voice. 'I didn't hear anything.'

'It rang. Ask not for whom –'

'How can you be so happy and wide awake this time of night?' She blindly found her way to the sink, parted the hair on each side of her face, and then, with a stifled shriek, dashed water into it. She turned, dripping, toward Jake and pulled the towel from his hand. She mopped her face with it and emerged with her cheeks pink and her eyes wide open. 'So that's how you do it. Cold water.'

'What won't they think of next?' Jake said. 'That terrace here faces the bay, doesn't it?'

'Uh-huh.' She trailed after him through the bedroom to the terrace. 'Jake, when will you be back? What time?'

'After it's dark. Good and dark.' From the terrace he could make out the speedboat docked below, the white hair of the man at its wheel. 'Looks like my cab is already here, sweetheart. Put the chain back on the door when you let me out and get back to bed. What's the most important thing not to do while you're here.'

'Not to do? Get sunburned on any of my important parts.'

'Try again.'

'Not to go out of the door. I know that. Jake, is it all right to call you up at the house?'

'No calls to me through the hotel switchboard. Write me a card instead. I'll read it when I get back here tonight.'

'I'll write you a whole letter. It's a shame not to use up all that expensive stationery they've got in that desk inside.' She folded her arms around his neck. 'But it wouldn't say anything you don't know. And it would be spelt all wrong. Jake?'

'I'm still here, sweetheart. But I shouldn't be.'

'Yes you should, because there's something I want to ask you, and it'll only take a second. I mean, it's something I made up my mind never to ask you, because I know how uptight you are about saying it, but maybe you're not any more. Do you know what I mean?'

'Despite your tongue-tied way of putting it, I know what you mean.'

'And you won't mind if I ask it?'

'Try me.'

'All right, I will. Do you love me, Jake? You don't have to say it exactly like that, if you don't want to. You can just say yes or no.'

'What if it's no?'

'Then I won't believe you, because I think you do.'

'I think so too,' he said.

55

In the boat, as it moved out into the bay, he said to the skipper: 'Know anything about the Everglades? Ever do any cruising around there?'

'Done a little alligator poaching in my time, when the

competition wasn't so stiff. Can't say it's a place to go cruising around in. Swamp buggy's not much of a pleasure craft.'

'What about a town called Crosscut there? Ever hear of it?'

'Been there. But it wasn't what you'd call a town then, and I got my doubts if it is now. Dozen of them cabins like Daniel Boone's, general store, gas pump, and that's it. Mostly old-timers there, and none of them friendly. Kind of inbred.'

Jake said: 'What about a place near it called Dobbs Hammock?'

'Don't know it by name. Outside of some of the big ones, one hammock is like another. Patch of dirt sticking up out of the sawgrass with a couple of trees on it. Only difference is some are hardwood, some are pine. Why? You interested in getting to this Dobbs Hammock?'

'I might be.'

The man steadied the wheel as the boat bounced over a heavy chop in the deep-water channel past Dodge Island. He said: 'Got anything to do with Cubans?'

'No. Why Cubans?'

'Because a bunch of them's out training again in those parts, looking to get even with Castro for the Bay of Pigs. Friend of mine might take on the job of finding this Dobbs Hammock for you, but not if it's in a training area. Last time, he rode some TV news people out to see what them Cubanos was up to and got his buggy shot full of machine-gun bullets by mistake. Almost got his ass blowed off. But if you're not heading into that kind of territory, he'll take you on. You just tell Mr Magnes when and where.'

Jake said: 'I'll keep it in mind. And how about you? Available for another taxi job tonight? Same run, but earlier. Say about ten o'clock?'

'And pickup next morning at five?' The light suspended over Milt Webb's lawn showed clearly from far out in the middle of the bay. The man switched off the boat's searchlight and cut the motor down.

'Pickup at five,' Jake said.

As soon as he got into the house, he looked over every door and window carefully, checked the phones for bugs, and then caught up on his sleep until eight o'clock when the Daystar service help arrived to take over the house and gardens. He cajoled a cleaning woman into making him breakfast, then retired behind the locked door of the study with the morning paper. At nine he phoned the architect in New York who was contracted to convert his recently acquired brownstone to high-rental apartments and told him to hold off on all plans.

'Changes, Mr Dekker?' the architect said in the tone of someone prepared for the worst. 'Or selling the place for a quick turnover? Remember, my contract specified – '

'No, I'm not selling. But instead of all five floors being rentals, I want two of them for myself. A duplex layout.'

'A duplex? Mr Dekker, I've already put in a month's work on those plans. We'll have to sit down together about this. If you're at the building now – '

'Not now,' Jake said. 'I'll set up a meeting with you in a week or so.' He put down the phone, and an instant later it rang. Magnes said: 'That you, Dekker?'

'Yes.'

'Look, what did that Spanisher tell you about the house in Belle Glade? That it was absolutely for sure a present to Mrs Thoren from her father?'

'Not absolutely or for sure. She just mentioned it. Why?'

'Because now I got three guys working over the territory there. And this new one I put on got a brainstorm to look through deeds on file there to see what property is listed under either Sprague, which was the father's name, or Thoren, which is hers. No dice. Could it be your Spanisher told you the wrong town altogether?'

'No, she sounded too sure of herself for that. She said Belle Glade, and she said the house was a gift to Mrs Thoren from her father. Wait a second. There is one thing she might have had wrong. The king of thing she might assume. Papa's usually the one to give gifts like this, but suppose in this case it was mama? The house could be listed under her mother's family name, not her father's.'

Magnes said: 'So what name is that?'

'I don't know. But if Mrs Thoren was brought up around

there, there'll be school records with the information on them. She might have even been born there, so it would be worth looking up birth records too.'

Magnes sighed. 'Dekker, you live two doors from these people. If you could get the kids talking, or if you could maybe get in and take a look at the family Bible or something – '

'I don't trust this Raymond Beaudry enough to go snooping around there. And the kids are over at the university until late afternoon. You have to get on it now, Magnes. Tell two of your men to move on it right away. The other one can keep scouting around.'

'If that's how you want it. How does our girlie like it at the Argyle?'

'Our girlie likes it fine. Call me back as soon as you have anything to report, good or bad. I'll be waiting here.'

The call came a little after two o'clock. Magnes said: 'We got her. Like you figured, there was a birth certificate for Charlotte Sprague, and the mother's name was on it. Hoagland. And this property out by the lake is registered in that name. So my boys snooped around it, and there was the Mercedes locked up in the garage. The aggravating part, they already been by this place, but there was a jeep parked in front of the garage, and the name was Hoagland, so they just kept going.'

'Have they got it staked out?'

'One of them is laying low in a car on the road between the house and the town. The other two got themselves a boat like they're fishing, because it's the same as where you are on Daystar, the house is right on the water, and all the action is in back of it, away from the road. So they spotted this back porch with long-range glasses, and that's where we got a problem. There's not one woman. It's three of them, and two ain't easy to tell apart. The third one is dumpy and always running in and out, so she's probably help around the house. But both of the others are like you described the Thoren woman. Skinny, rundown-looking, grey hair, wearing big sunglasses. Does she have a sister maybe?'

Jake said: 'I don't know. She might have. Or it could be some old friend from around that neighbourhood.'

'Yeah, but whichever it is, Dekker, the boys don't know who to move with or stay with. They want a couple of recent photos to work from. You got anything in the file that'll do?'

'No, all Maniscalco could get me in that line was the newspaper picture taken at Thoren's funeral, and she was wearing a veil. Mrs Ortega has some snapshots of her in an album, but they're from way back when.'

'Still and all – '

'Still and all, we can waste too much time hunting up a worthwhile picture, if there is one around. I'll tell you what I'll do. You said the town is only seventy or eighty miles from here. I can be there in less than two hours and spot the woman myself for your boys. If she's out of sight when I get there, I'll try again first thing tomorrow morning.'

'No,' Magnes said. 'This is, *tokkeh*, too much of a gamble. The one thing those hoods ain't caught on to yet is we know where the woman is hiding out. Blow that, and they'll move her some place else. We took this much time to get where we are? So let's take a little more time and see if we can't get identification without you going up there. The way they're watching you, the minute you drive past North Miami they'll know you're heading upstate, and they'll have a good idea why.'

'I didn't figure on driving. We'll charter a small plane, make the jump in no time, and be back here for supper. We arrange the charter for a jump to Key West or the Bahamas, but when we're off the ground we head for Belle Glade. You can fix me up with a plane and a hungry enough pilot for that, can't you?'

'I can, but I'd just as soon not. What is this, Dekker? You've been playing it so beautiful all along. Now all of a sudden it's panic time? Maniscalco told you you had to deliver the goods tomorrow?'

Jake said: 'If I can, I will. We've got every piece lined up on the board, Magnes, and I'm not sitting around for the next few days waiting to jump them. I'll identify the woman for your guys today or tomorrow. Right after that, we put the crunch on Dobbs, and then get him together with her. Then she either signs a release, or he signs a detailed statement about Walter

Thoren – meaning Walther Stresemann – for the newspapers. It'll all be done a lot quicker than if we waste time hunting up pictures of the woman.'

'It's your case, Dekker, so we'll do it your way. But tell me only one thing. Are you positive that when it comes to the showdown – when the woman has to pick up a pen and sign away two hundred grand – she'll do it? Are you so sure she's that much scared about everybody finding out about Thoren? After all, he's already dead and rotting in hell, the *momser*. And what he was and what he did before she ever met him is not her fault.'

'She'll sign. She must know by now she'll never see anything of that two hundred grand. It's all earmarked for Gela now, and it doesn't hurt that much to sign away somebody else's money.'

'I only hope so,' Magnes said. 'All right, I'll meet you at Opa-Locka airport in an hour. That's where the plane is. And hungry pilots more than you can count.'

The identification was made from a cranky little outboard moored on the lake a quarter mile away from the house and pitching wildly in the wake of passing speedboats. Jake sat in the bow, trying to mask the binoculars as much as possible with his hands and to keep a fix on the house despite the bobbing of the boat. Magnes gloomily sat amidships, an unlit cigar in his mouth and a fishing rod in his hand. The brisk, collegiate-looking young man who had picked them up at the Belle Glade airstrip sat at the motor, trying to keep the boat headed into the wavelets coming at them from what seemed every direction. Almost an hour of this, and then a woman came through the screen door of the house and stood on the veranda, looking down at the newspaper she was holding. The veranda soared out of view, back into it briefly, and out again. Jake braced his elbows on the side of the boat and steadied the glasses on target. Charlotte Thoren. But not merely haggard now. More like a death's-head.

He handed the glasses to Magnes, who passed them along to the man at the tiller. 'That's her,' Jake said.

The man sighted with the glasses. Then he opened the bait box at his feet, put the glasses into it and took out a movie camera. He attached a Zoomar lens to it, sighted again, and ran off a few feet of film. 'Got her good,' he said, and Jake said: 'Now all you have to do is stay with her.'

On the plane back to Opa-Locka, he said to Magnes: 'Tomorrow we hit Dobbs. That man of yours who ferries me to the Argyle said he has a friend who knows his way around the Route 94 section of the swamps. I'll be seeing him tonight and booking a trip for tomorrow. Will you be in around eleven or so tonight?'

'I'll be in all night. I got a lot of resting to make up for.'

'Then after he drops me off at the hotel I'll have him phone you about what arrangements we made. About when and where to meet me.'

'Do I have to? Look, Dekker, I already seen all the swamps I want to see. And if Dobbs don't want to play ball with you, he won't play ball with me either.'

'He'll play ball with me. But you got friendly with the old guy who lives next door to him in Crosscut. We might need him to steer us to this hammock, if Dobbs is laying low there when we show up. So stay home and wait for a call. And remember, you're laying it on Thoren this way. You're helping kick apart that whole job he did, signing up for the insurance and faking the accident.'

'True,' said Magnes. 'And the name is not Thoren. It's Stresemann.'

56

The speedboat showed up at Daystar promptly at ten. Jake waited until it quietly slid away from the dock and was aimed in the direction of the Venetian Causeway, then laid a restraining hand on the skipper's shoulder. 'Don't turn on the speed yet. I want to talk to you.'

'I'm listening.'

'I want to book your friend for that trip I told you about. Dobbs Hammock, somewhere around Crosscut.'

'When?'

'First thing in the morning. What do you do after you drop me off at the hotel? Go back to the marina?'

'Yep. Watch TV if there's a cowboy picture on. Maybe play gin with the night watchman. It's a good place to kill time.'

'Then as soon as you get back there, phone Magnes and tell him about it. I want you to meet him somewhere along the bay and bring him to the Argyle in the morning. Your friend from the boondocks has a car, doesn't he?'

'Beat-up old jalopy. Not much for comfort.'

'We won't worry about the comfort. He'll pick up Magnes and me at the hotel and take us out to wherever he keeps his swamp buggy. When I turn up the guy I'm looking for, your friend'll drive us from there to Opa-Locka airport. That's the whole deal. What time does it get light in the morning?'

The skipper ruminated briefly. 'Sunup'll be about six. Say a quarter to six.'

'Then have Magnes and your friend meet me on that dock at the hotel at quarter to six. Pass that along to both of them tonight. Now you can get this thing moving. Let's make speed.'

They made thunderous speed from there to the Argyle's dock, but this time it was not deserted. A small group was gathered on it, the men in dinner jackets, the women in evening gowns, taking in the night time view of the bay. When Jake stepped ashore all of them glanced at him and then stared openly at the skipper's patchwork, lacquered face. He ironically saluted them before he swung the boat away from the dock.

And unlike the night before, the hotel lobby at this earlier hour was well filled, the Midwestern twang predominating over the hubbub in it. Jake worked his way around the crowd, toward the bank of elevators. As he passed the registration counter, the clerk who had signed him into the hotel took notice of him. The man did an almost comical double-take. 'Mr Majeski?' he said. He didn't sound too sure of it.

'Yes. What is it?'

'Well, I suppose – ' The man's face now registered open bewilderment. 'But then you're all right? There wasn't any accident?'

Jake moved up against the counter. 'Who said there was?'

'Why, the police officer who called for Mrs Majeski about an hour ago. He told me you'd been badly hurt in a car accident, and he had been sent to take her to the hospital.'

From behind partly open doors across the lobby came a clatter of cutlery, a beehive hum of voices. Rising over the noise, barely audible, a small, sad voice was singing a French ballad. A bulky, red-faced man in a dinner jacket standing near the counter said, 'Oui, oui, ooh la la,' and the group around him, beefy, freshly sunburned men and rigidly corseted women with blue-tinted grey hair done in neat little waves, all laughed.

Jake said to the clerk: 'Did she go with him?'

'Yes, she did. But if it was a mistake, she should be back by now.' The man turned and flicked an eye over the pigeon-holes in the rack behind him. He looked again, more closely. 'I don't understand, Mr Majeski. She isn't back. Both your room keys are in your box.'

Someone pushed up to the counter beside Jake and said irritably to the clerk, 'Now looky here, Ramos – ' and Jake said softly, 'You can see Mr Ramos is busy, can't you?' The intruder glanced at Jake, got a full view of his expression, and said placatingly, 'Why, sure. I didn't mean – ' He drifted further down the counter to bring his troubles to one of the other clerks.

Jake said to Ramos: 'This police officer wasn't in uniform, was he?'

'No. But of course I asked for his identification. He was a detective attached to the Miami Beach force.'

'What was his name? Did you notice it?'

Ramos was looking increasingly worried. 'I'm afraid not. Actually, there didn't seem any reason to. And with the amount of work at the desk here this evening –'

'But you did get a look at him.'

'Yes. A youngish man. Not too prepossessing, really. Dark

complexion. Eyes rather close together, a thin moustache. Not prepossessing at all.'

'And what did you do when he told you why he was here? Just send him upstairs?'

Ramos looked shocked. 'Oh, no, sir. There's a routine in such cases. We call the room and announce a visitor will be coming up. And where it's a lady, we send the housekeeper with the officer. If she's a bit delicate, might faint –'

'And that's what you did in this case?'

'Yes, sir.'

'When you spoke to Mrs Majeski on the phone, how did she sound? What did she say?'

'Well, now that you bring it up, that was a bit curious. It almost sounded as if she expected my call. She told me she'd be down at once, but, of course, the hotel doesn't want – that is –'

'The hotel doesn't want people fainting in the lobby. So you did send him upstairs. But with the housekeeper.'

'Yes, sir.' Ramos leaned over the counter. Almost inaudibly, he said: 'Mr Majeski, is there any reason –'

'No. But I do have some big-shot friends around here who are great on practical jokes. Better give me my room key.'

Ramos handed it to him. The worry was gone from his face. His expression was now one of sympathetic disapproval. 'This kind of joke is in pretty bad taste, sir. If you don't mind my saying so.'

'No,' Jake said, 'I don't.'

He pushed open the door to 15C carefully, as if it were going to be snubbed up short on its chain. It wasn't. It swung halfway open, showing the sitting room brightly lit by the chandelier. The bedroom was fully lit too, as was the bathroom. The black chiffon nightgown was on the bathroom floor along with one bedroom slipper. The other slipper he found under the bed. The bed itself had been turned down. Its coverlet was rumpled, and on it was a comb, long golden hairs caught in its teeth, and two paperback books. One was a mystery, the other was Eldridge Cleaver's *Soul on Ice*.

He checked the walk-in closet. The two valises and the flight bag were still there, and, from what he could make of it, the dresses they had contained. The rest of her things were stuffed untidily into dresser drawers. The one item definitely missing was the coat she must have exchanged for her own at the airport. He finally found it rolled up tight and shoved into a wastebasket. He opened it up. It was a cheap cloth coat, badly worn, its lining frayed.

He picked up the phone and gave the operator Magnes's number. The throat-clearing he heard over the line when the connection was made might have been Magnes. The voice that followed was not. 'Hello. Who is it?' It was a drawl that came out in a hoarse whisper. Not the Deep South drawl. More the speech of the native Floridian from this end of the state. And it sounded apprehensive.

Jake said: 'Is that you, Dobbs?'

'Me? That's right. Yes. Is that you, Mr Dekker?'

'You know damn well it is. You've been waiting for this call, haven't you? Where's Magnes?'

'Well, he – Look, Mr Dekker, you got to come over here now. I'm supposed to tell you that. Come over here right now.'

'Not a chance. I'm not going anywhere until my wife is back where she belongs. Now put Magnes on the phone. Or better yet, if Gela's there, put him on.'

Dobbs's voice became anguished. 'Mr Dekker, I'm here all by my lonesome, and you have got to be here when Mr Gela calls in because that's what he says to do. And I swear I ain't looking for trouble with you, but I have to do what he says. And he says don't you do nothing foolish, and it'll all be settled right away.'

'Where's my wife now? With Gela?'

'That's right. And that other feller's with them too. I tell you the truth, I didn't want any part of this, but you don't fool around with people like them. So you come over here, and everything'll be fixed up quick. Mr Gela already called in twice. He's waiting for you to get here, and he's getting hot at me like it's my fault you don't. The quicker you do, the better for everybody. Especially your wife.'

'I'll be there,' Jake said.

57

He travelled back to the house on Daystar by cab. There, he took Aiello's automatic out of the closet, loaded it, and thrust it into his belt. From what he saw in the mirror, it did not make too obtrusive a bulge when he buttoned his jacket over it.

When he crossed the bridge to the Beach in the Jaguar, he saw that for the first time in more than a week, no car fell in behind him. He parked a block away from Magnes's hotel. From across the street he could make out some people in the lobby sitting in orderly ranks, undoubtedly watching the TV set there. He scouted the side street along the hotel, found a service door, and went up to the roof on foot. He crossed the roof as noiselessly as he could and positioned himself beside Magnes's door, his back aaginst the wall, where he would be out of sight and range of anyone opening the door. He rapped on the door with the gun barrel.

It was pulled open almost at once, and a skeletal figure stood outlined there, peering into the darkness of the roof. 'Mr Dekker? That you?'

Jake swung around, planted his hand against the out-thrust face, and shoved hard. The man was catapulted backward into the room, hit the armchair there, and went sprawling. Jake thrust his shoulder against the door with enough force to slam it against the inside wall of the room, but no one was behind it. He stepped into the room and shut the door.

The man slowly getting to his feet could only be Earl Dobbs. He was tall and cadaverously thin, with outsized hands and feet emphasizing the narrow dimensions of him. He wore a fine silk suit, badly rumpled and stained; its jacket hung slack from his shoulders as it might from a too-small hanger. He was pale-eyed, sharp-featured, lank-haired, and unhappy-looking. 'Now, Mr Dekker – '

Jake levelled the gun at him. 'Where's Magnes?'

Dobbs's eyes involuntarily flickered in the direction of the bathroom door. 'Now, Mr Dekker, I can't blame you for being riled up, but there ain't any sense taking it out on me.'

'Open that door.'

Dobbs backed toward it. 'I purely wish you wouldn't point that thing at me. You know you don't figure to go shooting me, the way things are, but there's all kinds of accidents can happen with a gun.'

'Open it.'

Dobbs opened it. From where Jake stood, the bathtub was in clear view, taking up most of the space in the closet-sized room. It was a large, old-fashioned tub set on claw feet and was almost full of water. It was long enough for Magnes's naked body to recline at full length just below the surface. The face stared blindly at the ceiling, the dental plate for the lower jaw was thrust halfway out of the gaping mouth. Jake motioned with the gun, and Dobbs hastily pulled the door shut. 'Now, Mr Dekker – '

Jake said: 'You're a brave man, aren't you, Earl? Turn you loose in an old folks' home, and I bet you'd be a real hero.'

'You got it wrong, Mr Dekker. I didn't do that. I would never do a thing like that. I tell you I got a heart for old people. That was Mr Gela done that. And the other one.'

'Aiello?'

'That's the one. They done it. And not even on purpose. All they wanted for him to do was tell where your wife was around here, and they had to keep ducking him and ducking him until he would. He was sure one stubborn old man. And he wasn't drownded. It was his heart give out right after they made him telephone to your wife. So you can't even rightly say they done it.'

Jake said: 'How did they know my wife was still in town? They saw me take her to the airport, didn't they?'

'They surely did. And soon as they knew about it, they phoned up some people in New York to be waiting when she got off the airplane. That lady you had making believe to be your wife told them who she rightfully was real quick. I don't think they hardly had to get mean with her at all. She just spoke right up.'

'Old men and women,' Jake said. He thrust the gun into his belt, neatly straightened his jacket over it, then suddenly backhanded Dobbs across the face. The impact flattened the man against the wall. He cried out and covered his face with his crossed arms when Jake raised his hand again. Jake lowered the hand. 'For a guy without any guts, Earl, you've really got yourself in deep. Where's my wife now?'

'Mr Dekker, I swear I don't know.'

'You want to try that bathtub on for size?'

'They didn't tell me where they are with her. Mr Gela only said he'll keep calling up, and you'd be here sooner or later so he could talk to you. And he said rough as you might want to be on me, he could be just as rough on your wife, and you'd know that. Mr Dekker, you better know that. Mr Gela has a mean streak from his neck clear to his tail. And that other one ain't any better. Only Mr Gela is worse, because he's smart too. And he's got big men backing him up. They all put their heads together, and you just can't get around them.'

'What big men? Frank Milan and a lawyer named Katzman?'

Dobbs kept his arms before his face. 'I ain't supposed to say any names.'

'I said them. Do you mean Milan and Katzman are cutting in on the blackmail money?'

'I don't know about that, Mr Dekker. All I know is they're in the company.'

'What company?'

'Well, the company that lawyer made up. When Mrs Thoren gets that insurance money she puts it all in the company, and they take it out. That makes it all lawful and regular.'

Jake said: 'Sure it does. All right, put your arms down. Nobody's going to hurt you. Not as long as you talk sense.'

When Jake seated himself on the edge of the table, Dobbs warily lowered his arms. Blood trickled from his lip. He touched it and said reproachfully: 'Looks like I'm already hurt.' He fumbled in his pocket, came up with a crumpled and dirty handkerchief and pressed it to the wound. 'I can't even blame you for wanting to take it out on me, Mr Dekker. I got no hard feelings against you for it.'

'I said as long as you talk sense. I suppose you're an officer in this company. The one that's going to divvy up Mrs Thoren's money all regular.'

Dobbs heaved his shoulders in a self-deprecating shrug. 'Well now, I don't really rate that big.'

'How much do you rate? Ten dollars' worth out of that two hundred thousand?'

'Well, a lot more than that, Mr Dekker. A lot closer to ten thousand.'

'Five per cent? You can be bought cheap, can't you, Earl?'

'Well now – '

'Five per cent of your own two hundred thousand for doing all the dirty work. You're the one who found out Thoren was really Stresemann to start with, you're the one who had to mail him those dog-track tickets, the one who had to get the money from him every month, the one he would have killed if he could. He did try to kill you, didn't he?'

'Yes, sir. Almost did over on the hammock, wartime.'

'I don't mean then. I mean after the blackmail started.'

'Then too,' Dobbs said in an aggrieved voice. 'He was purely poison, that man. Before Mr Gela took over he tried to run me down with his car right in front of my rooming house two different times. And he was the one who brung money into it. That day at Bayside Spa, I had him on the rubbing table and remembered who he was, I says without even thinking, "You're Stresemann," and for all he turned sheet-white when he heard that, two seconds later he says to me, "It's worth a lot of money for you to forget it." ' Dobbs tapped his chest. 'That man put a bullet through me here when I was a runty kid back in the swamps, so it was only God's goodness I even lived to tell about it. And he gunned down my uncle right there while I was looking, even when he'd laid him out already with a crack on the head. Just aimed right between the eyes while he was laying there and let him have it. And now when I was willing to let bygones be bygones and settle for cash, all he wanted to do was lay me amongst the daisies. Purely poison, that's all he was.'

Jake said: 'What do you think Gela is? That money from

Thoren should have been all yours. How much did Gela ever give you of it when he took over? Did you know he got up to where he was squeezing ten thousand a month out of Thoren?'

Dobbs shook his head. 'No, sir, I didn't know, and I didn't care. Mr Gela says to me, he says: "You do things my way, and you're good for one thousand dollars cash money each and every month of the year." That's a pile of money, Mr Dekker. A man can live like a king on a lot less. I ain't saying Mr Gela ain't poison, too. I'm only saying he gave me more than I ever looked to get in this lifetime. And the way he took care of things, I didn't have to be in a sweat about getting run over by a car before my time. No sense being greedy and dead.'

Jake said: 'But Thoren's the one who's dead now, so there's no chance of getting run over by him any more. And ten thousand dollars for the final payoff is too cheap. You're the big man in the company. Without you, Gela and his friends don't have anything to sell. They don't have any way of putting pressure on Mrs Thoren. Be smart, Earl. You're worth at least twice what they've promised you. And you don't have to shop around for it. Play ball with me, and you're going to collect twenty thousand.'

'Mr Dekker, I am purely glad to hear you say that. It shows you don't bear hard feelings, and I am dead set against hard feelings. But playing ball ain't exactly what it would be. It would be more like kicking a hungry bull alligator square in the snout and watching to see what happens whilst you stand there.'

'Thirty thousand,' Jake said softly. 'All in tens and twenties fresh from the bank. Do you have any idea the kind of pile that makes when you stack it up in front of you, Earl?'

Dobbs hitched his shoulders uncomfortably inside his jacket. He worked his hand over his face. 'I tell you the truth, Mr Dekker. Long as Mr Gela's got your wife put away somewheres, I don't rightly see what you can do for yourself, much less me.'

'I can have you on my side when the showdown comes. And with a gun in your pocket. Once we get my wife loose from Gela, we're home free. I've got a billion-dollar company backing me up, Earl. And the police and the FBI. What's wrong with collecting thirty thousand for going along with law and order? Or are you against law and order?'

'Me? No, sir, Mr Dekker. I am a law-and-order man all the way. I don't hold with none of the crazy things niggers and long-hair kids get away with nowadays. But I can't rightly see what doing a widow woman out of her insurance money got to do with law and order. And no hard feelings, Mr Dekker, but that's what your company aims to do. You have got to admit it. If your company wasn't so tight about paying off that woman, you wouldn't be down here at all now. And brung along your wife and put her in such a pickle.'

The phone rang, and Dobbs started at the sound of it. It was Magnes's outside line, and the phone itself had been taken from its place of concealment under the bedside table and laid on the bed. Dobbs said worriedly: 'I guess that's him, Mr Dekker.'

'Answer it.'

Dobbs sidled along the wall to the bed, giving Jake a wide berth. When he picked up the phone it was almost engulfed by his immense hand. 'Yes, sir?' he said anxiously, and then in a tone of relief: 'Yes, sir, he's here all right.' He started to offer the phone to Jake then put it to his ear again. 'Yes, sir.' He slyly glanced at Jake. 'That's what he done, Mr Gela. Both ways. Bloodied me up, and then said he'd give me thirty thousand iffen I played ball with him. No, sir. You know me. I like it fine the way it is.' He held out the phone to Jake at arm's length, his other arm going up before his face in that protective gesture. 'He wants to talk to you now, Mr Dekker. Now you remember he got your wife there.'

Jake took the phone. 'Gela?'

'You took your time showing up, didn't you?' Gela's voice was uncannily like Frank Milan's, a rasping growl. 'What were you doing, Dekker? Trying to figure more angles? You ought to know you finally run out of angles.'

'Maybe. Before we hash it out, Gela, I want to talk to my wife. Put her on.'

'Come off it. This cute little piece of tail's not your wife.

292

And you're not on Guaranty's payroll. You're strictly on your own for a fifty per-cent cut of the insurance. And nobody had to knock this broad's teeth loose to get her talking about it. She told it all by herself to that nice detective who was taking her to the hospital. So don't get up a sweat about it, because there ain't a mark on her. Not yet.'

'Put her on, Gela. I want to hear her tell me that.'

Elinor's words came out in a rush. 'Jake, it was Magnes! He called me up, and he told me you – '

'Never mind that,' Jake cut in sharply. 'Are you all right?'

'Yes. But, Jake – '

Her voice was cut off so abruptly, it was clear someone had clapped a hand over her mouth. Gela said: 'Now you heard her.'

'I heard her,' Jake said. 'What's the deal?'

Gela said: 'I'll make it short. I got the home number of your insurance guy Maniscalco up in New York. You meet me right now where I am, I put in a call to him, and I listen to you tell him the case is all washed up. Thoren died in an accident, and you found that out for a fact. So the insurance cheque better go out first thing in the morning. Then we all sit down and wait for it to show up here.'

Jake said: 'And what do I get for being so helpful?'

'If you're lucky, a long, happy life full of little blondes like this one. What the hell do you expect to get for it? A loving cup?'

'Don't be thick, Gela. If I make that call, I'm out a hundred grand. And I'm already out twenty grand for expenses. If you're making me a partner in this, let's hear how much I salvage out of that dough.'

'Nothing.'

'Look, Gela – '

'Don't try to snow me. When that cheque hits the mailbox here, you and this dame can take off wherever you want, and the books are closed. After that, all you have to do is keep your mouth shut about it. And you will, Dekker. Because if you don't, not only will I tell Guaranty I bought you off, so you'll be washed up in your line, but a guy I know in the phone company just done a job for me and turned up a couple of bugs planted in the Thoren house. And if you don't think Mrs Thoren'll stand up in court and swear you had to be the one who planted them, you don't know how close she listens to me. You wouldn't like that, Dekker, not the way they run the jails down here.' Gela's voice took on a note of exasperation. 'Jesus Christ, you been banging heads with me for almost two weeks now. You really think you'd wind up with anything but a busted skull to show for it?'

'Maybe I still do, Jake said.

'Sure you do,' Gela said contemptuously. 'Your trouble is you can't get used to the idea you just blew a hundred grand. All right, you want a little time to get used to it? It's late as hell now anyhow, and it comes to the same thing if you talk to this Maniscalco tomorrow morning, soon as he gets into his office. Only thing is, Aiello'll be looking out for your broad until then, and he got no use for you at all. But if you want to put in the rest of the night kissing that hundred grand goodbye, you can tell that monkey with you to pick you up at eight in the morning and bring you to Dinty's. He knows where it is.' Gela waited a few seconds, then said impatiently: 'Come on, Dekker, make up your mind. Right now or in the morning? Me, I always say when you got to get a tooth pulled, do it quick. Even if the bill comes to a hundred grand.'

Jake stood there, sweat starting to bead his face and trickle down his forehead. He swept it off his forehead with the back of his hand, but it was immediately there again.

Suddenly Gela said: 'All right, Dekker, then it's first thing tomorrow,' and slammed down the phone.

'Hold it!' Jake said. 'Gela – !'

It was too late. The only sound he heard now was the monotonous, unbroken buzz of the dial tone.

58

He wheeled on Dobbs, who shrank back terrified. 'Where was he calling from? Where is he staying?'

'Mr Dekker, I told you I don't know. I swear I don't.'

'Crosscut?'

'No, sir. Not to sleep over. He lives fancy, and it's all broke down there.'

Jake gripped the man's tie at its knot and pressed a thumb into the bulging Adam's apple. 'Where does he live fancy?'

Dobbs's mouth gaped wide as he fought for breath. His hands flailed at Jake's face until Jake banged his head against the wall. Groaning, Dobbs clapped his hands to the back of his head. 'I don't know, Mr Dekker. Some hotel up a ways on the Beach. But I don't know what one.'

Jake said inexorably: 'Where's Dinty's? And don't say you don't know, because he told me you did.'

'Yes, sir, I do. But if you'll only let go –'

Jake flung the man away from him. 'Well?'

Dobbs rubbed his throat and drew a deep breath. 'That's in Crosscut, Mr Dekker. It's the general store there.'

'You sure?'

'Yes, sir. Store ain't much, but Dinty's the one markets the alligator skins for folks around there, so he does all right.'

Jake said: 'The store has a phone, doesn't it?'

'Yes, sir. The onliest one there. And I know the number, if you want to call up. But nobody'll be there. Not this time of night.'

'Call up anyhow.'

Dobbs did, while Jake held the phone. There was no answer. Dobbs said pleadingly: 'That ain't my fault, Mr Dekker. I told you nobody would be there this time of night. Not Mr Gela, for sure.'

'For sure,' Jake said dully. He sat down on the bed and considered the pattern of the worn linoleum underfoot. Then he looked up at Dobbs. 'Gela said you were to take me out to Dinty's at eight in the morning. Do you have a car here?'

'Yes, sir, Mr Dekker.' The answer came out loud and clear. It was as if thought of the car was a stiffener for the man's spine. 'Big T-bird.'

'You know where the bridge is to the Daystar Islands?'

'Yes, sir.'

'Then meet me down the block from it at eight. Now get over to that table and empty your pockets onto it.'

'Mr Dekker – '

Jake stood up, and Dobbs hastily started turning out his pockets and emptying their contents on the table. Among them were two rings, one a plain gold band, the other with a diamond set into it, a heavy, old-fashioned watch on a chain, and a jewelled Masonic pin. Jake placed these apart from the rest of the litter on the table. He said: 'Did you lift the money out of his wallet too?'

'No, sir, Mr Dekker.'

'I'd like to believe that, you goddam ghoul. All right, take your stuff and get out of here. Fast.'

He locked the door behind Dobbs and went to work combing the room for any papers or tapes concerning Thoren. A half hour of this indicated that Magnes had either kept no such records or had not kept them in the apartment. In the end, he put everything back as he had found it, stored the valuables in the top drawer of the dresser, and left the apartment with its lights burning.

It was almost two when he got back to Daystar and made himself a cup of black coffee laced with cognac. At six he made himself another, and then went in to shave, cutting himself badly in the process. At seven-thirty he went into the study, sat down, and put his wristwatch on the desk before him. When the minute hand marked exactly seven forty-five he dialled the operator and asked for the police.

He said to the man who answered: 'This is not a gag or a crank call. I want to report a kidnapping.'

'A kidnapping? What's your name and address?'

'Jacob Dekker, Daystar Island Number Two. The kidnapped person is my wife. She was –'

'Hold it. Hold it.'

A few moments later another voice came on the line. 'Mr. Dekker?'

'Yes.'

'Lieutenant Brittenum here. You reporting your wife was kidnapped? You're sure of that? It's not just a case of her failing to show up some place she was supposed to be?'

'No. She was taken from the Argyle East Hotel by a man pretending to be a detective on the Miami Beach force. His name is Anthony Aiello. He gets his orders from someone named Gela who –'

'Angelo Gela?'

'Yes. Frank Milan's nephew. His friends call him Pooch.'

Brittenum said heavily: 'I see.' His voice became wary. 'And what do your friends call you?'

'I'm not tied in with your local mobsters in any way, Lieutenant. And I just got a call from Gela discussing ransom terms. We're supposed to finish the talk at a place called Dinty's in Crosscut on Route 94. The general store out there. I'm leaving for there now, and I want you and your men to move in and grab everybody in sight right after I get there. Dinty's. I'm driving a Jaguar coupé. You'll know I'm there if you see the car parked by the place.'

'Oh sure. Except for one thing, Mr Dekker. Crosscut's in Monroe County. That makes this Monroe's jurisdiction. Now you call the police in Key West –'

'Key West? That's way to hell and gone out in the ocean. What have they got to do with this?'

'Look, Mr Dekker, Monroe County happens to be one great big empty hunk of swamp run from Key West. And it takes time for anything to be done from there. So don't you go chasing right off to Crosscut. You call Key West, see how much time it'll take them–'

'You call them, Lieutenant,' Jake cut in explosively, 'because I'm leaving right now. You call anybody you want, just as long as I'm covered when I get there.'

59

The cream-coloured Thunderbird parked near the corner of North Bay Road was badly scraped and dented, rust patches showing through the scrapes and dents. Jake pulled up beside it and motioned Dobbs to join him in the Jaguar. Dobbs put his head out of his window and said brightly: 'Kind of thought we'd be going in my car, Mr Dekker. No reason why not. Save yourself gas that way.'

'Get in here,' Jake said.

Dobbs resignedly obeyed. 'You know the way, Mr Dekker?'

'You'll show me the way.'

The traffic was heavy until they were past midtown Miami. On the Tamiami Trail, it was heavy until they were clear of the shabby commercial area it cut through inside city limits. After that, there were fewer and fewer cars to be seen along the way.

The road ran straight to the horizon as if laid out with a ruler, a canal to the right, a flat green waste to the left. Dobbs, an eye on the speedometer which registered a steady fifty miles an hour, shifted restlessly in his seat now and then. Finally he said: 'You can open her up now if you want, Mr Dekker. It's like this all the way to 94.

'You in any special rush?'

'No, sir. Not if you ain't, Mr Dekker.' Dobbs sat for a while in silence. Then he said hopefully: 'I purely wish you didn't have such hard feelings against me. Mr Dekker. I tell you the truth. I can't stand anybody having hard feelings against me.'

Jake glanced at him. 'You're all heart, aren't you, Earl?'

'Maybe you don't rightly think I am, but that is the truth.'

'If you line up with me against Gela, I'll know it's the truth.'

'Well, I wouldn't go that far, Mr Dekker. But look how I got lined up with him to start with. All of that come from not wanting anybody to have hard feelings against me.'

Jake said: 'Don't hand me that. You went to him with the

story about who Thoren really was. He never came to you about it.'

'Well now, it shows how even somebody smart as you can get wrong ideas, Mr Dekker. Fact is, he come to me. I was working the kennels at Flagler track then. Not handling or anything like that, just feeding and cleaning. And somebody pointed me out to Mr Gela in the stands once, so he come over and asked me what dogs looked good that night, and after that he asked every night about it. So when I got that first money from Mr Thoren, and I showed up at Flagler with my new suit and betting twenties instead of twos, Mr Gela thought I hit some big winners and was holding out on him about them. He had real hard feelings against me because of it. So I went and told him how I got the money, and before I was done I told him all about Mr Thoren. About him being Stresemann. That is the truth, Mr Dekker. You think it ain't, you are misjudging me something awful.'

Jake said: 'Not as far as your brains are concerned. What do you think'll happen when Gela's phony company gets hold of the insurance money, and you ask for your share of it? He'd cut his own mother's throat for a dollar. What do you think he'll do to you for ten thousand?'

'Well now, Mr Dekker – '

'And I'm still offering you thirty thousand. Honest money. Money you can be sure you'll get.'

Dobbs thought it over. Then he regretfully shook his head. 'Except for one thing, Mr Dekker. Him and them people he's with, they run the works. And that makes his money a lot realer than yours.'

Route 94 was a straightaway continuation of the Trail where it suddenly angled off northward. A gravel road, washed out in spots. As they passed what looked like a frontier outpost, Dobbs said: 'That there's Pinecrest. Crosscut's only couple of miles more.'

It was a slow couple of miles on that washboard road, even slower on the deeply rutted track that diverged from it and plunged into the depths of the swamp. The track wound through stands of cypress and pine, around thickets of under-

299

brush, and ended in a clearing before a large shanty-like structure. The building sagged at one end, and it's wall there was supported by a pair of two-by-fours braced against it like flying buttresses. Broken panes of glass in its windows had been replaced by cardboard, the sign over its door, *Dinty's Gen'l Store,* had been so weathered by time and riddled by buckshot that it was almost illegible.

The area around the gas pump in front of the building was evidently the local parking lot. There were several cars there looking ready for the boneyard, a couple of work-worn, nearly derelict pickup trucks, and a gleaming black Cadillac convertible. There were no electric lines in sight. The only sign of communication with the outside world was a telephone line looping through treetops to the eaves of the store.

There were no other buildings in sight either, but when Jake had followed Dobbs up the three creaking steps to the store's porch, he could make out the rough-hewn log walls and tar-paper roofs of some cabins half hidden in the undergrowth.

The store was dimly lit by what sun the windows allowed in through their few remaining glass panes and by a kerosene lamp hanging from a rafter. There was an overpowering stench in it of kerosene, stale beer, and decayed meat.

There were two men in the place. No question about the one with long sideburns and in white turtleneck shirt and snugly fitting, high-waisted slacks being Gela, because the other, except for the narrow-eyed shrewdness of his face, was cut to the same mould as Dobbs. That one wore overalls, grey chest hair sprouting over them, and leaned on his elbows behind the counter. On the counter lay a shotgun, its twin barrels aimed at the doorway in which Jake stood. The man's outstretched hand rested on the narrow part of the gunstock, his forefinger on the trigger guard. When he spoke his voice had the identical twang and drawl of Dobbs. 'Took you long enough, Earl.'

'That is the truth, Dinty. But we come in his car. And I told him – '

'Never mind that,' Gela cut in. 'It looks to me like he's packing a gun. Get it.'

Dobbs apologetically removed the automatic from Jake's

belt and laid it on the counter. Gela motioned to Jake. 'The phone's over there in the corner.'

'I see it,' Jake said. 'But I don't see the girl. Where is she?'

'She's around. Don't worry about her. Stick to business.'

Jake said: 'I don't see Aiello either. Is he with her? That would be stupid, Gela.'

'I told him to lay off her, so you got nothing to worry about. She's all right. And the sooner that insurance money gets down here, the sooner you're both out of this.'

Jake leaned against the door frame and folded his arms on his chest. 'No phone call to anybody until I see the girl. And not long-range. I want to see her close-up and talk to her. Then you're in business.'

Gela turned to Dinty. 'You hear that? Go on, tell him she's all right,' and Dinty said, 'She's all right, mister. I took them out to the hammock myself last night, and nothing could have happened to her there that she didn't want to happen.'

Jake looked from one to the other of them. Then he said to Dinty: 'I see you've signed up with the team, too. How does it work? He cuts you in on this, and you cut him in on the alligator poaching?'

'You're stalling, Dekker,' Gela said warningly.

'No, I'm standing pat.'

Gela stared at him, gnawing at a hangnail on his pinkie.

Jake said placidly to Dinty: 'You're out of your mind if you let this guy in on your alligator racket. A month from now he'll be running it, and you'll be skinning hides for him, a dollar an hour.'

'Sure, mister,' Dinty said.

'Think it over,' Jake said. 'He's already half way to making you partners in blackmail and kidnapping, in case you don't know the whole story. Be smart. Aim that gun his way and step out of this mess right now. Whatever he's paying you, you can count on a lot more from me. All you have to do is say how much.'

'Sure, mister.'

Gela spat out the hangnail he had been working on. He said to Jake: 'I already talked to that secretary in Maniscalco's

301

office first thing today. I told her to have him stand by for a call from you. He's waiting, Dekker.'

'He'll keep. I'll get around to him when the girl is right here where I can see her.'

Gela started to gnaw the bothersome pinkie again. Finally he said: 'You want to see her, you'll go where she is. Not here. She stays under cover right there until this whole thing is settled. You'll have plenty of time with her then, because you'll be staying there, too.'

'Dobbs Hammock?'

'Wherever. I don't know why the hell you're making it so hard on yourself, Dekker. This thing would run smooth as silk if you wasn't such a donkey. But I know you got some kind of idea to get her here and make a break for it. Then what happens? You both get gunned down. Nobody wins, everybody loses. Is that using your brain?'

'How about using yours, Gela. You've got these two rednecks here along with you and Aiello. Do you really think I'd try to make a break for it against those odds? But all right, I'll do it your way. I'll go where the girl is. Let's get moving on it.'

They left Dinty behind his counter and moved single-file along a narrow, spongy path to the waterfront, Gela bringing up the rear, shotgun in hand. Three swamp boats were moored to a dock there along with several rowboats. In the muck of the shoreline was a litter of broken oars, rusted beer cans, and empty gasoline tins. The swamp boats were flat-bottomed skiffs, square at the bow and riding low in the water. Mounted on a platform in the stern of each was a heavy-duty automobile motor powering a wooden airplane propeller of ancient vintage.

Gela pointed Jake to a seat in the bow and then seated himself beside Dobbs, who took the controls. As Jake settled down, trying to keep his feet clear of the slimy water rolling from side to side in the boat's bottom, Dobbs poked him in the shoulder and shoved a wad of grimy absorbent cotton into his hand.

'What's that for?' Jake said.

'Noise, Mr Dekker. Better stuff it in your ears real tight.'

Jake was still holding the cotton in his hand when the motor kicked over. The sound was ear-shattering. It racketed through the head so violently that it was like a physical hammering on it. Jake hastily thrust a wad of cotton into each ear and wedged it in as tight as he could. It took some of the hard edge off the noise.

The skiff moved across open water towards what looked like a solid wall of sawgrass. Jake flinched involuntarily as it dived into the grass, but there was no feeling of impact. As the boat knifed forward, the grass simply parted before it as if without substance and closed up again behind it with no signs of having been run over or through. Minute after minute of this, moving almost as fast as the speedboat had in Biscayne Bay, but here there were only occasional patches of open water, many more patches where the water was so low that they were skidding over mud flats.

The only landmarks in sight were occasional islets rising a foot or two above the water and with stands of trees on them. At one point, after cutting sharply around one of them, they entered what looked like a man-made canal, a dark brown ribbon slicing through the endless green, but instead of traversing its length, Dobbs, as if tuned in to a directional finder, suddenly banked the boat hard right into the wall of sawgrass again. They tore through it full speed, and then were in a broad lake of comparatively deep water, judging from the way only the tips of the sawgrass showed above its surface.

Centred in the lake was a hammock with a stand of dead pines on it. The hammock was about twenty yards long, maybe half that in width. Under the pines was a cabin. Near it was a dock in ruinous condition. Dobbs pulled the boat up to the dock, stepped ashore, and tied its line to a post. When he cut the motor the silence left the ears ringing. The heat, dispelled by the breeze raised when the boat was moving fast, closed down immediately. The sun was like an auger drilling through the skull; the dampness raised a sweat on the body which instantly saturated every inch of it. It was like trying to breathe in a steam room.

Aiello, shirtless and badly wilted, waited on the dock a short-barrelled revolver in his hand. Elinor sat on the ground in the shadow of the cabin, her back against its wall, her knees drawn up, her hands clasped around them. She looked at the boat with no sign of interest on her face, then rested her forehead on her knees.

Jake pulled the wads of cotton from his ears and stepped up on the dock, Gela's shotgun trained on him every move he made. 'Five minutes,' Gela said. 'That Maniscalco's probably already wetting his pants wondering what you want to talk to him about.' He motioned to Aiello. 'Come on in the boat. You too, dummy,' he told Dobbs. When they were aboard, he said to Jake: 'Get the point? You try any kind of trick, we pull out of here. Maybe we'll be back in a couple of days with a bucket of drinking water and some eats, maybe not. I'm not pulling any bluff, Dekker. This is all salty water you're looking at, and there's not much to eat or drink inside there, so unless you want to see what it's like to get by on salt water and fingernails, you be a good boy.'

Passing the open cabin door, Jake saw that the furnishings inside consisted of a canvas army cot, and a couple of dirty mattresses on the floor, straw oozing from them, and, in lieu of a table, some boards laid across a pair of sawhorses. Even outside the place there was a reek of mildew from its interior.

He walked up to Elinor and stood looking down at her. 'How are you?' he said, and she gave him a barely perceptible shrug. She did not raise her head from her knees.

He said: 'Did that guy give you any trouble here?'

This time she raised her head but still refused to look at him. 'Yes.'

'Bad?'

She said tonelessly: 'Soon as they left us here last night and went away, he told me I had to do what he wanted. I said no, so he tied me up, and we did it that way.'

'He's number one on my list,' Jake said. 'Gela is number two.'

'How about Magnes? He's the one called me up and said you were in the hospital. And that a policeman would be coming to take me there.'

'I know,' Jake said. 'But they made him do it. He held out as long as he could. He's dead now.'

'Dead?' Elinor looked dazed. 'And I thought he sold out.' She let her head fall back against the wall of the cabin in a gesture of total exhaustion. 'I got to thinking everybody sold out when the time came.'

'Ellie.' Jake squatted down before her, trying to make her eyes meet his. He cupped her chin in his hand, but she wrenched her head away. 'Ellie, don't be like this. You know how I feel about you. It hasn't changed any. Don't talk as if it has.'

She said relentlessly: 'I was next to Gela when he was on the phone with you. He told you to come right over, and you didn't want to. You knew what could happen to me, but you were thinking about the money.'

'Ellie, he hung up while I was wondering about what move to make. If he hadn't hung up that fast – '

'You were thinking about the money. If you came right over, nobody would have touched me. But you knew that as soon as you said you'd do whatever Gela wanted, that was the end of the money. So you couldn't make yourself say it.'

'Jesus Christ, you can't boil everything down to black and white like that. If you only think it over – '

'I did. All night long.' Now she looked squarely at him. Her face was smeared with dirt and blotched with insect bites. 'There was just too much money, that's all.'

'Doesn't it mean anything that I've blown it all by calling in the cops before I came out here? They might even be moving into Crosscut now. Once they do, this thing'll be all over the papers, and that's the end of it for me. I knew that, and I still called them in.'

'That was nice of you,' Elinor said.

'God almighty, what do you want from me, baby? I'm trying to show you – '

'Don't. Just get me out of here. Not on account of us, on account of my kid. I want to be back with him. If anything happens to me, it'll be a bad scene for him. Just get me back with him, and we're even.'

'And what about us?'

Elinor slowly shook her head. 'There wasn't really any us. There was you, and there was this dumb Polack who thought you were something special. But she'll never be that dumb again.'

'Sweetheart, when we're out of this bind –'

'No. Never again.'

Gela called from the boat: 'All right, Dekker, how about it?' and Jake stood up. He took Elinor's arm and pulled her to her feet. 'You heard the man,' he said. 'Let's go.'

He led her to the dock. Aiello was already out of the boat and standing there, the short-barrelled pistol ready in his hand. He showed his teeth in a smile. 'See how people learn things, Dekker? No more automatics. And this makes just as big a hole.'

Jake disregarded him. He looked down at Gela and said: 'You double-crossed me, Gela. You'd better call Maniscalco's secretary again and tell her he won't have to wait around for me to get in touch with him. No sense his wasting time on it.'

'Yeah? What the hell's this all about?'

'You said you gave this ape orders to stay away from the girl. Either you were lying to me, or he doesn't think much of your orders.'

Gela squinted at Aiello. 'Is that the truth, Tony?'

'Ahh, Pooch, for chrissake, she was looking for it.'

Gela said disgustedly: 'If you ain't something. But no more of that, you hear? This is a business deal, so you make like business only. You got that straight?'

'Sure, Pooch.'

Gela turned back to Jake. 'All right? You heard me tell him, and you heard him say yes. Now let's get going.'

'Not without her,' Jake said. 'Either she goes with us, or I stay here.'

Gela stared at him, then spat into the water. 'You at it again, Dekker? Still playing hard to get?'

'Put yourself in my shoes, Gela. If it was your girl, would you leave her here alone with that horny bastard? Especially after what already happened?'

306

Gela said contemptuously: 'If I was in your shoes, I wouldn't have her hanging around me while I was on any job.' The barrels of the shotgun shifted in a small arc from Jake's belly to Elinor's. 'That's one reason I'm giving the orders, and you're taking them. Anyhow, you'll be back here right after that phone call. I think Tony can hold out until then as long as your girl don't wave her ass too hard at him.'

'No deal,' Jake said.

'Then she can stay here alone.'

'Except for the snakes and the alligators? Still no deal.'

'You're getting under my skin, Dekker. Who the hell are you to run things the way you want?'

'That's easy. I'm the guy who's ready to help dump the jackpot in your hand. It looks to me like you're the one who wants to do things the hard way. I don't see why. We both know you're coming up a winner, and all you have to do is pull the handle. Why keep splitting hairs until then?'

Gela dug his fingers into the back of his neck as if trying to ease a stiffness there. The dead silence around them was suddenly broken by the sound of a plunge and spatter out in the middle of the water. Gela instantly wheeled in that direction, the shotgun already at his shoulder. Aiello spun halfway around in a crouch, pistol aimed at the emptiness beyond the boat. Jake took one quick step toward him, then froze in his tracks as the pistol came around to confront him again, an inch from his chest.

Dobbs pointed at a V of ripples out in the water. 'Grand-daddy alligator,' he said. 'I told you they was all around here, Mr Gela. But you leave him to me. Twelve-gauge might just tear up his hide. Sooner or later I'll get him out all in one piece.'

Gela followed the progress of the ripples with fascination until they disappeared among the sawgrass. Then he faced around. He took in the tableau made by Aiello and Jake. 'Son of a bitch,' he said to Aiello, 'you can't take your eyes off this guy for a second, can you?' He crooked a finger at Elinor. 'Get in this thing. Sit there in front of me.'

Impassively, Elinor took the bow seat beside the one Jake

307

had occupied. Gela rested the shotgun on the back of the seat, the muzzle thrust into her spine between the shoulder blades. With great deliberation he cocked both triggers, the snap of them loud in the air. 'You hear that?' he said to Jake. 'You make one little wrong move, and I leave it to you what happens. Now sit there next to her. That's right. And remember, Dekker, you rock the boat, there won't be any ladies getting out of it the other end of the line.'

60

There were no police to greet them at the other end of the line, only a pair of gaunt and mangy hounds who trotted down to the water's edge, tails wagging furiously, to sniff their ankles until Dobbs sent them howling with a couple of hard kicks. The sun was directly overhead now, the humidity oppressive enough to have everyone open-mouthed and gasping as they toiled their way along the muddy path to the store. Only Dobbs seemed immune to it.

In the store, Gela handed the shotgun to Dinty and took in its place the automatic that had been removed from Jake. He said to Dinty: 'Any chance of somebody walking in on us now?'

'Might be.' Dinty jerked his head at the few shelves of groceries along one wall. 'That's my business. Selling things to anybody walks in.'

Gela said sardonically: 'Sure it is. But I don't want anybody doing it while we're taking care of this. Go out on the porch and keep them away. Take along that gun to show them you mean it. Same goes if they try sneaking up to look through the windows.'

Jake said to Dinty: 'What did I tell you? You thought you were a partner in this deal. All you are is hired help.'

'Do what I tell you,' Gela snarled at the man. 'You stand there listening to this guy, he'll talk you deaf, dumb, and blind. And close that door when you go out. Make sure it stays closed.' He waited until his instructions had been carried out, then said to Jake: 'You can stall just so long, Dekker. Now let's get to it.'

It was an old-fashioned dial phone, an upright with the dial set into its base, which stood on a shelf in a corner, along with a tattered directory. Nearby was a small round marble-topped table surrounded by four wire-backed chairs, all looking as if they had been salvaged from a bankrupt soda parlour. On the table was a checkerboard, the checkers scattered over it. Gela swept them to the floor and planted the phone on the table. He motioned Jake into a chair with the automatic, then pointed to the chair directly opposite. 'You sit there,' he told Elinor. 'Keep that gun in her back,' he instructed Aiello, 'and if he tries anything, don't even give her time to be sorry about it.'

Jake said: 'Would it be considered trying something if I ask for a drink for the lady and me? A couple of bottles of anything cold and wet?'

'Soda pop and beer,' Dobbs said. 'But it's all warm. Only get ice here when the delivery man feels like it.'

'Warm'll do fine as long as it's wet.'

Dobbs looked at Gela, who nodded. 'And bring me one too.' He sat down beside Jake. 'You know what to tell this Maniscalco?'

'Sure. That the case is washed up. The evidence shows Thoren was killed in an accident. The company better pay up right away. Only, where do they make payment, Gela? If you keep Mrs Thoren stashed away –'

'She's coming back to Daystar tonight, so don't you worry none about that. And you better make it sound a lot more convincing to him than you just did to me. Like, for instance, if they try sitting on that payment any more and this goes to court, one of the things that'll come out is about those bugs you planted over there. That'll be nice to get in the papers, won't it? A great big insurance company planting transmitters all over a widow's house so they can screw her out of her money. Think that'll make Maniscalco see the light quick?'

'It'll help. But what he'll want to know most of all is why I'm so sure all of a sudden that Thoren really did die in an accident. I've been telling him for ten days straight I knew it was suicide, so what made me change my mind overnight? Did your friend Katzman work out an answer to that one too?'

Gela said warningly: 'Watch out the way you say people's names, Dekker.'

'Then I take it he did. What did he come up with?'

'Something solid. There's a doctor up in Palm Beach makes a million on the side taking care of rich dames who get themselves knocked up when they don't want to. Guy name of Ahearn. He'll say Thoren went to him a couple of times last year because he was worried about blacking out a lot lately. Even happened when he was driving once. He went to this Ahearn instead of his family doctor because he didn't want the family to find out.'

Jake said: 'And Ahearn has cooked up some records about this?'

'He'll have 'em.'

'And he'll stand up in court and swear to it?'

'He'll do what he's told. He better, if he wants to stay in business down here.'

Dobbs put the uncapped bottles of soda before them, the red stuff in them foaming over to puddle on the table. Elinor, her body rigid, Aiello's gun prodding into the nape of her neck, made no motion towards hers. Gela took one mouthful of his and swallowed it with revulsion. He wiped his mouth with the back of his hand. 'Any more questions?' he said. 'Anything else to get straight before I put the call through?'

Jake shrugged. 'Probably nothing Katzman hasn't already thought of.'

Maniscalco's voice over the phone was thickened by his head cold, but jubilant. 'Jake, you back in town? You got the release? Remember, I owe you and your girl a dinner for it. Tonight we can –'

'No dinner, Manny. I'm calling from Florida. And it's bad news.'

It took a few seconds for this to sink in. Then Maniscalco said hopefully: 'Very funny. One of these days you'll give me a heart attack with that sense of humour.'

Jake said: 'I wish it was a joke,' and Gela took hold of his wrist and turned it so that the receiver was angled away from his ear. Gela's head was almost against his. 'I was on the wrong track all along, Manny. I was looking so hard at the blackmail angle that I didn't go deep enough into the medical end.'

'Medical end? What the hell are you talking about? His doctor said he was in perfect shape. So did ours.'

'Because he may have been when they examined him. But for this past year he was having bad blackouts. He was even warned it would be dangerous to keep driving under those conditions. I heard all about it yesterday from the doctor he went to in private so the family wouldn't know. Guy named Ahearn in Palm Beach. He's got the records of the visits and the diagnosis right there. And Mrs Thoren's lawyers have copies of them ready to bring into court. It's no use, Manny. All you can do is okay the payment as quick as possible. Maybe cool them off that way.'

There was a long silence at the other end of the line. Then Maniscalco said in a hoarse whisper: 'As quick as possible. Are those your orders, Jake?'

'My advice. And don't take that tone with me, God damn it. Do you think I'm any happier about this than you are?'

'That's what I'm wondering. Like if the lady knew she couldn't collect a dime from us because you could prove a motive for suicide, she might go to you with a real interesting offer. Maybe fifty thousand for her, and all the rest for you. Maybe even less than that for her, as long as it's something. That couldn't possibly have happened, could it, Jake?'

'No, it couldn't. Because any motive I proved wouldn't stand up for one second against that doctor's report. Manny, if anybody else said something like this to me, he'd wind up with a busted jaw, I'm not holding it against you only because I can imagine how you feel right now.'

'No, you can't. You had this case wrapped up already. You as much as told me that. All of a sudden you're completely licked. But did you put in any time checking out that doctor? Do you know for a fact nobody reached him?'

'Manny, I did what had to be done.'

'I don't believe it. You're not kissing off any hundred grand because some doctor that's nowhere on our records pulls a report out of his hat to show you. Not you, Jake. You'd want to put in plenty of time on him and his report before you signed off for good. You'd have the guy checked out from here to medical school before you bought that kind of goods. And you didn't even have time so far to start back-checking him, did you?'

'Manny –'

'Don't try to oil me. I'm saying there's something smelly going on down there, and I'm not okaying any payment until I know different. You hear me? You stay where you are, because I'll be down there in a few hours. I'm taking the next plane out of here. I want to see you and that woman and that doctor. The one who can do card tricks with medical records. If I'm wrong thinking what I do, I'll write all three of you an apology.'

Gela's lips were compressed into a bloodless, angry line. He suddenly clamped his hand over the mouthpiece of the phone. 'The bugs,' he whispered. 'Start selling, Dekker. Make it good.' He removed his hand from the mouthpiece, and Jake said into it: 'Save yourself the trip, Manny. And the letters. She found out about those bugs I planted there. Step on her toes now, and she'll go looking for a court case just to get even. The only way out is to make that payment. And fast.'

'You mean that was the deal? She doesn't prosecute for those bugs you planted, and you pay off by buying her a doctor's report that can cost Guaranty two hundred thousand? Or was it your pal Magnes who did the buying? The hell with that. I'll still be down there this afternoon. And with a couple of lawyers along.'

That was the end of it. Jake sat there with the dial tone buzzing in his ear and Gela gripping his wrist. When Gela slowly released his grip, Jake dropped the receiver on the hook. 'It looks like the gentleman doesn't want to co-operate,' he said. 'Now what?'

Gela savagely gnawed at a fingernail. 'The guinea son of a

bitch. You'd think it was his own money he was hanging on to.'

Jake said: 'He doesn't hang on to his own money that hard. And I've seen him in action. When he gets nose to nose with Mrs Thoren and that doctor, they might not hold up very long.'

Aiello said to Gela with concern: 'This is no good, Pooch. Maybe you should talk it over with the *capo*.'

Gela glared at him. 'Shut up and stay out of this.' He looked at Jake. 'So what's your idea?'

'Let the girl and me go, so I can work on him. I never double-crossed him yet. I think I can convince him I'm not doing it now.'

'Maybe you. Not the girl.'

'Both of us.'

Gela slowly shook his head. 'Not her. I keep her until that dough is in my hand. Every dime of it.'

He started from his chair at the blast of a shotgun outside. One barrel, then, an instant later, the other. He stood momentarily poised for trouble, but relaxed in the silence that followed. 'The crazy bastard. He's supposed to keep them away, not blow them away.' He motioned at Dobbs, who was standing at the counter. 'Go on, tell him that.'

'Yes, sir. He is sure one gun-happy old man,' Dobbs said, but before he could move, the door swung open and Dinty stepped into the room, shotgun in hand, a large, foolish grin of embarrassment on his face. He stood like that for a moment, then, with the grin still fixed on his face, dropped to his knees, sagged forward, and went down full length on the floor.

Gela leaped toward the door, Aiello pivoted toward it. Jake already had his hand around his bottle of soda. It made one turn in the air, spraying soda, before it struck the side of Aiello's head, butt first, with the sound of a melon being struck by a hammer. Aiello went back and down, the gun skittering across the floor, and Jake landed on it full length the same instant that Gela kicked the door shut and levelled the automatic at him. He saw the automatic buck in Gela's hand, felt the white-hot spike drive through his thigh, and it took all his strength to squeeze the trigger of Aiello's gun. Gela doubled

313

over, his hands clutching his belly as if he were nursing a bad cramp. He was still standing like that when the door flew open and three men burst in, carbines at the ready. Only then did he finally go down in a huddle on the floor.

The men were cut along the same lines as Dobbs and Dinty, and, while not in uniform, they all wore similar ten-gallon hats made of straw, the brims turned up high on the sides. They looked around the room, and the oldest of them, white-haired and potbellied, said with awe: 'God almighty.' He squinted at Dobbs, who stood back against the counter, hands held high in the air. 'That you, Earl?' he said unbelievingly. 'You mixed up in this here kidnapping mess, too?'

'Yes, sir, Sheriff. But right on the bottom of the pile, you might say. I don't even know how it come about. It started off different, but it just got out of hand.'

'It sure as hell looks like it did,' the sheriff said.

61

Up to now, Crosscut had seemingly been a deserted settlement. Now suddenly, there was a gathering of ten or twelve male inhabitants on the porch, a silent and stoney-faced audience, while the sheriff bound Jake's thigh tight enough to cut off all feeling in the leg and Dobbs made chatty identifications for him. From among the gathering, the sheriff commandeered a pickup truck and driver. A couple of mattresses were stacked on top of each other in back of the truck, and Jake was tenderly laid on them. A doubled-over mattress was placed on the other side of the truck as a seat for Elinor. The youngest of the deputies, a lanky, freckled boy who looked a year or two shy of voting age, was assigned to see them back to town and make sure of their comfort and well-being along the way.

He hovered over Jake and called warnings now and then to the driver when the truck bounced in the rutted track leading to Route 94 and then over washouts in 94 itself, but when it reached the smoother surface of the Tamiami Trail he perched himself on the tailgate. 'Won't be so bad the rest of the way,' he told Jake. 'Ain't like an ambulance, but it takes a godawful time to get an ambulance out to these parts. And you don't rightly rate a 'copter for that kind of hurt. Clean hole, and just enough bleeding. They'll fix you up in the hospital without no trouble at all.'

'Maybe,' Jake said. He looked at Elinor, who was sitting against the side of the truck as she had against the wall of the cabin on Dobbs Hammock, knees drawn up and arms clasped around them. 'There's a big empty yard in back of the brownstone,' he said. 'It could be fixed up into a great playground for the kid.'

'No,' Elinor said. She turned her head away from him and kept her eyes fixed on the emptiness they were travelling through.

After a while she started to cry. Almost soundlessly at first, then, with teeth clenched and nostrils flaring, in long, shuddering sobs. It went on until the boy sitting there on the tailgate glanced worriedly at Jake to see what he was going to do about it, and finally undertook to do something about it himself, assuring Elinor in that gentle drawl that there really weren't no call to take on like that, ma'am, because you couldn't rightly call that bullet hole anything more than a flesh wound, that's all it was, a flesh wound, and it would heal quick and clean, that was for sure.

Patiently telling it to her over and over as if he were comforting a heartbroken child, and it didn't do any good at all.

More about Penguins and Pelicans

Penguinews, which appears every month, contains details of all the new books issued by Penguins as they are published. From time to time it is supplemented by *Penguins in Print*, which is a complete list of all available books published by Penguins. (There are well over four thousand of these.)

A specimen copy of *Penguinews* will be sent to you free on request. For a year's issues (including the complete lists) please send 30p if you live in the United Kingdom, or 60p if you live elsewhere. Just write to Dept EP, Penguin Books Ltd, Harmondsworth, Middlesex, enclosing a cheque or postal order, and your name will be added to the mailing list.

Note: *Penguinews* and *Penguins in Print* are not available in the U.S.A. or Canada

Other Stanley Ellin titles in Penguins

The Blessington Method

'You are either a criminal or a practical joker. Either way,
I'd like you to clear out. That's fair warning.'

All the same, Mr Treadwell is soon in touch again with the
blandly sinister Mr Bunce. Soon 'The Blessington Method'
is all set to solve a very tricky problem. A problem you may
well share with Mr Treadwell.

The rest of this collection is equally dazzling, just as
haunting. Robert taunts his teacher to suicide; the murder
of a racketeer sends a man's mind back to a day in
childhood when the criminal's fate was decided; Mr Kessler,
the soul of conformity, leads a very odd life from nine to
five . . .

Each of Ellin's stories grips like a vice. Once read, they
settle obstinately in the mind. Start one now . . . if you dare.

Not for sale in the U.S.A. or Canada.

The Valentine Estate

Late one sultry April night Chris Monte was in a tennis shop on Miami Beach, re-stringing a racket and day-dreaming of fifty thousand dollars. Then a girl walked in and apologetically offered him fifty thousand dollars to marry her. Thus activating the carefully drawn plans for his murder . . .

Not for sale in the U.S.A. or Canada.

Also available
Speciality of the House